MW01167405

Born in Edinburgh, Scotland in 1946, Leslie Hunter began his banking career in 1962, and in 1970 he and his wife, Ann, joined the world of international banking in Nassau, Bahamas, and then the Cayman Islands. In 1975, they moved to Richmond, Virginia, where Leslie managed the trust and private banking affiliate of a leading regional bank. Leslie and Ann's early retirement years were split between the USA and their home at Bridge Castle in Scotland. Leslie recently completed a trilogy of historical fiction, of which *Bodotria* is the first of the three novels in the series.

Dedicated to my wife, Ann.

We began our life's journey together in Scotland, the land of our birth, and the inspiration for this story.

Leslie Hunter

BODOTRIA

AUSTIN MACAULEY PUBLISHERS™

LONDON * CAMBRIDGE * NEW YORK * SHARJAH

Ordering Information
Quantity sales: Special discounts are available on quantity purchases by corporations, associations, and others. For details, contact the publisher at the address below.

Publisher's Cataloging-in-Publication data
Hunter, Leslie
Bodotria

ISBN 9798889102175 (Paperback)
ISBN 9798889102182 (Hardback)
ISBN 9798889102199 (ePub e-book)

Library of Congress Control Number: 2023917865

www.austinmacauley.com/us

First Published 2024
Austin Macauley Publishers LLC
40 Wall Street, 33rd Floor, Suite 3302
New York, NY 10005
USA

mail-usa@austinmacauley.com
+1 (646) 5125767

Prologue

The centurion in charge of the soldiers looked up and saw a broken figure of humanity, whose cries of pain were an ineffective relief from the agony of his impalement on the wooden cross. Rough metal nails hammered through the palms and the ankles bound him to his tree of death, and he inevitably slumped down and forward, so that it was increasingly hard to draw breath.

A centurion and four Roman soldiers were assigned the responsibility of ensuring that the Jew on the cross, Jesus of Nazareth, would die his death in the manner prescribed by Pontius Pilate. Sedition, rebellion, and insurrection were not trivial matters. Less than a day on the cross was normally about as long as it took for death to end the horrific suffering, and this prisoner was hardly less mortal than the other two men on their crosses who had also dared to break the laws established by the Roman authorities in the lands of Palestine.

Remnants of his purple robe lay around the base of the rude cross, where some of the angry mob had tormented the prisoner while he hung above them, before being chased away by the guards. The crucifixion of a criminal was an excuse to give vent to a public display against authority, more so than any particular disposition toward the prisoner. And yet there was something different about this man.

In the late morning, the agony of his wounds from the scourging of the whips was palpable. Later, as his body adjusted to the shock, there were periods of calm and lucidity, when his murmurings and incantations were soft and almost conversational, as if he was speaking to someone. There was never any malice toward the soldiers, who from time to time were unsettled by the face of the Jew that both sought and gave compassion. No soldier wanted to be on the detail assigned to a crucifixion, the cruelest of deaths, learned from ancient Carthage.

The strengthening sun shone unmercifully as he moaned in and out of consciousness, while the weight of his body and the stress on his joints did their work. The centurion made sure that his soldiers were attentive to their patrols, so that Jews were no longer allowed in the vicinity of the crucifixions. He did make an exception for two women, who the centurion took to be the mother and sister of the Jew. They were granted time to say their final words, but were restrained from giving him food or water. The young girl collapsed in her apparent grief, and had to be helped away by one of the soldiers.

There was a process for death by crucifixion, and the Romans were masters of the craft. If the centurion sensed that the death might take longer than a day, he would adjust the angle of the cross to make it more difficult for the prisoner to breathe. First one thief, then the other, was lowered to the barren ground on his cross, and ripped from the nails that held him captive. A soldier sent by the centurion to his unit at Herod's Second Wall brought a detail to carry off the bodies for disposal, as the sun's rays slipped over the hillside of Golgotha.

In the late afternoon, Jesus of Nazareth finally appeared to be in the throes of his death, but in a sudden period of consciousness he cried out for help, and asked the centurion to send for his follower, Andrew. The Roman, being a soldier but a man of compassion nevertheless, fought his better instincts and dispatched one of his men with haste.

Just as it seemed that it might be too late, as the Jew appeared to be increasingly delirious with pain, Andrew hurried across the rocky hillside to the crucifixion site, under the watchful eye of the centurion, and approached his Master. "My Lord, I am here with you, it is Andrew."

Jesus spoke in a voice as broken as his body, racked with pain, and said, "Andrew, my brother. You were the first of my Disciples, and you are my Apostle for all the ages. You were the best of men, and your righteousness shall live on in those who descend from you."

Andrew was agitated, and struggled to understand the words of Jesus. "What does this mean, Lord? For I have no wife, and have resolved to devote my entire life in your service, and to the word of God."

There was no response. The sounds of anguish and pain from his Master became elevated and urgent, as he suffered from the worsening stress on his broken body. Suddenly, the centurion told Andrew to leave, as the end was near. He had seen enough crucifixions to know when the dying had run its course. The rest of his guards would soon be called to take the body to Pontius Pilate for his dispensation.

With one last questioning look at his Master, Andrew turned away and took the narrow path down the side of the hill to find his fellow Apostles.

On the hillside of Golgotha, no birds sang.

Chapter One
Patras

In the time before history, there were people inhabiting the high lands of the interior and the deeply indented coasts of a vast and rugged peninsula at the southern end of the Balkans. They knew nothing of the Mycenaean culture that went before them. They knew nothing of a place called Greece, which was a kettle not yet boiled. But they settled, established communities, created villages and then towns around strategic locations, and in time became linked by custom and commerce into a society of City States, of which Athens, Corinth, and Sparta became pre-eminent.

War came to the peninsula known as the Peloponnese around 431 BCE with the military adventures of Philip of Macedonia, and his successor Alexander the Great. After the death of Alexander, the Hellenistic age saw the City States grow in size and influence, but they too inevitably succumbed to Roman rule, in 146 BCE. Within the Peloponnese, Sparta was the center of power and influence but, change being a Hellenistic constant, the City of Warriors began a gradual decline, and then it was Corinth that ruled the roost. The town of Patras on the northern coast of the peninsula was close enough to hear the cock crow.

In the ten years since the Crucifixion, the Apostles took up the cause of spreading the word of God, in the service of Jesus Christ. The ministry was in its infancy, and the Apostles were at the vanguard of a popular movement that the peoples at the eastern end of the Mediterranean would adopt in greater and greater numbers, and which would add complexity to the administration of the lands that were under Roman rule.

It was a pleasant summer morning in Patras, on land and sea. To the traveler on the escarpment above the town, making his lonely way along the dusty ridge, there was a sense of hope that he might find new customers for his leather goods. Out on the channel separating the peninsula from the mainland, where the winds were often favorable but just as likely to be pernicious, a fisherman wiped the spray from his eyes and focused on the breakwater that led to the harbor, anxious to get his fish to market ahead of his competition. The promise of custom was a prize hard fought for in the Peloponnese, and for those who tried and failed, there were also those who prevailed and prospered. There was life in the ordinary in this town, amid the curtain of security imposed by the occupying Romans.

A crowd of people at a corner of the main street listened to the preaching of Andrew, an Apostle of the man the Romans called the King of the Jews. An imposing physical presence always gave him the advantage when among his fellow men, but still he addressed the crowd from an elevated position on a bench, so that he could clearly see and be seen. And what they saw was a tall, well-built, good-looking man, with olive colored skin, and light blue eyes that spoke to a break somewhere in his Semitic lineage. The women in the crowd were glad for the chance to be entertained, and the rugged and handsome look of the preacher provoked a few asides and comments among the younger women. Too soon, they would need to move on about their daily tasks and chores, and a few moments of relief and chatter with their friends were welcome diversions. He looked as if he could be Greek, although it was pretty common knowledge that he was once a Jew, and was now proselytizing for some new kind of faith.

A sudden quiet over the crowd caused a woman's voice to reach a larger audience than she intended. "I tell you what, it would be a lot easier if all we had to do was pray to one God, instead of the many that we have to appease every day." That got a nervous laugh from many in the crowd, and suddenly the preacher stopped his preaching, and focused his gaze on the woman, with his piercing blue eyes. He had clearly heard her words. She froze in embarrassment.

His voice was strong, with a cadence that didn't threaten his audience as much as drew them in to feel his message. "Yes, it is easier, but life is not just about taking the easy way out. I want to tell you about Jesus Christ, the son of God, the only God." There was no doubting the intensity of his belief, as he paused before slightly elevating his voice. "I knew him as a living, breathing person, who brought a message from God for all of us, that there is a better life for us on Earth if we follow his teachings. I was with him when his mere touch

11

was enough to cure the sick. I was there when he raised a man from the dead. And I was with him when he was willing to suffer in death rather than repudiate his message of faith and hope in a new religion. He was crucified. He died for our sins. And I was there when he was resurrected as a living breathing testament to the power of the Lord, before ascending to Heaven. Believe in Him, and your life on Earth will be fulfilled. Believe in Him, and you will have eternal life in Heaven."

Amidst the whispers and murmurs from the crowd, as they passed their comments and asides to their friends, the woman turned away from the preacher, embarrassed to be the focal point of his sermon. She hid behind her shawl as she made her way through the crowd on her way to the fish-market. Behind her, she heard the rising voice of the preacher as he began to ask questions of his audience, in an attempt to engage them.

Later that afternoon, Andrew made his way home toward his modest house in a courtyard of small mud bricked buildings, close to the busy harbor of Patras. The narrow sand-filled track was wide enough to accommodate a wheeled cart, but more often than not was used by pedestrian traffic. The path ahead was clear, as he took out a faded red cloth from his tunic and wiped the sweat from his brow, and pondered the strange existence that he led, as if to question yet again the life that he had chosen, no, had been given, by his Master, Jesus Christ. For the last ten years he had traveled through many of the lands bordering the Black Sea, spreading the Gospel, before settling in the Peloponnese. He had kept his faith absolute in the face of many tribulations, as he reflected upon the journey he had taken.

Andrew turned along the pathway that led up to the small settlement and looked out from the high ground to the panorama of blue and green in the melding of sea and land across the Gulf of Patras. Once again, he thought about that day in Golgotha, when his Master had spoken to him from the Cross. He had never shared this with anyone, and kept hoping that one day he might receive a sign that would help him understand what Jesus told him, and why. It had been many years since his last time in Jerusalem, and he had only sporadic contact with his fellow Apostles since his marriage to Magdalena, a Greek citizen from Corinth.

When he reached home, he began to ready his small boat so that he could fish the nearby waters, and if lucky enough he might be able to trade the catch with his neighbors. Although the fishing was better in the early morning, he sometimes had good luck in the evening, and the calm sea augured well. Suddenly, he heard Magdalena call from the distance, as she returned from a visit to one of her friends. In a few moments she fell into his embrace as she spoke excitedly to her husband. "Andrew, I have something to tell you. I can't wait, I am so happy."

Andrew wrapped his arm around her as he brought her into the small rectangular room that was their living and sleeping space. The only other room in his house was even smaller, and used as a stable of sorts for his two goats. Her news that she was pregnant came as no surprise to Andrew.

"Magdalena, you are even more beautiful than ever." He held his wife closely and tasted the sweetness of cloves from her breath as they kissed. On another day he would have closed the door as a signal to his neighbors not to disturb them, but he reluctantly broke off the embrace so that she could talk.

While Magdalena told him about her visit to the midwife, confirming her pregnancy, Andrew was trying to think through what this change in their lives would mean for his ministry. Although Jerusalem continued to be the focal point of all the activities of the Apostles of Jesus, the fact is that most of them were spread throughout the land of Palestine, and only managed to keep in touch with each other through the growing body of converts to the faith. But first, he had to talk to Magdalena.

He looked into the eyes of the only woman he had ever truly known, and only ever loved. She was taller than most women, with perfectly formed features. Her brown eyes, coal black hair, a small brown birth-spot just below her left eye, and a figure that was the envy of her friends, made for a striking example of femininity. He could not but help caressing her shapely body, which curved out behind her, as it curved out from her chest, and Andrew was both nervous and elated as he spoke.

"Magdalena, I too have something that I need to share with you. In some way it is a burden that I have carried for a long time, as I have struggled to make sense of it." Andrew quietly told her of his message from Jesus as he was dying on the Cross, and of how he had kept this to himself for all these years, not knowing if it would make him different from the other Apostles, and how this might be perceived by them. There were strong personalities in the group, and he did not want to cause any trouble among his brethren.

"While I don't really know why Jesus spoke to me the way he did, I have come to believe that whatever the reason, it can only be for the best. It never occurred to me before then to even think of marriage, and then you came along and it seemed so right."

Magdalena teared up, and burrowed her head into him for the security and comfort that he always brought when they were together. She loved him without reservation.

Andrew looked up for a moment, and in that moment, he suddenly felt the relief that came with the sharing of the message from Jesus. For the first time he felt inspired, rather than intimidated. Perhaps all Jesus wanted to do was just to thank him as the first of his followers, and free him of any implied bondage to the faith that would prevent him marrying and having children. Could it really be that simple? He squeezed Magdalena's broad shoulders as he stepped back and let her go. "Magdalena, as usual you have solved my problem just by being here. Now, I need to find some fish to feed my hungry wife and child!"

The commanding presence of the Sun over the Peloponnese began to weaken in intensity as it lowered over the western sea, and for those who fished her waters, this was a last call for action.

As Andrew made his way down to his small boat that was tied to an anchor on the sand, his thoughts eventually focused on the task at hand. Fishing in the open sea was not the same as fishing in a lake, and while his nets were able to trap the small shoals of sardines as they ran, he needed to line fish in order to land mullet and bream. Andrew put his effort into the pull and push of the oars, as the running tide made his work more difficult. His keen eyes constantly roved across the water. Fishing for men was how he thought of his ministry, but fishing for the table took him back to a place faraway, where his missionary journey had begun, by the shores of Lake Galilee.

Magdalena was adored by the many families who lived in the small settlement, and shared the surrounding patchy but resilient grass where their livestock grazed. Some were Greeks citizens who had received the word of God through Andrew, although most still worshipped in the old ways. There were even a few Jewish families who clung to their faith and their belief that they would all return to Jerusalem one day, but felt the need to hedge their bets. The rivalry over their respective religions was never a barrier between these Jews and Gentiles, living in close proximity, and sharing a sense of community.

It was her neighbor Sarah who looked after Magdalena on those days when she was unable to manage a full work-load, and had to rest. The daily life as a follower of Christ and a wife meant that Magdalena not only had to organize the household affairs, such as the barter for food, cooking and cleaning, and working the vegetable plots in and around the courtyard, but she had also had to support Andrew with his ministry. As she approached the full term of her pregnancy, she did as best she could, but for the last few days she was unable to move easily, and was relieved to let Sarah take care of the household duties, in addition to her own.

And then late one afternoon her water broke suddenly, and she felt the sharp stabs of pain that signaled the movements of the impatient child inside her. As she lay in obvious and growing distress, Andrew arrived home early, and hurried to her bedside, feeling a different pain, as he called for Sarah to tend to his helpless wife. Before the sun set, she had delivered a baby boy. Sarah had told Magdalena many times that her hips were made for birthing, but that had been of little comfort during the agonies of the delivery. At last, she felt a release from the blinding pain, and lay back on the bed as she settled loving eyes on the small naked bundle that she had delivered.

"Here you are, Andrew, you should cut the cord now." Sarah passed Andrew the knife that had been cleansed in the fire, and he quickly cut through the flesh that had chained his son to his mother, and now was no longer of any utility. Andrew was thrilled to hold his newborn son, but taken aback by his gray eyes.

There was no doubting his black hair however, sprouting irregularly across his head, and when Sarah told him that the gray eyes would probably turn blue within a few months, he was content. As Andrew held his tiny child before passing him to his mother, he could feel the racing heartbeat. He had produced a son, and in some way, he had his Master to thank for it. He had already decided to name his son Andreas, to acknowledge Magdalena's heritage, yet still bless his child with his own name.

As time went by, Andrew continued to build a reputation as a priest of the new religion that he preached, and their domestic life was tranquil and happy, as they made their life together in the service of Jesus. Andreas became a fit and handsome young boy, who was loved dearly by his parents. Yet while their lives were filled with the peace and quiet of domesticity, the world outside their home was changing.

The Romans ruled their Empire with a heavy hand, yet were generally accommodating to the role of religion in the lives of their subjects. Through the practice of Syncretism, Rome accepted that all religious beliefs, philosophical teachings, and government systems could be compatible only within a controlled political environment, such as that imposed by the Roman Empire. Andrew understood the paradox that it was the very presence and dominance of the Romans that enabled him to travel as a missionary of a faith that directly contradicted the Roman ethos, and yet be able to speak freely of his cause.

However, within the many sub-divisions of the Roman occupation there were inevitably those who pushed the rules to satisfy their personal biases. Andrew had to pick his way carefully on a daily basis, as he sought to spread the word of God without upsetting the various levels of authority in the towns and villages throughout the Peloponnese, and occasionally across the Gulf into the mainland.

He could usually be found by the Jewish Temple in Patras, either speaking on the corner from his allotted bench, or conducting services that gave structure, discipline, and orthodoxy to the converted. He was tolerated by the older Jews of Patras, who clung stoically to their established beliefs, while the younger people took a more open view and were not afraid to engage in dialogue with him. As Patras was an important sea-port as well as a market town for many of the smaller towns and villages throughout the area, there was a steady stream of visitors who came by the Temple for news and entertainment as well as religious instruction. The faith of Jesus of Nazareth was no longer an aberrant child of Judaism.

One afternoon, shortly after Andreas had his eighth birthday, Andrew was sitting on the ground near the breakwater wall mending his nets when he looked up to watch a ship entering the harbor. The curved prow and single white sail were typical of the trading ships that worked the eastern Mediterranean, and the helmsman seemed glued to the rudder as he went about his business. Suddenly, as the vessel tacked to make the final run in to the dock, he saw a familiar figure waving and shouting to him from the deck.

"Andrew, it is me, Philip. I have news from Jerusalem." Andrew had no trouble recognizing his friend, the Apostle Philip, and was overjoyed to see him after so many years. The ship slowed as it approached the aged wooden planking of a pier that was set in the water, her docking ropes on the aft side pulled by the dock-hands to fight the settling of the hull as it rudely met the bulwark of the pier. Yet even as the boat docked, Andrew was apprehensive to know why Philip was in Patras.

They embraced warmly by the side of the dock, and Andrew picked up the bundle of belongings that had been dropped over by the young deckhand. "Come Philip, we have a lot to catch up on since we last met." Andrew led him along the shore toward his house, as they both laughed together and renewed their friendship. "My house is just along the way, and I'll be happy to kick out the goats and give you a place to lie."

As Philip chatted on about his journey from Jerusalem, Andrew could not help but think back to their early childhood in Bethsaida, their baptism by the Baptist John, and their journeys with Jesus across the lands of the Jewish people on their way to Jerusalem.

Magdalena and Andreas heard Andrew's voice in the distance, and waited by the door to greet the stranger who was with him. "Magdalena, Andreas, this is my friend Philip, and he brings news from Jerusalem." Magdalena hugged this man Philip, of whom she had heard so much, and went to the kitchen area to prepare some food for him, while he ruffled Andreas' hair and told him how much he looked like his father.

Soon the men were delving into a heap of fresh oysters, that needed a touch more salt than that provided by their own jellied mass. Andrew also added a healthy measure of wine vinegar, having picked up the habit on his journeys around the Black Sea. Andreas was happy to listen to the men talk, and he hung on to every word, having grown up with his father's stories of Jerusalem, and his childhood by the Sea of Galilee.

After a while they took a seat outside to enjoy the cool of the evening breezes as they swept in from the western side of the Gulf, and into the welcoming embrace of the residents of Patras.

Andrew had decided to deal up front with the issue of his marriage. His many years in the backwaters of the Roman Empire had sheltered him from regular interaction with his fellow Apostles, but now there was no way to avoid the issue. "Philip, you need to know that my marriage to Magdalena and the birth of my son Andreas is no impediment to my service on behalf of our Lord. I am as committed as I ever was."

Philip smiled, and slowly shook his head. "Andrew, this is no issue between us or our fellow Apostles. Many of our brothers in Christ are married, and have children too." Then with a smile he told Andrew of his own wife Julia, and their daughter Leah.

The relief that Andrew felt was almost overwhelming. That last conversation between Andrew and Jesus need never be an issue between Andrew and his fellow Apostles. The blessing from his Master was between the two of them, and in his heart, Andrew had hoped all along that this was the intention of Jesus, when he spoke from the cross at Golgotha.

Philip then began to tell Andrew why he had come to Patras to seek him out, and to ask that he accompany him back to Jerusalem to attend a meeting of the Apostles. In the years since the resurrection of Jesus, and his ascension, the Apostolic missions carried the message of Christ from the heart of this new religion in Jerusalem to the larger world. However, there were schisms developing among the Apostles, especially since the inclusion of Paul of Tarsus, whose conversion on the road to Damascus had portended an impact of breathtaking proportion on the followers of Christ in how they would manage their ministry.

"In the early days it was so much simpler. We attended to the poor, healed the sick, and spread the word of the Lord among the people of the Galilee, Samaria, and Judea. Now we have to deal with a myriad of other ritualistic issues that are part of our Judaic heritage, such as whether or not circumcision has a role in the conversion of non-Jews to our new faith."

Philip was visibly moved as he sought to impart to Andrew just how divisive the feelings were among the Apostles on not just these issues, but on so many other matters that dealt with the practicalities of establishing the message of Christ as a religion of the people.

"Andrew, we need you in Jerusalem to help us decide how our teachers should teach, and how our followers should follow. We need to meet together, all those who value the word of our Lord Jesus above the rituals of the Temple, and reach a concord that allows our Gospel to thrive and prosper, and not wither as a vine lacking the water of life to sustain it."

In the way of Andrew, he asked for some time to dwell upon the matter. Andrew was proud of his ministry that was based in Patras, but also included many of the rural regions of the Peloponnese. He wanted to show Philip how it was organized, so he took him to evening prayers to introduce him to the growing number of Romans, Greeks, and Jews who had accepted Jesus Christ as their Savior. His congregation was overjoyed to meet someone from

Bethsaida on the Sea of Galilee, who had known Jesus Christ, and they were anxious to hear of how the movement was growing. There were often questions asked by his own congregation about many aspects of dogma, and Andrew always had a difficult time with such issues, given the long time that he had been away from the center of the faith in Jerusalem.

Once Andrew made up his mind about the need to go to Jerusalem, it was an easy decision to ask his friend Abydos to run the ministry in his absence. He drew inspiration from the excited reaction of his congregation to the convocation in Jerusalem, and he could understand why. It was a validation of their faith, and a reminder that they were all part of something much larger. Soon Andrew and Philip, walking slightly ahead of Magdalena and Andreas, made their way home. It was a beautiful evening in a part of the world that was truly blessed. Twilight drew a soft cover over the Peloponnese, as the people turned from their daytime activities and made their way home to the farms, villages and settlements around the town.

Before committing to Philip, Andrew needed to speak to Magdalena, and get her blessing on his plan. At his suggestion they took a walk together along the nearby shore, and after a spell of unusual silence from Andrew, Magdalena stopped and turned toward him. "Andrew, what's the matter?"

He looked at her, and held her close, as he raised the issue that he knew would be a difficult one for his wife to accept. He asked her to agree to let Andreas go with him to Jerusalem. "Andreas has a burden to bear as the son of an Apostle of Jesus, and this is a chance for him to see the Holy City of Jerusalem, and meet those who were closest to Our Lord."

It had not occurred to Magdalena that Andrew might want to take Andreas with him, and her first instinct was to shake her head in consternation at the thought of her young son undertaking such a journey. "Andrew, are you sure you want to do this? There are so many things that could happen, I just can't imagine it." Andrew didn't take issue with his wife, and hugged her as he told her to let the matter lie for a while. He knew it was a big decision.

Andrew left to join Philip and Andreas, who were in the courtyard among a group of friends and neighbors. They were curious about Philip, and anxious to hear news from his travels. After a while the adults engaged the children by playing dice games, juggling oranges, and talking in jest and in earnest about their daily lives.

Later, Magdalena and Andreas lay in bed together with their voices in whisper, as they talked about the trip to Jerusalem, while Andreas lay fast asleep in the nearby bed. "I suppose that it would be a good thing for Andreas, even though I tremble at the thought. I would rather come with you both, but I must be here for Sarah. She will likely deliver her baby by the next full moon, and she is depending on me to help."

Magdalena lay still for a few moments, then turned toward Andrew. "Just promise to bring him back safely." They lay quietly for a while, till sleep came.

After breakfast, Andrew, Magdalena, and Philip talked at length about the journey to Jerusalem, and Philip was able to reassure Magdalena that there would be a welcoming group of families of the faith who would look after Andreas. "Your boy will be well looked after, Magdalena. There will be lots of children for him to play with, so please don't fret."

Within a few days they had planned their journey overland to Corinth, where they would be able to secure passage on the same trading vessel that had brought Philip to the Peloponnese. Andreas was excited about this adventure, but also sad to leave his mother for the several weeks of time involved in the trip. When the day came for them to leave, Magdalena was able to keep her composure enough to hug Andreas and give him words of encouragement. "Stay close to your father, Andreas, and everything will be fine. Just come home to me safe, that is all I ask."

Chapter Two
Jerusalem

The five-day trip, following the northern coast of the Peloponnese by well-traveled Roman roads, was uneventful, and the accommodating weather of summer made the journey palatable. When they reached the outskirts of the city of Corinth they turned south, and crossed the narrow neck of land that led to the port of Cenchreae on the Saronic Gulf. Philip recognized the ship as it lay in the harbor, tethered to the massive stone wall. The vessel was carrying mixed cargoes of foodstuffs to Ephesus in Asia Minor, where they would refill the hold with goods destined for the Judean coast. Most of the space on board the ship was taken up by cargo and crew, but there were a few places set aside for passengers. The Captain was happy to see Philip again, and made a fuss of Andreas, as he tried to take in all that was going on around him. "Looks like I've found myself a young lad with keen eyes who could handle a spell up in the basket," he said to Andrew, in the hope that the father would agree, and after a few words between father and son, Andreas was soon climbing the ropes to a perch on the main mast.

After unloading at Ephesus, on the far side of the Aegean Sea, the hold was filled with sacks of grain, which obviated the need for ballast. The hull settled into the depths, promising a more stable vessel for the onward journey. They were bound for the port of Caesarea on the Judean coast, after rounding the island of Cyprus, by following the coast of Asia Minor. It was a journey made many times by the Captain, but was never easy, and always required diligence as well as favorable winds that were usual at that time of year. Going around Cyprus to the north added miles to the journey, but avoided the difficulty of crossing the open sea.

Andreas reveled in his assignment, and then one day the Captain told him to keep his eyes on the horizon, as they would probably make landfall soon.

"We'll change tack now and leave the open sea for the coast. If I have my calculations right, we should be somewhere off the mainland near Caesaria."

"Land ahead, land ahead!" screamed the excited voice from the basket, as Andreas announced to the Captain and crew that they were within sight of the port of Caesarea, in the Province of Judea. The voyage had been uneventful, but the passengers were ready to set foot on dry land again, and eager to get to Jerusalem.

The last stage of the journey was along the well-traveled Roman road south from Caesarea along the coast, and then inland across the Judean Hills to Jerusalem, and the enthusiasm of Andreas kept Philip and Andrew motivated for the last few days of their journey. Every little village and town that they passed through had a synagogue, and more often than not there were a number of Jews present attending to one part or another of a religious ceremony. They kept themselves to themselves, and when the open road gave way to the climb up to Jerusalem, they stopped for prayer and thanks before finally arriving at the western walls of the city. Philip's home was a few streets over from the Temple Mount, and close to the rooms that were being readied for the Council meeting.

Andreas was thrilled to be with his father in Jerusalem, but spent his days with the many children of the other Apostles, while the men were deliberating on the issues that had led to the need for a Council to rule on many of the matters of dogma that had arisen in the course of the last few years. All roads led to the Temple on the Mount, and the children were free to run and play in the streets around the Temple, even although they were no longer part of the Jewish faith. There were shops with all manner of goods for sale, and the narrow streets were crowded with visitors and residents jostling for access to the stalls of the shopkeepers.

While Andreas played with his new-found friends, Andrew was able to meet up again with his fellow Apostles, including his brother Peter. He was a careful listener to the debates and arguments of the Council members, but found himself more often than not being swayed by the words of Paul of Tarsus. Paul was not one of the original Disciples, who followed Christ before his death, and witnessed his resurrection. However, through his force of personality and abilities to argue and orate, he was clearly seen as one of the leaders of the early church.

One day Paul sought out Andrew and asked to spend some time with him. They moved to a private section of the rooming house. After a warm embrace Paul asked, "who is this young man?" as he stepped across the room to acknowledge the presence of Andreas.

"I am happy to meet you, sir," said Andreas, as he took a seat by the door and sipped from a cup of water that his father had brought for him. Andrew and Paul spent a while in low conversation, as they discussed the matters that were before the Council, and it was clear that they agreed on many of the issues that were in debate.

Then Andrew asked Paul if they could talk about a personal matter that was important to him. "I believe that you are a Roman citizen, even though you are from a Jewish family in Tarsus. Is that true?"

"Yes, that is so," said Paul. "My family was able to acquire the right of citizenship some time ago, and were that not the case I fear I would have been executed long before now." Paul went on to tell of how he had been sentenced to death on two occasions, and each time he was set free when he was able to prove his status as a citizen of Rome, who were exempted from capital punishment.

Andrew took a deep breath and glanced at his son as he spoke to Paul. "As you know, I minister in Patras on the Peloponnese, and while it has been a long time since we felt persecution by either the Greeks or the Romans who predominate there, I sense a change in the temperament of those who oppose us, and object to our proselytizing. My wife is often taunted by Roman soldiers because of her marriage to me, and it seems as if the stronger we become as a movement the more we have to fear from the authorities in Patras and Corinth. I am worried about what will happen to my wife and son if something happens to me. I would like to be able to tell them that you will speak for them, and use your rights as a Roman citizen to protect them from harm should that be necessary in the future."

"Be comforted, my brother," said Paul, "you can tell your family that they live under my protection as a Roman citizen. It is the least I can do for such a good and steadfast servant of Jesus." The two men spent another hour in conversation on the matters before the Council, before Andrew led his son away to their lodgings. He had a feeling that this was an important development, and would someday make a difference in the life of his son. It was this concern that had prompted him to bring Andreas with him to

Jerusalem, and to meet the only one of the leading members of the Council to have Roman citizenship.

The next few days followed a familiar pattern, as Andrew joined in the Council debates while Andreas played along the streets and around the Temple with his new friends. One afternoon, Andrew stepped out of the meetings and went to join Andreas at a shop belonging to a friend in the Lower Market, at the foot of the western wall built by the Jewish King, Herod the Great. Earlier that day Andreas and his friends had climbed the stairways and alleys of the stone walls to reach the plaza above, and looked down over the city below.

However, as a Gentile, he was prohibited from access to the Temple itself, and his father had warned him to be careful not to get in trouble with the authorities. Even Andreas, as a young lad, could understand the seriousness of the many signs around the main Temple ordering non-Jews not to enter, on pain of death.

"Andreas, come join me, I want to show you something." Andreas embraced his father happily, and stepped along in his shadow as they walked along one of the streets below the Temple Mount. This was a section of the city that Andreas had not seen. The busy street markets soon gave way to a crudely marked roadway that led to a corner of the Second Wall, also built by Herod, and a gate that led to a rocky path along a hillside to the site of the crucifixion. The Romans had long decided to ignore the significance of the site to the Christian community, and merely took steps to ensure that it stayed the way it was, an out of the way and undevelopable piece of land.

Andrew held his son's hand tight when they neared the spot where Jesus was crucified, as he re-lived the final moments of their last time together. "Andreas, this is the site of the crucifixion, and the place where I last saw Jesus before he died on the Cross. Let us pray together before I tell you something that you must know." After their prayers, Andreas listened carefully to his father, whom he had never seen quite so serious, as Andrew told him of the blessing from Jesus that had been given to him, and those who would come after him.

Father and son sat for a while together on a rock next to the spot where Jesus died. Andrew was able to reflect on that terrible day, and finish his thoughts with a sense of contentment rather than the confusion and uncertainty that he used to feel. "Andreas, not only was I blessed by Jesus, but you are too, and everyone who follows from you. This is not easy for a young boy to grasp, but you are special, and have already been chosen by our Lord to be a force for goodness throughout your life." As they rested on the hillside of Golgotha, they heard a chorus of birds singing sweetly in the late afternoon sunshine.

After a while, they re-traced their steps to the city streets, and joined up with a few of the Christians who were enjoying a break from the deliberations of the Council. The talk was all about the decisions that would be made tomorrow on the many matters of debate that had engaged the Council over the course of the last several days. Andreas quickly found his friends and joined them as they ran through the markets and stalls of the Holy City.

James was the recognized leader of the Christian community, and it was he who announced the findings and conclusions on behalf of the Council members at large. However, there was now no doubt that Paul was the galvanizing force of the group, who saw as his mission the expansion of the faith in the lands surrounding Palestine, and the endless borders thereafter. The controversial issue of circumcision had been settled, as it would no longer be required of Gentiles that they be circumcised before entering the Christian faith.

This was a major concession by James, and a victory for Paul. There were other elements of the old Jewish faith that were required of converting Gentiles, but none as cathartic as this. Henceforth, James would lead the proselytizing of Jews in the Holy Land, and Paul would carry the word to the rest of the world.

After one last meal of thanks together, the Apostles retired to their various places of rest for the evening, and Andrew walked with his son through the quiet streets of the city to their rooming house. His last conversation with Paul reflected the warmth that had developed between the two men, as they promised to keep in touch with each other, and to meet up again if their Apostolic journeys permitted.

The next morning Andrew and his son said their goodbyes to his brother Peter, then Paul, Philip, and the other Apostles, before heading out of Jerusalem on the road to the coast, and the port of Caesarea. Andreas was a boy of eight years old when he started this journey with his father, and as they began the long road home together, he seemed to his father to have left his childhood behind. He walked with a stride and a purpose that belied the boy, and foretold the man.

They were lucky to find a ship at Caesarea that was bound for Antioch, a busy port city at the north-east end of the Mediterranean Sea, and the Jewish Captain and owner of the ship was happy to give them a berth in exchange for the coins of the Roman Empire that Andrew gave him, severely depleting his resources. After an uneventful passage along the eastern coast-line they docked at the port for Antioch, and Andreas pondered their next journey while Andrew walked with him along the quay in search of a vessel bound for Ephesus, or better yet, Corinth. The streets were crowded.

Aside from the usual plethora of Jewish merchants and traders hawking their wares, there were strange looking people with slanted eyes and short hair who went about in groups, as if ready to attack the shopkeepers against the prices of the goods that they coveted.

Hearing the sound of a voice calling his name, Andrew turned around and saw the Jewish captain of the vessel that brought them to Antioch. He was perspiring freely as he approached them, and told them that he had secured a charter to carry a group of Roman soldiers and conscripts to Corinth, and would be able to give them passage. Andrew quickly presented a false emotion of disdain for the offer, while secretly he was thrilled that there was a way home quicker than he had imagined. "I regret that I only have but a few coins of silver left from our journey, and one gold coin of the Emperor Claudius. You may have the gold coin, but I must keep the silver to feed us when we meet the road to Patras."

The Jewish captain would ordinarily have waived away the offer and demanded a more realistic price for the journey, but he had been impressed with the way in which the traveler had conducted himself on the first voyage. He was clearly a man with a good heart and an honest disposition, and his sermons to the Judean crew during the journey to Antioch were as honey to a bee. His stories and parables of this new faith that was spreading throughout the region were so simply told and yet so binding to the soul of the listener that his motley crew of lower-class Jews were entranced by his words, and the spirit with which they were conveyed. "You followers of Christ drive a hard bargain, my friend, but I will do for you and your son what I would do for no others. Come, let's return to my ship and break some bread together."

When they returned to the vessel the Roman soldiers were loading their gear and supplies, and Andreas was entranced by the military weapons and equipment. Andrew quickly surmised that the soldiers were made up mostly of conscripts, and young ones at that, so he approached the soldier who was giving the orders. "Good day, my friend. My son and I will be traveling to Corinth, and as he is but a lad of eight years old, I hope he will not be in the way of your men as they go about their work."

"Rest easy," replied the soldier, in a friendly tone. "Once we are under way, I'll make sure the lad is not put out by these young conscripts, who will soon be turned into soldiers of the Empire, once I get them on the parade grounds in Corinth."

Andrew was relieved that the Roman seemed an agreeable person, and his first concerns about the presence of Roman soldiers were alleviated by the warmth of the response. He ventured a question to the Roman. "These are young men indeed to be headed for conflict. What age must they be to join the Roman Army?"

The Roman laughed as he replied. "Let's just say that your own lad has about seven or eight years to go before he would have the pleasure of volunteering for service, although we often go through periods when conscription is a necessary tool to keep the engine that is our Roman Empire in a steady state of progression. That is the case with these young Jews, fresh from the fields of the Judean hill country, and my job is to get them through training and into one of the legions by this time next year. I fear I have a challenge on my hands, but hard work, discipline, and two meals a day can work wonders."

The sentiments of the Roman were a bit disquieting to Andrew, as he pondered the future of his young son in a land where the occupying army kept a tight grip on their authority over the subjects of occupied lands, known as the Peregrini, and maintained a forcible policy of compliance by the people to the many edicts from Rome. He motioned for Andreas to join him, and they talked quietly together of their time in Jerusalem, while leaning on the stern of the ship, and watching the hillsides of Antioch fade away in the dimming sky.

The voyage took several days, as the ship made its way along the channel separating the island of Cyprus from the mainland, and then weaved its way through the islands guarding the entrance to the Aegean Sea, that sparkled in the bright and certain sun. The winds were out of the north-west, so the captain had to work his men hard to keep the sails in the best position to tack across the open waters.

Andreas was an eager spectator, and made friends with one of the conscripts, an older Jewish lad named Isaac. His family had reluctantly agreed to let him go after being assuaged by the payment of a standard fee from the Roman Captain, who brought his troops to the village with orders from the Prefect in Caesarea. Isaac had been sad to leave his family, but excited to have the chance to see something other than the Judean countryside, and the flocks of sheep that required his vigilance at all times. He had an unusual characteristic. He was not intimidated by his Roman superiors.

"So, Isaac," said Andreas, as they sat together on some bales of straw that were there to feed the animals in the hold of the ship. "What will happen once you have finished your training?"

"Well Andreas, we are supposed to complete our basic training in Corinth, but after that, we have no idea. I fear my head and my heart will be put to the test before the year is out, but I have resolved to be strong, and to be silent. The Romans take me for a peasant, but I know who I am, and I will learn even more than they think they are teaching me."

Over the several weeks of the journey Andreas and Isaac became good friends, with Isaac happy to play the role of an older brother as they climbed the masts together, and tried to identify the many islands that littered the mouth of the Aegean Sea. The sight of leaping schools of dolphins soon became commonplace, and the boy and the young man whooped and screamed together as the fish swam and cavorted alongside the ship.

Andrew was able to gain the confidence of the Roman in charge of the soldiers, and was soon holding regular religious services for the crew and the conscripts, who were mostly Jewish by birth, but of varying degrees of commitment to the faith. He preached to them not as a priest, with a litany of scripture and rules from Judaism, but as a humble fisherman who was chosen to meet and follow the man who was called by others the Messiah, or the King of the Jews.

"Jesus did not acknowledge those words," said Andrew. "I followed Jesus among the hills of Galilee where he preached to the people, and my faith in the Lord through him became complete."

It was the simplicity and authority of Andrew's preaching that affected his listeners, and he never failed to be uplifted by the willingness of people to reach out for a firmer grip on the spiritual part of their lives, given their lack of control over the realities of their daily struggles in bondage or servitude.

The Roman soldier was happy for his men have some relief from what otherwise would be a long and difficult journey, and likewise the Captain had no concerns about what his crew got up to when they were off duty. Andreas and Isaac could always be found in the group of listeners, until they were inevitably distracted by a movement on the horizon, or the noises of the animals in the hold of the ship.

The small island guarding the entrance to the Saronic Gulf came into view as Andreas and Isaac peered from the bow of the ship. "Look, there is the lighthouse!" shouted Andreas, as they both scrambled up the riggings of the mast to get to the prized look-out spot. The blue waters of the sea turned to green as they entered into the gulf and gained on their destination of Cenchreae, the port of Corinth.

The two friends were able to spend a few moments together before the Roman soldier called for his men to muster in preparation for disembarking. "I wish you well, Andreas," said Isaac, as the two of them grasped each other's forearm in the way of the Roman army. All around them the crew was busy securing the ship to the dock.

"Do you think you might get to Rome one day?" asked Andreas, while his friend gathered his few personal effects in a small satchel that he had brought as a parting gift from his mother.

"I don't think I would care much for Rome," said Isaac softly. "I think I am bound for the ends of the Empire, and to tell you the truth, that is a better place for me. I yearn for the open spaces at the end of a long road. My military training will be tough, but it will make me a better man." Isaac stared off into the distance as he pondered his future, as if it had only then become apparent to him that his life from this point on was always going to be determined by someone else.

Andrew joined Andreas to escort him off the vessel, and gave a warm hug and a friendly wink to the young man who had been such a friend to his son. "Goodbye Isaac, and be vigilant. You have a strong arm and a good heart. I will pray for you."

Andrew and Andreas retraced their steps along the coast of the Peloponnese on the last part of their return home, and the olive groves and vineyards along the trails and among the hills, were as a welcome mat laid out to greet the two travelers home again. Andrew had already decided to take advantage of the quiet time together to talk to Andreas about the future. By the time they reached the small village of Aigio they settled in to a dry cave on the hillside, and Andrew sent his son to gather wood for the fire, so that they could have their last meal together before taking the road home to Patras the next day.

The whole plucked chicken that Andrew had negotiated from a grateful villager for the few remaining pennies he had left, was set carefully above the fire, and they took turns in moving the meat around to get the best of the heat and the least of the flame, as they chatted together. Ice cold water from a nearby stream and some sweet figs and grapes were all they needed to settle their appetite before they slept. Finally, after the meal was finished, Andrew told Andreas of his concerns for their future. He could see the increasing level of prejudice against the growing Christian community.

"I am worried, Andreas, because it is the very nature of my mission to convince people, all people, to let Jesus into their lives, and embrace the faith." He looked deeply into the embers as he continued to talk. "We are seen as a minor irritation to the Romans, who have no high regard for their own faith, with its countless and aimless gods, but the more we build the movement in and around the prefectures of the Empire, the more likely there is to be a push back against us."

Andrew reached out and grasped his son's shoulder, as he told him that the Apostles of Jesus were all potential targets of the Roman authorities, and that this concern could only get worse as the movement grew. "I worry for you and your mother, so you need to be careful, and to always be ready if I am arrested. There is a larger purpose to your life, Andreas. Remember, wherever you go, you must be a force for goodness."

Andreas could not help but look fearful before his father. He wanted to say something but was not sure what to say. He loved his parents, and knew enough to know why his father was worried, but had no concept of how to deal with such a situation, if his father was arrested, or worse, killed. "Just tell me what I should do, Father, is there some place we should go?"

"Yes, there is, Andreas. If that time ever comes, I want you to reach out to the Apostle Paul, in Jerusalem. Paul is a Roman citizen, and because of that he has certain rights and protections that he can use on behalf of you and your mother." Andrew went on to tell his son that they should head immediately for Corinth, and reach out to any of the brothers of the movement, who could be found at the main temple. "They will know how to get you passage to Caesarea, and then to Jerusalem, and you should take comfort from your knowledge that you have already taken such a journey, and know what is involved."

Andrew told Andreas to go ahead and get settled in his blanket, as they had a long walk tomorrow if they wanted to be home before dusk. A crop of mosquitoes gave them an uncomfortable time while they tried to stay under cover, then just as quickly disappeared into the moonlit night.

The two figures rounded the cliffs to the east of the city of Patras, and made their way home with a spring in their steps. Magdalena was scrubbing some clothes in a basin, and wondering, yet again, when she would see her beloved husband and son. Suddenly she heard the shriek of a gull as it left its perch on the sea wall after being disturbed. She looked up into the distance and saw two figures, outlined by the glorious red and gold of a dying sun from over her shoulder, and her heart began to pound.

Chapter Three
Maximilla

The young man who gathered the sail of the small boat did so with the skill of an experienced fisherman, yet with half a mind on matters other than his return to the harbor of Patras. That was often the way of a sixteen-year-old, mixing dreams with reality, or just pushing the moment away for a glimpse of the future. And always, a return to the present. Andreas pulled the oars back into the well of the boat and held the rudder in line to reach out and grab the weathered ropes lining the ancient wooden pier at the end of the harbor. He had a catch that represented fish to sell, and enough left over to eat, and he smiled to himself in anticipation of his mother's pleasure.

The small harbor near the narrow neck of land that separated the Greek province of Achea from the mainland was busy with fishermen returning with their day's catch. The horizon was dotted with white, salt encrusted sail-cloths, inching across the dark blue sea. Not many were as happy as Andreas, who had learned his trade well from his father Andrew, the evangelizing preacher who had established a growing and influential church of his converts to Christ in Patras, and the surrounding area of the Peloponnese. Andrew was indeed a fisher of men, zealously engaged in spreading the word of a God that had revealed Himself in the life and death of Jesus of Nazareth.

The soft rain that had fallen for most of his journey across the channel disappeared, and the warm embrace of the evening sun took over. As always, there was quite a crowd of people from Patras and the smaller villages in the area. Andreas strapped the basket of fish to his shoulders and headed for the market stall, and to the customers who came to trade goods, services, and money for the fresh fish of the Gulf of Patras. He found his usual spot next to the stocky wife of a carpenter, and gave her a hug as she stepped over to welcome him.

As usual, he was left with more than half of what he caught, but there was enough in the way of bartered bread and meats to please his mother, and he would surely find a neighbor or two who would be glad of a contribution of fish to help feed their families. He picked up the basket by the strap and slipped it over his shoulder, then headed for home.

Andreas looked fondly at his mother from a distance, as he saw her sweeping the front of their modest home in preparation for their evening meal together. It was a constant battle to keep the grounds free of the droppings of all the small animals who lived in and around the buildings, and while the cats could be trained to some extent, the dogs, goats, and chickens saw no difference between the hard clay on the floor of the house and the sandy area out front. His father would not be home until tomorrow, as he was visiting some nearby villages and homesteads, preaching to believers and talking to others who had yet to make the commitment to the new faith.

As Andreas dropped his basket, his mother Magdalena embraced him warmly on the crude patio area outside their front door. "What little fish ran to your nets tonight, Andreas, and how many big fish did you let away?"

"You know mother, that I am irresistible, even to the fish." She laughed as he made fun of himself, even though he was just acknowledging how much she loved him. He was only sixteen years of age, but already was the object of attention from the young women of the town when they went to the Temple. He was still growing, and would surely one day match his father in height. His skin was the color of rich honey, unlike the olive veneer of his father, and the creamy mix of olive and sand that highlighted the skin of his mother.

Magdalena busied herself with preparing the evening meal as Andreas relaxed for a while on the wooden bench that his father had built on the day that his son was born. The Peloponnese of Greece was the only home that Andreas had ever known, but he was aware that there was a larger world out there, and his voyage to Jerusalem as a boy had instilled in him a yearning for something different in his future than the life of a fisherman in the Gulf of Patras.

His father hoped that he would one day take over his ministry, but Andreas had larger ambitions, and struggled to respond to his father's urgings to immerse himself in the church. He thought back to his friend Isaac, who sailed with him from Antioch to Corinth, and wondered where he might be by now. He could be in Rome, Sudan, the Silk Road to China, or the north-western edge of the Empire, at the end of the known world. Such was the reach of Imperial Rome.

Andreas was a keen student, and had just completed his final studies in the schoolhouse that was attached to the Temple. From now on he would fish the seas to make a living, and help the household, while he continued to study the old religion of the Jews, and the writings and sacred texts that were preserved at the Temple.

The belief system preached by his father incorporated the stories and parables of Jesus that were fundamental to the establishment of the new faith that he had brought to this part of the Peloponnese. Andreas had noticed a change even in the last two or three years in the large number of Greeks and Jews who had converted, so that the church now had its own building attached to the Temple, and every day there were activities and events that helped disseminate the word of Jesus.

The following day Andrew made his way carefully down the mountain pass, tugging on the rope that was tied to his donkey. The addition of a pack animal had made easier his frequent journeys throughout the Peloponnese, as he carried gifts of food and wine that were provided by his followers to distribute among the poorer people who lived in the mountains and valleys, far from the Gulf of Patras. He always came back with a lighter load, and it seemed that even his donkey was less demonstrative and more pliable today, as if to reward his master for the absence of a burden on the way back.

Andrew smiled to himself at the thought, then glanced over to a nearby ravine in time to see an eagle swooping down to grasp an unsuspecting rabbit or rat from the scrub. *That might just as well be the eagle of Rome,* he thought, *picking its prey from a position of strength.* He quickly took that thought and made up the basis of a sermon, then quickly discarded it as being too contentious. This was the part of his travel that he liked best. When he was out on his own in the hills, and had time to think.

Andrew's church in Patras had grown significantly in the last few years, and Andrew was pulled in so many directions as he tried to balance his responsibilities to his community. He was a seeker of truth, who helped his followers deal with the day-to-day happenings in their life by a blend of realism and faith. He was a healer, who did not have the divine power of his Master, but still had a depth of practical knowledge about sickness and disease and how to treat them that made a difference in the lives of his congregation. He was an Apostle of Jesus who carried the message to the people, in the towns and villages of the Peloponnese and up in the mountains. He also had to run the business affairs of the church, which was no small task given the size of the congregation. He was also a husband and a father, who never forgot the blessing that had been bestowed upon his family by Jesus, as he whispered to him on the Cross at Golgotha.

As he reached the lower elevations of the hills, he could see a gorgeous carpet of color ahead, where the seasonal wildflowers had burst through with impatience after their months of suppression. With the color and the life-giving qualities that the flowers provided to the insect world below and around them, in this temporary kingdom the bees reigned supreme. They buzzed and busied themselves around the treasure of nectar that lay in the hearts of the flowers, and was the reason for the presence of so many hives, put there by the families who built their homes between the stream and the field.

Andrew paused to exchange some cheese and vegetables that he had left in his pack, for a measure of honey wrapped in a cloth that was still damp, lying by the side of the trail. This was a time honored trade, that spoke to the trust among the people of the Peloponnese, and it was never violated.

Andrew finally connected to the main road into Patras from the east, and soon approached the town center, and the sprawling temple buildings that served as a community center for the Jewish faith. It was also a home to the plethora of gods who looked after the Greeks and the Romans. The Romans, like the Greeks, believed that divinity was spread among several godhead figures, and the only way to be safe was to worship enough of them often enough to gain protection from adversity.

As he gained the entrance to his church, he was greeted by his friend Abydos, who motioned him over to a sheltered spot to speak to him in confidence. "Andrew, there is a situation that we need to deal with. These last few days the wife of the Roman Proconsul, Aegeas, has visited our church, and has been seeking an audience with you. She has attended services here for several weeks hidden behind her veil, and wishes to become a follower of Jesus."

This was an unexpected turn of events, and while Andrew saw every conversion as a victory for his ministry, he immediately thought about the larger implications if she was accepted into the faith. A convert must initially be baptized by Andrew, and must promise to conduct his or her daily life from that point forward in accordance with the example set by Jesus.

It was hard enough for simple people of the land to abide by the conventions of the faith, but it was quite another to imagine that the wife of the Roman Proconsul would do so openly without causing some kind of disruption to the uneasy peace that prevailed over this small part of the Roman Empire.

Andrew turned to look out over the crowd of followers who had just heard that he was back in the church, and were anxious to see and hear from him. Then a lady approached from the benches in front of the altar, where she had been praying.

"May I call you Andrew?" she whispered, as she approached him in deference, and yet with a confidence that only the privileged class could present. She was wrapped in a cloak of dark purple muslin, with a white knitted scarf untied around her neck, and flowing black hair held in place with a white sash.

"That would be fine," said Andrew, "If I may address you as Maximilla?"

She was taken aback that he knew her name, and Andrew let her know that the wife of the Roman Proconsul was a difficult responsibility to hide, and that he had seen her many times at civic events, although mostly from a distance. She smiled at this gentle provocation, as she could tell that he was really trying to make it easier for her to explain herself.

"I have attended services here many times, and kept my head covered, but I know now that I feel called to join the faith of those who love the Lord Jesus, and desire nothing more than to worship him and live a life in accordance with his teachings. Will you accept me into your congregation?"

Andrew replied in a soft, guarded tone. "Maximilla, are you sure that this is what you want to do?"

She knew exactly what he meant by the question. "I have no doubts, Andrew, and my husband will just have to accept it."

He knew he could not deny her, but he still felt trepidation as he conceded to her request. "I will be happy to administer the rites of baptism that will signify your commitment to our faith, and our faith's commitment to you. This can be done soon, as there is already a group of people who, like you, wish to join our church, and be baptized in the waters of our Gulf of Patras. This coming Sunday at mid-day is when I plan to hold services, where the River

Haradros flows into the Gulf. You have made a brave decision given your circumstances, but you'll be welcomed by our congregation."

Andrew took his leave graciously, and stepped over to join the group of people waiting patiently to welcome him back after his journey, anxious to find out what news he had from the hinterland. He did his best to circulate among the group, demonstrating the patience that was his hallmark, and finally he was able to make his way home. He said farewell to Abydos, who took the donkey to the nearby enclosure, where it would remain until some member of the congregation had need for its services. It was the many small acts like this that endeared Andrew to his followers, as he sought nothing from his ministry other than the opportunity to give.

The citizens of Patras were quick to move out of the way of the Roman chariot when it made its way through the town, toward the nearby hills overlooking the Gulf, as the charioteer flicked his whip expertly to keep the horses safely in the middle of the winding roads. Maximilla was lost in thought, and had no care for the steep hillsides that climbed to the villa of the Proconsul, where her husband Aegeas was no doubt waiting for her to return, so that he could chastise her again about her meddling with the religion of the Christians.

To her thinking, Aegeas was as Greek as the Oracle at Delphi, and yet he fulfilled his role as the senior member of the Roman government in the Peloponnese as if he were born in Rome, and not Corinth. Maximilla was carrying a burden in the form of a sickness in her eyes that kept her in pain for much of the time, although to her husband it was just an excuse for pity, which he abjectly refused to dispense. She knew he used his position of power to suborn young women to better satisfy his needs, and he had encouraged Maximilla when she first spoke of her interest in the Christian faith. Now that she was clearly captivated by it, he was suddenly jealous of her fascination with not only the religion, but the preacher who led the church.

As if to add complication to the quandary she was in, her brother Stratoklis was the one who had introduced her to the church, which he had joined almost from its modest beginning. He was a business partner of Aegeas in a shipping venture, owning trading ships that plied the coastal ports of the mainland into the farthest reaches of the Ionian Sea, and he was caught between the tension of his Christian faith, and his secular world that was intimately involved with the Roman Proconsul and their profitable business partnership.

Maximilla stepped wearily off the chariot at the door of the villa, and prepared for the usual verbal challenge of her husband at times like these, when she came home from a late afternoon service, after leaving him to eat his evening meal alone. He was not quite secure enough in his philandering to bring any of his women to the villa, and his trysts were normally conducted at the Roman Administration building in town.

As she entered through the ornate double doors and entered the large room, she was happy to see her brother sitting in conversation with her husband. Stratoklis saw the resolve in her face and looked questioningly at her as she hugged him closely, then administered a perfunctory kiss to her husband, who chewed angrily on a mouthful of soft nuts from a bowl on the table.

"I had planned to tell you in confidence, Aegeas, but it is probably better that you both know that I plan to be baptized this coming Sunday into the faith of the Christians." Her words seemed to echo in the silence. Stratoklis was secretly pleased, but knew how difficult this would be for his brother-in-law, who drew a measured drink from his wine glass as he considered his response.

"Maximilla, you may think that you answer to your own conscience on spiritual matters, but the fact is that you are now a Roman citizen, the wife of the Proconsul, and it is your position that will dictate how you pray, not some newly found preacher from the land of the Jews."

This was what Maximilla expected, and she knew that this was a matter that was much more significant than the perfidy of her husband, and his expectation that she will look the other way from his sexual assignations, in the tradition of the Roman elite. "Be that as it may," she replied testily, "But my conscience is mine to manage, not yours."

She looked over to Stratoklis with a shrug of her shoulders, then squeezed his arm briefly as she headed past him to her chambers, paying no attention to Aegeas. She was relieved to have it out in the open. Where it would go from this point forward was yet to be determined, but she now had a faith to temper her doubts, and a focus for her prayers.

The two men in the room looked past each other, as men do when their emotions are in conflict, and a fork in the road opens up to put their convictions to the test.

Chapter Four
Andreas

In the way of things, a year in the life of a young man like Andreas seemed to pass so quickly. For Andrew, the growth in the church had actually caused his life to become a bit less frenetic, and a lot less conflicted with the tugging responsibilities that were prevalent even a year or so ago. There was a sense of legitimacy to the church, ever since he had established a group of Elders to bring structure and organization to what had previously been a simple evangelical movement.

As always, there was purpose to his decisions, and in this case, he was already looking to the future. Prior to settling in Patras, Andrew had traveled throughout the lands of Asia Minor as the first Apostle to spread the word of his Lord. He had never forgotten what it was like to travel all the way round the Black Sea and preach to the poor, help heal the sick, and give hope to so many people of disparate faiths and beliefs, and many with no moral compass other than the misguided direction of a local despot. It was in these environments that Andrew felt tested by his Lord, and knew the joy of success that came from the faith and belief of the converted.

In order to prepare his church for his likely prolonged absence, Andrew had asked the Elders to appoint one of their members to head up the church in Patras. The Elders had in turn selected one of their most fervent and dedicated believers to take on the responsibility, the Roman citizen Stratoklis, who was overjoyed at this signal from his fellow converts of his obvious devotion and commitment to the church.

Andrew had relished the past few months, as he observed his church and their members, growing and flourishing in the goodness of their works. He had discussed with Magdalena his calling to undertake another Apostolic mission, and although she was terrified at the thought of his absence for a year or maybe longer, she knew that this was his calling, and that Andreas would be there to take care of her.

Meanwhile the Peloponnese was a hotbed of political activity, as the curtain of authority that was the Roman Empire drew a deeper fold over their subjects to the east of the imperial city of Rome. Proconsul Aegeas was consumed with anger at the protests of the people complaining about the high cost of bread, as if he was responsible for a disappointing harvest. There had been petitions and appeals to the Roman Administration for relief from taxes, which he had brushed aside, and as the news spread around the Peloponnese, there had even been a few street demonstrations. These he had quickly put down, with a few carefully selected arrests of the loudest of the mobs, and a clear threat from his soldiers that an act of force might soon follow from the mere show of force projected so far.

Compounding the social unrest was the growing popularity of the Christian movement from the Apostle Andrew's church in Patras. Aegeas had just returned from one of his periodic trips to Rome, where he was one of several Governors chastised by the Senate for permitting the followers of Christ to become a serious religious movement that was capable of upsetting the carefully balanced administration of the Empire. When the Senate spoke, the echoes reached the Emperor Nero. Aegeas felt vulnerable, which was a strange feeling, and now he needed resolve to show the Senate he was up to the challenge.

This nonsense had to be dealt with now, he thought to himself, as he prepared for disembarking at Patras after a long journey home. He hadn't worked so hard and applied himself so diligently to the service of Rome that he was willing to risk it all for peace in the family. His wife's conversion to the Christian faith after her baptismal in the waters of the Gulf was a direct insult to his own authority.

She appeared to have been cured of failing eyesight by her immersion in the waters that the priest Andrew had somehow made holy with his blessing, and now this word was spreading among the people, as a further insult to the validity of the temporal and secular power of Rome.

It was time for action, and his thoughts turned on a sudden recollection of the wife of the preacher Andrew, whom he had noticed in town on the way back from one of his trysts. After barely satisfying his lust on a skinny Jewess prostitute, he saw a beautiful full bodied mature woman near the market by the town square, linked by the arm with the preacher Andrew, and a young man likely to be their son. So, this was the wife of the troublemaker. Aegeas remembered that day well, and now as he lurched along in his chariot on the winding road to his villa, he hatched his plans and quieted his passion, to be satisfied later.

It was in this troubled political environment that Andrew made his preparations for his Apostolic journey, and although he admitted to himself of doubts about the timing of his mission, he always resolved them by his faith, which was pure, absolute, and made no compromises.

He had carefully chosen three of his followers to accompany him, who had language skills from the areas that he planned to travel in, and what with food supplies, equipment for bedding, pack animals, and a necessary stock of gold and silver coinage to be raised from donations, there was much to be organized. On the first day of a new week, Andrew busied himself with preparations, while Andreas was repairing a neighbor's roof, and his mother worked around the courtyard.

Magdalena was the first to notice the dust and noise in the distance, which she soon recognized as a group of Roman soldiers marching in formation along the coastal road in the direction of their community. A sudden feeling of dread came over her as she called on Andrew and pointed to the Roman soldiers. "Could they be coming to us?" she said softly to Andrew.

"There is nothing to be done, Magdalena, and nowhere to go. If they are coming for me, you need to stay close to Andreas." At that, their son joined them in the courtyard, having also seen the Roman soldiers closing in on the settlement. Within a few moments the cluster of houses was quiet, as their neighbors moved indoors, hoping that they were not the focus of the soldiers' attention.

Soon the troops approached the house, and Andrew could see that they were made up of two conturberniums, but were commanded by a centurion, rather than a lower-level officer. The sixteen-man troop was brought to a halt, then stood down while the centurion approached Andrew, beckoning to four of his men to come with him.

"I have orders from Proconsul Aegeas for the arrest of the preacher Andrew." The Roman was as imperious as the Empire that he represented, and drew his short sword as if to put an exclamation point on his statement.

"I am Andrew, and yes, I am a preacher, but since when has that been a crime against Rome. My message is one of peace. How could I possibly challenge the might of the Roman Empire."

A glance from the centurion was enough for four of the soldiers to approach Andrew, and tie his wrists together with rope, while a cart drawn by two horses was brought up from behind the squad. Andrew was pushed into the cart and tethered to one of the posts, and a soldier led the horses to the head of the line, to begin the journey back to the Legion barracks in town.

Magdalena watched powerlessly as Andrew was taken away, and she turned sobbing in quiet pain into the arms of her son, now more than a head taller than his mother. Having secured Andrew without protest, the centurion suddenly pointed to Magdalena, and the next group of soldiers approached her quickly and wrestled her away from Andreas, who was held at bay by the soldiers. She was likewise bound by her wrists, then led toward the cart to join her husband.

The first of the soldiers pushed Andreas away, as he tried to stop the men from taking his mother, then Andrew shouted, "Andreas, do not provoke these men. We will get this sorted out in town. Tell the others to seek an audience with the Proconsul."

Andreas stepped away from the men, and let his father know by a nod of his head that he had heard his words. He was shaking inside, but he tried to stay calm, knowing his father would want him to. The conturberniums had regrouped, and once in formation the men shuffled into step with each other, as they followed the cart along the road to town.

In twos and threes, the neighbors re-appeared and tried to comfort Andreas, while he closed up their home and prepared to go to the Temple, to tell Bishop Stratoklis of the arrest of his parents. His mind was racing with all of the possibilities. He could not bear to imagine that his parents might be harmed, and tried to tell himself that all would be well, as he set off hurriedly to follow behind the Roman soldiers and the cart carrying his parents.

After telling Bishop Stratoklis the news of his parents' arrest, he set off on his own toward the section of town where the Administration Buildings and jail were located. He passed by the buildings a few times to orient himself to the layout, and noted that the jail appeared to be at the side of the building, separate from the administration chambers, and connected by a narrow walkway between the building walls. The jail had only one street level door, and Andreas found a spot where he could observe what was going on. He gathered his cloak around and covered his head and all but his eyes, as if an indigent resting after too much wine. In this way he saw the comings and goings of soldiers and citizens as they entered and left the prison in order to fulfill whatever required them to be there.

As dusk fell Andreas saw a cart pulled by two horses make its way along the street, and the driver jumped down from the seat and fastened the reins to a post at the door of the prison. After a few knocks, and calling out "slops", the door was opened by the jailer, who beckoned the unfortunate city worker into the building, so that he could attend to his task.

The door stayed open, and every few minutes the slop man would appear with two buckets of slops which he emptied into large containers on the cart. When he had completed the last trip, the door was closed behind him and the driver jumped up into the seat and motioned the horses to move ahead. Andreas assumed that this was a nightly occurrence, and he now knew how he might gain entrance to the jail. He took the loose security as just a sign of the vanity of the Romans, then rose quickly and hurried away, heading for the church building where he could be sure of a place to rest the night.

The commodious stately villa of the Proconsul glittered brightly in the late sun, from its lofty perch on a hill overlooking Patras. Suddenly, Aegeas was awakened by a hammering on his bedroom door, as Maximilla vented her rage at her husband, who had imprisoned the champion of her new faith, and even his wife, on charges that were ridiculous.

"Aegeas, how could you do this?" she cried, "He is a man who does nothing but good, and yet you put him and his wife in prison. You must let them go!"

Aegeas opened his door, and Maximilla brushed past him into his chambers. "This is not your business, woman! This new religion is a pretext for subversion of the very foundation upon which the Roman Empire is based." Aegeas held himself erect and strong as he pointed his finger at Maximilla and continued his harangue. "The very assertion that there is one God somewhere who outranks the gods who have served the Empire so well is nonsense. It is nothing more than a ploy for creating unrest among the people, and it has no place in my Peloponnese!"

He turned away as if to dismiss his wife, and he tasted victory as she swallowed defeat. He could not help but throw out an aside, to goad her some

43

more. "Change your ways, Maximilla. Give up this false religion and let the people see your rejection of this faith. Maybe then I will turn your Christians free, and watch them give up on their following, and leave our people in peace."

"That will not happen, Aegeas, because Andrew would never let it happen. Once you believe, you cannot deny. My faith is in my Lord, and I trust in His purpose that has brought us to this place. I will have no more to do with you." She stormed out of his chambers, and left him to think.

Her response was as expected, and Aegeas thought little of his wife's recriminations, as he took comfort in the plans he had drawn to show his resolve to the Senate in Rome. The priest will be put down. That is that. We shall see how resolute is his faith when he has to live out his remaining time on a cross. So be it.

Later that morning, Aegeas met with his counselors and his senior commander of the Legion based in Patras. "This is a military matter that needs no courtroom justice. This priest has been conspiring to discredit the gods in favor of one God, and causing social unrest. An unsettled populace gives cause to those who would conspire against the right of Rome to rule in their lands. The charge is sedition, and the verdict is guilty. There will be a crucifixion tomorrow."

Aegeas looked around the room at his men, and saw them fall in line as they took it in turn to support his orders and espouse his argument. Aegeas dismissed his counselors to discuss military issues with his commander, and they quickly left the room, pondering this strong and decisive action by their leader. This was no time for disloyalty, and they all knew it.

Magdalena was alerted by a noise from along the corridor. Her cell was just a few feet square, and contained a rudely fashioned bed, a pot to use for her toilet, and a small opening with bars on the wall near the ceiling that she was not quite able to reach. A soldier jangled some keys as he opened the cell door, and beckoned her to follow him, after first securing her wrists.

The soldier led her up a narrow staircase that connected the lower elevations of the barracks with the Proconsul's office suite. He knocked cautiously and announced his presence, requesting permission to enter with the prisoner.

Aegeas was thrilled when he saw Magdalena up close. She was beautiful, and a luscious fruit about to be picked. He could hardly wait, but first he had to make her compliant. "So, you are the wife of the preacher, but that is only when you are outside of this room. In this room you are mine, to do with as I please! Do you understand?"

Magdalena was about to protest when he quickly cut her off by seizing her jaw in his fingers and pulled her close to him. "You do as I ask, and I will let your preacher live. Do you understand?"

Her eyes answered the question, then she nodded her head, saying nothing. There was nothing to say. He prodded her in the direction of his bed-chamber.

Aegeas took his time disrobing Magdalena, until she stood naked in front of him. She was a woman in the prime of womanhood, and he could hardly contain himself as he pushed her on to her back on the bed, and rose up into her. Her lack of response was of no concern to him, but merely indicated that she was in his complete control. He lost himself in the lust, and thrived in the soft and yielding folds of her body.

By mid-afternoon Aegeas had indulged himself again, and solved every mystery her body had to offer. He was not concerned about any repercussions, as it would never be made public.

Fortified by his ravishing of the preacher's wife, he summoned his jailer to take her back to her cell while he dealt with her husband. Once in his office he summoned the head of the Legion, his Legatus Legionis, and laid out his orders for summary justice on the charge of sedition. The preacher was to be crucified in the public square the following day at mid-day.

Given the growing support of the church by its many members, there could be trouble in the streets, and the commander soon left to meet with his officers and plan for the events that would follow. While due process was required for a citizen of Rome, a transgressor in matters pertaining to law and order in the community had no such rights, and fell under military discipline.

Aegeas sat in his couch and ruminated on the day's events. It was a pity that she had to be killed. He had tried to think of a way to keep her around for a while, but knew that he would be pestered by the Christians, who had already petitioned to meet with him about the arrests. He had taken the best of her that day, and she would likely be of no more use to him after the preacher was dead. Better to deal with her now.

Later that afternoon as the jailer was doing his rounds, he stopped at the cell where Magdalena was held. The cell door was slightly open, and he quickly drew his knife without thinking. He pushed open the door with his foot and saw the woman hanging from a rope of cloth tied to the bars of the window. He could see that she was dead. And this was no suicide. She was not tall enough to reach the bars. The rope had been fashioned from a length of cloth that had clearly been cut from her dress, and with no sign of a knife in her cell there was no doubt that she had been killed by someone else, and probably a group of men.

A heightened sense of fear quickly gave way to the realization that the Proconsul must have had something to do with this, and that the best thing to do was to leave her alone, and report her death in the morning to the man who killed her. In a state of panic, he left the door ajar as he quickly left the scene.

The fall of dusk added context to the silence in the streets, as Andreas hid in a nearby culvert. Soon the slop cart turned the corner at the top of the street, and slowly made its way down toward the prison door. As the slop man knocked his usual knock and offered his usual salutation, the door was opened by the jailer, who returned to the privacy of his room, where he could at least shut the door against the stench delivered by this nightly performance.

Andreas moved quickly over to the doorway, and prepared to enter several few paces behind the slop man, who stopped to fill his buckets with the contents of the pail resting against the door of one of the cells. The slop man moved along to the next cell, and in this way made his way along the corridor, filling his buckets as he went, from pails that were full to others that were almost empty. Before Andreas had moved into the corridor, the jailer suddenly reappeared and quickly moved toward a cell door that was partially open, and pulled it closed. "This one is empty," he said to the slop man, who merely shrugged and went on his way along the corridor.

Andreas had a premonition, and tiptoed silently to the cell door as the slop man turned the corner to the next row of cells. He looked through the bars on the door but could not see inside, and he was not certain enough to call out to whoever was in the cell. At intervals along the walls there were flaming torches of pitch secured in their iron rings, and Andreas quickly freed one and held it close to the bars. After a few moments his sight adjusted to the light, and he faced the horror that was the hanging body of his mother. He turned away and slumped over, and yet still had the presence of mind to stop from screaming. As he beat the walls with his fist he moaned in denial, and cried to himself in agony.

In a closed section of the prison, no more than fifty feet away from the dead body of his wife, Andrew lay on his cot and shivered in the dampness of the dark space. He worried about Magdalena more so than Andreas, as his son had been left untouched by the soldiers. He didn't know the underlying motive of the Proconsul in arresting Magdalena, and tried to convince himself that she would be seen as an innocent and released from custody. He had no such thoughts for his own fate, and he sought relief in prayer and contemplation.

Andrew had no qualms about the likely outcome of his arrest, and was ready to face whatever lay ahead with unshaken resolve in the cause that had brought him to this place. He prayed for his wife and son.

Andreas bolted from the prison building and ran until he was out of breath, sobbing and almost choking with the emotion that spilled from his body. He found a quiet place near the city gardens, and slumped over in grief and pain at the memory of his mother. After an hour or so Andreas was able to gather himself and think not of what had happened, but what must happen now. He had only ever known a life of kindness, sharing, and compassion, and now he felt nothing but rage and revenge in his heart. He let the strange emotion take over his mind, as he thought about what to do next, where to go, and even why.

Finally, he rose with a certainty of movement and purpose as he strode through the silent streets of town, and he soon reached the stockyard of the church, where he quickly located a length of rope from one of the stalls. Soon he was heading for the road that led to the south and into the hills beyond Patras. Everyone knew the hillside villa of the Proconsul, perched on a rocky and secure outcropping high above town, and alone in its splendor.

Finally, as he came within sight of the columns surrounding the villa, he saw the winding path that led from the villa on to the trail down the hill. He took one last look at his surroundings, then doubled back to find a secure refuge for the night.

Andreas slept a fitful sleep, and stirred at the first light of dawn. The path was a defined track with wooded sections and bushes on either side, thinning out as it gained ground, and Andreas back-tracked until he found a spot that would be perfect for his purpose. He searched among the trees and found a thick section of a newly fallen tree limb that fitted his grip, and using his fisherman's knife that he was never without, he whittled it into the shape of a hefty weapon that would surely serve its purpose.

47

After a while Andreas heard the sound of horses in the distance, as the Proconsul's chariot made its way through the gardens and on to the track down the hillside. Aegeas sat within the chariot as his driver stood in position and flicked his whip to keep the two horses in line on the journey toward the town. There was much to be done, and Aegeas felt a nervous energy as he planned the day's events that would show his power and demonstrate his authority.

The chariot slowed as it approached a rocky outcrop, and Andreas leaped out from the side and swung the club with all his might at the helmeted head of the charioteer. He went down within the echo of the strike on the metal helmet, and as he slumped to the ground Andreas drew his knife and jumped in front of Aegeas, who had hardly time to realize what was happening.

Grabbing Aegeas by the collar of his robes, Andreas held the knife close to his throat and motioned with his head for Aegeas to step down from the chariot, then forced him to the ground with the point of his knife. He quickly looped a rope around his neck and secured it to the wheel of the chariot. Cutting a length from the rope Andreas tied his ankles to the other wheel, rendering Aegeas incapable of movement. Turning to the soldier, who was still unconscious but breathing, he tied his arms behind his back and left him lying on the ground.

Aegeas was scared and almost in shock as he came to terms with his predicament, and realized that he might be killed.

"Fear not for your life," said Andreas, "It is not within me to kill another human being, and this is but one of the many differences between us. You will not die today, but you will be left with a message that you will carry for the rest of your life." He then cut a short piece of cloth from the robes of his captive, who was wide eyed and panicked at his predicament, then quickly thrust the piece of cloth into his mouth.

Andreas placed one hand round the neck of his prisoner, resting his head on the ground, and adjusted the grip of his knife, which was razor sharp, then set to the task. He placed the tip of the knife on the forehead and cut through the skin until it was deep enough for his purpose, then carefully drew the blade to carve the sign of the fish into the immobile face of his captive.

Aegeas screamed silently as the pain shot through him while the knife point did its work, and streams of blood drained into his eyes from the wounds. Andreas took his time, as he firmly imprinted the sign that had stood for the followers of Jesus from the time that his father was a fisherman on the Sea of

Galilee. It even had a name. Ichthys. When it was over, Aegeas knelt close to the soldier and felt his shallow but steady breathing. He had no wish to kill him, and the blow to the head had served its purpose. He would live.

There was no need to ponder his next move, as Andreas had already planned his escape from Patras, but first he had to see Bishop Stratoklis. He cut one of the horses loose from the chariot, and taking one last look at the bloody face of the Proconsul, he mounted the horse for the ride back into the town, before the Romans were aware of what had happened to their leader.

Early that morning the streets of the town leading to the Roman Administration building began to fill with the people of Patras, as the news spread about the arrest of the preacher Andrew and his wife. Andreas picked his way as quickly as he could through the crowds heading for the center of the town, and soon arrived at the church, where he saw Stratoklis in conversation with some of his fellow believers. Andreas dismounted then strode quickly to his bishop, who had become more like a beloved uncle over the last few years, and threw his arms around him, as if to clutch at something stable.

"Andreas, you are not safe here in Patras, and I have no doubt that Aegeas has already arranged for you to be taken into custody. He wants no trace left of your family, and he will already have told his soldiers to find you and bring you to him. Abydos has a horse waiting for you. You must leave Patras, and never come back. Andrew was clear in his instructions to us that should something happen to him, you must leave with your mother to find safety with the Apostle Paul. Now that you are alone, you need to quickly leave and seek the safety and protection that Paul can provide."

Andreas had no doubts of what he had to do, but was distraught with the thoughts that he would never see his mother again, not even in her death robes, and his father would soon die a horrible death about which he could do nothing. He looked at Sratoklis as if to question his advice, then shrugged his shoulders in acquiescence, his heart pounding. So many thoughts were pulsating through his mind, and yet there was a certainty to his expression as he looked at Stratoklis, then embraced him with an intensity borne out of so many emotions.

There was a moment when Andreas tried to speak, then choked up, but after a deep breath he told Stratoklis that his mother was dead. "I don't know what happened at the jail, but I think someone killed her. It might have been the Proconsul himself." Andreas spoke evenly and unemotionally as he described what had taken place on the track leading to the villa of the Proconsul. The old man and the young man held hands together for a few moments, and then Stratoklis motioned over to Abydos, before he turned again to Andreas.

"Take the mountain track that leads to Corinth," Stratoklis told him, as he helped Andreas mount the horse that had already been packed with provisions for the journey. "When you get to Corinth make your way to the port at Cenchraea and look for our ship 'Fair Winds' that lies at anchor, taking on supplies for her next voyage. Tell Captain Petrakis that I sent you. She is set to sail for Ephesus and if you go now, you will have enough time to get there before she leaves port. Once in Ephesus you will be able to make your way onwards to Jerusalem. Aegeas would never think to look for you on one of his own vessels. Here is a purse of coin."

Later that morning, Aegeas finally arrived at his offices in the town, having been rescued by a platoon of soldiers sent in double time to find him. His advisors had been at his offices since early morning, and had waited for his arrival. Eventually they sent the soldiers to his villa, where they found him bloodied, but in no danger.

After applying a bandage to his head, he changed his robes and took his seat on the replacement chariot, seething with rage and anxious to dispense with the preacher and show his authority to those who would challenge it. The orders of the Senate were clear. Stamp out this challenge to the law and order of the Roman Empire.

As he expected, Stratoklis and Maximilla were waiting on his arrival in the courtyard in front of the Administration building, along with dozens of their fellow Christians. The activities of the Roman soldiers in setting out what was obviously a crucifixion site in the market-place sent shockwaves through the entire town, as the citizenry came to see what it was all about. This was unusual, crucifixion being such a horrible and distressing sight, that the common people were usually shielded from it, by placing the cross away from public places.

"Aegeas, this cannot be true, please do not do this," pleaded Maximilla, as Stratoklis grabbed Aegeas by the sleeve to get his attention. Immediately a Roman soldier pulled Stratoklis away from the Proconsul, but Aegeas motioned the soldier to release him, and nodded to the sergeant to let his wife and his brother-in-law pass through with him into the building.

Once inside and away from the crowd, Aegeas said to them both, "Quickly say what you have come to say!"

Stratoklis looked earnestly at his business partner and the husband of his sister, and sensed the rejection before he had a chance to form his plea. "Aegeas, this is not the right thing to do. Andrew is a man who cares nothing for the privileges of power, and has no plan to usurp the Roman order. He is interested only in the welfare of the people, and in bringing to them a new message of hope. He cares nothing about the political affairs of men, and is no threat to Rome or its possessions."

Aegeas stayed silent for few moments, then looked up angrily at the people who had until recently been at the center of his life, and who had through their own actions helped to create this situation. "My orders are clear, and there is no room for challenge or defiance to a military order. Your beloved preacher goes to the cross at mid-day. Oh, and by the way, his wife chose to take her own life rather than wait for the mercy of her husband's accuser, which I would surely have given."

Stratoklis and Maximilla were prepared for this announcement. They both feigned shock and distress, as they did not want Aegeas to know that they both were aware of what had happened to Magdalena. They turned to each other and embraced, distraught with the news of what was to happen next. Stratoklis slowly turned away from his former partner and friend, and pulled Maximilla with him. He had a responsibility now to the members of the church to lead them through this tragic development, and they first had to stand strong in the face of the crucifixion of their beloved Apostle Andrew. The congregation of their church in Patras now numbered almost one thousand. He was their Bishop, and would soon be the leader of their church.

Andrew was led out to the town square, and secured in a pillory with his back and legs exposed to the soldier who carried the scourging implements— whips that had iron balls tied a few inches from the end of each leather thong on the whip. In short order the soldiers began the methodical process of flogging his victim, so that the iron balls caused deep bruising to the muscles, and the leather thongs cut into the skin. It did not take many strikes for the skin to break, and soon the blood began to flow from the many cuts.

As the soldiers stopped to offer Andrew sips of wine mixed with myrrh, a traditional elixir in the Roman dance of death, he asked to speak to the centurion in charge of the soldiers. "Soldier, you know who I am and why I am here. Let there be God's mercy in your heart to allow my crucifixion to be on another cross than the one that carried my Master at Golgotha in Jerusalem."

"You make no sense. I have no other cross to give except that which awaits you now." The centurion moved closer to Andrew, who again whispered to him that he could not face death on the same cross as his Master, as he was unworthy of such a glorious death. Just then, Aegeas arrived at the scene, and approached the centurion.

"Ask this man to admit that there are many gods, and that his master was nothing but a Jewish pretender who really wanted to lead the people to uprising and dissent against the Romans!" ordered Aegeas. Following these orders, the centurion challenged Andrew time after time, but he would not yield to the request, and merely repeated his Lord's Prayer.

"He does not deserve a last look at earth!" shouted Aegeas, and ordered the soldiers to change the cross so that Andrew would be tied upside down on a Crux decussate, an X shaped cross that was rarely used.

In this way Andrew's final wish was granted, and the crucifixion was delayed while the soldiers reset the cross so that the prisoner could be secured in a position that had his legs pointed to the sky and his head toward the ground. Once the soldiers had tied Andrew to the X-shaped cross, they then applied the nails through his feet and through his wrists, and lifted the Crux decussate into position.

As the soldiers did their work, the crowd of people in the square reacted in different ways. The more extremist Roman sympathizers chanted loudly, "Death to the Jew!" while the majority of the people kept their feelings to themselves, either in fear of reprisals or from the sheer horror of the spectacle. For Andrew, it was the death he always wanted, believing that anything less a death than the way of his Master would be a failing. His followers were aware of this, but were nevertheless shocked by the horror of his chosen path. Following Stratoklis, the Christians left the horror of the crucifixion to the Romans, and returned to their church to pray.

While the justice of Rome was meted out in the town square, Andreas was heading away from town into the surrounding hills, on a journey that would take him first to Corinth, and then far away from his home in Patras. His black steed was a handsome animal, with a strong and steady gait that still required the occasional nudge of encouragement along the narrow and exposed ledges of the Aroania mountains. As he reached the end of a rocky plateau that curved around into the inland hills, he looked back in the far distance and saw the crowds around the marketplace, and the central area where his father was dying, if not already dead.

Andreas dismounted, and secured the horse to a convenient wild pear tree. He had to pray, and soon gave himself up to his communion with his Lord, as he had been taught to do since a child. He cried with the pain of his loss, and for the souls of his mother and father, who had given him life and love in the fullest measure. He also contemplated the blessing that Jesus had bestowed on his father, which would now be his to fulfill. To be a force for goodness.

Chapter Five
Paul

The major port city of Ephesus was just as Andreas remembered it from his journey to Jerusalem. The harbor was full of ships of all descriptions, some of them clearly in the service of the Roman Empire, but most were there for the maritime trade that was the lifeblood of the eastern Mediterranean.

Only the scholars of biblical times were aware that this was the city of the Labrys, the double-sided axe of the Mother Goddess, which adorned the palace at Knossos on Crete. And the site of the Temple of Artemis, destroyed by fire on the night that Alexander the Great was born.

The ship's Captain was a fellow Christian, and a close friend of Bishop Stratoklis. He was only too pleased to carry Andreas to safety, and on landing had given him directions to the center of the faith in Ephesus. Andreas patted the horse's head and whispered a few words before handing the reins to the Captain. He was headed for the church that was the physical and spiritual home of Christianity in this part of Asia Minor.

Andreas soon reached what was obviously an outdoor ceremony attended by many hundreds of people, all with their attention focused on the preacher, who stood on a raised platform, and spoke his message to the quiet and respectful audience that was transfixed by his oratory. Andreas recognized the Apostle Paul almost immediately. There was no mistaking the small stature, bald head, hook nose, and crooked legs of the converted Pharisee known throughout the eastern Mediterranean as Paul of Tarsus. Andreas was elated at this fortunate turn of events, and settled down in a clear space among the crowd to listen to the rest of the sermon.

When the service was concluding, with the usual rituals and liturgy common to the emerging church, Andreas made his way to the edge of the platform behind Paul, and waited for the last few words of the Lord's Prayer.

He called Paul's name and when Paul turned around, he was unsure of Andreas until he spoke, and then he quickly embraced this young man whom he had last seen as a boy. "Andreas, it is so good to see you, you have grown so much. Tell me. How is your father. Is he here with you?"

Andreas quietly told Paul of the deaths of his mother and father. He had arrived ahead of the news, which traveled surely but not always quickly in this part of the world due to the distances between the major population centers. Paul immediately embraced his young friend, in the most human of comforts, and after a few moments he summoned his church leaders to gather so that he could tell them of the events in Patras. He knew they would be shocked to the core, and then alarmed at the prospect of further recriminations against the Christians. Meanwhile he arranged for one of his followers to take Andreas to his rooms, and to organize a place for Andreas to bathe and rest until they could meet at the supper table.

Later that night the two men were able to relax and talk about all that had happened in their lives since their first meeting in Jerusalem. Paul knew that Andreas had come to him for a purpose, but there was time enough for that. Tonight, it was necessary to listen to Andreas as he spoke about his mother and father, and shared his grief.

After a day or two Andreas asked Paul if they could walk together, so they set off along a trail that led into the hills surrounding Ephesus, and when they found a picnic spot by a clear and cold stream coming off the high ground, they stopped for a drink and to share a meal.

"Paul, I need your help to do what I want to do, and I hope that you will agree," said Andreas, as they sat down together on the soft grasses. "I have not yet the calling of an Apostle, like my father, but I know that one day I might, and if that time comes, I will gladly commit my remaining life to spread the word of God. As my father led, so I followed, and while I have committed to lead my life in accordance with the teachings of Jesus, it is not yet my remit to preach and minister. That is for another time and another place.

"The further I am away from Patras, the less likely it will be that the Proconsul will find me. The safest place I can be right now is deep in the arms of Rome, and the way to do that is to join her army, and become her soldier. It is the last thing that would be expected, and the one thing that will lead me to the far distance, and to freedom."

Paul was a skillful speaker, but no less a listener. He observed the calm and measured way that Andreas spoke, and saw the commitment to such a radical course of action. There was no fear in this young man; only an evident determination to take control of his life after the traumatic events of the last few days.

Paul took his hand in a firm grasp as he responded. "I'll be glad to help you, and here's what I suggest. I'll provide you with a letter that you must carry to the Roman Proconsul in Caesarea, Governor Felix. He is a powerful man, who authenticated the Roman citizenship of our family. He has the power to make it possible for you to make a new start, and he need not know of your troubles in Patras, only that you wish to serve the Empire and see the world."

The young man and the old man made their farewells early next morning, as Andreas carefully stowed the letter of introduction in his satchel and set off down the hilly road to the harbor. He was now familiar with the coastal and island shipping activities in this part of the eastern Mediterranean, and was confident that he could work his passage to his eventual destination in Caesarea.

Later that morning, Andreas once again boarded a ship in the harbor of Ephesus, only this time he was alone in the world, and about to change his life in so many ways. He was no longer a son of loving parents. He could no longer live openly as a practitioner and advocate of his faith. He was to all intents and purposes a Roman, and if his plans were fulfilled, an occupier of his ancestral home. All in the hope that he could one day travel to the farthest parts of the Empire, recover his faith as a believer in Christ, and spread the word of the Lord. He carried a special responsibility that weighed heavily upon him, that gave him a singularity of purpose from such a simple mandate given to his father. That his descendants would be a force for goodness, wherever they might be.

Andreas made his way unsteadily down the gangway in the port city of Caesarea. The sea voyage had tested his mettle due to stormy weather patterns that seemed to dog the ship as it made its way by the conventional trade routes that took it around the island of Crete to the south and west, and then on an angular path across the open seas.

There were few places in Judea more impressive than the port city of Caesarea in the time of the Roman Emperor Nero. It was not always that way. Sitting at a strategic point of land between the older ports of Dora and Joppa, the prevailing south-west winds would often compel ships from Egypt to ride at anchor in the open sea, so menacing were the force of the winds off the Judean coast. King Herod the Great dipped heavily into his treasury to build the huge breakwaters that extended out into the sea, but the transformation made possible a safe harbor, and the city had grown significantly by the time of Emperor Nero. The lighthouse was a wonder of technology, and the two large towers guarding the entrance to the harbor were at either ends of a heavy forged metal chain, that could be stretched between them to prevent ships from entering.

Andreas' petition to Governor Felix would determine how he would spend the next part of his life, if not the rest of his life. He felt a nervous energy, and had to steel himself into a positive and determined frame of mind as he made his way toward the Governor's Palace, which stood in its magnificence at one end of the harbor. He had no reason to believe that word of the recent events in Patras would have reached Ceasarea by now, and he felt secure in the knowledge that he would not be recognized.

Approaching the gatehouse, he beckoned to one of the two guards, and was rewarded by a snarl as the guard stood across his path to the entrance. "Who are you, and what is your business at the palace?"

"I am a Greek citizen who carries a letter of introduction addressed to Proconsul Felix, and would like to speak to the Captain of the Guard." Andreas stood to the full measure of his height that gave him advantage over the man, and said no more, as the guard eyed him suspiciously then turned away to report to his superior across the courtyard.

Andreas was soon waved over to the Guardhouse, and once again he explained who he was, and the reasons for his desire to see the Proconsul. The Officer of the Guard left him in the company of the soldier, and a few minutes later he entered the formal palace residence of Proconsul Felix, where he presented himself to one of the Advisors, and whispered the reason for the visit, just as the Proconsul himself appeared from the door of his main office.

The Governor, hearing the story, held his hand out for the document, and quickly scanned the contents, noting the name of the sender, Paul of Tarsus. Felix had a memory of an important and influential family of Pharisees in Tarsus who had sought and received Roman citizenship. The request was to conscript the bearer of the letter into the Roman Army, as the young lad had recently lost his family and had decided to begin a new life for himself far from his home. Paul's letter was solicitous in the extreme, and Felix was quick to scribble his signature on the letter approving the request. If only every petition from wealthy Jews was as easy to deal with.

Within a few minutes Andreas was standing before the Officer of the Guard, while he completed the paperwork and formalities of his conscription. Voluntary enlistment was not something that was too common in the Roman Army, but every new conscript was one less that the Officer of the Guard had to find in order to meet the goals set by someone in faraway Rome. He then told Andreas that he would join the next available training unit, which would likely be here in Caesarea. The battle-hardened officer liked the look of the young man, and passed on a few words of encouragement. "Take my advice. Pay attention to your training. When you are on the front line, it is kill or be killed."

Andreas nodded his appreciation, while another soldier was summoned to take Andreas to the Armicustos so that he could be given the proper kit and basic weaponry. There was no turning back. The requirement to kill or be killed was contrary to all that he had been taught by his father, but what choice did he have. He was willing to face the issue if or when he had to.

In the late spring of that same year, when the Feast of Pentecost was about to enliven the people of Jerusalem as they celebrated the giving of the Laws to Moses in the Sinai, Paul made his return to the city, and thereby completed his third missionary journey. His travels in the last two years had taken him all around the eastern Mediterranean, and he had finally docked at Caesarea a few days ago, then journeyed through Judea to Jerusalem. He had made this journey through the green Judean hills so many times, and never failed to be inspired by the beauty that nature had bestowed on the land God gave to the Jewish people.

While in Caesarea he stayed at the home of Philip, his fellow evangelist, where he was asked by a man named Agabus, a prophet, to lend him his belt, which he did. Agabus then bound his own hands and feet with the belt, and gave a prophecy that the Jews of Jerusalem would bind the man who owns this belt and deliver him into the hands of the Gentiles. The prophecy caused consternation among Paul's followers, who pleaded with him not to go into Jerusalem, but Paul had no fear of the future, and made plans for his departure in time for Pentecost, and a re-union with his brothers in Christ.

Jerusalem was a hotbed of religious controversy when Paul made his way through the gate at the residential quarter of the upper city, and returned to the place that was the very center of his faith.

There were several members of Paul's entourage who had converted to the faith in faraway places, and had journeyed with him to see Jerusalem and the Holy Land. They were mostly Gentiles from Asia Minor, and were overcome with emotion to be so close to the center of the Christian movement, whose formative doctrine was nevertheless embedded in the faith of Judaism. Later that day, he accompanied his converts through the old city and into the Temple Courts, and pointed out the various holy places on the Temple Mount, many of which were inaccessible to all but those Jews who had completed the rites of purification before entering. Of all the courts, the most holy was that of the Devir, which could only be entered by the High Priest. Unlike the other courtrooms, this place was empty and devoid of garnishments, so that it was filled only by God.

At any festive occasion the Temple Mount was crowded with people, and while some came to participate in the symbolic acts of their religion, there were many who just wanted to be there, and enjoy the hustle and bustle of the crowds. As Paul and his followers were about to leave the Temple area and descend into the city proper, he was accosted by a group of Jews who demanded his arrest. The ringleader of a group of Jews from Asia Minor who hated Paul cried out to the crowd. "Men of Israel, help! This is the man who teaches against the only true faith, and he has brought Greeks into the Temple and defiled this holy place."

The religious tension in the city was palpable, and the accusation was enough to stir the crowd into action, as they accosted Paul and his followers and demanded an explanation. As Paul tried in vain to respond, a riot soon erupted, and within a few moments a mob had seized him, dragged him off the Temple Mount, and began to beat him. The Roman soldiers policing the exterior of the Mount rushed over to sort out the rabble, and were able to free Paul from his captors, only to bind his wrists and escort him toward the nearby barracks.

As Paul was led away, he pleaded for permission to speak to the people, but his attempts to placate them were barely heard over the noise of the crowd, and the Roman soldiers, fearing that the riot might start again, pulled Paul away and into custody.

The soldiers in the barracks set about the task of securing him to the bench, as they prepared to apply the metal tipped whip with enough intensity to secure a quick confession, as was typical in the treatment of non-Roman citizens.

"Stop this now. I am a Roman citizen and I demand to be released!" shouted Paul, and on hearing this, the centurion in charge of the soldiers motioned to his men to stand down, while he considered the situation. "You are a citizen of Rome, and yet you wear the attire of a Jew and worship on the Temple Mount," he said carefully, as if interrogating the man before him. "This is a nice trick, but not many can perform it."

Just then the Commander of the soldiers entered the barracks room, and was quickly apprised of the situation. The centurion was glad to be relieved of responsibility for the Jew, and he gladly stepped aside. The Commander had no need to raise his voice, as he was accustomed to an attentive audience. "Tell me who you are, and on what basis you claim Roman citizenship?"

"I am known generally as Paul of Tarsus, and was born in the free city of Tarsus, which automatically makes me a citizen of Rome, as I am sure you know. I also had my citizenship authenticated by Proconsul Felix, who now commands from Caesarea, but who once held office in Cilicia, where we met. I am sure he will be glad to confirm my status."

The Commander was satisfied that the scourging was not yet necessary, but there still was the matter of the accusations by the Jews against him, so he remanded Paul in custody for the night, as much for his protection as the interests of the government in the maintenance of law and order in the city.

On the following day Paul was taken before the Sanhedrin—the Supreme Council of the Jews, composed of seventy Elders plus the High Priest. This council met in the chamber of hewn stones, and Paul was brought in and stood on trial before the leaders of the Jewish faith. The arguments raised back and forth between the Elders and Paul, as he took issue with each of the accusations, and replied forcefully, and on occasion with a lack of grace not customarily directed to the Elders. When a group of Elders who were Pharisees realized that Paul was one of their own, they appeared to waiver on some of the issues, igniting the wrath of the Sadducees in the group, so that the end of the day saw no resolution of the matter.

Paul was taken back into confinement for the night, and in the morning was preparing to return to the Temple to continue his interrogation when word came of a plot to kill him, hatched by a forty strong group of Jewish zealots.

The Commander realized that the situation was getting out of control, so he made a command decision to have Paul moved to Caesarea where he could answer to the charges before Proconsul Felix. He prepared a petition to the Governor explaining the facts of the case, and requesting that Paul be tried there, as security in Jerusalem was compromised by the volatile nature of the charges.

That evening, Paul, by now deemed an important prisoner, was escorted out of Jerusalem by a Roman military formation of two hundred foot-soldiers, two hundred spearmen, and seventy horsemen, who guided their mounted prisoner on yet another journey along the road to Ceasarea, only this time to a trial before Proconsul Felix. When they reached the town of Antipatras, where they would encamp for the night, the foot soldiers were ordered to return to Jerusalem, now that the initial danger had passed.

Paul whistled softly to himself as he rode on the horse behind the cavalry, his hands secured by a rope, on the road from Antipatras toward Caesarea. The city walls rose before them on the last leg of the journey, and after an authorized passage through the southern gate the troops headed in the direction of the former palace of King Herod the Great, where they could turn over their captive and rest at the local garrison.

It had been easy duty, once they had left the dangers of Jerusalem behind them. Keeping order between the Jews and the Christians was becoming a serious problem throughout the lands of Israel, and there was relief among the men to be rid of their charge, with time to enjoy the taverns of the city for a night before their return to Jerusalem.

King Herod's palace was now the home of the Proconsul, Governor Felix, and he was finishing his daily meeting with his staff when he was interrupted and handed the written request from Jerusalem to take custody of the Jew, Paul of Tarsus, and to deal with the dispensation of justice in the matter.

Governor Felix pondered the strange co-incidence that had yet again brought the Jewish preacher Paul of Tarsus to his attention, only this time on a matter that had serious implications for the man who, in the years since they first met, had become a leading member of the movement of followers of Jesus of Nazareth. He knew fine well that Paul was a Roman citizen, and that he would be able to uphold that particular claim, but the dispensation of a verdict on a case that had everything to do with religious doctrine was not a simple matter.

A verdict on either side would leave him open to question from the other side of the argument. These issues often resulted in the protagonists taking to the streets, and he did not need the headaches that came with civil unrest, and the consequences that came from Rome. The deputation of Jewish leaders would be arriving from Jerusalem in a few days to testify against Paul, and they would expect justice to be meted out there and then. He needed some time to think.

Paul was taken to one of the better cells in the prison that was next to the guard's station, and so had adequate light, with a separate table and chair in addition to the wooden bed-frame that would keep him elevated from the cold hard floor. As Paul lay down to rest, he reflected on some of the many tribulations that he had experienced on his journeys, and took some consolation in the relative comfort of his confinement. He remembered the five times that he had been subjected to the lash by fellow Jews. The freezing nights in the mountains of Asia Minor, as he and Barnabus journeyed among the Gentiles.

The time when both of them were sentenced to be stoned in Iconium, barely escaping with their lives, after the intervention of the good people in the streets, who challenged the orders of the civil authorities. Being beaten in Philippi with his brother Silas, and escaping jail only because of an earthquake that caused the prison doors to open. As Paul meditated on these past events of his life, he had to smile to himself at the predicaments that he had been in, and the ways in which his Lord had provided rescue.

His faith was built on a sure foundation—the rock that was his belief in Jesus Christ, and the House of his Lord that gave him shelter. There was nothing that he could not endure in the service of his Master, and the teaching of His way. In short, he was a fanatic.

Within a few days, the deputation of Jewish Elders from Jerusalem arrived, and Governor Felix convened the trial. After a few hours of accusations and recriminations from both sides, Governor Felix was not convinced that the Jewish Elders had a substantive case, but he was unwilling to show obvious support for Paul's testimony. After all, the Jews were omnipresent in the land of Israel, whereas the Christians were but a minority sect. This was a situation that needed to be taken off the boil, and the best way to do that was to defer judgment for now and keep Paul imprisoned.

Let the Elders go back to Jerusalem leaving Paul still in jail. Let some time go by. In the meantime, there was always the chance that Paul might be willing to pay for a favorable verdict, with some of the money that was rumored to have found its way into the coffers of the new church, from the conversion of wealthy Jews and Gentiles.

Having determined a course of action, Governor Felix gave it a few more days to percolate before bringing Paul once more under guard into his chambers, for some private conversation about Paul's new faith, with the intent of drawing him out on the possibilities of there being some kind of payment made in exchange for freedom. Paul soon realized that Governor Felix had reverted to type in seeking personal gain from his position of power, and he duly refused to be drawn out on the issue, and kept the dialogue on his agenda alone.

After a few attempts over the course of several days Governor Felix gave up on his charge, and Paul remained imprisoned, but with freedom of movement within the jail itself, and access to visitors, food, and drink. Governor Felix was playing the game, and one of the ways to do that was to placate the players, and defer the decision until events provided a fortuitous solution. The days turned into weeks, then months.

Chapter Six
Caesarea

Andreas missed his parents so much, and on this summer day, when the relentless sun chased all but the children of Caesarea indoors, and he had a few moments of introspective during his spell of guard duty, he finally acknowledged to himself that his grief had run its certain course.

Whatever pain and suffering they had endured, it was over, and that burden that they carried in the last few moments of their lives had become his to bear. For the several months that he lived with this grief, he woke each day to its inevitable presence. Today, while nothing had changed, everything was different. It was time to get on with his life, and to do that he must accept that the path ahead would require him to be fully invested in his role as a soldier of Rome.

He had seen enough of the Roman military doctrine on training and building their armies to know that he had to work within the system. He had to become a better soldier than the rest, so that he could influence the future course of his service, and ensure that the larger purpose of his life was fulfilled.

His training regimen and lowly status required constant attention to the dictates of the army and the whims of his commander. He had made a few friends among his fellow Auxiliaries in those first few weeks, but none that he could trust with the truth. He was Andreas, the Greek Christian from somewhere in the Peloponnese, and that was as much as his comrades new about him. The entire training class numbered around 125 soldiers, and for the duration of their training they were housed in special barracks on the outside of town, and separated from the regular army that was made up of Roman citizens.

The order to stand down and partake of their lunch rations got a quick response from the recruits, and they sat in a rough circle together and passed the water jugs around while they munched on their bread ration and the inevitable cheese, figs, olives, and blueberries.

Soon the chance to make small talk and jest drew out comments and observations from the more voluble of the soldiers, including a young scrawny Jew from the hills around Nazareth. "Hey Andreas, looks like you win the big foot competition," said the upstart, directing his remark to Andreas who was sitting across from him, and not in a position to respond with a slap on the head, or other recrimination.

"Oh really, Silas," responded Andreas with a smile on his face. "That's so that when I kick your skinny arse, I won't miss."

Just as the group was laughing and talking among themselves the sound of a bugle pierced the air around them, announcing the return to guard duty. Andreas placed his arm around Silas and playfully held his massive fist up against the small pointed chin of his new friend, as they assembled in ranks to come to attention, and take their assigned places around the center of the town.

In this way the first few weeks of his training passed quickly enough, and after a while Andreas began to enjoy the hard physical effort that had to be put into long marches, increasingly in double time, and the physical exercises and challenges that were part of the process. In the early weeks of his training, it was all about marching in formation, as one of the most important military strategies of the Roman Army was its ability to move faster and more effectively than the enemy. The line of soldiers was expected to be kept in formation at differing speeds, and every other day there was a march of twenty Roman miles that had to be completed in five hours. This was the training schedule, but the goal was to cut that time and keep formation, and there was competition among training units that was almost a natural outcome of the process.

In the evenings the men had a chance to relax in the bunkhouse, unless they were on the rotation for evening guard duty, and there soon built up a sense of camaraderie among the men that the training was designed to foster. Assigned tasks were always shared by small groups working together, and there were no outliers among the men to cause dissension or tension within the ranks. Andreas was on good terms with everyone, although Silas and he tended to hang around with each other, and involve their fellow recruits in the banter and small talk that typified their evenings in confinement.

All this changed with the arrival of a late addition to the training group, a sulking brute of a man named Caleb, who had been arrested for violent behavior in his home town of Sidon on a number of occasions, and the judge eventually solved the town's problem by having him conscripted.

Within a few days he began testing his fellow recruits by bullying those who were physically inferior, and after two weeks among the group he was widely disliked. It was only a matter of time before he picked on Silas, the smallest of the recruits, and Andreas was ready to intervene on a couple of occasions but was waived away by Silas, who tried to disarm Caleb by making light of his actions. Caleb was not of a mind to go up against Andreas, who was physically imposing, and he backed off his vindictiveness toward Silas, but carried a simmering antagonism toward the two friends.

By the end of the hottest of the summer months, the exercise schedule was changed, with the introduction of a daily session of physical exercise, in between the interminable marches, and this involved racing against each other, long jumping, and high jumping. There were also weekly sessions on the beaches, where not only did they swim, but they were raced against each other, starting in the surf, and ending high up the raised beaches of resistant sand. It was the introduction of muscle building exercises that set Andreas apart from the rest of the men, as he attacked the series of push-ups that were designed for both chest and arm muscle development.

On a rainy and windswept morning, the group was taken to a special training ground, that had just been set up in the form of an obstacle course. The men had watched it being put together by some of the regular army members of a Caesarean cohort of Roman troops, and were curious to try the course, as it would be something a bit different from their regular routine.

As the sergeant lined them up near the start of the course, he asked for two volunteers to try out the obstacles as the rest of the men watched, and Andreas was quick to signal his willingness to take on the challenge. Two other hands went up at the same time, and the sergeant motioned Silas and Caleb forward, quite happy to have three of the men try it out. Caleb pushed his way to the starting line and snarled a rebuke to Silas. "Stay clear of me, pipsqueak, or I may have to run you over."

"You'll have to catch me, Caleb. Everyone knows that the men of Sidon tire easily, as the women from there are so ugly there's no sport in chasing them." Silas took up his position on the line to the left of Andreas, who was between him and Caleb.

"Go!" yelled the sergeant, and the three men began their sprint to the first of the obstacles, which required them to crawl underneath fishing nets that had been stitched together to make one big net. It was no surprise to see Silas emerge first from the net, as his smallness was a clear advantage. He was first to begin his sprint to the next challenge, followed by Caleb, and Andreas was a distant third having caught his sandals in the netting, and had struggled to get clear of the tangled ropes.

Caleb concentrated on his pursuit of Silas, and after three other obstacles he was just a few yards from him, with Andreas a clear third. Silas was first into the water, and swam his way as fast as he could toward the wall of netting that lay perpendicular across the water, extending up to about thirty feet or so. As he reached up on to the net and began a rapid climb, he could feel the weight of Caleb on the net underneath him. As he got close to the top, he felt a hand grasp his ankle and pull him in a downward motion, and he frantically tried to keep his grip of the netting. Suddenly Caleb freed up his right arm and then swung a punch to the kidneys that took the air out of Silas, and then Caleb grabbed him by the neck and began to pull him off the wall of netting. In a few moments Silas felt the last of the netting slip through his fingers and was in freefall toward the water, landing with a splash in the murky pool.

Meanwhile Andreas had started his climb up the wall, and was lucky not to be hit by Silas on his way down. He focused on catching up with Caleb, and his superior arm strength helped him gain on his opponent, who had climbed over the top and was quickly moving down the netting on the other side. When he was close enough to the water, Caleb leaped out, and then began to swim to the far side of the pond. As Andreas dropped down the other side of the net, he saw Silas emerge from the water and begin to pick his way across to the side, where the sergeant had signaled him to quit the race and get checked out. Recruits were valuable pieces of equipment in the Roman Army, and he wanted to make sure that Silas was not hurt in any way from his fall.

Andreas turned around into the water and began to swim to the far side, where he picked up a yard or so on his opponent, and emerged in hot pursuit on the last leg of the course, which was a sprint over or around large pieces of rock that lay between the pond and the finish line. There was not enough distance left to give Andreas a chance of catching Caleb, and he crossed the line just a few seconds behind his rival, who had slowed to a jog and was making his way back toward the rest of the recruits.

Caleb braced himself as Andreas approached, expecting a challenge after the events of the past few minutes. He was astonished when Andreas came up to him and offered him an outstretched arm to be grasped and shaken as a sign of amity. "Well raced, Caleb, you deserved to beat me, and you probably would have beaten Silas too in a fair fight. Let's make sure that Silas is ok."

Caleb tried to figure out what was going on, as it was obvious that he had punched Silas to gain the advantage during the race. As he pondered his response, Andreas spoke to him again, only this time with a measured cadence that carried with it a daunting presence. "Look Caleb, what you did to Silas was not right. It was unfair, and it was not necessary. You would surely have beaten him anyway, and now your victory has been lessened by your actions. I know it, the men know it, and I suspect the sergeant knows it."

Caleb had been completely disarmed by Andreas, and was almost at a loss as to how he should act, not being used to conversation to solve disputes. He fumbled with the belt around his waist, then smoothed his long hair behind his neck. Andreas gave him the silence, and was rewarded by an outstretched arm. "Let's go and see if Silas is ready for another time round the track."

The two men joined the rest of the squad, and the sergeant looked over at Andreas, as Caleb approached Silas with an obvious apology, which thankfully the smaller man accepted with surprise rather than disdain, taking his cue after a nod from Andreas. The others quickly realized that something good had come out of something bad, and that Andreas had something to do with it.

After a few weeks they began weapons training, and they were given wooden weapons such as swords and shields with which to practice. These weighed at least double the weight of the actual weapons, as a training method to build strength and endurance. The weapons were employed against wooden stakes, and each soldier was trained in the various moves of strike and counter-strike. Andreas reveled in the challenge and physicality of this training, and he soon progressed to the more advanced stage of combat training, known as armature. Finally, each recruit was required to master the use of the spear, so that his hand-eye co-ordination and strength were developed to battle readiness condition.

Those who trained well ate well in the Roman system, and Andreas enjoyed perhaps as full and as healthy a diet as he had ever experienced. The training unit commander had seen them come and go over the years, and took pride in his ability to get the best out of the young men who were assigned to him for training, most of whom were reluctant warriors in the first instance. This young Greek Andreas was a refreshing change. He had rarely seen such motivation and commitment in a trainee, and his reports to the garrison commander were documented accordingly. Andreas was a natural leader, and deemed battle ready, if not battle hardened.

Chapter Seven
Ararat

The Port of Antioch, sometimes known as Seleucia on Sea, was a hotbed of activity when the boat carrying part of a cohort of Auxiliary soldiers from Caesarea docked against the harbor wall. Andreas called over to his old friend Isaac, with whom he had been surprisingly re-united on the voyage along the eastern seaboard of the Mediterranean. "I don't know about you, Isaac, but I am actually looking forward to getting back on the march again."

"Me too, Andreas, but it won't be long before we eat our words, as there's a long journey ahead to the front in Armenia." Isaac looked over at Andreas, and smiled to himself at the good fortune that had brought the friends together again after so many years, soon after Andreas had finished his training.

One after another, Isaac, Andreas, Caleb and Silas made their way down the gangplank and followed the crowd of soldiers heading for the rallying point, where they would fall in to begin their long march north and then east into Armenia. The 250 soldiers were a combination of experienced men and recently graduated recruits, gathered from the ranks in the Caesarea garrison to fulfill their orders to join up with the armies of General Corbulo, who had distinguished himself in Germania, and was elevated by a grateful Emperor Nero to Supreme Commander in the East. Armenia was truly a buffer state, within the Roman sphere of influence from the west, and right up against the Parthian Empire to the south and east. When the new commander surveyed his territories, he determined that he would need additional men and materiel from other parts of the Empire to fulfill his mission, and even the regional Proconsuls had to bend to the will of the General.

Isaac was an experienced soldier who had served on a number of missions from his base in Caesarea, and had the trust of his officers. He was given the chance to select his own group of Auxiliaries who would form a conturbernium, and march with him on the long journey to the mountains and valleys of Armenia, and he made sure that his three friends were part of his unit.

Isaac told his men to set their baggage to the side, including their spears— a weighted javelin and a light javelin—each known as a pylum, to be loaded on the accompanying wagons. This would enable the men to march with relative freedom of movement, but still have the basic defensive weapons ready for use in the event of a surprise attack. The intelligence reports had been shared with the men on the voyage to Antioch, and there did not appear to be the threat of any military action until they were well into the interior of Armenia.

The small children of the town were their first contact with the local civilian population, and the men were happy to share some of their provisions and water with them. Andreas looked at one little boy with interest as he skipped around the horses and baggage carts. He had obviously just learned to whistle, and was practicing this new sound to the best of his ability, with not much to show for it. Andreas beckoned him over with a wave of his drinking cup, and the young boy drank greedily of the cold and refreshing water. Andreas put his forefinger and thumb spaced apart into his own mouth, and the sound of the piercing whistle made the boy laugh, and try unsuccessfully to do it. Andreas spoke to him in Greek, and shared some bread and cheese with him. The boy reminded Andreas of himself as a child in Patras, and a flood of memories came to him, as he sat with the boy and immersed himself in the warm waters of reflection.

After a while Isaac assembled his group into marching formation, and they were soon heading out into the hills to find a suitable camping spot for the night. There were some two hundred miles or more to cover and less than ten days to do it in, if they were to meet the deadline established by General Corbulo for joining the other units, before the longer journey to the Armenian front. Failing to meet that deadline was not an option, as had been made clear by the General's Aide-de-Camp, who had brought the orders to the Caesarean troops.

The roads to the interior were easy to see and to follow, but were sadly lacking when compared to the Roman roads in places that were permanently occupied by Roman forces. However, there were always local people to provide directions and intelligence, in exchange for Roman coin. Andreas found the early going not too different from the foothills around Patras, but after a few days there was a distinct change in the topography, as the hills gave way to mountains, and the rivers were replaced by creeks and streams.

On one of the frequent water breaks, Silas and Caleb were talking, while Andreas was on a water detail. "Silas, it seems to me that Andreas has something on his mind, have you noticed?"

"Yes, and I think I know why," answered Silas. "I think he is trying to face up to the reality that he will be involved in serious fighting for the first time. He may not say much about his Christian faith and his beliefs, but I think he is trying to make sense of it before we are caught up in the fighting and the killing."

That night, after they had set up the tents, Silas and Andreas were sitting enjoying the peace under a sky that was an endless ocean of stars, and Silas asked his friend what was on his mind. "You seem to be in a world apart these days, Andreas, and we're worried that you have reservations about what you might have to do when we meet up with the enemy."

Andreas looked ahead with his eyes open and fixed in a stare, as if trying to focus on a shape in the distance. "I know from all our training that once in a fight it is kill or be killed, and I suppose I am still trying to understand what my Lord would have me do. To turn the other cheek is to lay open my heart to the thrust of a sword, and yet I know there is a larger purpose for me in this life."

Silas looked over to his friend. "Andreas, I have watched you in amazement ever since we first met in the barracks. Everyone in the billet knew that you were a leader of men. If your God puts you in front of an enemy soldier, it cannot be to end the life of one whose very purpose is to spread His word and bring people to His altar." That was as much philosophy as Silas had ever uttered, and he seemed to have even surprised himself. After a moment or two Silas smiled, and said, "Andreas, let's get some sleep."

At times like these, Andreas wished so much that his father was there to guide him. And yet the words of Silas were comforting, and gave him food for his soul. He lay awake for a while, fell into a dreamless sleep, then awoke to a morning light that shone with the promise of the coming day.

In a few days the unit reached Melitene, the rendezvous point with the greater army of General Corbulo, near a bend of the Euphrates that had been chosen carefully. The Auxiliaries, conscripted from the Empire, were directed to their allotted ground, and ordered to set up camp. All eyes were on General Corbulo, and while he looked over an assembled army of 18,000 soldiers and Auxiliaries, he sensed the larger audience that waited in Rome for news from the eastern front.

The throne of Armenia was now occupied by King Tiridates, who had proved to be an obstacle to the will of Rome since his accession, after the last series of Roman/Parthian confrontations. As General Corbulo considered his military options, he decided to take a cautious approach toward the king, and rather than pursue an all-out war, he thought it wise to engage in talks, to better take the measure of his opponent. He sent emissaries in concert with local leaders to carry the word to the king, who was about three days march away on the eastern side of the river.

He soon received a message of peace from an Armenian official, advising that the king had agreed to truce talks. The rendezvous site was about fifty miles upriver at the point where the Euphrates turned to the north before entering an inland lake. The king had announced that he would bring 1000 men to the meeting, assuming that General Corbulo would do likewise. The Parthians would be on the eastern bank of the river, on the other side from the Romans.

When King Tiridates and his men approached the meeting site and saw a much larger Roman army across the river, and dressed as if for battle, he withdrew his men during the night, and the Romans woke up to a silent landscape.

General Corbulo called a meeting of his senior officers to discuss strategy and plans, and there was a lively discussion as they talked about their options. After a while he stood up from the table and rattled his drinking cup against the surface, signaling his desire to speak to his men. "We need to send a message to the Parthians that there are always repercussions in thwarting the will of Rome. Absent an agreement to our terms, there can only be one response, and that is in military action. If we can get this puppet king and all his men to the field of battle the game will be over. He knows that, and that is why he stays away from us. We need to draw him out."

As General Corbulo finished making his point, he looked around the table, signaling his desire to hear from his commanders, and the Legatus of the Fourth Legion stood up and volunteered his thoughts. "General, I think the answer lies in the fortified strongholds that are scattered around the country, whose loyalty to Tiridates will only hold if they see that he is willing to stand up to Rome on their behalf. Let's choose a few strategic targets and destroy them. If this forces his hand, then we have him on the battlefield. If he chooses not to fight, he loses the support of the remaining forts and the people both inside and outside who depend on them for security."

Hearing and seeing the nodding of heads and sounds of approval from the men around the table, General Corbulo walked over to the maps that were hanging from the walls. Drawing his short sword as a pointer, he showed the locations of the main population centers, and the forts that protected them. These maps were the General's pride and joy, as they were a scarce resource in the Roman Army. Taking up half the wall space was an authorized copy of Agrippa's Map that had been commissioned by Caesar Augustus, and carved in stone in the heart of the Roman soldiers.

General Corbulo pointed at the section of the map that showed the location of Asia Minor, and spoke to his men. "Here you see the position of Armenia, and why it is important. It commands the entry way to the Caucasus, and is in the pathway south for the barbarians should they choose to threaten our Empire." He then moved to the side and pointed to one of the smaller maps. "Here is a map from the last time we campaigned in the heart of Armenia, and it shows a line of forts that extend to the capital of Artaxata. We know from our intelligence sources that these are fortified positions to safeguard the residents as well as the surrounding population. However, they are seriously undermanned, as most of the soldiers are with the army of Tiridates."

The more seasoned campaigners in the group quickly realized the strategy that their general had devised, as he continued his message. "It is roughly three hundred miles across the Armenian highlands to the Plain of Ararat, where the forts are strung out in a line along the valley toward Artaxata. Tiridates will be mustering his men for the journey, but he will soon find out his army are no match for ours on a forced march across the wilderness. I expect us to get there five or six days ahead of him."

The Roman army departed with banners lifted and flags flying on their march over the hills and mountains, and their mission to bring Armenia back into the fold of Rome.

Time passed with the relentless routines and demands of an army on the march. As they made their way across the wilds of the Anatolian hinterland, the conditions began to change, and what had begun as a fairly routine march across the central plains of the region became a challenge even for the highly trained Roman army. The soldiers were forced to wear an outer garment over their normal marching gear, to protect against the biting wind and the flurries of snow at the higher levels of altitude. There was no respite from the pace.

One evening, as Andreas lay in the tent with his friends, huddled beneath all that he possessed in order to stay warm enough to fall asleep, he prayed, as he had done every night of his life, and when it was over, he reached over to Isaac to get his attention.

"Isaac, I was told by one of the men today that we will cross the high mountains to the Plain of Ararat. Do you suppose that we will be near the mountain where Noah's Ark rested when the floods came to the Earth?"

Isaac looked out from the mounds of clothing that covered him near the rear of the tent. "Andreas, I have forgotten most of what I learned as a boy in the Temple, but the story of the Ark was told so many times that it is about all I remember. I know that the Elders always used to speculate about where the mountains of Ararat might be, and Rabbi Togarmah always pointed to the north and said that it was far away from the Galilee, on the edge of the world. I don't know about you but that pretty much describes where we are. Now, can I get some sleep?"

Andreas was amused by his friend, yet also excited that they might see a place that was so important to the Jewish religion, and therefore the followers of Christ.

It took General Corbulo's army a week to transverse the high mountain range guarding the central valley that was the Plain of Ararat, and once in the lower elevations he called for the camp to be set up for a prolonged stay, while he had his men scout the countryside for information about the enemy. Within a day or two there was a better mood around the various campfires, as the men reveled in the relative warmth of the daytime temperatures, and had little to do while waiting other than pull guard duty, or hunt for fresh meat.

While in this waiting period, orders came through for the men to sharpen their knives and swords, and make sure their shields were viable. This caused a certain nervous tension in the camp, as the men readied themselves for battle, in many cases for the first time. Isaac spent time with each of the men in his unit, giving them advice and generally keeping the mood positive.

At his daily briefing, General Corbulo met with his officer corps, to prepare them for the military action to come. "We shall march together to the first of these forts, leaving Colonel Flacus and his group to ready for their mission, while we advance to the second fort. Colonel Capito and his forces are assigned to this target, while I lead the rest of the men toward the third and most important of these forts, known as Volandum. I shall personally take command of this action, and when the fighting is over and we have command of the forts, we will regroup on the main road to Artaxata. Let's get our troops organized for these actions, and let them know there will be no mercy to those who would resist us."

Finally, the orders were given to break down the camp, and the soldiers were separated into three main groups in preparation for their missions. Isaac led his conturbernium to join with General Corbulo's group for the march across the valley toward the forts that lay waiting on the other side.

The plain of Arafat was hardly an apt description, as the men soon found that the terrain was sometimes rocky and uneven, and other times boggy and difficult for the baggage wagons to negotiate. However, there was a distinct trail that led across the terrain to link the various forts and military locations in the central valley, and within three days the first two groups had peeled off to position themselves for their attacks on the enemy strongholds.

The persistent fog meant that they could not rely on sighting their targets from a distance, and the General was relieved that he had spent worthwhile time and money on gathering intelligence on the lay of the land that held the enemy.

The Judean Auxiliaries were part of the group of soldiers that had been selected for early action. Silas had found this out from talking with another soldier, and lost no time in sharing this information with his friends.

"So be it," said Isaac, as he worked on his equipment along with the rest of the men. "This is a long way to come just to sit in the stern of the ship, so let's make the best of it. We only get paid once a year, so we do whatever it takes to make it safely back to Judea."

Caleb and Silas looked over at Andreas to see his reaction to the news, and were pleased to see him nod his head at the words from Isaac. "The way I see it, we have to deal with one fight at a time, and make sure we make it through to the next one." Then smiling, he said, "eventually we'll run out of enemies." His friends laughed along with him, and felt the camaraderie that only soldiers know.

General Corbulo called his commanders together at their campfire that evening. Their camp was positioned along higher ground with water available from the plentiful mountain streams. Bats crisscrossed the smoke from the fires as if angry at this intrusion on their dark spaces around the hills, while lingering mosquitoes enjoyed a rare feast from a host of donors. He didn't care that the flames might be readily seen from the higher ground. It was all part of his strategy.

After a few words of encouragement and praise for the officers and their men, he gave his final orders. "I want you to let your soldiers know what we expect of them. All three forts will be attacked on the same day, and the mission is simply to take control of the forts, and put all of the armed men to the sword. As for the women, you may let a few of your men know that you will be looking the other way. That should be enough to send a strong message to Tiridates." This was a privilege not always granted in battle, but the officers raised no issue with their general. The spoils of war were sometimes shared throughout the command structure of a victorious army, when there was enough to go around.

The following day, after a tough march over rising ground, the leading group crested a hill as the fog finally began to lift, so that the soldiers became aware of their environment, and the target that awaited them. The fort of Volandum was clearly visible on the crest of a steep and rocky hill, that dipped down in elevation, then rose up again in a double peak that crested at a much higher altitude. But the sight of the fort and the realization of the challenge that lay ahead was not the only surprise for the Roman army. In the distance lay a fabulous triangle of a mountain rising about fifteen or sixteen thousand feet above the valley floor, and covered in snow from half its height to the summit. This was surely Mount Ararat.

"Isaac, look. Isn't it incredible. It has to be Ararat!" said Andreas excitedly, as the conturbernium filed along the trail toward a large meadow defined by a meandering river, promising water for the camp and a suitable place for the encampment. Soon enough, the troops were brought to a halt and went about the business of setting up their camp. There was no mistaking their objective, as it sat high above them, and they could see the distant faces of the soldiers above and behind the walls.

The early morning sunlight announced the ubiquitous presence of Mount Ararat, and momentarily diverted Andreas from his thoughts. His deepest faith had been kept in another part of him for so long, ever since his life had turned upside down with the deaths of his mother and father. It was his faith that now seemed to have grabbed him and brought him back from a journey away from everything he knew to be real and true. He was troubled by the conflict between the faith that enabled him to endure, and the commission of acts of warfare that could require him to take a life, but he was not afraid of it. He prayed silently in the few moments of privacy before the trumpet call signaling the muster.

As General Corbulo took his breakfast with his senior officers he challenged them over the way to take the fort. "What we have to deal with is a fort that is defensively well positioned to sustain a long period of siege, but we do not have the luxury of time. We know that it is held by fewer than a hundred men, and we are many thousands, and yet they have the advantage. We know from intelligence that they are supplied with water from an underground clay pipe that is fed from springs in the higher ground, so they can hold out for several days if they have to. Artaxata awaits, and so does the kingdom. We need a plan, so I need ideas."

The general looked at his men expectantly, and then admonished them with disdain. "Talk among yourselves, talk among your officers, and even talk to the men if you have to. We need to take this fort, and quickly."

As is the way of men in combat and close proximity, the word of the general was soon heard and spread among the men. Most of the common soldiers did not relate to matters of strategy however, and looked at the standoff as a chance for a few days of rest before the ultimate order to storm the fort, which would surely come in due course. Andreas could only think of the difficulty of an armed assault on a well defended fort, and the likelihood of many deaths between the attackers and the people inside the fort, most of whom were innocent civilians.

Later that morning Andreas was on duty tending to one of the horses, and noticed how impatient it was to drink from the nearby stream. The trek across the Armenian highlands was hard work for Roman horses, unlike their Arabian cousins who were capable of carrying a thirst from oasis to oasis. Suddenly he had an idea, and quickly pulled the horse back from the stream. The horse showed its displeasure by rising and kicking its hooves in the air, but Andreas was able to pull it down and get it settled. Andreas walked over to the edge of the horse's enclosure and motioned to Isaac to join him.

"Isaac, I have an idea but I am not sure if it will work. You know more about horses than I, but what I do remember is that horses can smell water in the ground. I can just see my father all those years ago telling me how that saved his life when he was alone in the steppe, with no water for himself or his animal."

Isaac frowned momentarily, as if searching his memory bank, then replied to Andreas. "That is true, as I sometimes had to nurse a horse through a shortage of water on the way back from a mission, and it was uncanny how they could sense the water long before we reached it."

Isaac thought long and hard, and then said to Andreas, "I know what you are thinking Andreas, and it just might work. If we can keep a few of the horses from drinking for a day or two till they build up a real thirst, we might be able to follow them till they sense the presence of water in the ground. The way the fort is situated, the water supply has to come from the big mountain, and if we can walk the horses across the connecting ridge, we might get a clue on the location of the underground spring that gives life to the fort."

It took a few minutes to work themselves up the chain of command, but soon the two Auxiliaries were brought before one of the commanders. Isaac, as the senior of the two men, told the officer of the idea, and then both of them had to recount their experiences to support their convictions. The officer was quick to adopt a plan that might just be worthwhile, so he gave orders for several of the horses to be cordoned off and denied any food or fresh water. Isaac volunteered that it might take about three days for thirst to influence their behavior, so they were put in charge of the project, and told to stay close to the horses and keep them from any form of liquid.

Each day the horses became a bit more frenetic, and on the third day Andreas led a group of Auxiliaries on his mission with the six horses. The open and gradually rising land from the walls of the fort across to the slopes of the higher mountain were the obvious place to try and find a source of water, as any spring or pipe would have to cross it on the way to the fort.

Andreas chose a point that would take them across the fields but far enough away that they were safe from any weapons fired from the fort. They could see the soldiers at the top of the walls looking their way, but had no cause to stay hidden. "Let them see us," said Isaac, "and then let them wonder what we are up to. With luck, they will find out soon enough."

As they were about one third of the way across the fields, the horses began to act in an agitated way, and their minders were hard pressed to keep them under control. They began baying and pawing the ground in front of them, and after pulling them to and from across the section of the fields, the soldiers were able to narrow the area of ground that was the object of the horses' attention. Isaac signaled to Caleb, Silas, and the others to begin digging on a line that would intersect any water line from the mountain to the fort. After an hour of concerted effort, with the increasing noise of the frenetic horses to spur them on, the soldiers found the clay pipe, and on breaking it open, the flow of sweet mountain water on its way to the fort.

Isaac immediately sent for reinforcements, to tackle the backbreaking work of digging out the stream and diverting the underground channel away from the fort. The officer arrived on the scene to survey the progress, and turned away hurriedly to give the good news to the general.

In the fort of Volandum, the news of the break in the water supply spread quickly through the town, and the civilian residents, numbering well over two thousand souls, huddled together and in groups, and speculated on what would happen next. The head of the council, Artavesdes soon requested a meeting with the Parthian commander, and was told that there was to be no giving in to the Roman hordes. "Soon enough, King Tiridates will arrive with reinforcements and the Romans will be sent back to their seven hills."

By noon of the following day the civilian population was in an increasing state of agitation, as the mothers tried unsuccessfully to keep their children content, and the husbands talked furtively among themselves, but lacked the ability to do anything about it. That night, as the town lay quiet at the midnight hour, several of the leading townspeople met at the home of Artavesdes. It was clear that something had to be done, and quickly. After an hour or so of conversation, Artavesdes spoke to his friends and neighbors. "There are less than one hundred of these Parthian soldiers in our midst, and we number upwards of four hundred men. I think we can take over the fort and welcome the Romans. It is our only hope, and even though we are barely armed, we have the advantage of numbers."

He let his words lie among the men for a few minutes, while the conversations passed and the attitudes and mindsets of the men gradually emerged from the discourse. He sensed from the mood in the room that there was a strong consensus for action, and he allowed it to ferment before bringing it to the boil. "We can do this, men. We can overcome these Parthians as long as we act together. This is what we should do."

It took a few minutes to go over the plan, and then go over it again, but there was unanimity among the men, and a sudden sense of excitement and tension as they contemplated the task ahead.

Artavesdes once more called the men to attention, and laid out the plan. "I don't think we need to overcome one hundred Parthian soldiers, just the group of twenty or so who man the gates to the fort. All the rest are spread out along the perimeter, and if we act quickly enough, they will soon see how pointless it would be to respond."

He quickly ran through his plan, and the undercurrent of conversation was enough for him to bring it all to a head. "All we have to do is to overcome the Parthians at the gate, and open the gates to the Romans. Not only do we open the gates, but we march out together without weapons. They will see us as their allies, and the Parthians inside will have nowhere to hide."

The leader continued with his plan, forming it in his mind just before the telling. "There will be no sleep for us tonight. We need to split up and go round all of the houses and tell the men we need them to assemble in the streets before dawn. Then we will advance silently to the gates of the fort, and overcome the soldiers. Bring whatever weapons that are available, and tell the women to stay inside and keep the children safe. By noon tomorrow there will be water and food for everyone from the grateful Romans."

Early in the morning, as the sun rose and lit the eastern side of the great mountain of Ararat, clearly visible to the Roman soldiers stirring in the camp, there was a sudden commotion as the soldiers noticed the gates of the fort open up, and a multitude of civilians walking toward the camp with arms waving and loud calls of greetings and welcome.

General Corbulo was summoned, told of the news, and quickly mounted his horse to ride out to the scene. On being appraised by Artavesdes of the situation, he quickly arranged for a large formation of his troops to enter the town, and search out any Parthians who might still be there, as in all likelihood they would have left as soon as they realized what had happened. As for the civilian population, he admonished his officers to tell the men. "Let no man touch any of the women and children. They are under my protection, and must not be harmed."

And so, the siege of Volandum was over, almost before it was begun, and the way secure for the Roman army to continue on its march to the regional capital of Artaxata. For Isaac, it was a mission under his leadership that might get him a promotion up the ranks. For Andreas, it felt good to reflect that he was responsible for a peaceful end to a bad situation, without loss of life or harm to anyone involved. Now there was a march to Artaxata to be completed, and the conquest of another key part of Armenia that would bring it back into the Roman fold.

Chapter Eight
Bedouin

As the Roman camp broke up the next day, on a day when even the horses sensed a change in the air, word came that was a surprise to General Corbulo. One of the scouts who had been sent ahead of the trail to Artaxata came back to camp, riding hard, and dismounted on the edge of the general's tented area. He strode up to the group of officers and then, as if realizing his lack of authority among so many important people, addressed everyone and no-one in particular. "Begging your pardon Sirs, but Tiridates is ahead of us. He passed above us to the north where the valleys lead directly into the city of Artaxata, and his army is now assembled on the plain, about two days march from here." He was soon directed away by an Aide-de-Camp to where his unit was holding, and gathered himself so as to present his importance to the rest of his fellow soldiers.

Once again General Corbulo consulted with his senior officers, and discussed the military strategies that would offer the best chance of success, in a pitched battle that finally might just happen. His lantern jaw was both an object of ridicule among the officer's corps, and yet a sign of his authority when he addressed his men. "There must be a reason that Tiridates has avoided a direct conflict with us so far. It seems to me that he has no faith in his men, be they Parthians or Armenians."

The officers presented their comments and suggestions, in the manner that they had become accustomed to during the campaign, and it was clear that the General was respected by his men as a strong leader and a bold tactical commander. He eventually brought their conversation to a close with a firm and measured directive. "They will bring their horsemen to our line to break us down from the middle, while they try and get round our flanks. This time we will show them an unbreakable formation that puts our best soldiers as the outside of a hollow square, with our Auxiliaries on foot and on horseback forming the inside line right behind our Legionaires. The third line on the inside will be our other foot soldiers and archers, who will fire at will over the heads of our soldiers into the enemy lines ahead of us. Make sure your officers and men all understand their roles, and that our line will not be broken."

For the first time in the entire campaign the sounds of mutterings and exasperation could be heard as the officers made their way to their tents. Perhaps their favored commander had gone too far. This was a strange way to prepare for battle, and some if not all were suddenly second guessing their leader.

The smell of human sweat was a familiar consequence of an army on the march, and today was no different. As Andreas marched in formation with his fellow Auxiliaries, he knew that he was now headed for a pitched battle with enemy soldiers, and that the prospect of death was a clear threat. Once again, he wrestled with the demons that challenged his faith, as he contemplated the reality of one-on-one armed conflict where it would either be kill or be killed. Keeping perfect time with his fellow soldiers, he let his thoughts and his conscience run free, as if daydreaming. He saw the fertile fields of the plain and contrasted them with the graded hillsides in the Peloponnese, where a yield from the plantings was never assured until the last rain had fallen.

Here, it looked as if an abundance of crops was something certain, and the sun and rain had agreed to share enough of each other to bless the earth, and those who farmed there.

The command to halt by the out of breath officer of the line was automatically obeyed, and as Andreas adjusted his breathing to benefit from the rest period, he once again came to terms with the reality that there was a larger cause than this particular fight, and that the will of God sometimes must prevail even in the face of the evil of warfare. He was a trained soldier, and that training was designed to make automatic the ability to kill almost without thinking. He must condition himself to this dichotomy, and look to his prayers for inspiration and validation.

The unit commander ordered his men to add an extra layer of clothing, as they were heading into more snow and freezing rain on the plains of Ararat. He remembered the mucus from his nose freezing over the last time he had marched around Mount Ararat, and still had the scar to prove it. Once his men resumed marching, they automatically picked up the pace, so as to reach their overnight campsite, and a welcoming fire. The grateful citizens of Volandum had provided much needed food and supplies, and even the meanest of Auxiliaries knew that an army marched on its stomach.

By noon of the following day, the Roman army had formed the hollow square that was the order of battle chosen by General Corbulo, and each unit had been thoroughly briefed by their officers on their role. The Auxiliaries were overjoyed when they realized that it was the Legionaires who would form the front line, and this time it was the cream of the Roman forces that would face the enemy head on.

After a hard march of about one hour the formation was brought to a halt within clear sight of the Parthian army spread out along a line ahead of them. With the backdrop of a snow laden Mount Ararat, it was a beautiful sight to the eye, but a harbinger of death to the soldiers who waited for the orders to advance.

As General Corbulo looked out over the battlefield he expected Tiridates to send his cavalry in a mass attack on the leading edge of the Roman formation. Instead, he was surprised to see a smaller force of archers on horseback make a run at the Roman front, as if to test the enemy, and within a few minutes most of the skirmishes had played out with either the death or the retreat of the Parthians. Soon a larger force with the same intent charged the Roman line, and once again the Roman Legions held their ground, and dispatched the enemy with sword and spear in short order.

The few casualties on the Roman side were moved back into the open space at the hollow of the formation, and were soon attended to by the medical unit, while General Corbulo and his senior officers viewed the field from their vantage point. "This Tiridates seems to want to play chess, so let's give him something to think about. Tell the square to advance one hundred paces, then hold the formation at the ready for the next move."

In a few minutes the maneuver was complete, and while the Roman soldiers settled in to their new position on the field, the Parthians back-tracked, so as to maintain the same separation between the opposing forces. As they did so, there were gusts of wind and snow that portended a larger storm. In his tented headquarters, Tiridates vented his frustrations by castigating his officers, who had no option but to accept his recriminations, in the way that military men had already learned to do over the generations of warfare in the eastern fronts. Their commander was a king of his people, but not a warrior, and his military leaders had come to know and loathe his inability to lead. The change in weather darkened the field and it was obvious that there would be no more fighting on the day.

The Roman army set up camp on the inside of the hollow square, and tents were raised so that two thirds of the line was able to sleep for a few hours, while the other third maintained their vigilance in the darkness around them. There were sounds carried on the wind from the Parthian camp, but no way of knowing their movements. Eventually, in the early morning hours the pale sunlight revealed an empty campsite and no sign of the enemy. Once again Tiridates had opted to run rather than fight.

The city of Artaxata was open to the Roman forces, and they entered without opposition from an impotent citizenry. While the Romans displayed their full battle honors and standards in a colorful spectacle of strength and majesty, there was nothing to fear, as General Corbulo had decided to see out the rest of the winter garrisoned behind the walls of the city. The Romans set up their own administration in the municipal buildings around the square, and took control of all the food resources, to be apportioned among the local population as well as the Roman soldiers. Orderly governance of occupied territory was an art as much as a science, and the Romans had the measure of both.

Gradually the people emerged from their homes and hide-outs, as it became clear that there was no danger in the streets. The leading members of the city found each other and presented themselves to the Roman command as supplicants ready to pay homage. "As long as we are here, we will live as neighbors," was the word from General Corbulo, and so relieved were the Armenians that they failed to grasp the implication of his message.

As the winter months passed, Andreas worked hard at keeping a positive attitude in his dealings with his Roman superiors and the local citizens, with whom he interacted at various levels. He was sent on hunting parties into the Armenian highlands, and proved himself an able hunter of the many species of small animals that inhabited the hills and valleys.

There were rivers and lakes across the land that they occupied, and he soon recovered his skills as a fisherman, sending countless supplies of bream, trout, carp, and the much-desired catfish back to the city while he stayed on location with his fellow Auxiliaries. And all the while the majestic form of Mount

Ararat dominated the landscape, and pulled Andreas in to countless spells of contemplation and prayer, whenever he had the opportunity.

Finally, when the arrival of a warming sun brought the promise of Spring to the Plain of Ararat, General Corbulo gathered the city elders together. He thanked them for living and working as neighbors with his army, then gave them the news that the population must prepare to leave, as the city would be reduced to a crumbled edifice over the next several days. "Your gods gave you fields and streams enough to provide a constant harvest," said the General, "but the military significance of Artaxata demands that it be razed to the ground." Within a week there stood a line of rubble and dust, where before there was a fortified redoubt that had stood for hundreds of years.

The people streamed out of the city with their meager possessions strapped to their carts and animals, and dispersed into the distance. Their mountain of Ararat was the home of their gods, and their presence in its sight was their blessing. Their city was gone.

Once again, the Roman army was on the march across the Armenian highlands, although this time in a south-westerly direction that would lead them to their final military objective, the Armenian capital of Tigranocerta. The prospect of the final action of the campaign lay ahead of them.

They were only two days out on the campaign when the General's primary intelligence source, who had deployed his men across the Plain of Ararat, informed him that Tiridates and his men were off to the rear. General Corbulo now knew that taking the capital was but a formality, there being no viable resistance that could be brought to bear. Armenia had been his to attack. Soon it would be his to defend.

At the final overnight camp before the march into Tigranocerta, he met with his officers around a warming fire, under a canopy of stars that told their story in the forms and patterns that they made in the night-time sky. All military commanders were well versed on the map of the heavens, and it was just one more thing that the gods gave the people, to understand their place in the universe.

"To all intents and purposes this campaign is over. Tigranocerta lies defenseless but for her walls, and if we have to build catapults and assault towers to take them, it will add but a few days until its inevitable submission."

He turned to his scribe, who was always to be found on the outside looking in at these meetings, but ever listening. "Bring my proclamation to the Emperor

Nero that Armenia is ours. It has lain dormant long enough, and you may dust it off and get ready to send it to Rome." He had the taste of victory, and the meal would be but a formality.

The General continued his briefing, and, pointing to a parchment that was on his table, he told his men that the garrison of Caesarea in Judea had petitioned him to release the Auxiliaries that had joined his forces at the start of the campaign. "I am inclined to let him have his men back, as we have the large advantage of numbers." Turning to his Aide-de-Camp, he told him to tell the centurion in charge of the Caesarean Auxiliaries to ready his troops for their return journey to Judea, as their mission was now over.

When word of the discharge reached Andreas and his fellow Auxiliaries, there were many sighs of relief at the prospect of returning to their home base, which for all its challenges was nevertheless a pleasant enough billet, as long as there was peace in the land of Judea.

That evening Isaac attended a meeting of the troop leaders to discuss the plans for the return trip. The centurion addressed the group of about a dozen Auxiliary NCOs and Roman soldiers, pointing to some maps on the table. "I have looked at our options for our return journey to Caesarea, and plan to take a different route. One that will get us back quicker than the way we came. Rather than continue west across the Armenian highlands, we will march south and cross the Tigris at Marida."

The centurion looked around at his men and saw little reaction from them, apart from Isaac, who knew better than to volunteer any challenge. "The Proconsul will want us back in barracks as soon as possible, and I believe we can take a week off the return journey if we come down off the mountains at Marida, and then take a more direct route on a line that will get us to Damascus. It means crossing the Mesopotamian desert, but there are ways to travel between oases and rivers that will give us enough access to water. Beyond Marida, we will take on enough fresh water at Dionysias for the trek across the northern desert to Callicinus. That is where we will cross the Euphrates, and from there the hill country will provide for our needs. This also avoids a journey by ship from Antioch."

Isaac had experienced the Syrian desert on several occasions, as the garrison in Caesarea was invariably the source of additional men and materiel for the periodic campaigns to the north of Damascus. He was deep in contemplation as he made his way to his tent, and the gathering of his Auxiliaries, who were waiting for news.

Isaac gave them the orders with a minimum of fuss. "Once we cross this protective range of hills to our south, we will have a long and trying march across the northern Mesopotamian desert through Syria to Damascus. There will be few places to find water on the way, and the Bedouin people who live there submit to no-one, not even the Romans. We are heading into summer, and the sun can be merciless to those who would challenge the desert." He led the group in quiet conversation for a while, telling them some of his stories from his previous campaigns, as he tried to calm the nervous tension caused by his announcement.

Within a few days of marching in pleasant conditions, the topography of the land began to change, as the lush foothills of the mountains began to turn to patchy scrub and large sections of rocky and sandy landscapes. The impressive Roman built fortress at Marida watched over them as they took the opportunity to fill their water storage containers from the Tigris, after a full day spent ferrying men and provisions across the divide. There was one last ribbon of green that boldly tried to assert itself into the landscape, but soon succumbed to the encroaching desert. Within one day's march the conditions were markedly different, with extreme daytime heat and bitter cold in the evenings.

They approached the town of Dionysias from the north in the late afternoon, and crossed a small river-bed that should have been flowing with waters from the distant hills. This was the first sign that there might be drought conditions in the area, and the centurion brought his troops to a halt. He could just make out the town walls in the distance, and there were no Roman flags flying, or ensigns of the Legion that should have been occupying the garrison. He quickly sent two of his scouts to follow the river-bed toward the town and bring back information. They disappeared from sight in the twisting trail of boulders and faded vegetation that marked the course of the river. A short while later they returned with the news that the town appeared to be in the control of a group of Parthian soldiers.

The centurion pondered the options, none of which were good. He knew that the certain flow of the Euphrates lay about five days of marching ahead of them, but they only had a couple of days of water supply left for each man. There was no return, and any other direction would take them away from their destination. He told his officers to tell the men to observe half rations, and took up his position at the head of his men as he led them into the desert, guided by the setting sun.

By the third day the intense heat took its toll on the men, and with around two hundred and fifty soldiers carrying all their gear, and without horses, they were continually stopping to attend to men too dehydrated to march. The centurion came to speak to Isaac, whom he knew to have had experience of desert campaigns. "Isaac, you have been in this situation before. We now have eleven soldiers who cannot keep up, and I fear there will be several more if this continues. What can be done?"

Isaac thought for a few moments before responding to his superior. "Well, sir, the wadi bed that we are following west will probably lead to an oasis between here and Callicinus, and I would expect that we would arrive at a watering place within a day or two. There will be Bedouin there, and we should be able to pay them well for information. They care not for beads and baubles, but have a known hunger for gold. If we can somehow get to the Euphrates with their help, the conditions once we cross get much better."

Just as they spoke, one of the more senior of the Auxiliaries joined them from the rear of the column, and reported that several more of his men had collapsed. Without additional water supplies there could well be casualties. The Commander made up his mind and once again looked over at Isaac. "Choose two of your more able men and gather enough water from the supply truck to take with them. I need them to reach the oasis and arrange for some of the Bedouin men to bring us water as soon as possible. Tell the Bedouin they will be well rewarded but only after they have got us over the Euphrates. Here is some Roman gold coin to show them."

He summoned the purser, one of the few Roman citizens among the group, and told him to give Isaac enough to gain the attention of the Bedouin. "You say there are two days of travel to reach the oasis. I need your men there tomorrow, and back here the day after with water supplies and help."

Isaac saluted the order, and nodded in the direction of Andreas, and then Caleb. "You heard the order, men, so get ready to go. Carry only a night blanket against the evening cold, and as many water bags as you can." Within a few minutes the two men set off along the dry bed of the wadi in the direction of the oasis.

Andreas told Caleb how they would approach the march. "We need a comfortable pace that we can sustain, rather than a quick pace that might elevate our heart rate and cause distress. Let's help each other to keep moving, and we will take regular water breaks. There are a few more hours of daylight to endure, but once the night falls, we will make better time. There will be little sleep tonight, my friend."

The relentless sun finally slipped over the flat horizon ahead of them, and they had to slow down in the darkness to make sure they kept to the wadi, for if they lost the trail there would be little chance that they could complete their mission. Before long, the inky blackness yielded to the light from the stars, as they twinkled from one end of the sky to the other, and the two men were able to keep to the narrow course. Their pace quickened, and for hours at a stretch they matched each other's steps, staying within the contours of the wadi, and lost themselves in their own thoughts.

Finally, Andreas said to Caleb to take a break, and the two men took shelter in a rock-strewn gully, and relished the long draughts of water from their supplies. It was warm from the residual heat, but that was of little concern. "Let's get some sleep here, Caleb. It will be dawn soon, and a couple of hours of sleep should be enough to get us through the rest of the journey."

Andreas watched Caleb slip into a deep sleep within a matter of minutes. As much as he wanted to close his eyes and nod off, he could not help but think about their situation, their mission, and the chances of being able to reach find water resources and Bedouin help. Finally, he willed himself into a calm and peaceful place. Within a few minutes, he too was fast asleep.

From a large crack between some rocks a black irregular form made its way among the debris toward the sleeping men, having felt the vibrations when they lay on the ground. Flicking its tongue back and forward to provide its sense of smell, the desert cobra lay still, confused by the strange odor that was new to its experience. The round eyes took in shapes and saw color as either black or gray. At that moment Caleb stirred in his sleep, and moved his hand across his chest. The strike was straight to his exposed throat, and Caleb shot up from the ground. The cobra had its teeth locked on the skin and flesh for the few seconds it took to release its venom. Caleb was able to pull the snake away from his body even as he felt the venom pulse through his veins. Andreas stirred with the noise, and then leaped up as Caleb called out in pain.

He realized immediately that Caleb had been bitten by a snake, and called out to his friend, "Caleb where did it get you," as he pulled his knife out from his legging, ready to open the wound and try and extract the venom. Caleb's hand on his wound indicated the area that had been bitten, and he was already going into shock. With a strike to the neck there was no way for Andreas to cut out the poison.

In his heart, Caleb knew that there was nothing to be done. If the strike had enough venom to kill him then he would die. If he was lucky, he might just feel the symptoms, but would recover in a few hours.

"Andreas, I can only wait it out. Leave me here and head on along the wadi. You will get to the oasis in a few hours, and bring help. The Bedouin will know what to do." Caleb had turned pale with the pain and nausea, and his muscles began to twitch uncontrollably.

Andreas made his friend as comfortable as possible, and left a blanket on the ground with a few rocks to hold it down as a marker. He split the supply of water bags between them, and with a last look at his friend he began his journey to the oasis, and the Bedouin who might somehow be able to save his friend.

After several hours of marching in double time, taking his bearings from the stars, as he used to do when he fished the waters around the Peloponnese, Andreas noticed a gradual change in the ground surface, where there now appeared occasional plants among the scrub of sand and stone. The sight of a lizard sunning itself on a rock was no longer unusual, and the scurrying of insects large enough to be heard told Andreas that he was closing in on his destination.

He saw a dust cloud on the horizon, which soon showed as a group of men on horseback, and prepared himself for their arrival. They would want to know first if he was a threat, and if not then perhaps an opportunity. He positioned his short sword over his shoulder so as not to pose a challenge, but yet still have a ready defense, if needed.

Andreas raised his arms in the air as they brought their horses to rein, and greeted them in his native Greek language, explaining that he was a Roman army conscript on a journey to seek help for his fellow soldiers. Andreas had little faith that they would understand him, and yet the apparent leader of the group, who had dismounted, nodded his head in awareness.

Sensing that he must explain himself before asking for anything, Andreas talked slowly but firmly as he told them of the situation with his unit who were stranded in the desert, and then of his fellow soldier who had been bitten by a snake, and was a few hours ride east along the wadi.

Andreas knew that the ways of the Bedouin were unpredictable, and it all turned on whether or not they perceived him to be a threat, or a guest. To his surprise the Bedouin leader quickly offered Andreas his horse so that they could travel to their village, and he motioned to one of his men to make room for him to double up. As this was happening, Andreas expressed his thanks with his hands and said, "God bless you" almost without thinking, as he often did. The Bedouin leader then looked at him intently as he asked Andreas if he was a follower of Jesus.

"I am," Andreas answered emphatically, and this seemed to generate a smile that traveled around the group of men. The leader motioned to Andreas to nudge his horse and join the group, as they rode to the village, without the tension that was evident when they met up a few moments ago.

When they reached the village, he was immediately offered cold water again, and then hot spiced tea brewed over a wood fire that was strong and sweet, and welcome. In short conversation with the men, he found out to his amazement that many of the Bedouin tribes had given up their old ways of polytheism, and adopted a new spiritual life as followers of Jesus. The men had a smattering of Greek in addition to their native Aramaic language, and Andreas was able to communicate easily and effectively in both.

After surprising Andreas by giving his name as Abraham, the two talked almost as if they were friends. Andreas explained that the Roman army would be grateful indeed for the help of the Bedouin in providing water and leading the men out of the desert, and over the Euphrates. While Andreas and Abraham talked, his men were assembling a group of camels that would take them to Caleb, and then the rest of the unit. They also organized the filling of animal bladders with water, and loaded them on to several horses that would follow the main group, although at a slower pace.

Within the hour the Bedouin leader gave the signal to begin the journey, and Andreas found himself adjusting to a camel ride for the first time, and being surprised how easy it was. He still looked oddly out of place as the group made its way along the wadi. Each man wore a wrapped turban on his head, and at least two pieces of outer-garments protecting his skin. Only the eyes were exposed to the merciless sun, as they constantly searched the distant sky-line.

The first indication was a hazy movement just above the horizon, and as they urged their camels across the scrub, they saw what Abraham had suspected all along. Desert vultures had found a ready bounty in a dead animal, and a large one, based upon the number of birds swooping up and down, as they punched their pointed beaks into the flesh and soared up and away only to return for another attack. The flock had a hierarchy no less ingrained than that of the tribes with whom they shared the spoils of the desert. The shrieks and cackles from the lesser birds signaled the rules of the pecking order, that always showed when there was prey on the ground.

Andreas recognized the shape of the garment still lying on the ground near to the spot he had left his friend, surrounded by the excited birds of prey. A few of the Bedouin dismounted expertly and chased the carrion away from their feast. There was a bloody mess of skin, flesh, bones that was no more than an outline of Caleb's body mixed with the torn remains of his clothes.

Andreas dismounted unsteadily from the camel but could hardly bear to look. He could only sink to his knees and pray for the soul of his friend. Caleb had spent most of his life causing problems for others, and only a simple act of kindness and compassion from Andreas had somehow turned his life around. And now it was gone.

Andreas asked for a few of the men to help him dig a hole in the desert, and they were able to wrap the body in cloth before placing him in the ground. The Bedouin men looked around the wadi for rocks and boulders that they used to cover him before heaping on the soil and sand, and then more rocks and boulders. As Andreas said a few words of prayer to himself he saw the Bedouin men follow his benediction, and in a few moments, it was time to mount up, and continue toward the main group of soldiers.

In the middle of the night, Abraham called a halt and told everyone to catch some sleep until dawn. Andreas fell asleep almost immediately and had to be prodded awake by one of the Bedouin men in the morning. The tea pots were already bubbling on the fire, and Andreas had already acquired a liking to the sweet Bedouin potion, which helped him shake off the lethargy and re-invigorate him for the journey ahead.

After some hard riding for most of the morning, they eventually came upon the rest of the soldiers as they lay around the wadi area, trying to get some relief from the mid-day sun. Andreas approached the centurion and told him that the Bedouin leader, Abraham, was willing to help them reach the

Euphrates, and provide water and provisions on the way from their village at the oasis. The more seriously dehydrated men were given first priority for the fresh water, and it was not too long until everyone had received some relief from thirst, and a portion of different meats and vegetables that the Bedouin had brought with them as a stop gap, until the additional supplies arrived on horseback.

The centurion asked Andreas to stay with him while he spoke with Abraham, and Andreas motioned to Abraham to sit by a fire so that they could drink tea and talk. The centurion picked up on the signal from Andreas to observe their custom, and they spent a few minutes asking personal and family questions until it was appropriate to talk about how the Bedouin could be of service to the Roman army.

After two or three cups of tea the business had been taken care of, and Andreas was able to go back to his unit and tell them what had happened to Caleb. The most affected was Silas, who had formed a close friendship with the man who had inflicted such pain on him when they ran the assault course, and it was no surprise when Silas rose from the fire and pointed to his tent, announcing an early night.

After a while Andreas stood up and stretched, as he suddenly realized how tired he was. "Isaac, I think I'll get some sleep. I'll see you in the morning."

Andreas signaled his departure to the other men as he shuffled over to his tent, as if the effort was more than he could deal with. His emotions had taken a hit from the cruel death of his friend.

It took some time to break up the camp the following morning, as the officers sorted out the men between those who needed help to travel and those who had recovered enough to march in formation. Eventually the entire party of rescuers and rescued took their allotted place in the line and set off on the journey to the Bedouin village, and then the onward journey to Callicinus and the crossing of the Euphrates.

Andreas was given special permission to travel with Abraham, after the centurion had surprised him that morning with a visit just as his conturbernium was about to fall in to begin the march. "Andreas, I need you to stay with Abraham and make sure that he is content with our arrangement. I can tell that he trusts you, and I want to be sure that he stays on our side. I have the currency he craves, and we have a need that only he can satisfy." Andreas stood to attention as his leader spoke to him, and quickly pulled out of the line while glancing over to Isaac, who nodded his approval.

Soon Abraham and Andreas were riding side by side near the head of the line, and finally had a chance to talk. "Abraham, I was so surprised when you told me that you and your people were followers of Jesus, how did that happen?"

Abraham had been expecting that question, and smiled as he responded to his fellow Christian. "I was in Damascus about three years ago, after accompanying some traders from the east, and fell upon a preacher in the street, who was asking the people if they wanted to be saved, and how there was a son of the one God at that very moment in Judea calling the people to his side. I was with a few of my men, and asked them to wait with me while we listened to this strange man. He was small of stature, with a hook of a nose and no hair on his head or face, yet he mesmerized the people who stood and listened to him as he spoke of his belief in Jesus of Nazareth."

Andreas knew right away that there could only be one person who fitted that description. He was impatient to tell his friend that he knew the preacher, and that he had been a close friend of his father, but waited while Abraham continued to speak slowly and reverently about his conversion. "We Bedouins have always been spiritual, and it probably is a result of our life in the desert. When I look up at the sky above the flat and empty land around us, especially at night, the beauty of the heavens goes straight to my heart, and I wonder where the stars came from, why their journeys around the sky are so predictable, and how they were formed. Surely, they were not crafted by plenitudes of gods, each owning a piece of the heavens, and all in competition to present their stars to the people below, as if to force them to choose."

He stopped speaking for just a moment, as if to frame his thoughts carefully, not having had to justify himself in such a way before. "We have known of the Jews and their beliefs for as long as we have lived in the desert, but we never had a calling to become Jewish, just as they never called us to take their faith. This man—Paul, an Apostle of his Lord Jesus, told us that the same God of the Jews was calling for all men to join a new way of faith, and to worship in the way of his son on earth, Jesus of Nazareth, who He sent to save us from our own sin. I felt the holiness of his spirit, and felt blessed to take the Son of the one God into my life, and His teachings into my heart."

Andreas was moved by the words and the emotions of his new friend. "Abraham, I also know the preacher Paul, who became a disciple of Jesus not long after my own father. In many ways he is the reason that I am here today." Andreas went on to tell the story of his life in Patras, who his parents were, and what happened to them, and how Paul had become a major influence in his life because of a promise to his father. As the camels cantered along the wadi in the merciless heat of the day, the two men hardly noticed.

There was the prospect of an easier journey ahead of them, once they were across the Euphrates, and until then Andreas was assigned to accompany Abraham, in relative comfort. Once they reached his village the march was halted to allow treatment for some of the men who were sick and unable to make the onward journey.

The Roman commander was relieved to have reached the safety of the village, and asked that Abraham and Andreas meet with him to discuss the onward leg to the Euphrates, the transport of the sick and infirm soldiers to Damascus once they were able to travel, and the payment of Roman gold for the services of the Bedouin Abraham and his men. Andreas was relieved to see his commander live up to his promises, and the sharing of tea outside the home of Abraham set the seal on a productive conclusion to a mission that could have ended in tragedy.

Chapter Nine
Voyage

The soldiers of the Auxiliary force that halted in formation outside the garrison of Caesarea bore little resemblance to the troops who had marched out to their ship to the beat of a drum just a few months before. Their numbers were reduced in ranks, due to the casualties of the heat and the dehydration that followed from the journey across the desert. Eventually those missing ranks would return to the garrison, but for those who entered the gates on this day, as a rag-tag bunch of men who were visibly weakened and stressed by their experience, it was a relief to be back in barracks.

As they marched along the access road to the garrison, and under the massive stone aqueduct that carried fresh water to every part of the compound, they could see and hear the huge crowd in the hippodrome. A full house of 10,000 spectators cheered and roared at the gladiatorial competition among the best of the Roman army. The blue sky was the backdrop to the palaces, temples, theaters, gardens, and walls that were built to the specifications of King Herod the Great, in ostensible tribute to Caesar Augustus. The garrison was at the northern end of the harbor on the rising land, and stood as a sentinel to the Jewish king's legacy.

The mission Commander, Quintas Julius, was welcomed by the camp Commandant, Caius Tiberius, who brought him into his quarters for a debriefing. The two men, long friends from their service together, shared a meal as they talked. It took a long time for Quintas Julius to describe the mission that had taken him and his men across the Anatolian plateau and back, but eventually they relaxed as they shared some wine, and the talk became easier. Then Caius Tiberius said to his friend and subordinate, "Have you heard yet of the appointment of the new Proconsul in Caesarea, who joined us last month after Proconsul Felix was recalled to Rome?"

"No, that is news indeed, my friend. Who is he, and does he rule with a sword or a handful of flowers?"

"Well, he prefers to be addressed as Governor Festus, and it's a bit too soon to tell how he rules, as he has spent most of his first few weeks in Jerusalem. Hopefully he will stay within the walls of the palace, and leave the running of the military to the soldiers." The familiarity between the two friends was quite unusual in a military structure that was highly defined, and could only be revealed on those few occasions when privacy was assured.

As the two men exchanged wine and wisdom in the military quarters, Governor Festus was dealing with the thorny issue of the fate of the Apostle Paul, whose innocence or guilt of defilement of the holy places of the Temple on the Mount had landed in his lap, now that his predecessor Proconsul Felix had returned to Rome. He had gone to Jerusalem to investigate the case expecting a rather easy time of it, but it turned out to have many twists and turns, and as a man of principle he was troubled by the contradiction between the simplicity of the charges, and the complications of the argument.

Seeking a means of shelter in such a high-profile case, he had requested the intervention of the Judean King Agrippa, who had arrived at the palace in Caesarea to interview the prisoner and help determine the rendition of a proper judgment. The beautiful woman who escorted the king and shared his bedchambers was Bernice, his sister. This Jewish king had spent most of his life in Rome, in the shadows of the Emperors, and now that he resided in Judea to rule as king, he still lived as a Roman.

After reviewing all the evidence gained from his visits to Jerusalem and Caesarea, even King Agrippa had expressed doubt about the viability of the charges, but with the added observation that as Paul had already appealed the case to the Emperor in Rome, there was no way now to stop due process. To Rome he must go. Governor Festus had smiled to himself as he thought about the insistence of a Jewish king for a Roman decision on a matter of dogma and religious practice between Jews.

The following morning Governor Festus received his debriefing of the Armenian campaign from Caius Tiberius and Quintus Julius, and the several hours of the telling was interrupted only for food and drink. It did not take long for the men to recognize that this Governor was deeply interested in military matters. Finally, when the matter of the campaign was dealt with, the Governor addressed his centurion.

"Quintus Julius, you have served us well as Commander of the Auxiliary forces that supported General Corbulo in Armenia, and I have heard good reports on the quality of the men who served on this mission. I have a special assignment for a centurion and a small but effective group of Auxiliaries. You will have time for some rest and recreation after your long campaign, but within a few weeks I need you to accompany the prisoner, Paul of Tarsus, to Rome, where he will face the justice of the Emperor. Pick your men and prepare accordingly."

Later that day, after Quintus Julius had met with Isaac and told him of the imminent departure to Rome on a special assignment, Isaac made his way to the barracks housing where he found Andreas and the rest of the men cleaning weapons while they waited their turn for the evening meal. "Well, Andreas, you and me and the rest of the men did such a good job in Armenia, that we have been picked by Proconsul Festus to escort your Christian friend Paul to Rome. Can you believe this! I signed up thinking I would end up at the edge of the empire, and now I will be heading straight for the belly of the beast! I cannot believe it!"

Silas and Andreas looked at each other and shrugged their shoulders almost in unison. "Isaac, what difference does it make if we dig ditches and clean stables in Rome or in the farthest reaches of the Caucasus," said Silas, "When the Roman's play, we dance. It matters not what they call the tune."

Andreas mulled over in his mind the implications of this news, and took a few moments to speak, while his friends waited expectantly, yet not knowing what to expect. "To see Paul again would be wonderful, and I would rather that we be entrusted with his care than any of the rest in the barracks. As to Rome, it may be the end of a voyage, but I plan for it to be the start of a journey."

Isaac raised his eyebrow and looked at Andreas with interest, as his friend responded. "Isaac, I would think that Rome opens up a lot more possibilities than it closes. It is at the center of the Empire, and the best place to understand the boundaries. You were first to give me the idea that the further from Rome the better, but now we will have the chance to know the enemy. I say, let's go with God, and find out what there is to know about our mighty benefactor."

Several weeks later Centurion Quintus Julius boarded a vessel in the harbor of Caesarea, in order to inspect the ship that would take them as far as the Anatolian Harbor of Myra, from where they would transfer to another vessel for the onward journey to Rome. It was a single masted cargo vessel that had mixed grains and food stuffs in the hold, as well as rough cut marble blocks that were destined for a construction project in Myra.

There were boxes full of amphorae from the coasts of North Africa, and wines from the hills of Judea. Fortunately, there was a reasonably sized passenger section that would provide enough comfort for himself and his prisoner, who was to be accompanied by two friends. The enlisted men of the conturbernium would make do with a space on the deck, or maybe below if they were lucky.

Pronouncing himself satisfied, Quintus Julius made his way back to barracks to pack his bags for the voyage. Maybe this assignment would be the one that would get him the promotion that he badly wanted. Ah, well, Rome does things in her own time, so what was the point of speculating. His thoughts returned to the logistics of the voyage. He and his men would by necessity be armed, but he did not expect to need them on what should be a fairly uneventful journey to Myra in Asia Minor, and then onward to Rome.

The Apostle Paul spent the last night of his confinement in Caesarea packing his minimal personal effects, of which the most precious were his biblical texts. He often read, meditated, and prayed, until the early hours, and would fall asleep making up parables and lessons, as if he were delivering a sermon in the morning. On this night he slept the sleep of the dead, and rose with a spring in his step. He was on another Apostolic mission, only this time he would deliver his message into the heart of the pagan.

For Isaac, Andreas, Silas, and the five other enlisted men there was a sense of excitement at the prospect of an unusual assignment. Andreas was awake before the morning bugle, and spent the time in prayer. He knew intuitively that everything about his life until now was preparation for something special in the future. He no longer speculated about his father's experience with Jesus on the Cross, like he used to do. It was really quite simple. He had received the word of God through his father, and no matter how the future unfolded there was a purpose to his life.

His Savior did not die in vain, and neither did his father and mother, as long as he lived his life with a moral compass that was testament to the divinity of his Lord, and the righteousness of his father, Andrew.

Centurion Quintus Julius and his party of Auxiliaries were waiting at the dock at the appointed hour to take control of the prisoner, Paul of Tarsus, and the two friends who had been given permission to travel with him to Rome. As

Paul passed the line of soldiers, he was amazed to see Andreas among the men, standing at attention and looking straight ahead. He had often thought about Andrew's son, having spent his time in Caesarea in a comfortable if quiet incarceration. As he reached Andreas he stopped, and turning around toward Quintus Julius asked if he could pray before leaving Judea.

After a nod from the centurion, Paul took off his outer robe before kneeling on the ground for one last time. He gave his tunic to Andreas with a look that was a clear message of greeting from a friend to a friend, and Andreas took the robe with a knowing look and the faintest trace of a smile. After Paul and his two friends finished their prayers, they boarded ship, and within an hour the Captain gave the signal to leave port.

The west wind that followed the curve of the Egyptian coast was welcomed by the ship's captain, who had one more stop to make, in Sidon, before the final leg of the trip that would finish in the port of Myra, in Asia Minor. He was obligated to carry the Roman military party as far as Myra, and then they would become someone else's problem.

The second leg of the trip required another ten days of hugging the eastern coastline of the great sea while on a northerly heading, and then turning west with the coastline at Cilicia, where the coastal currents would provide enough energy for the single square-rigged mast of the small ship to reach Myra, in Lycia.

After several days of waiting around at the Roman garrison outside Myra, the party finally embarked on a large grain carrier that was destined for Rome. The passenger quarters were adequate for Centurion Quintus Julius and the three Christians, but the Auxiliaries were given a corner of the main hold in which to stack their personal effects and their bedding, close to the ship's crew. Andreas was hoping to find a way to speak to Paul, but he knew that he would have to be patient.

It did not take long for the monotony of the trip to wear heavily on the centurion, his three captives, and the men in his conturbernium. After passing the island of Crete on the eastern side, they stalled in weak winds and were stumbling along the coast toward the safe haven of Phoenix when there was a complete change in the weather. The centurion and the captain watched the storm develop as the winds were spun by the high mountains of Crete and thrown out again into the sea around them in a violent gale that was now coming at them from the north-east.

The captain ordered the sails to be trimmed, and with expert use of the rudders was able to point his ship in a northerly direction, so that the wind from the north-east would cause them to drift to the west. There was no rest for the crew, who followed the captain's directions in a constant battle to keep the ship stable in the unpredictable wind gusts and the incessant rain.

There, then ensued a miserable journey of about two weeks across the open sea, until they finally approached the island of Malta, almost five hundred miles from Crete. It was the sight of waves crashing on a shoreline in the fading light of the evening that worried the Captain, and after conferring with his senior officer, he gave the order to lower the anchor to try and halt their drift on to the shore.

The night passed with no rest for anyone on board, as the ship was battered by wind and wave. As dawn unfolded, they could see a sandy beach facing them, so the Captain ordered the anchor ropes to be cut so that the ship could run on to the beach, but as soon as the axes thudded through the hemp cord into the wood the ship lurched forward and ran aground on a sandbank that lay just below the surface. The bow of the ship was propped up on the sandbar while the rear gradually disintegrated from the force of the waves.

There was no orderly arraignment of passengers and crew to leave the vessel and make for the shore. It was mayhem, with the wind and waves combining in a joint attack on the men, as they jumped from the ship in an effort to get to shore. There was wooden debris everywhere from the break-up of the vessel, and some of the men were able to latch on to a spar or a beam and be carried onshore by the morning tide. Others had no option but to swim their way to the shore, as it was not that far from the sandbar to dry land.

Centurion Quintus Julius had shepherded Paul and his friends to the side of the ship, and told them to jump overboard and make their way to shore. He then went to check on his men, and found them pulling some of the crew members out of the hold, while the part of the ship that was still intact was bucking up and down from the waves. Isaac signaled with his thumb when the last of the men were out of the hold, and then the centurion signaled them to go overboard and pointed to the shore.

Just as the last of the men were waiting to judge the waves, so that they could jump safely into the turbulent sea, Andreas looked back at his centurion and saw him knocked down by a thick beam of wood that had been wrenched from its socket and fell to the deck. Isaac turned round when he heard Andreas yell, and saw his Commander's body slide down the sloping deck into the sea. They both hauled themselves along the deck as far as they could then jumped down into the sea in the area where their centurion had gone down.

Isaac grabbed a floating beam and pointed to Andreas to dive under. Just then Quintus Julius emerged from the sea on the crest of a wave, clearly unconscious, then was sucked down again. Andreas pumped his legs to get some kind of traction in the waves, and when his commander surfaced again, he grabbed his tunic and held him upright in the water, while Isaac made his way over to them using the beam as a float.

They were somehow able to get Quintus Julius between them, and hoisted his upper body on to the beam, while pumping their legs to steer away from the debris and toward the shore. As they tried their best to move in tandem, their commander vomited suddenly, three times in succession, and then they saw him breathe in and move his head above the water. Once he had regained his composure, he was able to help his two men propel the beam forward and after several minutes they felt sand under their feet, and the final battering of waves that spewed them up and on to the shore.

The first to reach out to them as they crawled up the beach was Paul, who had witnessed the events as they unfolded, and stood helpless while the action played out in the sea before him. "Andreas, my son, I was praying for you. Let's find a spot to rest for a few minutes, and we can talk."

Quintus Julius was close enough to observe Paul speaking to the young soldier, and looked over at Paul for edification, but Paul merely smiled and held his young friend's arm while they ambled to the foreshore and sat down to rest.

Isaac addressed the Commander with a bit less formality than normal, given the unusual circumstances that had brought their voyage to a halt. "Sir, Auxiliary Andreas is an old friend of Paul of Tarsus, and has not seen him for many years. Please let them have some time together. All our men are accounted for, but I see the Captain over there, so I should see if he needs our help."

"Before you do that, Isaac, I must thank you and your man Andreas for saving my life. You put yourselves in danger to do that, and I am thankful. You can be sure that I will advise my superiors of your actions today."

Isaac nodded his head and mumbled a soft "Yes, Sir" as he moved away toward the Captain of the ship, to see what he could learn of the situation, and what might happen next. By the following afternoon the storm had abated, and the Captain organized his men to salvage what they could from the vessel, which lay battered and wrecked on the sandbar. Isaac and his men worked with the sailors, and foraged along the foreshore for anything that could be used in the making of a temporary camp on the island. They stumbled upon a huge cave, that was above the high tide mark, and after reporting this finding, the group of survivors followed them back to a place that would become their home for the next several weeks.

Three months later the shipwreck survivors boarded a vessel to continue their journey to Rome, and eventually they landed at the Roman port of Puteoli, for the final trip overland to the city state of Rome. There were no fatalities from the shipwreck, although the Apostle Paul was the only person who was not surprised by this good fortune. He had prophesied this, as they passed the island of Cauda near Crete. And then, during their stay on the island, Paul was bitten by a poisonous snake, and the islanders took this as a sign that he was a special man. The sailors who remembered this called it a miracle, and some were converted to Christianity during their time in Malta.

Centurion Quintus Julius adjusted his military cloak one last time before entering the gates of the Roman garrison, just a few miles from the port of Puteoli, and summoned one of the guards to take him to the commander. Within a few minutes he was seated around a table on a veranda and enjoying a meal of fresh meat and fruit, with a smooth and sparkling wine of local vintage. In the time-honored tradition of military men, the two officers exchanged stories and experiences of their lives in the service of Rome, while Isaac's conturbernium and the three captives were provided a lesser menu of food and drink in the soldiers' mess.

Isaac was back in a familiar place, leading his men toward another destination in the service of Rome. The group that left the garrison had been stocked with supplies, replacement clothes, and uniforms, which gave them a new energy as they made their way along the graded access road, that would join up with the Via Appia on the road north. Isaac had joked with Andreas about being out of shape from marching, and Silas taunted both of them as they felt the summer breeze at their backs on the first stage of their journey to Rome.

Centurion Quintus Julius and his captives were mounted on well-groomed military horses provided by the garrison, and the conturbernium marched in time to the trotting pace of the horses in the short distance ahead of them. It was early summer in the south of the long distinctive peninsula that was home to the Italic peoples, from the Alps in the north to the tip of the peninsula in the south, that jutted into the Mediterranean. But of all the ruling city states, it was Rome that people thought of as the heart and soul of Italia.

Within an hour of their departure, they joined up with the main road that would eventually lead them into the heart of Rome. This was a road like nothing they had ever seen before. The base was entirely of tight-fitting stones that were apparently laid over a bed of smaller stones and mortar, and it was slightly crested to allow for run-off from the plentiful rains. There were drainage ditches along each side, and protective walls, to keep the ditches intact. Their leather boots made solid and level contact, and gave out a collective sound as they marched in unison.

The town tucked around the crest of a hill in the distance was their destination for the night, and by the time the group reached the town walls, the sun was on the decline, and they saw the town fire-lights flickering as they marched through the gate. They set up a temporary camp in the main square, near to the well, and as their commander walked around and talked to some of the local men, the others settled in for the night.

Andreas was able to spend time with Paul, and tell him of all that had happened since he had escaped from Patras; things that he did not feel safe in talking about when they were shipwrecked in Malta. When the centurion returned, he looked over at Andreas and the three captives, and moved over to his own camp, as if to sanction their meeting. Being able to talk about his mother and father with someone familiar was so pleasurable, and the two men talked well into the night, after the other men had retired. They both knew that their journey together would end in Rome, but what that meant for each man was God's plan, and their faith made submission a gift.

The breaking light of the morning played on the travelers, as they rose from their slumbers, and dressed for the resumption of their journey. As Andreas splashed some water from a bucket on his face, he looked across at a movement close to the well, and saw the most beautiful woman he had ever seen. She was slowly turning the handle to draw up her bucket that was filled with water, and was straining with the effort, her breasts strained against her skin-tight dress, giving definition to her gorgeous profile. He walked over and placed his hand over the handle, so that she could remove hers, while his smile wished her good morning.

He never knew her name, and they never spoke a word, but Andreas was entranced by her beauty, and knowing that there was nothing he could do about it, he finished hauling the bucket up and slipped it off the rope, placing it next to her wheelbarrow. She smiled her appreciation with a blush, sensing the people around the square watching her and the young soldier. Andreas nodded and turned away, looking secure and confident to the onlookers, yet inside he was filled with emotion, and did well not to show it.

As he marched off together with his fellow soldiers that morning, now the best of friends after their times together, he could think only of the young woman, and her beauty. As he spun tales to himself that always ended with the reality of the next step on the road north, he remembered the young women in Patras, and the way their looks, their clothes, their words, and their very being captivated him.

But this was something different, and he could only place her as a singularity of beauty that he could aspire to knowing, but perhaps never experience. It may not have been love at first sight, but it was the expression of an emotion that had been hidden for many years, almost by necessity, and now was embedded in his consciousness. The day seemed brighter, if that was even possible.

Three days later, Centurion Quintus Julius led his group into the marvel that was Rome. His service over many years had taken him to so many notable places, yet none were the equal of this city. The wide streets, the beautifully sculpted stonework, and the statuary of the gods, gilded the homes, public buildings, and temples.

For the Apostle Paul, he knew that he had arrived at the heart of the beast, and that he would die here. His mission for the Lord and His son Jesus could find no greater challenge, and he knew that this was where he was to be tested in the extreme. The rendition of a verdict by the Emperor could never be in his favor. The Jews of Jerusalem had their tentacles in too many places around the vast Roman Empire. No, the game was not about his trial. It was about a podium where he could preach, and a people that needed to hear the word of the one God.

Isaac told his men to stand easy while he checked with his centurion at the end of their journey into the city. They had passed a central garrison on the way in from the south, and would return there as a base, while they received their orders for their return to Caesarea.

Just then, Centurion Quintus Julius beckoned him over, and asked him to bring Andreas to him. In a few moments the two friends stood before their commander. "Isaac, you and your men have served me well, and I feel a special debt to you and Andreas. I am not without influence in Rome, so before we part, is there anything I can do for you two men once you are back at your base in Caesarea."

Andreas quickly processed the words of his Commander, and saw the opportunity immediately. Here was a way to the world beyond Caesarea, beyond Rome, and the chance to bring the word of God to those who lived where Rome's authority met the resistance of nations beholden neither to Rome, nor God. To a place where his ministry should be, and would be. Before Isaac could reply, he spoke up to his officer. "Sir, Isaac and I have speculated many times about the future, and we both crave the opportunity to travel to another part of the Empire, where we may have the chance to become citizens of Rome through our service in one of the Legions far from Judea. Our life back there is pre-ordained, and once we finish our lifetime of service we will be pastured in the hills around Caesarea, with a small pension and at best an aching back. Surely, there is a chance to repay Rome with our service against the barbarians, and earn the right to citizenship while we are able to enjoy it."

Quintus Julius was impressed by the eloquence of the young soldier, and had no real argument with their preference to soldier elsewhere. It was true that Auxiliaries had every likelihood, given a long and faithful service, of becoming regular legionnaires and citizens after soldiering in the far north-west.

"How about you, Isaac? Has your young friend spoken out of turn, or does he speak for you?"

"Sir, we have spoken together many times about our future service, and we are both of a mind to go forward, rather than back."

Centurion Quintus Julius had the ability to enable the request for his two men to transfer, and was pleased to be able to do this for two exemplary Auxiliaries, and settle a personal obligation in the Roman way. The two friends left to make their way back to barracks, and the prospect of some Roman ale that Silas had somehow managed to procure.

As a full moon on the longest day of the year shone on the seven hills of Rome, Quintus Julius relaxed with some old friends, while he anticipated with pleasure the assignation for later that evening, that he had arranged with the wife of a fellow officer serving a long way from Rome. He was, after all, in Rome, and would do as the Romans do.

In the place that would one day be known as the eternal city, Paul had arrived from a holy city to which he would never return. He would die in this place. The only uncertainty was how soon. And yet he was in high spirits, as he dined with his two fellow travelers, at the home of one of the Jewish leaders in Rome, which had an already sizable Jewish population. Several of them had been summoned to meet Paul, and brought with them their pride and their prejudices. Here at last was the writer of the Letters to the Jews in Rome. They knew much about him, but there was so much more to know, and a few of the men were ready to resist his words as blasphemy. The others listened intently to his every word, while nervously fingering their prayer beads.

Some were surprised at how small and insignificant looking he was. Some were put off by his quick actions and the hardness of his voice. Others were transfixed by his oratory. All were changed by the man, for he was like no other evangelist they had ever met.

By the time the evening was over, and Paul and his two friends were back in the custody of their Roman guards, the die had been cast. The Jews would make of him what they would, and he trembled in the excitement of the cause, and the finality of the outcome.

Andreas could not believe how easy it had been for Isaac and him to break their assignments to the Caesarean conturbernium and transfer to a new group of Auxiliaries, who were destined for service in the distant island of Britannia. They both had to surrender their private papers that contained their service records, colorfully embossed with the various seals applied after each mission. These were duly returned after notation of their new status as members of an Auxiliary Cohort assigned to the Ninth Legion, currently serving in the distant island that had resisted Roman occupation for over a hundred years. When Andreas remarked how surprised he was that the transfer had been quickly accomplished, Isaac laughed a little, as he muttered to Andreas. "I have seen enough of the Roman military way to know that they always get the paperwork right, whether the battle is won or lost."

Andreas felt a nervous energy from the hope and the doubts about the future. They slept in the barracks alongside the men of their conturbernium for the last time, including their dear friend Silas. Centurion Quintus Julius had written his report and recommendation, and the two men who had saved his life were bound for Britannia, where the land ended and the endless sea began.

Chapter Ten
Boudicca

The fleet of Roman ships was easily spotted by the lookouts on the green island the Romans knew as Vectis, as soon as the ships showed over the horizon. Vectis was calved from the land that birthed it some ten thousand years before, when the larger mass of Britannia separated from the continent of Europe, by the rising waters from the great melting of the northern ice cap. As the land was cleaved from the continent, the island formed as a fragment of the country the Romans would call Britannia.

One of the ships in the fleet of Roman military vessels contained a number of conscripts from the hills of Judea and the plains of Israel. In their midst stood a young man whose impressive physical build and presence belied the lowly status of his rank. Andreas of Patras was an imposing figure as he stood alongside the other soldiers on the ship, waiting to receive orders for the imminent landing on the shores of Britannia. He was a head taller than most men, and carried himself with confidence. Andreas listened with interest as the centurion addressed his soldiers and his complement of Auxiliaries. Just a few paces away stood his friend and fellow Auxiliary Isaac, who was the leader of the conturbernium.

While Andreas stood with the other soldiers at ease, listening to the centurion give his orders for the landing in the harbor, his thoughts drifted to what might await them in the province of Britannia. For Isaac, it was simple, reasoned Andreas. The Roman occupation of his native land of Judea was well organized and highly regulated. There was no chance to escape other than a lifetime of service under duress and servitude. Isaac would take his chance on serving in the newer parts of the Roman occupied lands, where there might be opportunity for another chance at life as a free man.

For Andreas, his motives were a bit more complex, and by his own recognition, not really developed to the point of certainty. Although Andreas had been captivated by Isaac's plan, it was the events in his home town of Patras that had caused him to enlist in the Roman army, as a subterfuge following his attack on the Roman Proconsul in Patras, Governor Aegeas. He reasoned that serving as a soldier of the Roman army was perhaps the safest place to hide. Now, in the second year of his service and with an active campaign in Armenia behind him, he had developed his skills as a soldier, but that could only be a means to an end. He was his father's son, and knew that one day he should recognize his calling to carry the word of Jesus, not just as a tribute to his father, but as an absolute expression of his deep commitment to the faith.

Andreas suddenly felt an inner sense of conviction that touched a nerve, and coalesced around a simple proposition that appealed to his conscience. He had grown up in the church. He had been to the hillside of Golgotha, and prayed with his father. His father was the first of those who were called Apostles, and had received a special blessing from Jesus in the last few hours of his natural life, that extended to Andrew's lineage.

No matter how long it took, he would one day become a preacher of the faith, and carry the word to the barbarians who still dared, in their innocence and their pride, to stand up against the power of Rome. His would be a message of salvation that would give their lives purpose, and their death meaning.

A sharp command from the centurion brought Andreas out of his reverie, and he quickly came to attention as the final orders were given for disembarking at the port of Chichester, a natural and protected harbor on the south coast of the island of Britannia.

Andreas looked out over the calm waters of the creeks and inlets that provided safe harbor to Romans and Britons alike. "A fine place to cast a net, Isaac. Do you think I'll have a chance to test my skills?"

Isaac was engrossed in watching a heron make its laborious take off from the marshes, and reluctantly turned round to his young friend to answer. "I don't think so," ventured Isaac. "As we may not be here long enough to afford the opportunity. I have a sense that our Roman friends brought us here for a larger purpose than sea trout and perch." Isaac laughed aloud as he wrapped his arm around the shoulder of Andreas and pointed him in the direction of the gangplank, and the stores of supplies that were waiting to be unloaded.

Within several minutes, the soldiers had disembarked, and Andreas was able to stretch his legs as he got used to the feel of solid and stationary land underneath his feet, after weeks on the moving vessel. It was only a few days ago that they had completed the crossing of a huge bay on the west coast of Gaul to reach the mouth of the channel, and the journey had tested the sea legs of everyone on board.

Suddenly, all of those memories were dismissed, as he looked around with interest at his new surroundings. The summer sun was warm and pleasant rather than hot and uncomfortable, and yet the noise and hustle and bustle of the port area reminded him of Patras, when the fishing boats came home from extended voyages into the Ionian Sea. The screeching and cackle from sea birds of all sizes surrounded the many boats and ships around the harbor, and there was a whisper of waves breaking from a distance.

As a Roman port and garrison, there were Romans a plenty going about their business, no differently than their comrades throughout the provinces and dependencies of the Empire. But it was the local people who interested Andreas, and they were easily recognized by their simple clothes and their language. They dressed much the same as the folks back in the Peloponnese— the women in one-piece dresses and the men in trousers gathered at the waist, and a long-sleeved shirt or tunic that on some men was as low as the knee.

It was the loud colors that surprised Andreas, and red appeared to be very popular, especially among the women. But yet they were different in appearance, being lighter in skin color, and many with red or light colored hair.

Andreas focused on a group of young women sitting outside a market area, chattering and gesturing in a language that made no sense, as he listened in. Most were plain, some were handsome, a few of the older ones were portly, but then a select few were stunning. Andreas thought wistfully for a moment of the young woman he had helped at the well on the Via Appia. The sight of so many young and fetching women was such a pleasant surprise, and he suddenly realized how much he had missed in the past two years as a soldier, either in the garrison or on campaign.

His transition from son of the Apostle Andrew to an Auxiliary soldier of the Roman army kept him separated from the opposite sex, and there was much he had to learn, with no opportunity to do so. He had heard talk in the barracks that the leadership were relaxing their ban on marriage for serving soldiers, but this would not apply to Auxiliaries. Once again, he reflected on the circumstances that had brought him to this place—the son of an Apostle of Jesus, with a special blessing that could only be fulfilled if he one day married and had a child, who would bring an innate sense of goodness to the world in which he lived, just as he was bound to do.

A call to order soon brought Andreas back to reality, and in a few moments, he was part of a detail carrying goods and weapons to the Roman fort at the edge of the town, where the road to Londinium began. The performance of menial and simple tasks was always delegated to the Auxiliary soldiers, and Andreas carried his load without any outward expression of dissent.

Inside, he carried his resentment as a prison sentence that had a long prospect of confinement, but would one day lead to freedom. Without that steadfast and unquestionable belief, his life would hardly have meaning. Soon he was whistling a long-lost tune from the Peloponnese, and gazing at the young women as he passed along the busy streets of the port town.

Andreas was surprised to see that the barracks inside the fort seemed to have been built to a high standard, and no less than he was used to. There was the usual mix of natural stone and manufactured bricks that were built up to form solid walls and some of the roofing. There was a water distribution system that provide not only drinking water throughout the complex, but a drainage system for the latrines that carried the waste away efficiently and effectively. He was actually able to smell the perfumes and scents of the woodland shrubbery that grew everywhere unchecked, as if prescribed by the builders of the fort to render a more pleasing accommodation.

There were plots of gardens laid out among the buildings, and he inhaled the scent of honeysuckle that was ubiquitous among the vines and vegetables.

Later that evening, as Andreas was cleaning his possessions, Isaac called a meeting of the conturbernium to pass along the orders to his men. The group of eight soldiers came to attention quickly through force of habit, and then were told to stand easy while Isaac looked them over carefully before speaking. "Listen up men. We appear to have arrived on this island in time to join in the fighting."

There was an audible groan from the men.

"I know, I know. We were all hoping for a quiet time to re-adjust to our new location, but that is not to be. We will join with a group of about eighty or so Roman soldiers who are also assigned to the Ninth Legion, so in a few days we will begin the march to the town of Longethorpe. It is a distance of about sixty miles or so to Londinium, where we will have to ford the river, and then another 80 miles north to Longthorpe, where the Ninth Legion has a major base."

A few mornings later the men assembled after breakfast to join the eighty members of the Roman century under the command of a centurion. Andreas marched in formation behind Isaac as a cool wind out of the north-east was a constant companion for the first stage of the journey, and it lay directly in their path all day. In the late afternoon they set up camp in a sheltered area close to the main road, which was well marked due to its constant use. Andreas was curious about the local people, and had asked around the barracks to find out what he could before they left on the journey. The local tribe was the Atrebates, and apparently, they had maintained a cordial relationship with the Romans going back to the early Roman Conquest under a Roman commander named Julius Caesar.

The camp was close to a hamlet where a few wooden houses indicated the presence of locals, and soon enough some of the younger children wandered over to tease some food and drink from the soldiers. The blonde hair and pale blue eyes of a young beauty who could only have been about five years old, captivated the group of men, and soon she was singing to them, oblivious to the fact that they could not understand her, although she made it clear her name was Tessa. Her older brother soon moved over to take her hand and lead her back to the house, where her mother stood half hidden by the door, trying not to be noticed.

Andreas wondered how the people worshipped, or if indeed they had any belief system. He had seen no obvious signs of idols or god tributes, and could only wonder at the possibility that some day they might become Christians. It was insights like these along the way that kept his resolve intact. All of this was just a means to an end.

In the late afternoon, when Andreas was returning to the camp with a water barrel on wheels that was filled on a regular basis from small streams and rivers, he came across a few of the children from the hamlet. The brother of the young girl recognized Andreas, and called out to him in broken Latin that he could just about understand. "Hey soldier, do you want to see the bones?"

Andreas had no idea what that meant, but merely grinned at the boy, and said, "Sure, as long as it doesn't take too long."

The young boy and a couple of his friends led Andreas over to a rocky outcropping, and moved some bushes aside to reveal the entrance to a cave. Enough of the sunlight reached the interior that Andreas could see a pile of bones of all shapes and sizes, including a skull staring endlessly at the wall of the cave. It was probably some unfortunate tribesman who had been injured, and made it here only to die of his wounds. He had no idea of the circumstances that had brought these bones together, perhaps thousands of years before, when this land was occupied by hunter gatherers.

The larger bones were part of the skeleton of a man killed by an animal with strong and powerful jaws and sharp teeth, and the rest of the cache of remains would one day be identified as remnants of pigs, horses, deer, hares, and birds. For now, it was a playground for little boys, and the source of a Roman coin or two from passing strangers like Andreas.

After breaking up camp the next morning, the soldiers were soon into their marching rhythm across the hills and valleys which the locals called the Downs, and by late afternoon they had reached a Roman fort on the south bank of a major river, upstream from the city of London. Rather than ford the river that night, they camped in the comfortable barracks and started the day early by lining up ready to load their baggage onto the barges that were hired and paid for with valuable Roman coins that were accepted currency in the Romanized parts of Britannia.

Andreas was surprised that many of the people seemed to have a basic knowledge of the Vulgar Latin that was spoken by most of the Roman soldiers, and were quite capable of understanding their subjugators.

A torrent of rain welcomed Isaac as he lined his men up for a quick drink and some food, while he primed them for the rest of the day. "There is a lot of uncertainty about what is ahead of us, and we have received new orders to march to the River Cam and join up with some regulars from the Ninth Legion. There is a fortlet on a place called 'Castle Hill' and the Roman soldiers based there may need additional arms and support."

The men were quickly dispatched to ready themselves for an aggressive march in a north-easterly direction toward the fortlet on the Cam, in the territory of the Trinovantes, the neighboring tribe to the Iceni.

Isaac spotted the centurion and went over to ask him about the change of plans, and was surprised to be told that only the conturbernium was being diverted to the Cam. The other Roman soldiers would head to Longthorpe to join up with the main force of the Ninth Legion.

In the midst of the uncertainty, the weather improved to dispense warm breezes and bright sunshine, as the small group of soldiers headed for their destination. Isaac welcomed the pleasant conditions but worried about the assignment. It was unusual to send Auxiliary forces independent of the Roman soldiers, if for no other reason that they might defect. Grudgingly, Isaac had to admit that this was an unlikely proposition so far from home, and perhaps the Roman command realized this and believed it was a gamble worth taking. Still, it was strange.

Isaac shared his concerns with Andreas at the earliest opportunity, when they stopped at a stream to drink and fill their canteens from the cold gurgling water. "You know, Andreas, we could be heading into some trouble with this assignment. I overheard some of the Roman soldiers talking about the change in orders, and laughing about us heading toward the Iceni, while they continued to the main barracks at Longthorpe."

"Isaac, your intuition is usually pretty good, and it's strange that they let us march on alone without escort."

"Well, there's not much to be done except to follow orders, but we should be extra vigilant as we approach the fort. It is located next to the Trinovantes town of Camulodunum, and they are supposedly in league with the Iceni. There is a Roman fort under construction at the half way point of our march, at a place called Caesaromagus, and we should be able to shelter there for the night, and march the remaining 30 miles tomorrow."

Later that day they reached their stopping point at Caesaromagus. Sure enough, the buildings and construction works were well advanced, and there were about a dozen Auxiliaries mixing cement and building up the layers of stones and bricks in the familiar Roman style. There were local people out in the fields working and getting the most out of the late afternoon sun, but no sign of any Roman soldiers. Isaac approached one of the Auxiliaries, who laid down his mortar board as he approached. "Good day, soldier, we are heading to the fort at Colchester and wanted to rest here overnight."

The soldiers motioned for the squad leader to come over, and soon the two men were chatting easily with each other. Isaac sensed that his counterpart was already out of his depth in leading the small group of Auxiliaries, who were used to always being told what to do and where to go. Suddenly one of the men shouted from a half-built tower, that there was a soldier on horseback heading their way. The men watched the dust in the distance take shape as the rider closed in on the fort, and he soon pulled up to dismount before the group of men.

"I bring news from Colchester. The fort has been attacked by the Iceni, and there are only about 200 Romans left alive, mostly civilians and retired soldiers who are barricaded inside the temple. There are thousands of Iceni, and I was lucky to get out alive."

Isaac presented himself to the soldier and asked him to tell him as much as he knew about the situation. Since there did not appear to be anyone of leadership authority among the Auxiliaries on the construction detail, Isaac took control of the situation, and ordered that all the men assemble along with his conturbernium.

"Listen up, men, we need to pull out of this area and head for the headquarters of the Ninth Legion at Longthorpe. The Iceni tribe of Queen Boudicca has joined forces with the Trinovantes at Colchester, and there are thousands of rebels who are part of an uprising against our army. If we head north, we may be able to get word to the Ninth Legion headquarters, so let's gather our weapons and traveling supplies. We'll march through the night with only minimum stops for rest and food, so take only what you need for the journey, and for battle if necessary."

Isaac asked the messenger to stay by his side on the march, having established that he was familiar with the territory and would be able to lead them on the most direct route to the Legion headquarters. It would be a fifty-mile hike over relatively flat terrain. The soldier seemed a competent man, and Isaac was confident that they would be able to make the journey in as short a time as possible.

Once they were on the open road, the soldier was able to give Isaac a more complete report of recent events among the tribes of the east, who were rising up against a Roman administration that had taken a firm grip of the southern areas of Britannia in the last 100 years or so of occupation. The problem, it seems, was Boudicca.

Three months before.

Governor Suetonius Paulinus had spent the last few months gathering news and reports from around the occupied territories. He had taken the measure of his subjects in the south and east of Britannia, and decided that it was time to mount a campaign in the west, where the Demetae, the Silures, the Deceangli, and the Ordovices, hid behind the shelter of the Cornovii, and refused to pay tribute to Rome, nor acknowledge its sovereignty. The campaign had gone well, and the entire area had been brought to heel, but there remained the final objective. The island of Mona, sanctuary of the Druids, who still were a powerful unifying force against the Roman hegemony.

The dispatch of news from Procurator Catus Decianus about the death of Prasutagus was troubling, but hardly worth a change in military strategy. Let the Procurator earn his gold for a change and manage his responsibilities, while his legions completed the campaign in the west.

And after that, the push to the north. He would be the first Roman Governor to bring the entire island of Britannia to heel, and render his legacy worthy of the ultimate prize—Emperor of Rome. The many forts and vexillations in the south were under orders to send their officers and soldiers to aid the western campaign, and were left in the hands of trusted Auxiliaries to maintain a presence in the established areas of Roman control, among people who were used to follow.

The death of King Prasutagus of the Iceni tribe should have caused Governor Paulinus to think again, but he elected to leave his territories under-manned, while he was caught up in the larger theater of empire expansion. He boasted to his advisors as he led a discussion on military strategy. The Iceni were now led by a queen and two daughters, and hardly likely to show any resolve against their long-time superiors.

The ascendancy of Boudicca as Queen, on the death of her husband, proved to be a tipping point that the Governor had not considered, and if his advisors had thought of it, they were loath to speak out. Within a few weeks of her accession to the throne, she was openly challenging the Roman governing class, and the centurions who were plundering the resources of the tribe in the name of their Emperor. Unable to exercise any control of the Roman elite, she issued a request to Procurator Catus Decianus in London to meet with her, which he was required to do, and he left her waiting for an answer for a few days while she simmered in her anger, and he suffered in his ignominy. Eventually they met.

"My Lady Boudicca, I bring you condolences from Governor Paulinus on the death of your dear husband Prasutagus, who was a great friend of Rome. Please also extend my sympathy to your daughters." Procurator Decianus accepted the extended hand of Queen Boudicca, but did not kiss it in the time-honored tradition. He merely gripped it firmly as he feasted his eyes on the queen, and her ephemeral beauty, while trying to project the majesty of his office in a failing attempt at diplomacy.

"Thank you on behalf of our family and our people," said the queen, icily. "May I be the first to tell you that my dear husband has left half of his entire estate to the Emperor, and the other half to our two daughters, Damorra and Dasca, in the knowledge that eventually the entire estate will be vested in Rome."

Procurator Decianus was taken aback by this news, which was contrary to the standard practice that the Romans had instituted when they entered Britannia as an occupation force. "My Lady, this is not acceptable. It is inconsistent with the terms of our administration of the land of Britannia. The Emperor expects that the late King's entire estate will become vested in the Republic. Surely his last wishes have been misinterpreted."

Boudicca leaned a bit closer to the procurator, and bent her head to accommodate his lack of height, and her commanding presence. "Procurator Decianus, I think our family has been more than generous in the terms of my husband's disposition. My daughters are both likely to be claimed in marriage by Roman citizens, so one way or another Rome will get the rest of what Rome covets, as is the way of things. In the meantime, I have a kingdom to run as Queen, and there is much to be done."

The diminutive Procurator shook his head as if possessed of a tremor, while he gathered his thoughts in the face of this unexpected development. He had been looking forward to the additional responsibilities that the estate of King Prasutagus would bring to his administrative mandate, and the means to self-enrichment as the decision maker on all of the business affairs in the kingdom.

"Queen Boudicca, you clearly do not comprehend. There is no choice in this matter. There is no other way of dealing with the royal estate other than by conveyance in its entirety to Rome." Decianus had made his case in simple terms that a simple woman should understand.

"Procurator Decianus, let me tell you what has happened in the few weeks since the death of my late husband and King." Her eyes burned with hate as she looked down on him. "The Royal lands and properties are being appropriated by order of your Governor in trust for your Emperor. Your centurions are plundering the kingdom by random confiscation of the properties and possessions of my subjects, and my people are being evicted from their homes. Even your own slaves have looted the royal household. I demand that you act immediately to stop these acts of violence and vengeance."

Even in her antagonism, Boudicca could not help but reflect her obvious natural beauty. Her dark red hair fell in waves that lapped against her eyes and cascaded down her back. Eyes that were more green than blue. Her shapely figure was a matter of common discourse, and the root of many a snide remark on her husband's actual cause of death. Making comedy out of tragedy was not only a Roman predisposition. Taller than the average man of her time, she was the stuff of dreams.

Decianus drew in a deep breath in a failed attempt to give himself stature, and resorted to his usual response to aspersions against the Roman authority. "I remind you that you and all your people are subservient to the Emperor, and have no case to make against an occupying regime that has the force of law and the law of force on its side." He smiled thinly at having levied such a clever and appropriate rendition of the facts to Boudicca.

The Queen was quick to respond, no longer caring for the role of diplomacy. "How dare you deal with us this way. Our people have lived in this land for as long as time itself, and our rights have been trampled upon by you and your usurpers from Rome. I curse you and I curse Rome!"

Queen Boudicca took a step forward and looked down in disgust at her nominal superior, and this was enough to cause the Procurator to roar his disapproval with a call to his guards. Six Roman soldiers from outside the room entered quickly with their swords drawn, and forced Boudicca to back away from her protagonist.

Decianus had heard what he wanted to hear. "Enough of this nonsense. I have the authority of the Roman administration on my side, and the ability to dispense summary justice as a necessary tool, to ensure that there is peace. Until this matter is resolved I require you and your daughters to be remanded in our custody. Guards, arrest this woman and her daughters."

Boudicca was powerless to prevent the guards from following orders, and she was led from her home with her hands tied behind her back and her neck tethered to a wooden pole that the guards held between them as she followed along. Along the way her subjects were taken aback by this treatment of their Queen, yet unsure what to do about it. Word quickly spread of her incarceration. The other guards went to find her daughters, and by the time Boudicca had reached the Roman prison building, both Damorra and Dasca were in their custody. They were soon unceremoniously set free of their bonds, and bundled into a cell with their mother.

On return to his office, Procurator Decianus sat behind his desk and contemplated his next move. It was clear that Governor Paulinus was focused on his western campaign, and his reply to the dispatch from Decianus on the death of the King carried a clear message. 'Procurator Decianus, it has happened in the past that some tribes saw the death of their king and the transfer of the Royal properties to Rome as a seed of discord that grew into a harvest of treason. This must not happen with the Iceni. Even though there have been some precedents in the past, in this particular case Rome expects that the estates and properties of the King shall be conceded to Rome. You have my authority to dispense summary justice should that be necessary to maintain control over the tribe of the Iceni, from the Queen on down to the lowest of their serfs.'

Decianus pondered the intent of this message. Taken at its face, it was clear. He had the authority to do whatever it took to maintain law and order in the lands of the Iceni, freed from the responsibility of due process by trial for anyone who resisted the Roman authority. Who better to serve as an example of Roman justice than the Queen, and her daughters. How sweet it would be to exact a tribute from such a woman as Boudicca, who displayed in her maturity a beauty and appeal to a man's baser instincts that was even more promising than that of her comely daughters.

It was now a warm, almost sultry evening in Norwich, the capital town of the Iceni, and still Decianus stayed in his chambers and weighed up his options. At times like this he realized how alone he was. No friends that he could count on, and only fellow Romans of the governing class who each had ambitions, and whose every move was made from a selfish perspective.

He lay silent for a while, processing various approaches to the problem. How to teach a recalcitrant queen a lesson? There had to be punishment for her blatant disregard of the conventions that Rome applied on the death of a tribal king. Perhaps he should give her a choice. Suddenly it became clear, and he rose from his couch and summoned his guard. "I need three of my best soldiers to report here immediately. Ask centurion Janus to send them to me, as I have need of their services tonight." He poured himself some wine and ruminated on what to do next.

Decianus had barely placed the empty wine glass on the table when the three guards reported for duty. He quickly gave them his orders. "Go to the prison cells and bring me Queen Boudicca. Make sure you tie her hands. Leave her daughters in the cell, and two of you stay with them until you hear from me."

After several minutes one of the guards returned with Queen Boudicca, pushing her forward until she stood in front of her tormentor. Boudicca was powerless to resist but Decianus produced his dagger and waved it in her face. She had no choice but to comply. He then dismissed the guard, to wait outside the chambers until further orders.

"Sit here, my Lady, and let's discuss what needs to be done to resolve this unfortunate matter. I have a proposition for you." He pushed her backward and she collapsed on the sofa. He felt more in control when she was seated. "You have challenged the authority of Rome, and that is an act of treason. You do not have the right to a trial, but are subject to summary justice, at my discretion. I am willing to overlook your transgressions, but will require a small favor, or accommodation on your part. Lie down on this sofa, and do not resist. I can be easy to deal with when I am pleased, and I think you are more than capable of pleasing me."

Boudicca looked up at him with contempt, then spat in his face. Decianus carefully wiped the spit, and prepared to raise the stakes, just as he thought he might have to.

"You have one more chance to respond with the right answer," said Decianus. "Your daughters are with my men, who await my orders. Defy me again and I will pass the word to the guards that Damorra and Dasca are available at their pleasure."

Boudicca sat immobile on the sofa. She had felt for some time that a moment like this was coming, and had steeled herself never to compromise. She had even talked with her daughters about the risks that they were taking in going against Roman policy on the matter of succession. The people of her tribe had rallied around her, taking strength from her assertion of control, and she needed to keep their trust.

Boudicca had raised her daughters well, and they were both adamant that to give in would be the start of a slippery slope. She knew that her girls could deal with it. With a look of hatred and disgust at Decianus, she turned her eyes to the floor, and remained silent, in the knowledge of what it would mean for her daughters.

So be it. He had given her an easy way out, and she could have quietly returned to her castle with her daughters with no more said about it. Now she had increased the stakes, and he had no compunction about dispensing punishment to both the Queen and her daughters. It was time for a strong statement of the power that he had in the country that she still called her own.

Decianus summoned his guard from the hallway and directed him to return Boudicca to her cell, while he followed along. When they reached the cell Decianus motioned for the two guards to bring the daughters outside, and Boudicca was pushed on to a bench, still bristling with resentment and hate for her notional superior and his minions.

"Tomorrow at dawn you will be taken to the town square and flogged with one of the leather whips that speeds my chariot across your lands. Twenty lashes should be enough to remind you that you live here as Queen purely by the sanction of the Emperor. As for your daughters, I fear their punishment must be even more severe, as it is they who claim the land that rightfully belongs to Rome."

Boudicca was left alone, and felt powerless to change the course of events. She was scared for what would happen to her daughters, and also at the prospect of being flogged. She had to remind herself. She was Queen, and she would deal with anything. And she would have revenge.

After seeing the lock applied to her cell, Decianus motioned for the two guards to step over to him while Damorra and Dasca sat on a nearby bench, shaking with fear. "You are in luck tonight, my friends, Rome has a favor to ask of you. You may take these young women to an empty cell, and show them what it means to feel the power of Rome. Do not hurt them, just return them to their mother when you have had your way. There will be no repercussions."

There was no question that the guards would comply. Roman soldiers were not allowed to marry while still in service, and while sexual relations with the local women were not a problem with the army, as long as it happened off duty, it was easier said than done. The opportunity for sex, even if with a reluctant partner, was not to be ignored, and the guards were quick to seize the moment.

Decianus left the men to their favors and made his way back to his chambers. Tomorrow Boudicca would feel the lash for her stupidity, and the Kingdom of the Iceni would become yet another ward of the Roman state. Surely then this queen would give up her notions of resistance to Rome.

Chapter Eleven
Longthorpe

Dawn approached as a tired group of Auxiliaries emerged from a forested stretch of land that had slowed the men in their march toward Longthorpe. Andreas was just behind Isaac in the line, and was anxious to see what the light of day would bring, which would surely be tempered by the incessant rain. Soon Isaac called a halt so that the men could take a short break to eat something and drink from their canteens. There was no time for the niceties of warm grog and conversation, given the uncertainty of their position, and the unrelenting rainfall.

Isaac motioned the guide to join him as they sat on an outcropping of rocks and boulders, and asked him to lay out their location relative to the headquarters at Longthorpe and the Iceni capital of Caistor St. Edmund. The man, Bergamus, whom Isaac had come to like and respect after traveling with him for a few hours, was a citizen of Gaul who had been conscripted as a young man, and now had over twenty years of service under his Roman belt. He spoke the Roman tongue, and the common language spoken by the many tribes whose loose federation made up Roman controlled Britannia.

Bergamus cleared away some debris and weeds from an adjacent piece of ground, and picked up a few stones to use as markers. "Here, we are here," he said, placing a stone in the center of the cleared area. "We are about five miles south of Longthorpe, which is here, and some seventy miles to the east is the Iceni capital of Caistor St. Edmund, which is here. Colchester is about sixty miles to the south of the capital, so the three main towns form a triangle. There is no telling where Boudicca is, as she now leads the armies of the Iceni and the Trinovantes, which have been swelled by thousands of tribesmen." The stones laid down as markers told the tale.

Isaac looked at the rough map and added a rock to show London, on an extended line south and slightly west of Colchester by another fifty miles or so. "It seems to me that she will need to keep going, as her only hope is to bring in all the other tribes to the fight. If she stays in one place, Rome will eventually bring much larger forces to bear, so I would think she would head for Londinium, in view of its importance as a military center and port."

The men normally had no involvement in plans and strategy, but they had become a tightly knit group in the last several days, and they all sat together and paid attention to Isaac, who was clearly a leader of men such as not often seen in the Auxiliary forces.

Andreas spoke up, as he looked over to Isaac, then pointed to the rough map. "She will either try to get to Londinium before the Legions from Longthorpe get there, or maybe force his hand in battle on her own territory, in which case she might even now be heading north again on a line that would bring her to Longthorpe."

Isaac considered the idea for a moment, while he acknowledged the acuity of his young friend. "That's a good point, Andreas. There may be conflict going on right now and we have no way of finding out, other than by reaching Longthorpe, According to Bergamus, we are not much more than an hour's march from the fort, so let's be cautious as we approach the area. Let's clear the site here and see what waits us at Legion headquarters."

The spring weather brought another huge downpour, after a steady fall of rain that had dogged them on most of their journey north, and the men took it in stride as they marched resolutely toward their destination, each of them with their own thoughts, but thinking the same thing. Would they be back in the inevitable front-line position against a horde of warriors, before the day was out. The short discussion on the military options had reminded them of their situation. Each of them worked their way through the thought process as they gained on Longthorpe, and fought to dispel the prospects of battle, by reflections that were easier to bear.

Suddenly, as the column of men rounded a bend on the track north, they were faced with a river that had probably only days ago been an easily forded stream. Isaac and Bergamus conferred for a minute, and then Isaac addressed the men. "We need to divert across the fens to another approach road to Longthorpe, in the hope that it is passable enough. Bergamus says there is a road to the west of this location and a track to the east, either one of which will take us to the fort. It is important that we get through to the Legion in case they are unaware of the rebellion. Andreas, you and Bergamus go on ahead as quickly as you can along the eastern route, and I will lead the rest of the men in the other direction. We will eventually meet up at headquarters, but in the meantime, this should increase the chances that we can get news to the Legion sooner rather than later."

Andreas and Bergamus set off at an accelerated pace, each of them conditioned enough to able to make the extra effort to find a way through to their destination. They soon were plodding through the mud and rainwater that identified the fens in this part of Britannia. The entire area was crisscrossed by streams, which had burst their banks and spilled over to create a maze of fens and water, but as long as they stayed on line, they should eventually run into the track that would lead them to the fort.

The lightning bolts lit up the sky around them, but did little to illuminate the path through the fens, and the rain became torrential. Andreas couldn't help but reflect that this was a rainfall that would have brought joy to the farmers in the Peloponnese. Surely it would lighten up soon. The two men plodded through the forest floor as best they could.

They were not prepared for what happened next. The track below their feet suddenly gave way and they both found themselves in a pool of mud, gradually being pulled down. There was no purchase below their feet and they were both gradually sinking into what could easily be a bottomless pit. Bergamus called over to Andreas, who was only a few inches away. "Don't move Andreas, or you will just sink quicker into the mud. Try and stay motionless. We can only hope that there is a firm base near enough to hold us above the surface. If we have a secure foot-hold we should be able to gradually move to the side."

Andreas fought hard to control the panic as he felt himself inexorably pulled into the pit, and only the thickness and viscosity of the mud slowed the process enough for him to think about how to escape. Instinctively he reached out to Bergamus with his strong right arm, and told him to take hold. He was familiar with quicksand from his military duties in the desert, and if there was some way to hold Bergamus or push him to the side he might be able to be saved. He had no thought for himself, and instinctively tried to help his friend.

Andreas had a firm grip on Bergamus, and used all his strength to push against the mud. The more he pushed the greater was the suction power of the mud underneath him, but he struggled to get some leverage and somehow was able to get Bergamus close enough so that he was able to grab hold of the branches of some bushes by the side of the pit, and begin to pull himself toward the edge.

The movement by Andreas had quickened the suction of the mud, and Andreas was up to his neck. He quickly let go so that Bergamus could pull himself up to safety. He had to force himself to calm down in the face of the terror that was unfolding, with the brown viscous liquid just inches from his mouth. Suddenly he felt his feet touch something solid, and he felt himself settle against the bottom of the pit, with the ability to hold himself above the encroaching mud.

After what seemed an eternity, Bergamus reached the top of the bank. His small axe was still tethered to his belt, held in place by a clever knot of rope that was taught to all soldiers, so he unloosed his axe and quickly selected some strong branches to cleave from the surrounding bushes and trees. Picking a long staff of hard-wood, he extended it toward Andreas, who gratefully took hold of the end and began to pull himself toward Bergamus. This was an uneven match, and all he was doing was pulling Bergamus toward the pool of mud.

Suddenly Andreas shouted to him with an idea. "Bergamus, chop one of these small trees near the bank so that it falls in the pit, but don't cut through the wood completely. Leave enough that you can still push it down toward me, and as long as the limb is not severed, I should at least be able to get some support, and enough leverage to pull myself out."

Just as Bergamus began to hack away at a suitable tree, Andreas felt his feet begin to waiver as the base of firm ground below him gave way. He felt himself moving downwards again, with the mud now lapping his beard. His heart was racing as he felt the wet mud just below his lip when suddenly he heard and felt the tree give way and land across his shoulders. He grasped it instinctively, and looking over to the side he saw Bergamus using his rope to secure the tree in case the limb began to separate from the base.

Andreas began to pull himself upwards and outwards toward the bank, straining mightily against the countering pull of the mud. Gradually he began to move inch by inch toward the bank, and with each effort he felt himself rising above the surface, and able to breathe without fear that it might be his last.

Somehow, before his strength gave out, Andreas was close enough to the edge that Bergamus could help free him from the clinging mud, and he collapsed exhausted on the bank. He was utterly spent, and when he finally sat up it was to let the torrential rain clean the mud that was everywhere—in his eyes, his ears, and plastered all over his body. He gave a silent prayer to his Maker as he arose from the ground, with a hand from Bergamus.

After an hour or so carefully picking their way across the Fens, they ran into the track that led off to the road north, and the fort at Longthorpe. The two men felt better already, now that the rain had finally stopped. It was good to feel the warmth of the sun, and even the chaffing of a drying tunic, rather than soaked and clinging clothes. It was comforting just talking to each other, and when Bergamus tried to thank Andreas for helping him reach the edge of the pit, Andreas was quick to brush it off. His instinct to always do the right thing was a gift that he proffered at every opportunity.

They were able to pick up the pace now that the trail was defined, and the land around them began to rise and take on a more familiar landscape of fenced-off fields and cultivated plots of land. "I recognize this area," said Bergamus, pointing to a distant hamlet. "These small houses are at the junction with the main road to Longthorpe, and we should be able to find food and drink. The people are obliged to provide sustenance to Roman soldiers, but we may meet some resistance so we should be careful."

As they got closer, they saw a large group of soldiers on horseback appear from the south and dismount around an open area just short of the cluster of modest buildings. They carried the flags and standards of the Ninth Legion, and were clearly in disarray, with wounded soldiers strapped across the saddles of some of the horses, and other men lying on the ground and clearly injured.

As they reached the scene, Bergamus shouted out to get attention, and announced that he and his fellow soldier were Auxiliaries. A centurion looked up from a group of men that were huddled around a fallen soldier, and motioned for one of his men to question them. Bergamus quickly explained that they were on the way to meet up with the Legion at Longethorpe, and the soldier nodded his head toward the centurion, who turned away to continue ministering to the wounded soldier.

Suddenly, Bergamus placed his arm on Andreas and they both stopped, then Bergamus whispered to Andreas, "The wounded soldier is Petillius Cerialis, Commander of the Ninth Legion."

Andreas could see that an arrow had pierced the Commander's breastplate, and was stuck in position and buried in the right side of his chest. He was obviously in pain, and the soldiers were gathered around him but appeared to be undecided about what to do.

Andreas approached the soldiers carefully and caught the attention of the centurion, who was clearly discomfited at the condition of his commander. "Sir, I have had experience with arrow wounds before I was conscripted, and I think I can help this man. I watched my father treat this type of injury." That was as much information as Andreas wanted to give the centurion, who appeared to show relief at this chance encounter, then suddenly realized that he'd better check out this confident Auxiliary before giving him access to his commander.

"Where were you based?" he asked Andreas.

"I was part of a group that was sent to Rome from Caesarea, and then on to the fort in Chichester for assignment to the Ninth Legion," he replied.

"Who was the Commander in charge of the fort?" The centurion had served there, briefly on his arrival in Britannia.

"I am afraid I do not remember his name. We only saw him once when we were on parade before we began our march toward Longthorpe, but I do remember how he looked. He had a severe squint in his eye, which was the subject of ridicule among the men." Andreas reported this confidently to the centurion, who nodded his head, apparently satisfied. The fort commander at Chichester was indeed squint eyed, and the cause of many a jest among the men under his command.

The centurion waved his soldiers back so that Andreas could look at the wound. The arrow had penetrated the breastplate and then become stuck in position in the upper chest. As Andreas carefully moved the surrounding clothing and armaments to see the exact position of the arrow, he saw that it had become stuck at the point where it pierced the breastplate, and could not move any further through the body. The only way to help the victim was to push the arrow through the back muscles and out of the body, but that was not possible as long as the arrow was held firm by the breastplate.

Andreas quickly assumed control of the situation. He knew that wounds like this were easy to recover from as long as no vital organs were pierced, and the arrow could exit the wound. As a boy he had watched his father treat all sorts of injuries. Sometimes even Andreas did not know whether his father's skills were in doctoring or in ministering, but either way he had a reputation all over the Peloponnese for his treatment of the sick and the wounded. Andreas remembered a farmer from the mountains to the south of Patras who had been shot by an arrow fired by his brother in a hunting party. His father had dealt with the wound on the scene, and timely enough for the farmer to survive and recover.

"I need to separate the breastplate from the arrow, so have the commander lie still while I use my knife. This will hurt, so have him drink as much wine as he can stomach, and then have him take a rope between his teeth, as he will need to contain his pain as much as possible to avoid shock." The centurion motioned to his men, and in a few moments, he was able to put a flagon of wine at the mouth of his Commander, who drank down as much as he could before regurgitating some of the liquid in a painful eruption.

As this was happening, Andreas shouted over to a soldier who was standing close to a group of villagers watching the evolving scene. "Bring a jar of honey from one of the homes, and also some clean cloth so that I can dress the wound. Be quick." The soldier hurried to the task, and led three of the women away toward the houses.

Andreas pushed his left arm down and across the inside of the breastplate to locate the arrow, and then prized the breastplate back from the chest enough for his right hand to insert his knife in the space. Once he felt he had the knife in position, he nodded to the centurion, who positioned a few of his men around the body ready to hold the commander steady.

Andreas gripped with his left hand around the arrow shaft at the point where it had penetrated the chest wall then pressed the sharp knife-blade down and across the arrow, and it separated in two behind the breastplate. While the commander roared out in agony, Andreas kept hold of the arrow in the chest and carefully began to push it forward till it hit a bone of the rib cage, then gently moved it to the side before pushing again till it punctured the muscles of the back, and then pierced the skin to exit in a shower of blood.

Andreas examined the arrow and was relieved to see that it appeared to be smooth and undamaged other than the clean break from his knife. Any splinter left in the wound could cause infection. He used his knife to cut away the vest so that he could have clear access to the wounds. Andreas then compressed the open wounds on the chest and back while motioning for the soldiers to bring the honey, which he used to spread liberally around the bloodied skin. He then asked two of the soldiers to hold two of the cloths against the entry and exit wounds, while he looked through the rest of the material and found a length of white cloth that he cut into a long bandage.

He applied the bandage tightly around the chest weaving it above and below the shoulders to provide a firm compression, and tied it off under an arm pit as tightly as he could.

Andreas rose from his crouched position over the Commander, and deferred to the centurion, who quickly motioned for some of his men to carry the wounded General to a stretcher that his men had assembled, while waiting for Andreas to finish. "We have several wounded soldiers who need attention. Can you help?"

"I will do what I can," replied Andreas, and soon he and Bergamus were among the group of wounded to apply whatever care they could, with Andreas taking the role of doctor, and Bergamus acting as a liaison with the villagers, to assemble whatever medicines or healing herbs they might have available.

As the day passed Andreas was able to pick up the story of what had happened to the Ninth Legion. On learning of the revolt just a few days ago, General Petillius Cerialis had led his Legion toward Colchester, expecting to bring order back to the town before heading on toward London in pursuit of Boudicca and her tribal forces.

However, Boudicca had advanced toward Longthorpe knowing that she would have the advantage of surprise over whatever forces the Legion sent. Choosing the location carefully, her thousands of warriors lay in wait for the advancing army. They picked a part of the countryside that provided woods and hills around the valley below, through which the road led between the two towns, and they lay in wait for the signal to attack. Eventually an arrow was shot skyward trailing a bright red cloth that was easily seen, and the signal for blood to be shed.

The army was led by the Auxiliaries, followed by the Roman soldiers, and finally the cavalry group of about two hundred mounts, and they were taken completely by surprise when the tribesmen converged on the valley from all sides. There was no time to form a defensive position and the officers were at the rear of the legion instead of at the van, and in no position to prevent the outcome—a comprehensive defeat of the legion whose men were chopped down by the heavily armed tribesmen, led in battle by their charismatic leader, Queen Boudicca.

Two days later Isaac and the rest of the men finally made it to the fort, after being sidetracked around the river in flood. Bergamus made a fuss in telling Isaac the story of their escape from the mud, and their assistance to the wounded General, and as usual Andreas downplayed the events as nothing special.

Life at the vexillatio fort of Longthorpe then began to take on an element of regularity and predictability for the three soldiers, who now shared their billet as friends. The entire focus was on improving the defensive qualities of the fort, and at the same time guarding against another attack from the rebels. The situation also provided opportunities for them to pick up aspects of the local language, while referring to Bergamus for tutelage in pronunciation and meaning. It was one other way that they could pass the time.

Meanwhile Governor Paulinus had rushed his forces from the western campaign to London, and had arrived there ahead of Boudicca. However, it was clear that the defenses of the town were insufficient to withstand any type of sustained attack, so Paullinus withdrew his forces and headed north to the Midlands. He had a number of forts and vexillatios there to choose from, where he could gather his legionary forces from throughout Britannia, and organize war plans with his commanders.

Boudicca and her forces reached London just a few days later, with a force estimated to be in the tens of thousands, and whose numbers had increased with every mile they traveled through the countryside. The town was comprehensively sacked and put to the torch, marking another victory for the rebels.

By now Boudicca was riding a seemingly unstoppable wave of vengeance and destruction, and had captured the imagination of the tribes by refusing to let her own torture and the rape of her daughters stop her resistance to Rome. In the tribal society of ancient Britannia, there was no known precedent for a Queen to lead her people in battle, and not only did she lead, but she appeared to revel in her new found fame.

"I may be Queen because of my noble ancestry, but that is not why I fight. I raise a sword against the Romans as one who has lost freedom along with my people, who has been scourged by the Roman whip, and for the lost chastity of my daughters and the hundreds of others like them who suffered from the lust of our enemy. In this battle, we must conquer, or die."

With the smoke of a burning London behind them, Boudicca led her warriors toward the inevitable confrontation with the Roman Governor, and his professional armies. On their way north lay another concentration of Roman power in the town of St. Albans, and finding it similarly devoid of military defenses, the native host laid waste to the town.

Just as the lay of the land had opened up a way to victory for Boudicca against the Ninth Legion, so to would it proffer a means for the Roman armies to finally confront Boudicca and her rebels and comprehensively defeat them. The wily General Paullinus had studied the maps carefully and chosen a site to wage battle that would give his men the benefit of the high ground, the advantage of surprise, and the advantage of weaponry, particularly the long spears which they could discharge with accuracy and power. The Auxiliaries proved to be an effective fighting resource, coming off a campaign in the west that had honed their skills, and the lances of the cavalry merely added an exclamation point to the death warrant of the enemy.

Before the day was over, more than eighty thousand Britons were dead, including men, women and children who followed the army. Roman losses were negligible. As for Boudicca, she did not survive the day, and her body was found on the battlefield, facing the enemy. There were no marks of weaponry on her body, and she likely took poison rather than succumb to Roman steel. Boudicca's name, which means 'victory' would henceforth tell the lie.

Chapter Twelve
Journey

The Boudicca rebellion had come and gone, as Andreas and his fellow Auxiliaries remained on the base at Longthorpe, assigned to daily work parties charged with completing the defensive walls and related structures that were needed to serve as the regional headquarters of the Ninth Legion.

Andreas worked the broken-down rocks and stones into the limestone grindings and water, to create another layer of mortar to the walls of the various buildings inside the already constructed fortified wall of the vexillatio. It was monotonous work but there was a certain pleasure in creating something even so mundane as a wall, and Andreas applied himself steadily to the task, occasionally interacting with his fellow soldiers as they busied around the work site.

Hearing his name called from a distance, he looked up to see Isaac waving him over to the camp offices, and he set down his tools, washed his hands in a water bucket, and walked briskly over toward his friend.

"Andreas, we have been summoned to meet with General Petillius Cerialis. I have no idea why, but we have to report to his chambers at noon, and it is almost time."

Just at that, a centurion exited from the principia and walked over to the two men, who promptly stood to attention. "Follow me, soldiers."

It was the same centurion who had attended to the General when he had been wounded, and Isaac knew him to be Centurion Marcellus. They dutifully followed him into the barracks proper, and to the complex of offices and ante rooms that served as the administrative centers of the Legion. Waiting for them was their fellow Auxiliary, Bergamus, who shrugged his shoulders discreetly at them as he too wondered about the reason for this meeting.

They entered a room behind the centurion, and he gestured them over to a large desk in the corner, behind which sat the Commander of the Ninth Legion, General Petillius Cerialis, framed by the banners and gilded signs of the Legion. He looked to have made a good recovery from the arrow wound, and his dark eyes sparkled as he shuffled some papers around his desk, finally locating the one he was looking for. "At ease, men. I would like to talk to you about your next assignment."

He turned to a map behind him on the wall, and motioned the three men to come forward. "This big island that is roughly triangular in shape is Britannia, and this smaller island to the west is Hibernia. At the present time the Roman occupation has a rough border more or less two thirds of the way to the north of the big island. At the moment we have no immediate plans to occupy the small island." He stopped talking for a moment, while he peered closely at the map as if looking for a particular place, then he stepped away and returned to face the men.

"You will see on this map that there are noted the names of the tribes that inhabit each region. I see from your military records brought from Rome that all three of you can read and write, and my centurion tells me that you have already picked up some of the local language in your short time here. That is helpful, because it shows me that you are resourceful, and that is quality you will need for what I have in mind."

The friends glanced at each other as if to signal the same thought. "What exactly are we here for?"

The General continued as if he was teaching a class at school, rather than three experienced soldiers, but that was merely his way. "Now, you can see that the Brigantes tribe occupies the land just to the north of our current zone of occupation in the south, east and west. To their north lies the land we Romans call Caledonia. The Brigantes tribal region is not yet under Roman proxy, merely subject to a treaty. It is just a matter of time before they are brought to heel."

General Cerialis moved his chair slightly so that he could be seated again, and a grimace of pain was evident in his expression. He looked over at Andreas as he spoke. "I have you to thank for this pain, soldier, and also for my life. I know you were only doing your duty, but I appreciate it nevertheless."

Andreas didn't know if he was supposed to speak or stay silent, but it seemed like the right thing to do was to nod his head in a gesture of acknowledgement.

"Anyway soldiers, listen up. I did not bring you here just for a geography lesson."

All three men automatically stiffened their stance as an almost automatic response to a command from a senior officer, and paid close attention to the words of their Commander.

"From time to time the Roman army will call upon qualified members of their Auxiliary forces to serve as a special force, in military interventions where conventional force is not viable, for whatever reason. Rome has always preferred the use of Auxiliary in such situations in view of the higher chance of death or injury. This is a pragmatic course of action so as not to put fully trained and valuable legion soldiers at risk in dangerous operations. It is, shall we say, an occupational risk of the Auxiliary, but entirely justified by our military conventions."

"You three men have an assignment that will occupy your time for the next year. You will be on location in Caledonia, far from the legion, but you will still be accredited Auxiliaries of the Roman army. Bergamus, your end of service will be brought forward to the ending date of your mission, which will be Midsummer's Day next year. Isaac, you will be credited with three years of service for the one that you will spend in Caledonia. Andreas, you will also receive a credit for three years of service, so that when you complete this mission your total service time will be adjusted accordingly. These changes will be reflected in your military pensions."

The General paused briefly to make sure that the three men were following his words, and then continued. "In a few weeks, you will march across Iceni territory to the coastal village of Brancaster, where you will board one of our ships that will take you to Caledonia. You can see from the map that the country narrows in the middle, and on either side a major river allows penetration to the interior of the country. As you travel up the eastern coastline to Caledonia, the coast will eventually turn inland, and you will pass a distinctive uninhabited volcanic rock that juts up out of the sea less than a mile from shore. I am told it is easily seen in the light of day and is inhabited only by sea birds. That will also be your rendezvous point in one year from now, on Midsummer's Day next year. On that day you will make sure that you are on the rock, and you will be picked up by one of our ships. However, your destination is further upriver, at a point where a tributary of a smaller river joins with the main body of water, and it is there that you will take a small boat from the ship that will permit navigation in the shallow drafted waterway."

General Cerialis paused to pour water from a pitcher into a glass, then drank purposefully until it was drained. He was still weak from the trauma of his wounds, and decided to curtail this meeting and leave it to his centurion to brief the men thoroughly on their mission. "You may leave me now with Centurion Marcellus, and he will tell you what is expected of you. Good luck, and may the gods look out for you."

The General was content in the knowledge that the first part of his plan was underway. He knew that his transfer to Gaul was temporary in nature, and that he had already been commissioned to return to Britannia after this temporary posting. Then he would have the opportunity to regain the favor of his superior, Governor Seutonius Paullinus. He would present the Governor with an iron clad plan for a major Roman strategic move to invade the last remaining outpost of Britannia, and bring it into the Roman fold. His star would be on the rise, and the ignominy of his defeat by Boudicca would fade into obscurity. He might even succeed the Governor as the head of the Roman occupation force in Britannia.

"OK men," said the centurion, as he led them out into the compound. "Let's sit down round the table in my office and I will take you through the requirements of your assignment."

The table had numerous plates and dishes of fruits and vegetables that were more appealing than the version they were used to in their own mess. "There's no need to stand on ceremony, so eat and drink as you may."

Centurion Marcellus, whom everyone knew was but an acolyte of the Governor, already had an enviable reputation around the barracks as a man who liked his wine, but this was the first time that Andreas had interacted with him in any meaningful way, since the incident with the General.

Marcellus laid the main map out on the table so that they could refer to it when needed, and then began to speak. "General Petillius Cerialis will soon be moving to Gaul to lead some of our other Legions against the barbarians who still challenge our authority. Eventually he will return to the theater of operations here in Britannia. This assignment is merely part of his forward planning, should there be a time in the future, which is probably unlikely, when we would have to march our Legions north, and bring the entire island under Roman occupation and administration. So, listen up, we have a lot to cover."

Centurion Marcellus had prepared thoroughly for his instructions to the three soldiers. It was vital that they believed the mission to be non-threatening to the local tribes with whom they would interact. Only then would they be convincing when they dealt with the tribes, particularly the chiefs, who would surely be interested in the presence of Roman soldiers in their midst. The three soldiers took the imparted information at face value, and nodded in agreement. Encouraged by Centurion Marcellus, they began to partake of food and drink as they settled in for what was clearly going to be an intense discussion of their mission to Caledonia. Their host made it almost uncomfortable not to accept his copious offers of wine or ale, and he led by example, as he proffered a brief toast to the success of their mission, then breathed in the scent of the wine before swallowing it in one full gulp.

The men mumbled their thanks, probably because of the unlikely situation in which they found themselves, and sat down, eager to find out the details of their mission. Isaac was thrilled at the prospect of a year freed of the daily grind of soldiering, and just assumed that whatever they were required to do had to be an improvement on life as a second-rate soldier of Rome. Andreas too, was excited at this unexpected change in the direction of his life.

Bergamus, as someone who was quite at home with the tribal system of his adopted country, had no reservations about life at the edges of civilization. Especially as it lessened the need to bow and bend to the Romans on a daily basis. It would be nice to be free of command and control.

Marcellus brought their attention back to his briefing. "Listen up, while I take you through the objectives of the mission, and then we can talk about the logistics of the journey, both there and back. Here, fill your tankards with the richest ale in this wine-less landscape. And listen up, while I give you your orders." Isaac wondered if he repeated himself as a function of habit, or a function of wine. Perhaps it was both.

"The first thing you need to remember, is that the land to the north of the Brigantes is sometimes called Alba by the people who live there. However, we Romans know it as Caledonia, named after the main tribe that inhabits the north-west of the country, the Caledonii. I want you men to get in the habit of calling it Caledonia, so that we are all on the same page."

"The best way to think about what we need to know is to put yourself in the position of the Roman army on the march, with the objective of bringing the native population under our control, as we have done so many times and in so many places. What is the weather at different times of the year? Where are the populated areas in the form of towns and villages? How is the food supply provided? What do they farm, and what animals do they breed? How do they make war, and how do they make peace? Is there a noble class, and how does that relate to leadership of the tribes? Do they have navies, or any form of reliance on shipping? Who do they trade with? The questions just go on and on. And especially, Bergamus, we will need maps that include important details of local terrain, and how that might impact our military strategy."

Isaac was beginning to be impressed by the centurion's ability to cope with a clearly strong appetite for imported wine and local ale, and at the same time deliver a clear and concise message to his subordinates.

"We will have more time to get into the details in the weeks ahead, but here are the strategic aspects of this mission. We already have a peace treaty with the Brigantes tribe, who occupy large territories between here and Caledonia, and under the terms of that treaty we are obliged to help them if they are attacked by the Caledonii, the tribe that lives in the northern and western mountains. There is a history of military actions between these two tribal groups, and our support of the Brigantes is greatly valued by the tribe."

Marcellus stopped talking for a moment, to let his words sink in, and then spread his hands as if to calm his men, who were beginning to realize that this was no simple military exercise with a mission that could be accomplished in military style. This was a wholly different situation, and portended a mission unlike any other they had undertaken before. A sense of excitement was beginning to show in the three men, and this was just what Marcellus was hoping for. He had chosen his men carefully.

He raised his hands slightly to provide emphasis as he continued his talk. "The only warlike tribe in Caledonia are the Caledonii, and they are feared even by the other tribes that live in the central parts of the country. The other tribes are in effect a buffer state between the Caledonii and the Brigantes. It is in our interests to keep them thinking that way, so that we have flexibility should Rome at some point in time have to act on our treaty with the Brigantes. For that reason, when you present yourselves to the tribal authorities, it will be from a position of trust. Our interests are the same as theirs, which is to be ready if the Caledonii attack to the south, as their tribal lands and people would be the first obstacle to the Caledonii war effort."

The centurion realized that perhaps he was digging too deep into the politics of the matter. These were men not ordinarily accustomed to thinking in larger terms. "We will have time over the next few weeks to cover everything fully, so I will not burden you overmuch today, but I did want you to have a sense of what this is all about. Beginning tomorrow, this room will be yours to use as you prepare for the mission. I will spend some time with you each day, but you need to work as a team, because that is exactly what you will be once on the ground in Caledonia. I want all of your ideas for the proper scope of the mission."

Centurion Marcellus was pleased with the performance of the three men, who had woken up this morning completely unaware of the change that they were about to experience. He had watched them over the past few weeks, since first meeting Andreas and Bergamus, and had noted their friendship with the conturbernium leader, Isaac. He liked the cut of Isaac. He was a professional soldier and was already respected throughout the camp. Andreas was a gentle giant, there was no doubt. He was physically imposing, but it was his will that was overpowering, transmitting a sense of purpose and calm in every situation. The older man, Bergamus was a perfect foil to the two younger men. He was a font of information about all aspects of the tribes, and still had the hardiness of a regular soldier. Plus, he was a skilled map-maker, which would be a critical requirement of the assignment. Twenty-two-year veterans rarely made mistakes, being so close to the benefits of retirement and pension.

Then again, it was a pity that he had to mislead them as to the real objectives of their mission, but the stakes were too high to risk their complicity. They would take on the assignment unaware of the timetable for the invasion, believing it to be a preliminary assessment of the country many years ahead of a possible invasion. The information in the form of map-works and drawings and notations that they would collect would be invaluable to the Roman invasion force when it reached Caledonia, after the formal submission of the Brigantes on their way north. Only two men were aware of this; General Petillius Cerialis, and himself. The Governor had been quite specific. "When the mission ends on Midsummer's Day next year, the invasion planning begins." There was no need for Governor Seutonius Paullinus to be involved at this point. There would be time to manage that part of the plan.

After the surprise meeting, Isaac, Bergamus, and Andreas headed back to their barracks to put in a final shift on the construction detail. They would continue to bunk as normal, but now their daily work would take place in the shelter of the principia, and planning would replace plastering as their primary occupation.

That evening, Andreas lay on his bedding as soon as the evening meal was over. He felt the need to think for a while and not be interrupted by the normal chatter of his fellow soldiers. His mind was going in a dozen directions, and he soon reverted to a practice that he had developed while on active service in Armenia. He began to breathe slowly and deeply with his eyes closed, and once he could hear the steady beat of his heart, he was then able to channel his thoughts in an orderly way. It was the way his father had taught him how to pray. He could not help but think what his father and mother would make of the twists and turns in his life in the years since he had left the Peloponnese. He soon slipped into several minutes of prayer and contemplation until he was ready to give his attention to the mission, and what would be involved in the coming weeks and months.

Across the bunkhouse, Isaac lay contented with the knowledge that he would soon be free of the daily imposition of Roman orders, and in a place where he could live the life of a civilian again, even if the over-riding purpose was of a military nature. He could live a double life if that was what was required.

Bergamus lay in his bunk and ignored the cacophony of chatter and horseplay going on among the men around him. Once the mission was over, he would be able to return to his beloved Gaul. Only this time with the advantage of Roman citizenship, and income to keep him secure for the rest of his life. This new venture would bring him closer to the end game, and would give him a taste of freedom that would give his dreams potency, and substance to his aspirations.

The next several weeks flew by as the three men prepared for their mission in the north. There was a renewed emphasis on physical training, so that they would leave in prime shape for whatever they might have to deal with once they were in Caledonia. They spent time on learning the main language of the island of Britannia, which thankfully was understood by most of the tribes, even though they might have their own local dialects and variations. They had to replace their weapons, and become familiar with their use. There was also a need for new clothing, so that their clothes did not appear to be overtly different from most men in the north. It would not do to look like a Roman soldier.

The coastal town of Brancaster was strategic enough for the Roman invaders to covet its meandering access to the Iceni stronghold of eastern Britannia, and from her ancient harbor it was a straight sail to the south for the Roman province of Gallia Belgica.

On a warm summer's day in the time that would be known as the Uprising, a substantial procession of Roman troops approached the town from the east, toward the ships that lay in wait for them in the harbor. General Cerialis waved the annoying flies away from his face as he focused on the large Roman vessel that lay at anchor on a calm sea, whose customary waves were made impotent by the winding banks of the estuary. He knew that one day he would return to these isles, and set in motion his plan for a successful campaign against the Caledonii that would bring the rest of the island of Britannia under control, hopefully his control.

The defeat at the hands of Boudicca's rebels was unfortunate, but hardly enough to derail his carefully charted path to leadership in the Roman army. To be successful as a Roman often required a bloodline that was compatible with the interests of the time, and his uncle Vespasian in Rome gave him his pedigree. He was a bold soldier, and had no doubt that his strategies in the execution of war would ultimately be recognized and rewarded.

Anchored close to the mother ship was a smaller craft, readying for a mission that was but another step in his plans for the future. He had received favorable reports from Centurion Marcellus on the progress of the three men chosen to relocate in Caledonia, and gather much needed intelligence that would be critical to the pending assimilation of northern Britannia into the fold.

The large party of soldiers arrived at the harbor, and stood at ease, while the General dismounted and readied himself to board. He had one Aide-de-Camp who would travel with him to his next assignment on the eastern front. The rest of the cohort would travel back to Longthorpe, pending the appointment of a new commanding officer.

While the departure of the General entailed a few rituals and ceremonial proceedings at the harbor side, the three soldiers quietly made their way over to the small vessel that would carry them to Caledonia. Isaac, as the senior of the three men, spoke out in greeting to the sailor guarding the boarding ramp, and they were welcomed aboard.

Andreas looked over at Bergamus with a wry smile, as they surveyed the boat that would be their home for the next several days. It was hardly fitting to be described as part of a navy, as it more closely resembled a fishing vessel, but Andreas was always comfortable on the water, and looked forward to the sail north to Caledonia. They were shown the section of the hull that had been set aside for them, and the elderly and weathered captain eyed them cautiously as he waited for their attention.

"I am Captain Tiberius. We set sail before the sun goes down, so that we will be far from any rocks that might cause a problem. Once out in the stream, we will take our bearings from the Pole Star and follow her to the north. During the day we will sail closer to the shore, but not close enough to attract any attention. When we reach the great river that leads into Caledonia, we will need to be careful. I have sailed those waters before, and should be able to get you close to the mouth of the tributary that marks your drop off point."

It was quite clear from his expressions and the tenor of his voice that the Captain did not think much of his assignment, and even less of the men who were now in his charge.

"You seem to have more baggage than I was led to believe. My men are busy preparing for departure so you had better bring it on board yourselves, and see if you can find a space for it below deck. I don't want my sailors falling over it on the voyage north."

Isaac turned to his fellow soldiers and gave them some encouragement with a knowing smile, then spoke softly to them. "OK lads, let's bring on our gear and get settled in. We may as well get some rest tonight as there is no telling what we might face on the way north. He might have us scrubbing decks!"

There was a crew of six men on the ship, which looked like a small commercial carrier rather than any kind of military vessel. Andreas looked it over pretty carefully, and was satisfied that it was in decent shape for their journey. There was a small row boat with oars strapped to the rails, and he assumed that this would be their means of transport once they reached their destination.

Andreas figured that with a dominant wind from the north requiring them to tack, it would take them three weeks of sailing to get anywhere close to their target. Once again, he faced a long and tedious journey trapped in a boat. Fishing on the way would relieve some of the boredom, but that was about it.

He was thankful for the camaraderie of his companions, and he could always spend some extra time in prayer and contemplation.

Chapter Thirteen
Camelon

The days turned to weeks, and the weeks became days again, and soon the ship, with its distinctive yellow sails, made a definite turn to the west as it followed the shoreline around the coast. And there, dead ahead, was the huge volcanic rock that guarded the sharp turn to the river beyond. The river known by the local Votadini tribe as the Bodotria. The day was sunny and breezy and quite pleasant after the several days of storms, winds, and rain that was the norm for this part of the world, even in the summer months.

The rock was an impressive sight. It sparkled in white as if it was covered in snow. The captain was quick to point out that it was merely the accumulation of bird shit, in one of the few times he spoke of the mundane during the entire voyage. Still, his men had been pleasant to be around, and the food had been plentiful, if fairly limited in choice.

Isaac asked the captain to sail as close as he could, so that they could see the lay of the land, and how it might be approached, when it was time to rendezvous one year from now. "See, Andreas, there is a small beach of sorts on the eastern side, and it looks as if it slopes steeply down to the west from those cliffs."

Now they could see what the Captain was talking about. There were thousands and thousands of white sea birds, gannets most likely, resting on almost every piece of available rock, or careening around the sea waves, plummeting down to attack the shoals of fish that coveted the estuary waters.

"Well," said Bergamus, "At least it is easy enough to spot, and no more than a mile or so from the shore. As they made one final tack to pass the rock, they could see a huge opening that looked like a vast cave that might connect the east and west sides. Soon they passed the rock, and saw how the river began to narrow as they followed it to the west. There were signs of habitation on both shores, and small fishing boats dotted around the entire seascape, but no sign that their presence in the midst of the sea lane was of concern."

"Well, Bergamus," said Isaac, "This is when the work begins. You may as well try and sketch out the contours of the land as we head upriver. The only way you'll get that pension is if you bring the General his beloved maps!"

Bergamus laughed as he searched among his possessions for the writing materials that he had brought with him for this very purpose. He had a satchel full of sheets of papyrus, his precious bronze pen, and several inkpots made of clay. Enough, he hoped, to last out the year.

Andreas found a seated position at the point of the hull, and gazed out at the land of Caledonia on either side of their westerly heading, as he took his bearings. He could see low ranges of hills in the distance on either side, and then off to the south was a massive outcropping that sloped up toward a conical hill at its end. He automatically thought like a soldier, and immediately saw it as a key strategic location in that part of the country.

It was the month of June, and this far north in the late evening the sun was still vibrant in the sky. Andreas had been told of lands even farther north where the sun still shone at midnight, and then rose again within a few hours. On the north side of the river there were occasional signs of communal habitation, whether large villages or small towns he could not tell. The southern coastline seemed to be the more densely populated, with distinct roads linking places or communities.

In the distance they could see the land narrowing on either side, and they heard the Captain tell his men to prepare to hove to in the shelter of one of the few islands in the river around them. The captain addressed Isaac as they approached the narrow stony beach. "You and your men have your weapons, so you should land first, and make sure we have the place to ourselves for the night."

Isaac nodded in assent, and motioned for his two friends to arm up for the landing. Soon Andreas and Bergamus leaped into the shallow surf from the bow of the ship, and moved up the narrow beach. Within a few minutes they returned to report that the island was uninhabited, and would provide a safe haven.

Having arrived on a warm and sunny summer evening, they awoke next morning to a thick fog that brought visibility to just a few feet, and after stretching the breakfast time to about an hour there was finally a break in the weather. The fog began to roll back into itself, and finally revealed another sunny day, but cooler, with lots of clouds on the distant hills.

Once they had put out from the beach, the captain motioned for the three men to join him, and gave the tiller over to one of his men. "This is our last day in this God-forsaken country, and you won't see me or my ship again for another year." There was some comfort in the knowledge that their scheduled pick up would be by someone who knew the seas and the terrain, and regardless of his ill will and short temper, there was no doubt that he was a skilled mariner.

Captain Tiberius raised his voice a little so that his passengers and crew could all hear him. "Now that the river has narrowed, in a few hours we should reach the point where the small interior river joins the Bodotria. We will be more vulnerable to attack now that we are in shallower water so we need to be watchful."

"Captain Tiberius, I have a suggestion," said Isaac.

The captain looked over at him as if daring him to continue, but Isaac was up to the challenge. "Once we get close enough to the inlet, let's spend the rest of the day fishing up and down the main river, until it is dark. We can always use some extra provisions. Then, once the light has gone, we can drop our boat, load it with our gear, and row over to a landing spot while you spend the night in midstream, and head back the way you came in morning."

The captain came as close as he could to acknowledging this as a good idea, with a nod of his head and a grunt as he turned away. Soon they had set a few lines and began trawling up and down, prompted by Andreas, who was enjoying the task at hand. As they landed some plump, silver backed fish, the mood on the ship lightened, and even the captain seemed to relax, now that his mission was almost over.

Later that evening, the three men lowered their dinghy into the river, having already stowed their gear on board. There was a cleverly fabricated collapsible mast that enabled the use of a triangle of sail, as well as two sets of oars, and it was shallow drafted enough for exploring the smaller tributaries of the Bodotria. It would do for their purposes.

Andreas took the oars, and skulled them over to the center of the stream marking the entrance to the smaller river. On both sides of the confluence with the Bodotria there were mud banks that indicated the effects of regular tidal motion, easily seen by the light of a pale moon. Andreas pushed and pulled the oars enough to move them along the river with caution, in case they ran into any signs of habitation, or humans.

There was plenty of depth to carry the vessel upstream, and the river seemed to loop around in a generally westward direction. After a cautious journey of about an hour they reached a spot that had a small beach, more mud than sand, just after another looping stretch of water. Andreas guided the small boat over to the rocky shore and the three men set foot for the first time on the mainland of Caledonia.

Isaac helped unload their gear and made sure that their weaponry was easily available. There did not appear to be any sign of people in the immediate area, but a river tributary was a source of fresh water as well as fish, and a means of accessing the main river. He had no doubts that they would encounter some of the inhabitants once the sun was up, so he told his two men to get some sleep while he took the first watch.

Bergamus was on watch by the time that the dawn broke, and the men stretched themselves and looked around at their environment. A path led away from the beach through fields on either side covered in wheat stalks that still had a few weeks of summer to ripen before they were ready for reaping. The pathway led to higher ground, populated by a large number of small houses and buildings dispersed around the hillside, which appeared to level out in all directions at its modest summit.

As they stood together and looked over the landscape, they could see a group of men assemble in the distance, while one of them pointed their way. Soon the local men set off toward them, carrying their tools as weapons, clearly intent on defending themselves, if necessary, from the strangers on their river. Isaac prompted Andreas and Bergamus to drop the weapons that they had reached for automatically, and motioned for them to raise their hands as the men approached, and came to a halt a few feet away.

Bergamus spoke up in the Britonnic language that was the foundation of the languages spoken throughout the tribal system in Roman Britannia. "Good day, men, we have no bad intentions, and would like to speak with you and exchange information."

It was apparent that they understood him perfectly, and their leader seemed to relax a bit as he nodded to his men as if to express his approval. He was modest in stature, and dressed no differently than his companions, though he clearly exhibited an air of confidence as he responded to Bergamus.

"Good day to you. Did you come upstream or downstream of the Bodotria?"

Bergamus quickly surmised that the question was more about their background and allegiances than a mere exchange of pleasantries. The Votadini controlled the east, the Damnonii the west, the Selgovae the southern center, and the Veniconii the arc of land and hills to the north-east that was the frontier beyond which the mountains contained the warlike Caledonii.

"We came from the Bodotria after sailing up the Northern Ocean from the lands of the Iceni far to the south. We are on a peaceful mission for the Roman army. Not as soldiers, but as emissaries, to gather information that will be helpful in establishing trade routes and lines of communication. You will see that we have weapons, purely for defensive purposes, and will gladly surrender them to you until you are satisfied that we mean no harm."

The leader turned to his men and engaged them in low conversation, until he turned back to Bergamus.

"That won't be necessary. We have work to do in the fields around here this morning, but will gladly meet with you at noon at our village. We'll share our food with you, and talk."

By now the men had gathered that Isaac was the leader of the three strangers, from the way that Bergamus always looked to him when he responded to the questions.

Isaac saw this, and then spoke up in simple words of their native language that they were able to understand.

"I am Isaac, this is my fellow soldier Andreas, and our colleague Bergamus. We will gladly share food with you after the morning's work, and we'll fish the river this morning and bring whatever we catch with us."

This was deemed to be an acceptable truce, by the way in which the leader smiled as he nodded his head and said, "That is fine. I am Talorg, the leader of our community, and these are my friends, Nectan, Galan, Brude, Gartnaidh, and Drust. Just follow the path to our village, and we'll meet there."

The group of men turned away, each man raising his hand in an informal gesture that suggested friendship rather than enmity. Isaac replied in kind, and watched the men as they walked back toward the village, already thinking of what to say and what to do at the meeting.

Andreas was aware of an inner sense of excitement. In some respects, he had reached the end of his journey that began with his escape from Patras. He had literally reached the ends of the earth in Roman terms, and yet as he looked around him, he saw many of the familiar sights and sounds that he grew up with in the Peloponnese. There were fields and farms, villages and roads, orchards and vegetable gardens, all visible to the naked eye. For sure, the people looked different, with a preponderance of reddish hair and a fair complexion among them, but still, now and then, someone who had his own black hair and blue eyes.

He pledged to himself to try and keep the faith that had been instilled in him by his father, and to contain his desire to evangelize until he better understood the land and peoples of Caledonia. He knew from the preaching of his father that God was patient, and that the destination of belief often required a long journey in time.

As Andreas looked over at Bergamus preparing the line, nets, and bait for the fishing, he saw a man happy to live for the present, because he knew his future was not that far away. With another year of service, he would be discharged with a lifetime worth of wages, and allowed to return to his home in Gaul. Bergamus whistled cheerfully as he worked, and his optimism was infectious. Soon Isaac too, was caught up in the casual verbal sparring that denotes a conversation among friends, where trust in each other is implicit.

When the boat was ready to launch, Isaac suggested that they stay fairly close to their beach, so as not to stumble upon other inhabitants who might be less friendly. Andrea took the oars and coached his friends in the art of river fishing, and how best to catch some of the brown trout that were readily visible in the stream, all heading upriver to spawn and begin the cycle over again. After two hours or so they had filled a basket, and they landed on their beach in time to gut and scale the fish that they would contribute to the mid-day meal.

As they began the short journey of about half a mile to the village, they looked about to see the lay of the land. Immediately ahead was the village, around the side of a modest hill that leveled at an elevation perhaps one hundred feet or so above the coastal plan. The direction was to the south, and as far as they could see to the east and to the west the coastal plain was wider in parts than others, but eventually made way to the rising land to the south.

Behind them, across the Bodotria in the distance, there was a range of high hills that ran almost parallel to the river, guarded by a line of white fluffy clouds that softened the dark, grim, features of the hills at rest on the far horizon. It was mid-summer, and the fields of wheat and barley that would normally be ripening on the Peloponnese were several weeks away from maturity in the much cooler climate in these northern lands. Andreas was still caught up in the moment of his reflections, and felt an attachment already, as if the land had been waiting for him.

When they reached the settlement, there was a ceremony of sorts, at which Talorg introduced once more the five men from the morning, plus several men who had been working in a nearby field. There were men, women, and children scattered around the dwelling houses, and they all seemed cheerfully disposed to the strangers, and not in the least afraid.

Andreas was curious about the way the houses were built. They seemed to be made of turf sods laid on top of each other to form walls, and reinforced by rocks and stones that filled the cracks and any uneven aspects of the walls. There were planks of wood used to form an inside wall and to support a thatched roof structure, leaving an opening for smoke that was protected on the inside from rainwater penetration. He automatically compared them to the homes back in Patras, but if the healthy look and cheerful disposition of the natives were any indication, they seemed quite content in their domestic environment.

Once the fish had been given over to the women to prepare, the men sat around to talk. Talorg was full of questions about the newcomers, and Bergamus was an effective interpreter, introducing light heartedness wherever possible, to help assuage the men of their intuitive sense of caution. This continued over the meal, which was served with familiar vegetables, and a smattering of fruits such as apples, gooseberries, and raspberries. There was also a rough ale that had some taste of apple, and was pleasant enough to drink.

After a while Isaac addressed himself to Talorg, and in simplified language he asked him if he could address all of the men, through Bergamus.

"Talorg, we come to your land on a mission from the Romans who live far to the south, and who maintain peaceful relations with most of the tribes in that southern land, which they call Britannia. Rome is a city/state that is so far away that it would take about four months of traveling by ship to get there from here, and they are the wealthiest and most powerful state in the known world. We three men are from different parts of the world, all of which are controlled by the Romans.

"They know much about your land from previous expeditions, and occasional trading, and are aware that the large tribe in the mountains to the far north is aggressive, and might one day seek to attack the lands of the Brigantes far to the south of here, with whom they have a peace treaty, and an obligation to defend."

Isaac paused for a moment, to make sure that Bergamus finished the point, and noticed a few heads nodding, including that of Talorg.

"If this were to happen, they must first of all come down from behind their mountain strongholds and pass through here on their way south. It is in the interests of Rome that this part of the country be allied with Rome. We know that there is a history of occasional warfare between the Caledonii and the tribes to the south. We also know that there have been many trading operations from Roman Gaul along your coastal lands, that have brought benefits to your people. We are here to live peacefully among you while we gather information that would be useful to Rome if it is necessary to defend her protected allies throughout the rest of the great island. We come in peace, and we will gladly leave in peace if our presence offends you."

Bergamus translated Isaac's words as he spoke them, and when he stopped talking the men looked as one to their leader, who then addressed them in a low voice, while they listened attentively and signaled their point of view with nods, shrugs, and headshaking, and the occasional smile. Talorg then turned first toward Isaac, then moved his eyes between him and Bergamus, so that he could translate.

"Isaac, we know something of the Romans from the occasional travelers who pass by these lands from time to time, and we are aware that they are a great power. We have often spoke about them, when there are meetings with other tribes in our country, and so far, at least, we are inclined to encourage their trading activities that bring new goods and tools that help us improve our farming capabilities. There is also one other factor that we have considered, due to the tribal structure in our country. It would be easier to show you on a map."

Talorg motioned for a young man to fetch something from a nearby house, and he returned immediately with a large piece of slate and some chalky stubs, which he placed on a nearby table. Talorg signaled for the men to gather round, while he began marking out names and rough borders that clearly signaled the territories of the various tribes in Caledonia.

When he was finished, he pointed to the map as he talked. "There was a time when the four main tribes below the great mountains would argue and fight over the boundaries where they all met in the central carse-land between the River Clota on the west and the Bodotria to the east. Then, after a peace was negotiated, the tribal members in the central part of the country were allowed to come together as one new tribe, the Maeatae, and since then we have maintained our tribal lands as a buffer state friendly to all our neighbors on all side. We are obliged by treaty to be vigilant for any signs of the warlike tribes of the Caledonii from the north, and to report any such movements from a few key signal points at the extremes of our territory."

Isaac took advantage of Talorg stopping to drink from a metal tankard that was beautifully forged, as if its purpose was aesthetic rather than functional. It occurred to him that there might be more to this culture than implied by the rough demeanor of first impressions. "Talorg, are you the leader of your tribe?"

"I thank you for the compliment, Isaac, but no, I am the headman of our small village of Camelon, one of many scattered throughout our lands. Our leader is Constantin, and he lives a few miles to the north, at the edge of a great forest known as Torwood. I have already sent a message to him, and will take you to meet him tomorrow."

While ale was passed among the men, Andreas was trying to process this information, and how it might affect their mission. He was beginning to realize how important this knowledge would be to his Roman superiors. It would clearly suggest a strategy of appeasement with the main tribes, forming a significant military alliance against a common enemy.

Bergamus also was thinking about his role as the primary mapmaker of the group, and how helpful this information would be in producing accurate portrayals of the local geography.

Talorg had likewise taken the measure of the three men, and it was clear that they were who they said they were—important emissaries whose co-operation might be advantageous in times to come. He drank from his tankard with a flourish, and addressed the men once again.

"We control three main high points of land that provide security against incursions by the Caledonii from the north. One is Dumyat at the west end of the Ochil Hills, which guards the approaches from the north-western highlands, and from where we can signal to the Veniconii in the north-east. The other two are signal points which can be used to warn the other tribes. One is at Campsie, which is a signal point to the Damnonii in the west and the

Selgovae to the south, and the other is at Cairnpapple, which is a signal point to the Votadinii in the east."

Isaac absorbed this information with a great deal of interest. If only the city states scattered throughout the Roman Empire had the foresight and acceptance to carve a model for making peace among them, rather than self-serving politics that always ended up with the poorest of the people suffering the most, in the inevitable wars that began as territorial disputes.

He realized that the men were waiting for him to respond, and directed his remarks again through Bergamus. "Talorg, we have come to live among you if you will so allow, so that we may complete our mission in peace. I would like to proffer a bargain to your leader when we meet tomorrow. For some of the time we will be traveling in order to learn as much as we can about the country and the people, and we would like to base ourselves with your people here in your village. Then, as long as we are here, we'll provide labor in the fields, and whatever other form of contribution we can make to benefit your people. Andreas here is an expert fisherman. Bergamus comes from a tribal society in Gaul, and there could be no better teacher for your children. And we can all work with our hands."

Isaac had surprised the Maeatae men as well as his two comrades with this commitment, but it was easy to see that it was the right thing to do. There were smiles and heads nodding all around, as his words were absorbed by the men. The offer of three additional pairs of hands around the village would benefit everyone, especially at harvest time, when there was often a small window of opportunity to get the harvest in before it was spoiled by a frequent spell of bad weather.

Talorg responded firmly but cautiously to the offer. "Isaac, I can't speak for Constantin, as only he can decide on issues as important as this. He is a good man and a wise leader of our tribe, and he has strong relations with the other tribal chiefs. I don't think he will take issue with this proposal."

He then led the men to some of the houses so that they could meet the wives, sons and daughters who made up this small but clearly cohesive community of the Meatae village of Camelon. While there was not too much in the way of material possessions, there were no signs of poverty. There were carved wooden pieces of modest furniture, pottery goods, and metal-worked tools and implements. There were obviously skilled craftsmen or artisans in the tribe. Meeting a married couple with their young son reminded Andreas of his childhood in Patras, and the happiness he shared with his father and mother. For a moment he was back in his village again.

After the tour, Talorg led them to a house at the edge of the settlement. "This house is empty, and other than a good cleaning it is in fine shape. I will have some of the women prepare it for you, so that you can move in later in the afternoon. Tomorrow we will meet with Constantin. I'll travel there in the morning so that I can tell him of your arrival, and what we have talked about. Nectan will bring you there in the afternoon."

The three men were profuse in their thanks to Talorg, and soon headed off in the direction of the river to collect their gear.

The relative comfort of their first night sleeping on a bunk for some time was a welcome change, and they awoke early to the sounds of the animals in and around the settlement. It was a gray dreary day, with a soft sweet rainfall to nurture the crops in the fields. After they had eaten a breakfast with some of the men, Andreas took three of the young lads with him to fish along the banks of the river, while Bergamus brought out his papers from taking notes and drawing maps on the journey, to sort them in to some kind of order and refresh his memory. Isaac went with a work party to cut and gather wood. Time was precious in the long days of summer, so even the rain did not interfere with necessary community work.

Later that day Nectan led the three soldiers to a nearby barn, and Andreas was delighted to see that four horses were ready for their short journey to the chief of the tribe. The dull strike of a hammer echoed from a far corner of the barn, where the glow of a fire revealed a grizzled old man working a horseshoe into shape. The early rain had all but disappeared, and the weather was calm and clear as they set off. They could now make out the hills across the Bodotria, and Nectan pointed to the peaks of two mountains that had appeared to the north and west of the Ochils. "The valley between the hills and the mountains is the main access route north, into the lands of the Veniconii. They always have to stay vigilant against raiding parties of the Caledonii, from the mountains to their west."

Isaac had a rough imprint of the geography in his mind after the meeting yesterday with Talorg, and he was beginning to appreciate the strategy that the tribes had developed to counter the threat of the Caledonii. That northern valley would bear the brunt of any invasion from mountains. The system of signal hills that Talorg had talked about was clever. It would be interesting to see them up close.

Andreas waved away a host of small flying insects from his face as the four men on horseback ambled along the track to the north-west. These midgies were a curse, and a constant presence after the morning rain. The crossing of the river had been easy, with no need even to dismount, and the flat lands known as the Carse, were pleasant enough to canter through, and only occasionally requiring a detour to avoid mud flats and boggy ground.

The land began to rise off to their left, and the track veered across, taking the path of least resistance through the coastal plain. As the land steepened, the trees stood their ground guarding the ancient forest of Torwood, and the horses had to be prodded along as they nosed around the surrounding foliage that was damp and sweet smelling. Not much further along the track there was a young man waiting on them, and he led them on and upwards toward the settlement, with his flaming red hair an easy marker to follow. Then the forest gave way again to occasional trees, and rounding a corner the three soldiers were amazed at what lay ahead.

It was a stone built round tower, about sixty feet in diameter at the base, gradually narrowing to what looked like a diameter of around forty feet at the top, and where the stone walls stopped at a height of about sixty feet there was a conical thatched roof that fitted over the edge of the stones, presumably keeping the interior free from the elements. A plume of smoke arose lazily from a projecting stone chimney.

The land around the hillside had been cleared in all directions, and contained a settlement of perhaps fifty or so dwellings, similar in modesty and utility to those at the other village.

Waiting for them outside the stone building was a group of men from the village, surrounding their chief, and Talorg stepped forward to make the introductions to Constantin and a few of his men. The ale was waiting for them in cool stone jars, poured into tankards, and after a few minutes the necessary awkwardness of such introductions were past, and the men looked at each other with expectation and interest.

As the youngest of the three soldiers, Andreas would usually try to be the least noticeable, but his obvious physicality trumped his reticence yet again. There were more than a few stares in his direction, not only from the men in the group, trying to assess his presence should it turn to a threat, but from the

158

women of the community, who stayed a few feet back from the circle of men, but were clearly engaged in the scene being played out before them. Such black hair and blue eyes, in a frame that dwarfed the men around him. Life around the village had not been this interesting for some time.

Chief Constantin coughed discreetly, yet it was enough to bring the group around him to full attention, and addressed himself through Bergamus to facilitate the translation. "The people of the Maeatae are happy to welcome you three men as our first visitors from the Roman territory far to the south. We have often speculated about the Romans, and although from time to time we have traded with them at some of our ports on the North Sea, we have little in the way of direct knowledge. Talorg tells me that you are here on a mission, but not as armed aggressors. I was relieved to hear that."

He paused for a moment, then grinned from ear to ear, and suddenly everyone realized that he was making a joke in order to make a point. The atmosphere around the group quelled into a soft silence, as he continued his remarks.

"Talorg has shared with me the nature of your discussions, and let me first of all say that he has my full support and confidence. He tells me you are good men, and that is good enough for me. Now, you know of our unique role as the guardian of the pathways and roads that lead from the mountains into our heartland, and beyond. The news that there is a, shall we say, modest Roman presence in our midst will be of interest to our fellow tribes."

Constantin paused briefly to swat away some midgies, and there was not a sound from the group around him. He clearly had a presence among his men, who looked at him with respect, and some with awe.

"I believe that that proposal you made to Talorg is good for his village, and for our tribe. We need to know Rome before Rome knows us, and frankly I have no qualms about your mission. However, there is one thing that comes to mind." He looked over to Talorg with a smile as he spoke.

"I have long thought of moving my tribal headquarters to Talorg's village, which has now become a more central location, where the main trails into our territory intersect. This stone Broch that you see behind me was built hundreds of years ago, and is falling in on itself. Talorg tells me you men are familiar with construction methods. I have need of a new home, so perhaps the soldier, the mapmaker, and the fisherman can find a way between them of building a home worthy of the chief of the Maeatae while they get to know our people. What do you say, Isaac?"

There was only one answer, and Isaac laughed heartily as he shook hands with Constantin and extended his tankard for another ale. There was a sense of relief around the group, and soon the tables were being set up for an evening meal to celebrate the doings of the day.

In the natural order of things, the three soldiers shared a table with Constantin and Talorg, who were full of questions about the three men, where they came from, and how they ended up serving in the Roman army. It would be the first of many such conversations.

Later that evening, Talorg led the group of horsemen back across the Carse to his village, and chatted mostly with Bergamus, who occasionally shared some point or other with Isaac and Andreas. The most immediate need was to have his two comrades improve their language skills, and he made a note to discuss this in the morning.

Chapter Fourteen
Aberfeldy

The world changed for Andreas when he looked up from his workbench at the site of Constantin's house under construction, and saw the most striking young woman he had ever seen, who approached him on horseback and expertly brought the horse to a stop so that she could dismount.

For a moment he was back on the road to Rome, and the young girl who captured every bit of his consciousness for a fleeting moment in time. Many were the dreams born of that brief encounter.

While Andreas was still trying to decide what he should say, given his limited knowledge of the language, Bergamus stepped over from inside the frame of the house and welcomed her, as he helped her off the horse. He spoke with her for a moment or two, before turning to Andreas.

"This is Ninia, Constantin's daughter, and she is here to look at her new home. She wants to make sure that she is moving into a home and not a stable." Bergamus was jesting as usual, but his comrade was too flustered to notice the joke.

Ninia extended her hand to Andreas, as he willed himself not to put too much pressure into his handshake. They exchanged smiles, born of a shyness that would be the first thing they shared.

Seizing the moment, Bergamus produced a chair for Ninia so that she could sit by the workbench while he showed her the plan for the house. They had been told that the house should be big enough for Constantin, his wife, and his daughter, and large enough to accommodate guests. His wife was apparently in ill health, and stayed indoors most of the time.

Suddenly Andreas found the courage to speak up, and he did so with simple words in her language. Bergamus was called upon a few times to interpret, but otherwise he had to concede to himself that a conversation of sorts did occur.

It was obvious that Andreas was fascinated by this young woman, and Bergamus had to admit to himself; she was the kind of woman who caused older men to wish they were younger.

She had strawberry blonde hair to her shoulders, and two metal clasps in her hair that kept it from her eyes, which were a deep blue color. She was of average height among the other women of the village, and had to look up to him to engage him directly. "I hope you like the way the way the house is set out," he said, pointing to the parchment that Bergamus had appropriated when they were in the planning stages ahead of construction.

They walked around the site, and Bergamus pointed to the many massive stone blocks that were used to provide a stable foundation and the exterior walls, all of them transported by a horse-drawn cart from the Broch. The floor was of wood planks that were set on a bed of crushed rock and pebbles from the river, and they were just about ready to build the internal walls. As Ninia looked at the area designated as her room, she spoke to Bergamus and asked him if there was a way to build an extra window opening in the wall, with a solid covering that could be pushed out and locked in place to let fresh air into the room.

"I am sure, Andreas can figure something out," said Bergamus, as Andreas looked over at Ninia and smiled in acceptance of the challenge. Design and utility came easily to Bergamus, and this was his way of deferring to Andreas as an equal.

Just then Isaac returned, and after the introductions were over, Ninia told the men that she was pleased with the progress of the building, and would be sure to let her father know. Andreas retrieved her horse from its tether, and helped her mount the saddle. She smiled and waved a goodbye as she nudged her horse along the track toward the Broch. Her blond hair caught the afternoon sunlight as it spread over her back, and wavered in the cool breezes, adding exclamation points of beauty to her receding figure.

The men returned to their work, and their private thoughts, as they labored in the mild weather that had returned after a few days of rain and wind, which was not unusual in the carse-land, known as "the Carse", that separated the hilly lands to the north and south of the region identified as the home of the Maeatae.

A few weeks later, as they sat at an open table sharing an evening meal with Talorg and a few of his men and their families, Isaac took the opportunity to have a quiet conversation with him about their future plans. "Talorg, we will soon be at harvest time, and depending how the weather goes we may be lucky, and help get the crops in early before the onset of the autumn winds and rains that I am told are fairly predictable." Isaac paused briefly, always having to organize his thoughts, and render them in the local language.

"We will finish the roof of Constantin's house in a couple of days." The construction plans had evolved during the process and the abundance of shaped stone from the site of the Broch had greatly simplified things. The use of stones for the walls instead of turf had meant that there was no need to cover the walls with wood planks. "After that, it just remains to fill the gaps around the stone walls and the floor-stones with mud and clay, which can be done by the young boys who are always anxious to please Constantin, and of course, Ninia."

Talorg smiled as he noted the observation about the chief's daughter, and Isaac inched his chair a little nearer to Talorg so that he could talk in confidence. Both he and Andreas had worked hard on absorbing the language and were becoming proficient enough to make themselves understood without too many calls on Bergamus to help them out.

"Talorg, I have spent many hours studying the maps that you have provided, which have been a great help, as you can imagine. I think we need to travel north across the lands of the Veniconii and see the worth of the great mountains that contain the Caledonii, and then to the south-west where the Damnonii guard the western approaches to the river that means so much to them. From there it looks as if we can head east along the ridge of the Fells of Campsie that will lead us to the south of the Torwood and back to your village. What do you think?"

All the while Talorg was nodding his head, and it was clear to him that Isaac had a good sense of the lay of the land, and was able to form impressions of the nature of the landscape that would ultimately be of great value in laying defenses against the Caledonii.

"I think that's a good plan, Isaac. Now, your man Bergamus knows about our language and customs, as he is of the same stock as us, and that will be invaluable. However, I think you will need some local knowledge lest you find yourself immersed in one of the many bogs that nature has given us to host the bloody midgies!"

Isaac had enough experiences of the dreaded midgies by now that he could appreciate the humor, and the implication that Talorg would provide an escort from the village. "I will have Nectan accompany you, as he has journeyed the length and breadth of this land, and knows the boundaries that must be observed if you are to stay out of trouble with the Caledonii. Also, his wife has another baby on the way, so he may as well spend the next two months or so doing something useful. He is not much use to his wife right now, nor she to him!"

This brought a few guffaws and laughs from the men, as they pointed in the direction of Nectan, who was late for dinner. He quickly picked up on reason for the jesting, and elbowed his way in to the table with a knowing smile, and a red face. He was known as one of the most able and trustworthy men of his tribe, and Isaac was pleased at this development.

Within a few days the three Roman expeditionaries and their native guide, took their leave of the village, each of them on the back of valuable horses that had been provided by Constantin, and lately freed up from their use in bringing in the harvest. He had heard enough about the Romans to know that his tribe would be at their mercy, should they ever seek to settle in his lands, and there was no need to be antagonistic toward such a small and powerless group of scouts.

Better to host them and bend them to his will over time, than take umbrage at their presence. The Caledonii would always be a threat to the tribes of central Caledonia, and it would not hurt to have an established relationship with the Romans, even if vested in such tokens. He knew that the Romans were coming. It was just a matter of time.

The men packed their belongings, and some basic food supplies, in large cloth bags, which were slung over the back end of their horses. They each had an animal hide from the storehouse in the village, that would help to keep them dry in the face of the local rains that would often breach the uncertain canopy provided by the great pine forests. Their weapons, sword, small axe, and knife, were kept on their person, and they left the village with Nectan in the lead and Isaac at the rear, to a rousing cheer from the children. There was no need to push the horses, and an easy canter was as fast as they planned to travel. Nectan had estimated that the two-hundred-mile round trip would take at least one week, but Isaac insisted that they be prepared to spend a couple of weeks so that there would be time enough for exploration and reconnaissance where needed.

The journey would take them to the edges of the great mountain barrier, and they would have to steer clear of confrontation with the Caledonii, so as not to draw attention to the obvious foreign appearance of two of the men. Bergamus could pass for a member of any of the southern tribes, and his language skills would stand the test. It was Isaac and Andreas who had to stay silent, and if challenged Nectan would have to present them as visitors from the continent, looking for trading opportunities.

Almost from the start the horses sensed the chance to exert themselves in the fresh air of the late summer, and had to be constrained to keep a modest pace as they progressed across the carse-lands of the Bodotria. As the Broch lay close to their route north, they took the opportunity to bid farewell to Constantin, so they followed the same trail and soon reached the small settlement clustered around the huge stone building. They found Constantin sitting with Ninia, as they made plans for moving their household to the village.

At Constantin's urging they shared some of the local ale, which Ninia was happy to serve them, as they dismounted and tethered the horses. Andreas felt awkward in her presence, as he had not yet learned how to be natural in the presence of young women, never mind one so attractive as Ninia. For her part, Ninia had no qualms about projecting her pleasure at seeing Andreas again, as her eyes openly flirted with him. As her father talked with Isaac, she approached Andreas with a smile, and asked him if he was ready for the journey.

"I must admit to feeling more like a soldier when I am on the march," he replied, "but it does feel good to be on horseback again. Anyway, I am glad that we were able to get your house finished. I hope you like it."

"I can't wait to move in," said Ninia. "It will be fun living among our people in Camelon." As if a sudden thought had just occurred, she asked Andreas where he was from, and if he had family of his own waiting for him to return. As he was about to reply, Bergamus stepped over, and with a friendly punch on his arm brought their short and timid conversation to a close.

"OK Andreas, time to move on," he said, as Isaac shook hands with Constantin and turned toward the horses.

Andreas had just a few moments to awkwardly shake hands with Ninia, and project a smile that reflected his happiness and excitement about their brief encounter. What was left unsaid between them was deeper than their polite conversation would imply, and he could not wait to see her again. *But that would have to wait,* he thought, and he forced himself to re-engage with Isaac, Bergamus, and Nectan, as they mounted up and headed down to pick up the trail that led north toward the Highlands—already a common descriptor among the tribes who lived to the south of the great continental divide.

As if to give expression to the landscape that awaited them, the clouds suddenly opened up and there, to the north, at the end of the lower range of the Ochil Hills, were exposed two of the mountain peaks that formed part of the barrier of hills and mountains that contained the Caledonii. While it looked from their vantage point that the two mountains were an extension of the hills, they knew from their trip preparation that there was a separating valley that led in a north-easterly direction and contained the Veniconii. Their destination was the village of Doune, that lay about 10 miles from the base of the two mountains, Ben Ledi and Ben Vorlich. The men responded in tandem to the brightening sunlight, as the horses cantered comfortably along the narrow but certain trail to the north.

By mid-day they were closing in on a settlement clustered around the main crossing point of the Bodotria, at Stirling, just below the confluence of two of its main tributaries. For the last hour of the journey, they could see ahead a towering promontory at the end of a ridge that steepened to the north, and ended on what looked like a cliff. As they approached the fields around the settlement, Nectan led them toward another trail that led below the towering cliffs, to where it ended high above the surrounding countryside.

"We will cross one of the tributaries of the Bodotria and then pick up the other one, which will lead us due north to Doune," said Nectan, and in a few minutes they approached the meandering stream, and easily forded the churning water.

Once on the other side, Nectan motioned for them to halt so they could have lunch, and drink the fresh water. The skies were radiant blue, and the sun still high in the sky, as Andreas rooted in his baggage to find his fishing tackle, and eat his food while he fished the stream.

At times like these, when he could sit in the sun and work the currents, Andreas was never happier. Even although he had been forced to at least temporarily abandon his religion, and live a secular life far from home, he still had an inner conviction that he was on a path in his life that would one day open him once again to his faith in God. He prayed silently every day, and thought all the time about his mother and father.

The strike of a fish brought him out of his reverie, as he skillfully coaxed it through the currents so that the line would not snap.

"Hey Andreas!" shouted Bergamus, "why could you not have caught it before lunch, and we could have had fresh fish with our apples, instead of dry bread and hard cheese!"

Andreas nodded to his friend and smiled, as he unhooked the fish and expertly killed it, then swiftly gutted it into two half fillets that would stay fresh enough for dinner that night, as long as he carried them in a flagon of cold water. It took just a few minutes for the men to regroup on their horses and pick up the trail along the river, which flowed swiftly back to the south as they headed north.

Looking over to the north-east, they could now see where the Ochil Hills ended, and then further over to the north-west where the endless mountains began that separated the highlands from the valleys that were controlled by the Veniconii and the Damnonii. Nectan pointed over to a distinctive hilltop at the end of the Ochil range. "That is Dumyat, where we keep a lookout for any movements down from the mountains, and can signal."

In the early evening they saw signs of habitation ahead, with fields dotted with stacks of wheat, and a cluster of small houses built of turf sods. As they brought the horses to a stop, a woman came out of one of the houses, and on looking up at the strangers suddenly shouted. "Nectan, is that you, I had no idea you were coming!"

The men looked over at Nectan in surprise as he quickly dismounted and hugged the woman, who was clearly happy to see him.

"This is my older sister, Coreen," he said, as he introduced her to his friends. She looked to be around thirty, with a shock of dark hair carrying a few loose threads of gray. Her undoubted beauty had barely tempered with time, and while she went off to prepare her small house to accommodate her visitors, Nectan told the men of how Coreen had married into the Damnonii tribe several years ago, and just last year had lost her husband when he was killed by a band of Caledonii men on a cattle raid. The couple were childless, and Coreen, while still a very attractive woman, was not yet emotionally ready to find a replacement husband.

It was still an unusual experience for the three Roman soldiers to be in the company of the opposite sex, and they could not help thinking about her in their own terms. To Bergamus, she was a woman he would love to have met when he was much younger. To Andreas, she reminded him of his mother, which brought with it a whole host of emotions that he had to suppress for another time. To Isaac, she was simply beautiful. The men moved away as Coreen turned to enter her house.

While Isaac and Andreas busied themselves setting up camp in the small yard, and stabled the horses in a long wooden shed that looked as if it was a communal facility, Bergamus asked Nectan for his help in drawing his maps of the journey, which he would accumulate as the trip evolved.

Bergamus retrieved his satchel from his horse baggage, and set out some of his papyrus sheets that contained maps that he had already worked up, based on several conversations with Talorg. He selected one of them that had already been filled in, with the line of the Highlands running from south-west to north-east. And then, the broad central valley that began at the River Clota and ran to the north-east, picked up protecting ranges of hills on the eastern side, the Campsies and the Ochils, separated by the Bodotria. He asked Nectan to help him fill in markers for the rivers that fed from the hills and mountains and which emptied into the Clota to the west and the Bodotria to the east.

Bergamus made a marker for Camelon and Stirling, and then asked Nectan to mark the distinctive hilltop of Dumyat, and just to its south the cliffs and crags above Stirling. When Nectan marked their present location of Doune he could see that it had strategic significance, in the way that it was located in the central valley, with Damnonii to the south-west and Veniconii to the north-east, and had a number of elevated locations around to gain perspective. This would be a key location for a military occupation force to maintain vigilance over military movements from the direction of the mountains.

While the men busied themselves with the tasks at hand, Coreen tidied up her modest home, and found herself humming a song to herself as she went about her work. She stopped to look at her reflection in a polished piece of copper that was her only mirror, and realized that she had not looked at it in months. She had loved her husband dearly, but he was gone, and her extended period of mourning had sapped her energy and vitality. She knew this, but had only now admitted it to herself, all because of the unexpected presence of another man walking into her life.

She smiled at herself, then rummaged around until she found a comb that would put some life into her hair. Surely it would not be amiss for a woman to want to look at her best at such a time.

Later, Coreen entertained the four men with the hospitality of her home and her larder, in the only way that made sense, given the modesty of her situation. A fire was set in her small courtyard, and they drank from her ale supply, and used her fire to cook the meats and fish that they had brought or caught on the way. From time-to-time men from the village would stop by to see who was visiting, and Nectan introduced the men as visitors from across the wide sea, looking to assess trading opportunities.

As the sun began to drop, the midgies began to show, and Coreen went into her house then returned with a supply of pulp that had been champed into a stringy paste. She laughingly told them to apply it to their exposed skin, with the caution that it was a salve, but not a cure.

As the men finally rose from the fire to bed down for the night, Isaac helped Coreen carry some dishes and tableware back in to the house, and took the moment to thank her for her hospitality.

"Not at all, Isaac," she said, "I am just so happy to see Nectan again, and he obviously thinks highly of you, so that is enough for me."

He wanted to express his regret at the loss of her husband, but did not quite know how to do that in an easy and casual manner, in case he would not sound sincere. "Well, I am glad to have met you, and hope maybe we will meet again someday, perhaps when you visit Nectan at Camelon."

This was expressed more in hope than in confidence, so he was surprised when she said that she would like that too. She went to her room with some unexpected thoughts, and he lay for a long time before sleeping.

Later, after a restless attempt at sleep, Coreen put on her wrap and moved silently toward the cot at the end of the Shed, where Isaac lay asleep. She shook him carefully, willing him to wake up gently and not in panic, and then whispered softly to him. "Come with me Isaac, please, come with me."

The first time they made love it was with the passion and lust of two souls who had each known the best of it in the past, and who used each other to fill a void that had long been empty. The next time, it was with the passion and lust that suggested a sense of love. The future was never in play as they lay together that night. It was the present that mattered, and each other.

As they stirred in the moments before dawn, Isaac saw for the first time the many blue-colored tattoos that covered Coreen's body, each of them a link to some part of her life, and she took pleasure and pride in explaining each one, and what it meant. "Here is my tribe's mark, the very first I was given, when I was about five, and this one is for when I became a woman, which is my favorite."

The art was a singular blue that swirled and spiraled across her pale skin. "This one represents the Damnonii tribe, when I married, and this other one," which she traced with her finger across her midriff, "Is for love, represented by the shaped hearts."

She looked at him as if seeking his appreciation, and he smiled and brushed his lips across her breasts, as he tasted the salt of her skin and the scent of her womanhood. Pressing her down against the bed, he rose above her as she grasped him and pulled him into her. They coupled in a frenzy as if it was either the first time or the last time. When it was over, and they lay together, it would not be the last time. That much was clear.

The village came to life with the crowing and bleating of the animals, as heads popped out of windows, and children were sent to bring fresh water. As Isaac came out from the house and reached for his pack, he acknowledged the men with a nod, as they in turn greeted him as if nothing untoward had just happened. Nectan was un-phased, and happy for his sister, who had been in a state of depression for a long time, and had kept many a suitor at bay.

After breaking up their camp and attending to their horses, the men gathered to bid farewell to Coreen, and to a few of the men that they had spent time with. They hugged Coreen one by one, then mounted up to begin their journey along the hills and glens to the north-east, while Isaac and Coreen exchanged a knowing look.

Their destination was Aberfeldy, a village at the eastern end of a great loch. They would be even closer to the mountains, but there were many of the Damnonii spread across the fields and low hills of the Strath, as well as some of the more westerly locations of the Veniconii tribe. The Caledonii usually left them in peace, there being more profitable places to pillage.

After a long day spent riding in an easterly direction to the area around Inchtuthill, and then turning north to cross the Strath and take the well-used trail into Aberfeldy, the men arrived at the village, and set up camp in a traveler's rest area on the banks of the River Tay. They had picked up the pace on the journey across the Strath, stopping once to eat and drink, and the horses were clearly tired. The camp was a hive of activity, as there had been a cattle market that had brought many of the outlying farmers and smallholders into the village. The serious business of the day had been dispensed with, and now the men were eager to rest awhile, and enjoy drinking each other's ale.

Isaac and Andreas tended to the horses, and then took off wandering among the campfires. They were comfortable enough now with the language that they could get by if challenged. They also had the look of military men in their bearing, and no one seemed anxious to challenge them.

Meanwhile, Nectan and Bergamus settled down to discuss what they had seen today, so that Bergamus could make his maps and notes of their journey from Doune.

"It seems to me," he said, "that the Strath is favored with a fairly consistent ridge of higher land that runs parallel to the mountains on the other side, and it would be easy to establish watch towers at intervals to keep an eye on the Caledonii from the higher elevations."

"It is strange that you say that," said Nectan. "I have been told that there are ruins along the ridge at intervals that would have done exactly that, but they were abandoned a long time ago."

Bergamus pondered for a moment, then picked up from where he left off. "What would make more sense is the establishment of a garrison in a central location that would be a major deterrent to incursions from the mountains, and then a string of fortlets along the ridge of hills facing the mountains that form a line of defense. If I remember correctly from the other papers that you have showed me, the Strath continues to the north-east, with the mountains on the northern side and another low range of hills on the southern side."

He then turned to his maps, and the notes he had made that day. "The logical place for a legionary fortress would be here, in Inchtuthill. From there the military fortress can deploy troops either further up the Strath toward the north-east, or to the south-east into the land of the Damnonii, and the other tribes. There is one fairly consistent ridge that I think is shown as the Gask, that runs from Perth to Strageath. That ridge of land has strategic importance, and can be linked to the south at places like Doune, and even as far as Camelon."

Warming to his task, and his mind racing as he concentrated on the geography of Caledonia, which he had absorbed from the fairly simple maps and notes originally provided by General Cerialis, he looked over at Nectan as he pointed to one of the documents. "See here, the location of the three main sea-ways into central Caledonia. The River Clota on the west, the Bodotria on the east, and then further up the east, the River Tay. With the Roman army placed along the line of fortlets, a legionary fortress at a central location such as Inchtuthill, and control of the main rivers and ports, the Caledonii would never be able to control the heart of Caledonia, and would be stuck in their mountains, where they belong."

Nectan pondered the succinct military analysis, and even with his lack of specialized knowledge it did seem to make sense. Bergamus was writing feverishly on his papyrus, making notes and drawing symbols as he made sure he captured the main elements of his plan. It occurred to Nectan, not for the first time on this trip, but this time with edification, that the prospect of Roman soldiers across the only land that he knew was not some abstract notion, but might indeed come to pass.

When Isaac and Andreas returned, Bergamus was keen to share his thoughts and conclusions, and as Isaac looked through the mapping material, he could see the sense of it. "I think you are right, Bergamus. Better that we head to the south-west and see how vulnerable the Damnonii are to the people behind the mountains. We can leave the north-east for another time."

They awoke to a cooler day, and the prospect, if not the promise, of rainfall. Once again Bergamus produced one of his maps, and they huddled under a rough shelter to plan the day's travel. In a just a few miles they would arrive at the south bank of Loch Tay, and Isaac was anxious to get Nectan's opinion on what they might see as they traveled along the narrow loch, with the high mountains separated from them by the width of the loch.

"Our side of the loch is safe enough," said Nectan. "Although it is only just over a mile wide, the Caledonii tend to stay on the other side of the mountains, except for the fishermen who live in some of the small settlements on the far bank. They are a mixture of both tribes and tend to be left alone."

Soon they were on their way along the south bank of the loch, and taking advantage of the even terrain to go easy on the horses and let them dictate the pace. The sun burst through after a while, and showed off the beauty of the scene, which revealed a landscape so different to Isaac and Andreas than the dusty heat of the desert with which they were so familiar. The hills of Judea and the mountains of the Peloponnese were beautiful, but no match for the splendor and majesty in the deep blue of the loch and the light blue of the sky, and the many shades of green in the lush surroundings.

On the far side of the loch there were stretches of moorland fed by cascading streams, and then areas of cultivated lands rising gently into the mountainsides. Ferns and reeds and rushes covered the marshy soil at the lochside. Further up, the cleared land gave way to thick forest, and then above a line the trees gave way to bare or heathery slopes that melded into crags, crevices, and summits.

Later that day, as they approached the western end of the loch, they were amazed to find a small community of dwelling houses that appeared to be built on the water, about fifty paces or so from the bank. They could see people on the decks surrounding the houses, mostly children playing together or trying to fish with lines cast over the side. The houses looked to be supported by a circular ring of pointed wooden stakes that must have somehow been driven into the bed of the loch, and then used as a base for a wooden platform that served as a floor for the dwelling and a decking around. The houses were circular in shape, with thatched roofs, and appeared to be large enough for more than one family.

"These are crannogs," said Nectan, as he pointed toward them. "They have been used from as far back as anyone can remember. Originally the wooden causeway was built so that it could be withdrawn, for security purposes, but that is no longer necessary."

Just then they heard a cry from further along the trail, and they immediately nudged the horses into a faster clip, then drew in as they approached the scene ahead. A child was being carried carefully by a youth who was calling to someone on the crannog to come ashore and help.

Andreas was quick to dismount and approach the young man.

"My sister has broken her leg, and is in a lot of pain. None of the men are here right now. Can you help?"

The child was a girl of around four or five, who was crying hysterically from the obvious acute pain of the break. Andreas unhitched his clothing from the saddle and picked out his cloak, which he set down on a level part of the ground. He helped her brother place her carefully, and then looked closely at her injury just above her ankle. "Bergamus, tell the boy that her leg is broken alright, but at least the bones have not pierced the skin. And tell him to fetch his mother."

Andreas knelt at her side and held her shoulders still while he tried to comfort her. His whispering words may not have been understood by the child, but she was comforted, and her wailing cries reduced to a soft moaning as her eyes locked on Andreas.

Andreas turned his head to his friends and asked their help. He would need a basin of water to clean the leg carefully, and then a supply of willow bark. Isaac drew his knife and went toward a clump of trees in the hope that he might find a willow. They had seen plenty of them on their travels. Then Andreas turned to Bergamus. "I will need some clean linen cloth, so as soon as the mother gets here, see if she can provide some, or maybe one of the others can help." There was not much else to do other than comfort the young girl, until he had the materials to treat her.

"Well Andreas," said Bergamus. "This pretty thing probably fell off a tree. I'll get her something to drink from the house." He turned away and stepped on to the walkway leading to the nearest crannog, and returned in a minute or so with a jug. and a small cup.

Then there was a commotion from along the trail, as the mother and some of the other women hurried frantically to see the child. When she reached the spot, Bergamus told her what they knew, and asked if she had clean linen for binding the wound. She turned and spoke to a young girl, who quickly ran off toward their house.

Andreas asked Bergamus to tell the mother that he would need her help in comforting the child when he straightened the leg, and that there was no need to panic. The wound was internal, her bones were still growing, and in time she should make a full recovery.

Soon Isaac returned with a supply of willow bark, which he began to cut into strips that could be used along with the linen to hold the bone in place. All this while, the girl kept her eyes locked on Andreas, and grew quieter yet as he held her and whispered in words she did not understand, but which seemed to make the hurt go away.

Like his father before him, Andreas had a gift in tending to the sick and wounded. He could almost feel an inner strength and power from his emotions, that protected the young girl from whatever was causing the pain. He had seen this so many times in his father, and had come to realize that he too was blessed with that gift. He could not cure the sick, but he could help them with their pain, even if he did not understand why it was so.

With everything he needed around him, he rested the girl's head back on the cloak, and then gently but firmly placed his hands above and below the break, and straightened the leg. She did not react to the pain, but kept her eyes locked on Andreas. It was a closed fracture that aligned itself back in position, and he motioned for the mother to gently wash the leg while he held it in place. Meanwhile Isaac had been cutting the bark into strips, and Andreas used them to create a series of splints around her leg. Once in place, he nodded to Isaac, who began to wrap the linen cloth firmly around the splints.

While the child was being carefully moved across the walkway to her house, her eyes never left Andreas, and he waved at her as she was carried into her home. They waited together for a few minutes, while Nectan finished fashioning a set of crude crutches from the wood that Isaac had brought, which he handed to her brother, and then the four men mounted up to continue their journey along the loch.

There was a change in the air, and after a while the wind whipped up as if from nowhere. Soon they were pelted with a late summer rain that made the horses dance, while the men pulled their animal hides over their heads and shoulders. This was not the time to stop for food and drink, so they kept on along the trail toward their destination of Dochart, a village at the western end of the loch.

By the time they approached the end of the loch, visible in the clearing skies, it was late afternoon and they were hungry. There were scattered dwellings across the flat fields, and Nectan dismounted briefly to speak to two of the men, who clearly recognized him and were pleased to see him. While the three soldiers waited, the men brought some fresh meat, fish and vegetables, and waived away Nectan's offer to barter.

"We'll camp alongside the river at the end of the loch, where we'll have lots of fresh water and a sparkling waterfall to bathe in," said Nectan. This was welcome news, and within a few minutes they had found a good spot to set up camp for the night. Later, as the flames of their fire radiated a welcome heat that was enough to protect against what had become a cold windy evening, he asked Bergamus to bring his maps, and after selecting one from the set, he held it in front of him as the men looked down on the parchment, made luminous from the flames that darted in and around the sweet-smelling wood and acorns.

"From here we'll head due south, and keep the high mountains on our right. This general area abounds in mountains and lochs, but as long as we stay along the eastern valleys, we should not find trouble. The Damnonii in this area are a particularly fearsome bunch, and claim all the land on the eastern side of the great loch below Ben Lomond. The Caledonii have villages along the western shore, and claim sovereignty over the loch itself, so only they fish the waters."

As they finally got ready to bed down for the night, Nectan advised that they keep their weapons even closer than usual. "Like any border area, there are always petty disagreements that flare up between people who are neighbors, but not friends. This is rough country, and not like the pleasant pastures of the Carse, or the Strath."

The soft moaning winds in the night kept their nerves on edge, and as the youngest, Andreas felt a special responsibility to keep guard. It was a night that provided rest but not much sleep, and he was glad to hear the familiar sounds of the morning. At times like these, he could almost be in the Peloponnese. A tough day of riding, and occasionally walking, along the high passes, eventually brought them to the village of Aberfoyle, where they set up camp on the edge of the small settlement.

Their next destination was no more than fifteen miles, but would take them to the south-eastern end of Loch Lomond, and the closest point to where the Caledonii lived. As their horses ambled forward and out of the village, they reached a spot that gave a fairly good perspective on the surrounding landscape.

Drawing up his horse, Bergamus motioned to Isaac. "See there," he said, pointing to the east. "It looks like we are at the corner of an elbow of land that is at a divide between the mountains and the central plain. Let's take the trail over to the east. I need to make sure of my bearings."

After a while they approached another loch, and as they rounded the north bank Bergamus pointed up to a rocky outcropping, and reined his horse up the slope until eventually he dismounted and tethered it to a rough stone. He continued on for several minutes until he reached the top, and then was able to sit at rest and take in the view, which was quite dramatic. It was just as he had thought. He could see over an undulating landscape toward their first stopping point of Doune.

He made his way back to the men, who were enjoying the more hospitable weather, and a few cups of ale that they had picked up on their travels among the villages. Bergamus accepted the cup that was proffered, and enjoyed a swig or two before he told them what he had seen. "This spot is more or less on a direct line from here to Doune, then Inchtuthill, and on up into the Strath. This is worth remembering."

Soon they were back on their original route south toward the encroaching side of the great loch, and by lunchtime they had reached the village of Drymen, just a few miles from the water's edge. "It is better to stay here for the night," Nectan told the men. "We can take a look at the loch this afternoon, and return here rather than take a chance on camping too close to the Caledonii."

Chapter Fifteen
Dumbarton Rock

The men ate well, and rested for a while before gathering in mid-afternoon to have a look around. As usual, Nectan checked in with a nearby family to establish his credentials, and ask them to keep an eye on their camp. He had an easy familiarity about him that engendered trust and confidence, and it had made their journey so much easier and productive.

They set off at an easy trot toward the loch, and then at Nectan's bidding, they turned their horses to the north and picked up a trail on rising ground that soon had the horses breathing deeply and snorting as they exerted themselves. After a while Nectan signaled the men to dismount. "This is Conic Hill, and provides a good view of the southern half of the loch from the summit. Go ahead and follow the trail to the top, and I'll stay with the horses."

The soldiers enjoyed the chance to stretch their legs and exercise, as they bent forward into the slope and gained on the summit. The view from the top was incredible, showing the topography of the loch to be a long narrow triangle at the northern end, expanding to form more of a wider based triangle at the south end. Bergamus counted about twelve isles and islets strewn across the lower half of the loch, many with smoke coming from fires that indicated the presence of people.

There were also lots of small boats working their way in the winds, up, down, and across the deep blue water. These would be Caledonii fisherman, with undisputed access to the fishing grounds of a loch that Nectan had said was about twenty miles in length, although the top end was hard to see in the glittering panorama. Then the sun began to lose its brilliance, as it readied to disappear over the far mountains, before falling gently into the western ocean beyond.

The island that caught Andreas's eye was the largest of the group, and also the most northerly of the local group. Like the others it had a wooded interior, and small beaches and coves around the edges. There were signs of habitation in a few cleared spaces among the trees.

They soon met up with Nectan, and made small talk on the way down, and as they reached level ground Nectan took a trail off to the right. "We can circle back this way and you will see the water's edge. Although the land around here is flat and dry, almost no-one lives so close to the water, for fear of the Caledonii."

As they followed the meandering trail, they suddenly heard voices from the nearby woods, the sound of a woman screaming, and dogs barking from some kind of disturbance through the trees. Turning in that direction, they picked their way through the bushes and trees, then came across a man lying on the grass, and a woman leaning over him and screaming. As they approached, they could see blood coming from a wound in the man's torso, and Nectan hurried to dismount and talk to the woman.

Their daughter had been kidnapped by fishermen. The family had been rooting for mushrooms in the woods, and the Caledonii had taken them by surprise. They demanded that the young woman come with them, and when the father drew his sword, he was attacked by two of the men, who slashed him, while the other one dragged the girl through the underbrush toward the beach, and their boat.

Andreas could see that the wound was easily treatable, and comforted the father and mother, while Bergamus and Isaac reached into their packs to see what they had to treat the wound. Suddenly Bergamus remembered that he had a half-consumed bottle of wine from a previous camp, and he reached in and pulled it out. Removing the stopper, he applied it to the wound, which had spilled lots of blood but was not really that deep. The man groaned in pain, but was clearly relieved to get their assistance, and his wife was able to leave him to get some water from the nearby stream.

"Our daughter, they have taken our daughter. Please help us. They will have taken her to their boat, and headed for Inchclonaig. I have seen them before from the shore. They camp there from time to time." The father dropped his head suddenly, and his face tensed in grief.

"What can you tell us about their boat?" asked Andreas. "Does it have a sail, how big is it?"

The father drew a deep breath, and spoke in sorrow and pain, as if already conceding the loss of his daughter. "It is a small boat, with a blackened hull and one sail. They like to mark their sail with their talisman. This one has a fish crossed with a spear."

Andreas sat down next to the man, and spoke softly and clearly to him, looking to Bergamus for help should it be needed. "Listen, I think we can help you. If the boat has only just moved away, I should be able to follow it along the shoreline. Are you sure they will go to the big island?"

"Yes, I am sure. These animals don't like to share." As he said this his wife moaned in her grief, and Andreas wrapped an arm around her shoulder. "Try not to worry. I will see if I can get your daughter back, but I need to move quickly."

Isaac placed his hand on the arm of Andreas, and spoke softly. "What is your plan, Andreas?"

"I can make my way along the shoreline, and the island is only about five miles further up. I saw it today from the summit. I should be able to keep watch for the boat as it sails to the north. If I can get to the shore opposite the island, I can easily swim the two or three hundred yards across to one of the small beaches, once it is dark. From there, I will have to sneak up on them, and I'll have my short sword and knife at the ready."

Isaac was satisfied that Andreas was capable of handling this situation alone. Bergamus was too valuable because of his knowledge of the maps, and Isaac had to think of the larger picture, which also included keeping Nectan out of trouble. A small family tragedy was hardly enough to warrant putting the entire project at risk. At the same time, he knew right from wrong, and it was inconceivable that the fishermen could take the young woman away from her family with impunity. He knew Andreas well. There was only one answer, and that was to deal with the men accordingly, and restore the girl to her family. There was only one problem. Andreas had never killed anyone, not even in the thick of the Armenian campaign, or the Boudicca wars. He had never had to.

"Andreas, before you go. You know that a surprise attack on a larger force mandates that you kill quickly, as there is no time for disarming. You need to be willing to put these men to death. Are you ready for that?"

Andreas had quickly processed the implications of his rescue attempt, and was already in a place where he could reconcile taking life in the process of saving it. "Isaac, I can do it if is the right thing to do. My only concern is to get her back safely." Isaac offered his arm up to Andreas, who clasped it and sprung to his feet, and took off running toward the beach, dodging in and out of bushes and trees as he sought the shoreline.

In a few minutes, he approached the tree line along the beach, and turned right to head north, parallel to the shore. After a distance that seemed like a couple of miles, he slowed down and approached the edge of the trees, being careful not to show himself. There were a few boats scattered across the expansive waters, but only one with the distinctive talisman. He could see three men on board, and from their movements it was likely that the girl was lying on the decking, and restrained from moving. It was on a heading for the big island up ahead, and tacking its way toward the protection of their home base.

Andreas kept pace from the cover of the bushes and trees, and in about half an hour, he could see the boat tack a final approach to a small sandy beach on the island. While he wanted to get to the island quickly before the men raped the girl, he knew that it was foolhardy, as the sun was not yet down. He needed darkness to fall before he could swim across the calm waters, and he needed to make his approach from the landward side of the island, as the sun was setting on the other side, and casting a fading light upon the waters.

As if choreographed by nature, the last of the evening light brought out the midgies, and Andreas did his best to protect his exposed skin by soaking some of the leaves that he now habitually carried in his tunic, and applying them to his face, hands, and legs.

After a few minutes of discomfort, he finally felt confident enough to crawl into the water and begin to paddle silently across the dark surface of the loch. The water was freezing, and was enough to make his mind up that he would somehow have to get a boat for the return journey. It took him just a few minutes to reach the beach at the eastern tip of the island. Once on land, he wrung out his soaked clothing as best he could, checked his weapons, and began to follow the beach around the south edge, keeping well within the tree-line.

Up ahead, there was a small bay or cove, and the men were close to the beach, sitting round a fire, and already eating and drinking. They were a boisterous crew, and every now and then they would look over to where the girl was tethered to a tree, in anticipation. When the food was finished, one of the men drew out a pack of cards from his tunic, and set it down on a flat stone.

"OK lads, let's see who has the luck or the skill to claim first rights to the bitch."

They soon rearranged themselves around the stone, put some more wood on the fire, and began to play a game with three cups and two tiles, that was played in sequence, and required that one of the players win three in a row. Andreas had watched soldiers play this game over and over again when he was with the troops in Britannia. Sometimes it was over very quickly, but other times the mistress of chance dallied. Andreas felt the need to act, and quickly.

He believed that he could get to within a few yards of the men without being heard or observed. After that, it would be all about speed and efficiency. He did not sense that the men were particularly skilled or able to beat him in a fair fight. But there were three of them, and he would need to act quickly and surely.

In position, he drew his sword in his right hand, and his knife in the other. Then, when the men were fully engaged in their play, he leaped forward and covered the few steps between him and the men before they were able to rise. A slash of his sword on the run took out the closest man, and the same sword disabled one of the others, all within a few brief seconds. The third man had managed to get to his feet, and as he struggled to release his knife, Andreas knocked him over with an extended arm and he fell into the fire pit.

Screaming in agony, he rolled out of the pit as Andreas pinned him to the ground, and secured his hands behind his back with a piece of twine from his pocket. It was all over so quickly. They used to train for this in Caesarea, and it was all a matter of timing the sword movements, which was too precious a skill to let slip.

Andreas checked the three men more carefully. One was dead, the other looked as if he would bleed to death from a gaping wound in his throat. With a look over to the prone prisoner that told him not to move, Andreas hurried over to the young girl, who had been staring over at the scene, her shoulders heaving as she cried in fear. He quickly cut her loose from the tree, and motioned her to come with him.

Andreas helped her get into the boat, while he stepped back to the third man and turned him over on his back. He looked up at Andreas in fear of his life, as Andreas drew his knife and straddled him. Pinning his head to the ground forcefully with one hand, he used the sharp end of the knife to carve out the sign of the fish in his forehead. The man screamed in agony, and struggled in vain as an unyielding grip kept his head in position. Within a few seconds, the deed was done.

In a few moments, he was pushing the boat into the water, and rowing aggressively parallel to the side of the loch. The night was now dark, and the island silent, except for the area around the campfire, where a whimpering could be heard, had there been someone else to hear.

Andreas was able to speak to the young girl, who had a shock of red hair and a body shape that spoke more of a woman than a child. He asked her, "Did they hurt you?" and was relieved when she shook her head, and then smiled at him with teary eyes, as if to reward him for his actions in the only way that she could. Andreas was touched, and couldn't wait to deliver her back safely to the arms of her mother and father.

After a while, he asked her to point to the shore when they were close enough to beach the boat, and rowed silently and surely along the water's edge. Their careful pace took about an hour before they were at the right place to skim up into the beach, and leave the boat. Once they found the trail leading away from the loch, they picked up the pace, and turning a corner came upon Nectan, who had left the scene to check on Andreas, in case there was a problem. "Good job, Andreas," he said, with relief and sincerity. "Follow me. We are almost there."

The parents rose up as fast as they could to hold their girl and hug her, while Isaac looked over at Andreas, and nodded his head and rolled his eyes, as if to thank a higher power. He was safe, and back with them. Before they left, Andreas took a moment to take the girl's hands, and wish her well. She hugged him as she closed her eyes, with her body pressing against his chest, and cried softly. After an emotional farewell, the men mounted their horses, and headed inland toward their camp near Drymen.

The night passed without incident, and by mid-day they had found the river that fed off the end of the loch. All they had to do was follow the river south, and it would empty into the River Clota, at the town of Dumbarton.

The day had started with a rain-shower that stayed with them most of the morning, but after they sheltered long enough to have something to eat and drink, the sun broke through, and they were able to dry off before getting back on the horses. The land was full of the signs of people. Neatly ploughed fields, orchards, paddocks for their valuable horses, and well trampled fishing spots along the banks.

The land to the east of their heading began to rise, and soon became a range of hills that disappeared into the distance. At the suggestion of Bergamus, they picked up a trail that took them into the easy hills, and eventually they reached a smooth rounded peak that gave them a magnificent view of the land of the Damnonii. Nectan pointed out the distinctive hills jutting out from the river's end at Dumbarton, and they could see over the River Clota to another range of hills on the far side.

Looking over to the east, Nectan pointed to a range of hills in the distance, across the wide valley of the Clota. "Those are the Campsies, Bergamus, and the last stage of our journey will take us along the base toward the Carse of the Bodotria."

It was the view to the west and north that held Andreas's attention. The horizon was filled with endless peaks and mountain-tops, and home to the Caledonii. He wondered why they would be so different from the tribes of the central valleys. Surely, they were all one people when the land was first occupied. As he often did when he caught himself musing about matters not relevant to the moment, he pushed the thought to the back of his mind, for a later contemplation.

"Let's have something to eat and drink," said Bergamus, "And I'll spend some time on my maps. This is a perfect spot to add some details and improve some of my earlier renderings."

Within a few minutes, Bergamus was hard at work with his writing materials, correcting some of his earlier work, and creating some new perspectives on clean sheets of papyrus. Isaac and Nectan busied themselves with the campfire and the preparation of the food, while Andreas enjoyed the break, lying with his head resting on a convenient stone, which made him think of Jacob's pillow in the biblical texts of his childhood. He closed his eyes, and began to reflect on the journey that had brought him to this place at this time, and it almost seemed surreal.

Could it really be about three years since he had left Patras on the run? As always, his thoughts immediately brought forward the image of his mother and his father as he had last seen them. His mother's body hanging from the bars of her cell, and the distant cries of anguish from the crowd as they saw their spiritual leader, Andrew, suffer on the Crux Decussate.

As an Auxiliary at the van of the fight, he had been put in a position where he was obliged to kill, and yet he had never had to exercise that obligation.

Each time he suited up he resolved to kill the enemy if that was what he had to do to survive, but he never had to. And then, all of a sudden, in a matter of happenstance, he had killed at least one man, and probably two.

He knew his father had never caused harm to anyone, nor could his mentor Jesus of Nazareth. Their mission in life was clear and unequivocal, and was simply to preach the word of the Lord. They were not soldiers. They had never marched in formation, nor advanced on an enemy line, when a spear or sword or knife could appear out of nowhere and end their life. There would come a day when he would be in a position to trade his weapons for words of prayer. But not yet. It was not possible.

Isaac stirred him from his reflections with a prod, and he sat up by the fire, with a hunger and a thirst that was soon sated with the plentiful provisions that they had always been able to procure on their trip, like any other skilled hunters in such a bountiful land. They sat around the fire in quiet conversation, and from time-to-time Andreas or Isaac would ask Nectan for help with a word or a phrase, showing both the progress they had made with the language, and the distance they had yet to travel.

Picking a careful path down the hillside, they reached level ground, and rejoined the trail along the river. Once they left the hilly land behind, it was an easy ride toward their destination. The two hills that protected the town of Dumbarton now showed as one hill, with a distinctive peak and a rounded peak joined by a crevice in between. When they rounded the base of the hill, they saw how perfectly protected the town was, providing easy access to the higher elevations and immediate access to the river in the event of an approaching enemy. The harbor was full of boats of all shapes and sizes, and the people looked more prosperous than most of the other places they had encountered on their journey.

There was a stone built dwelling house around a ledge that lay above the rest of the town, and Nectan pointed it out as the home of the chief of the Damnonii, whose name was Balfour. Nectan had visited here on many occasions with Constantin, when the tribal chiefs met to discuss matters of security, and he was sure that Balfour would want to meet them.

When they reached the gardens of the house, Nectan told the men to stay, and approached a guard standing close to the door. They both disappeared inside the house, and then in a few minutes Nectan appeared again, waving them to join him. Once inside, they were taken to a central room that had a high ceiling, which had clearly been built in such a way as to let the smoke out and light in.

Standing by Nectan was the chief of the Damnonii and the Selgovae, Balfour, and he acknowledged their greetings with a smile and a warm handshake all round. He was a tall heavy-set man, with a stooped appearance as if he had a problem with his back, but with a bountiful smile that quickly put his visitors at ease. After the introductions, they were taken to a seating area, and gathered around Balfour to talk.

Bergamus told Isaac that he would translate for Balfour if needed, and after a few minutes of stilted conversation and a few difficulties in translation, they finally managed to get the timing right, so that Isaac could speak with confidence, and Balfour could understand with ease.

An hour flew by, and still the conversation flowed, as Balfour proved to be a talented ambassador, with the ability to make his guests feel important, and yet convey his own strength of character and the power of his office. He wanted to know all about the Romans. What did they look like? Was Rome on the sea? What did they call their leader? What food did they eat? In between, he would move off subject and ask about each of them. Where were they from? Were they married?

The give and take continued for an hour or so, then Balfour excused himself so that he could rest for a while. "Please make yourself comfortable in the annex that is always ready for use by visitors. Let's meet here this evening for dinner." He was careful to acknowledge all four men as he rose to leave, and there was no denying his dignity or his authority, which he projected without fuss or threat. *This was a man who was born to lead,* thought Isaac, *and one the Romans would do well to heed should they ever fulfill the expansion strategy implicit in their presence in his land.*

While Isaac and Bergamus checked out the bunkhouse, Andreas took the trail down to the harbor. The air around the town carried the salty tang of the sea, and Andreas was happy to be back in a port, with boats and a few larger ships anchored just off the stone-built pier. The people were obviously used to seeing strangers around the harbor, as they did not attract any undue attention. The white gulls shrieked and cried as they circled around the boats, looking for any easy pickings, and Isaac was hit on the shoulder by a fish that was lost in a skirmish between two of the birds.

This was enough to cause a laugh from his friends, and brought some attention from a few locals who were sitting around playing cards on an overturned barrel. It was a scene that could have been played out in Caesarea, or Tyre, or Antioch.

Later that evening, Balfour played host to his guests, and introduced them to his wife and family. They had all met Nectan in the past, and were favorably disposed toward them because of him. Their children hung around for a while, and then lost interest once the conversation turned to matters of commerce, government, and the military. They were soon peppered by more questions from Balfour, although he would often make comparisons to the ways of the Damnonii, and in this way they gained understanding from him that enriched their own observations.

After his wife and his brothers took their leave, Balfour rose to pile some fresh wood on the fire, then settled back down on his chair, with an effort to get comfortable. "What I find interesting, Isaac, is that the Romans would send a team of Auxiliaries into our country, not on a clandestine basis, but in the open, and in expectation that the soldiers would go about their business of gaining strategic information without any apparent concern that the men might be lost, or the information that they have would be compromised."

Isaac shrugged his shoulders, as he looked over at Balfour, and took a few moments to gather his thoughts. "This is the way of Rome, Balfour. They are the dominant power in the civilized world, and have had hundreds of years of practice. They send us here because to send Roman soldiers and not Auxiliaries would be to put their own people at risk. Better to lose us than the flesh and blood of Rome."

"But surely, they have to be concerned that they will get the truth from you, and not something you just made up, so you could get back to your regular life as a common soldier." Balfour was clearly not persuaded, and let his lack of conviction dangle in the air. A strategy he often used when trying to draw people out in his favorite game of politics.

"It is a bit more complicated than that," said Isaac, as he drew nearer to the fire, feeling a draught from somewhere at the back of the room. "We are from their occupied territories. We have no life ahead of us under their yoke that is worth living. A subsistence livelihood, a dependency on the local occupation forces to buy our food production, no say in our governance and society, and not much to look forward to in our later years. Then too, the prospect of our

187

own sons being taken from us and used as fodder for enemies, at the expense of their own soldiers and Auxiliaries."

Isaac paused and spat into the fire, before he continued his response to Balfour. "As an Auxiliary we take on a bargain with the enemy, yet it is a bargain that works most of the time. After a set number of years of service, which in my case is twenty-five years, I will receive my full pay in coin for that entire time in their uniform. Along with it, I will be given Roman citizenship, and from that point forward my family will likewise be Roman. How else do we have a chance to make something of our lives?"

The words hung for a few moments. Then Balfour pursed his lips and rose from his seat as if to signal the end of their meeting. "Ach well, Isaac, I hope you haven't made a bargain with the devil. Now, if you men don't mind, I will let you go and enjoy a night with a bit more comfort than you've been used to of late."

The men rose from their seats and shook hands one by one with Balfour, then left him by his fireside, as they made their way out and along the hallway and across the courtyard to their quarters. The light was failing, and the evening air was filled with rain, battering against the flagstones. The man on guard let them in, and resumed his position outside the door, while the men inside sorted out their sleeping mats and readied themselves for the night ahead. The bunkhouse was a large room that had eight bunks separated by wooden partitions, and a common room in one corner where there was a fireplace and a table with a few chairs. The room had lost its chill thanks to the roaring fire that had been set for them, and there were pitchers of ale, and even wine, on the rough table, and a large salver of meats and berries.

As dawn broke, Bergamus was up and about sharply, and brewed some tea to go with some of the food left over from the night before. There was a different tribesman on guard as he left the room, and indicated that he was going outside for a while, to climb the rock that dominated the area, and sheltered the cluster of houses around the Damnonii settlement.

Last night's rain had come and gone, and it was a pleasant morning that portended a fine day ahead. He soon found a pathway that meandered up and along the steeply sided rock, and he was just a bit out of breath as he gained the summit. There was a cluster of rocks that had been assembled as a rough look-out point, and he was able to stand on a level surface, and take in the marvelous views, in every direction.

Looking out to the west, he could follow the path of the River Clota as it widened and darkened in its claim on the landscape. He could see where it turned to the south and then it was lost in the distance. Opening up his satchel he withdrew his precious papyrus and concentrated on capturing the lay of the land and sea, using his artistic skills to set the proper proportions that would give meaning to those who might use the maps at some future time. He was no mere mapmaker, but rather a skilled cartographer, and soon his worksheet was covered in marks and signs and renderings that, when finished, would be of high value to a military user.

While he hunched over his makeshift tabletop, the countless seabirds in their endless playground swooped and dove and glided across the sky. From time to time, Bergamus would pause briefly, while he narrowed his eyes to gain a better focus on some detail that might better inform his work.

In a while he gathered up his belongings and made his way down the Rock, using his hands to keep his balance, and wishing he had brought his wooden staff that he kept tied to his saddle.

Arriving at the annex, he found Nectan, Isaac, and Andreas organizing the horses for the next, and final, stage of their journey. As he moved toward the door into the annex, Balfour appeared with two of his men, and extended a gnarled hand toward each man, one by one, and they felt the strength of his grip and the warmth of his smile.

"It was good to meet you, and to learn first-hand about this powerful country that you represent. Perhaps in my lifetime we might see some principals here in the land of the Damnoni, rather than some proxies," and then started to laugh as he lightened the moment by making fun of his guests. One by one they shook his hand and expressed their gratitude for his hospitality. Isaac spoke for all four men, as he thanked Balfour, and expressed a hope that they might meet again. They mounted, and turned the horses down the slope toward the trail, kicking up a spray of sand and gravel on their way.

The way ahead was clear. High land to the left, and straight ahead toward the rising form of the Campsies, then a heading east along the base of the hills until the carse-lands of the Bodotria announced themselves with wooded groves and legions of fens marking the boggy swathes, yet still protected from a rising of the land to the south. The midgies danced their endless dance, and the horses responded to the terrain, relishing the chance to lope along a flat and predictable trail.

It was late in the afternoon when the four horsemen revealed themselves from a dusty horizon to the youngsters of the village, who were playing a kind of ball game using curved wooden sticks to hit a round leather ball toward posts that were planted in the ground. The game quickly evaporated into a melee of cheering and clapping children, who recognized the four men and began to shout their names, as if in tribute. As Nectan hugged his boy and girl, his three journeymen headed over toward their house, waving their farewells to Nectan, and each with his own thoughts and impressions of their eventful journey.

Chapter Sixteen
Ninia

A few days after their return, the three men breakfasted on chunks of rough bread lathered in butter and honey, which had been brought to them by Nectan's wife, Sibil, as they made small talk among themselves. Once or twice, Andreas took out a red cloth from his tunic, and wiped the creamy butter from his lips. This was the only tangible possession that he had from his life in Patras, as it was in his pocket when he was forced to flee from home. It was now more of a rag than a proper kerchief, but it was everything to Andreas.

Isaac seemed to be in a particularly pensive mood, and when the meal was more or less over, he cleared his throat softly and the other two men looked at him deferentially, sensing that he had something serious to say.

"I have given a lot of thought about what we should do next. As you know, we have a pretty free hand to develop intelligence and knowledge about Caledonia in whatever way that we can. I have no doubt that we will be able to continue here as guests of Constantin and Talorg." He paused as if to reflect on his choice of words, then continued softly yet surely as he unveiled his plan.

"I think we should separate for the remainder of our time here, and arrange to meet up ahead of our rendezvous on Midsummer's Day next year. Bergamus, I want you to move to a base in the west, at Dumbarton, and your area of responsibility will be the lands of the Damnonii, including the sea access to the Isle of Hibernia. I understand that the Selgovae tribe have the same chief as the Damnonii, so they will be included.

"Andreas, you'll stay here in the heart of Caledonia with the Meatae tribe, and be responsible for developing intelligence on those areas controlled by the Meatae and the Votadini to our east. As for me, I'll move to the north, to the heart of the central corridor of land, called the Strath, that fronts the mountain stronghold of the Caledonii, and make camp among the Veniconii at their headquarters in Perth. That said, it also means that Andreas and I will have to pick up some of the work that Bergamus would normally do, with his mapworks."

Isaac paused to let his words sink in, and it was clear that his message was a surprise to the two soldiers. "I really believe that this is the most workable arrangement. If we stay here as is, we'll be consigned to further touring missions into the hearts of the tribal lands as we have just done, which will take time to organize and implement. Having our base of operations in the main territories means that we can each develop our intelligence on a continuum. We'll have the benefit of several months embedded in the regions, and what we learn will be of strategic value to the Roman Army should we choose to rejoin them, and will enable us personally to have options other than a return to military operations in Britannia." It was during several late-night conversations in their bunks that they had come to an understanding on this possibility.

Bergamus spoke first, and had no issue at all with the implications of Isaac's plan. "It hadn't occurred to me for us to split up, but it's not a bad idea. I do think we'll have a lower profile, as individuals far apart from each other." Bergamus was already thinking ahead to exploring the distant mountains to the west, where the River Clota claimed an ever-increasing share of the landscape, and the mystic island of Hibernia rose from the great ocean.

A sudden thought brought Bergamus back to the present, and the issue at hand. Their brief was to develop intelligence in general, and in particular, to render maps, drawings, and other manuscripts that described the lie of the land, and the implications from a military perspective. "You know, Andreas, one of the things that really registers in my mind as I think about our journey back from Dumbarton, is that right across the central pass between West and East, there is a natural line of the topography that would accommodate a defensive structure that has rising land behind, to the south, and flat lands enough to the north before the hills take away the advantage. Along that line is where the land to the south can be defended, and the enemy to the north can be contained. You might want to think about that as you organize your research."

"I like that, Bergamus," said Isaac, "Andreas can add that to his list of things to consider. Now, how about you, Andreas?" asked Isaac. There was really no need to even ask, given that Isaac had the command, but there was a long and deep friendship between them, and Isaac was hoping that Andreas would support his plan. Andreas had come such a long way, since their first meeting on the ship that brought them together at the port of Antioch. He was not surprised to hear Andreas respond with dispatch.

"I am fine with it, Isaac. However, I would add an additional element of advantage by making a bargain with Constantin. Let him share in our findings so that he knows what we know, and how that translates to our recommendations to our superiors. Therefore, when the Romans finally get around to extending the frontier, Constantin and the tribes he represents will know what to expect. This will ensure his support during the remainder of our stay, and may work to our advantage later. In fact, this should apply to the other regional chiefs. After all, they are supposedly our allies in the face of a common enemy, the Caledonii."

This brought a nod and a smile from Isaac and Bergamus both, as they immediately recognized the elegance of the strategy. Isaac stood up again to reach out to the men in turn, and extended his arm to exchange Roman handshakes, by grasping each other's forearms. Both men picked up quickly on the subtle jest, that could only come from men who now knew each other as they knew themselves.

"Oh," said Isaac, "It just so happens that Coreen lives among the Veniconni, and I will have the opportunity to see her again. You may as well know that I have every intention of pursuing her attention. We all know the regulations about Auxiliaries not being allowed to marry, but at least I will have time to deliberate, if she will allow." The grin on his face was ear to ear, and the other two friends laughed and slapped his back lightly at the friendly banter.

Andreas picked up the wooden platters from the breakfast table, and brought them inside the house for cleaning and storing, as he did every morning. As he tended to his tasks, he could only think how lucky he was to have been chosen to stay in Camelon, where he would still be able to see Ninia, and perhaps get to know her better. He had yet to see her since their return, but had thought of little else but her smile, her face, her figure, her golden hair… With a quick shake of his head, he put these thoughts behind him, and tried to focus on the new reality of living alone, as a spy.

There was no other word for it. He would have to come up with a work-plan to assemble the intelligence information that would be of value to the Romans should they turn their attention to Caledonia. He was now a bit more at ease knowing that what he was doing would not be against the interests of Constantin and his Meatae tribe, but would instead call for a focus on the existential threat of the Caledonii to not just the larger Roman aspirations but also to the several tribes of Caledonia that lived south and east of the Highland massif.

Later that morning Isaac headed over to Talorg's house, and sent one of the children inside to find her father. There were always children running in and around his house, and he was never sure who belonged to whom. Never had Andreas seen as many children with red hair. In a few moments, Talorg came outside, and motioned for Isaac to sit with him. Rather than divulge his plan to Talorg, Isaac thought it better to observe protocol and wait until they were together with Constantin. In a few words, he told Talorg that he had a matter of some importance to discuss with Constantin, and requested that Talorg make arrangements for them to meet, including Bergamus and Andreas.

An autumn breeze that spoke of winter had turned a pleasant morning into a chilly afternoon, and the four men on horseback sheltered under their cloaks as they took the well-traveled path toward the Broch. They were identified from a distance by a lookout, and waved on along the trail through a cluster of turf roofed houses toward the ancient stone Broch that would soon no longer serve as the home of the Meatae chief.

As they approached the ancient building, Isaac noticed how clean and tidy were the pathways and grass around the entire property. A flower garden formed a buffer with the hedgerows, and the profusion of bright flowers tempered the curved architectural lines of the ancient gray building. As they dismounted, the sweet fragrances from the hanging flower baskets provided a welcome to the home of Constantin, who appeared at the doorway with a smile on his face and his daughter on his arm. The chill in the air precluded sitting around the outside table, so Constantin motioned his guests inside the Broch, where a fire of peat bricks and smoking logs gave comfort to the large living room.

Once they were seated and had something to drink, the men exchanged small talk for a few minutes, while Ninia flitted in and out from the kitchen area. There was no sign of Constantin's wife, whom they knew to be ill and confined to bed most of the time. It was clear that Constantin regretted his lack of sons, yet clearly loved his only daughter. Someday there would have to be a new leader for the Meatae, and Constantin was always alert to the goings on in the various settlements who looked to him for leadership.

A small bird flew down from the high ceiling of the Broch, and flitted around the hearth, pecking away at the cracks in the wall, and interrupted Isaac as he was about to speak. Constantin shooed the bird away with a smile, and gestured with his hand for Isaac to continue. With Bergamus on hand should his lack of language skills prove a problem, Isaac spoke softly but surely as he outlined his plan. Having made his points with a growing conviction, he asked Constantin for his support, and for his help in gaining the co-operation of the other tribal leaders.

Ninia had already sensed that the men were ready to talk, and she crossed over to the stone staircase that wound its way in an ever-rising journey along and up the wall of the Broch, and disappeared into what was obviously another set of rooms. Andreas followed her enchanting form as she disappeared into next level, and was relieved to see that everyone else was focused on Constantin, as he poked the fire and gathered his thoughts.

This was an interesting development, and if Constantin put himself in Isaac's place, he had to admit that it was a sensible approach. Delegate responsibility and make the territorial assignments reasonable. Keep a low profile, and learn the ways of the people by living among them.

"Isaac, I can understand the thought process that has led you to this conclusion, although you must know that what may be good for you, and therefore Rome, may not be good for us, and the union of peoples that we represent." Constantin stopped for a moment, eyes on the three men, but it was clear that he had more to say.

"You have already shown us that you have our interests at heart. I accept that you seek to serve your colonial power in ways that complement our strategic goals rather than challenge them. We share a common enemy in the Caledonii. Our conflict is a product of a long history that for some time now has been silent. Yours is a function of political alliances, that may require you to face them as an enemy. I see no reason to stand in the way of your plans, and instead I believe it is in our interests that we continue our co-operation. So, that said, tell me how you plan to put this into effect."

Isaac stood up and stretched himself before the fire, then turned to reply. "Well, Constantin, before we do anything, we will finish up your new home, and get you settled in."

If there was ice to be broken, then that did it, as there was a marked reduction in tension in the room, as Bergamus and Andreas nodded their heads in affirmation. Constantin smiled, and Talorg soon followed. Isaac could now speak with more confidence as he outlined his plan.

"First, Constantin, we will have you moved in by the weekend. Andreas will work with Ninia on the logistics of moving furniture and belongings to your new home in Camelon. Once that is done, we will be able to split our camp, and Bergamus and I will prepare for our travels."

Isaac was now speaking at full throttle, as he set out his plan. "Second, we will need your support in providing horses for our journeys, and once more the assistance of Nectan in guiding us to our destinations. Myself, Bergamus and Nectan will travel together to Dumbarton, in the hope that Balfour will agree to shelter Bergamus. Then Nectan and I will head north toward Aberfeldy, although I believe that there is a town known as Perth that may be a more central location, and conveniently positioned above the flood plain of a main river that runs east to the great sea."

At this, Bergamus could not help but smile to himself, as he remembered that Nectan's sister Coreen had said that she had lived there in the past, and she was no doubt the source of Isaac's information.

"Third, we have no problem sharing with you and your fellow chiefs, any and all of the information that we develop over the course of this assignment. Bergamus has already begun to accumulate maps, drawings, and other renderings of the places of interest and the topography of the landscape in the tribal areas. Everything we learn is useful information from the perspective of a military conflict with the Caledonii, and while we think of it in terms of the Roman Army, it could just as easily apply to the tribes who share borders with a potential enemy.

"Finally, once I am settled, Nectan can bring the horses back with him to Camelon. Also, I would feel better if you, Constantin, would provide me with credentials that I will be able to present at some point to the Chief of the Veniconii, should I need them. This will also be true for Andreas, when he is ready to make contact with the chief of the Votadini."

Constantin took a moment to reflect, before replying to Isaac. "You can count on me to provide you with anything you need. Please keep the horses. We are fortunate to have more than we need to work the fields, and I know I will get them back one day." This was said with a knowing smile that acknowledged that theirs was a temporary stay in his territory.

"As to credentials for my fellow chiefs in the regions, it seems that you have already passed the test with Balfour at Dumbarton, and it won't take a moment to write something down for you to give to Chief Dunsin."

As he made to rise from his chair, he looked over at Bergamus with a smile. "I take it you are the mapmaker. I can never get anyone around here to take on that kind of responsibility, so I'll be happy to see what you come up with."

As Constantin said this, he rose stiffly, rubbing his lower back as he always did, and the men rose accordingly, and one by one shared a handshake, and a wish for good luck from their host. He moved over to a small desk and began to write a note to Chief Dunsin.

The men stood around for a few minutes, making small talk, and then Ninia stepped lightly down the stone stairway into the main room. As Isaac took the note from Constantin, Andreas moved over toward her and extended his hand. "Please visit us in Camelon as soon as you like, to see your house, and let me know what you need for moving in."

"Thanks Andreas, I will come to Camelon after lunch tomorrow," said Ninia, with a smile and a warm handshake that lingered just a bit longer than necessary. Linking her arm with her father, she watched the men mount up and turn toward the trail. By her side her father watched, and wondered.

The following day, on her way to meet with Andreas, Ninia pulled up on the reins, and her horse slowed down as she approached a group of children playing together on the grassy field just to the south of the village. Seeing her, the young girls dropped their skipping ropes and ran over to her, breathlessly competing for her attention as they greeted their chief's daughter. While she dismounted and hugged and kissed the girls, the boys picked up their hurling sticks and separated into the usual two teams who played against each other, chosen based on their location in the village.

Soon the game was on, and the sticks were flying as the boys fought for possession of the ball, and skillfully struck it toward the designated goal areas, searching for a winning shot. Leaving the girls to shout for their favorite team and players, Ninia led the horse around the field, and over to the site of her new home, nudging the animal along when it stopped to nose around and munch on tufts of green and glittering grass.

There she found Andreas, painting the trim around the doors and windows, using the vibrant blue woad that one of the villagers produced in enough quantities to meet the steady demand. It was used as a decorative make up, either applied to the skin as a motif, or as a protective and decorative coating on wood and stone.

Putting down his tools, Andreas smiled at Ninia as he took the reins and led the horse over to a tethering post. "Hello Ninia, let me give you a tour around the house, and you can let me know if you have any suggestions or advice," he said, as he extended his arm toward the front door, and followed her inside.

He was thrilled to see her again, and tried hard to stay calm as he took her through the house, pointing out the various decorative or utility features that they had installed. "You have to thank Bergamus for most of the ideas that we incorporated. We were able to get window spaces for every room by carefully selecting the old stones from the Broch and setting them to accommodate the wooden trim work that frames the window. And we built in closets and cupboards in all the rooms."

As Ninia slowly moved from through the house, envisioning which pieces of furniture to put where, Andreas followed along faithfully, acting as if his only thoughts were focused on the project, whereas in reality his mind was racing. Whatever it was he felt for her, it was something that he had never felt before. He just wanted to hold her, to look into her eyes, and for her to share those same feelings. No sooner had he reached a place of hope in his heart that she might feel the same way about him, he felt a self-inflicted wound of rejection, as the reality of the situation sowed its demoralizing seed. He stood still for a moment, and watched her move through the hallway door into what would be her bedroom. Suddenly feeling awkward, he stopped in place, and watched her step into the room.

Ninia was clearly happy with the work, and Andreas left her to linger and visualize where to place the various furnishings from the Broch, that would need to be transported to her new home. After a while she joined him downstairs, and they spent a few minutes going over the moving plan. It would require at least two trips from the Broch with at least two horses to pull the wagon each journey, due to the heavy wooden tables, chairs, sideboards, beds, and chests that comprised the bulk of their furnishings.

Finally, she moved toward her horse to un-tether the rope, and mount it for her journey home. As she placed her foot in the stirrup, Andreas put both hands around her narrow waist, and lifted her effortlessly up and across the saddle, while she quickly used her hands to stop her dress from sticking in the saddle. This was the first time that he had engaged in any form of intimacy with her, and she smiled her thanks as she gathered the reins and pressed her heels against the dark brown hide. "I'll see you on Saturday, Andreas. Come as early as you like. We have a lot of stuff to move." Andreas watched her retreating into the distance, waving to the children as she went, then bent to gather some tools before returning to his house. By the time she looked back toward Andreas, he had disappeared.

A week later, Isaac and Bergamus said their farewells to the villagers, and nudged their horses forward to follow Nectan into the trail that would take them on an angular approach to the Campsies, and then along the base of the hills in a south-westerly direction toward Dumbarton.

The steady clip clop of the horse's hooves seemed to match a drum-beat inside Isaac's head. He swallowed frequently in a vain attempt to combat the dry mouth, that was all caused by the heavy consumption of a village brewed drink from the celebrations of the night before. Talorg had organized a farewell dinner for the entire village of Camelon, and a number of the men brought out instruments and played their music while the children whooped and screamed among the ranks of their parents dancing in line. They all had to try to raise a tune from one of the sets of bagpipes that were the primary source of melody, and only Andreas came close, claiming that he had tried before back in the Peloponnese, on a similar instrument owned by a Turkish visitor.

Isaac engaged in conversation with Andreas, prior to stepping out into a soft rain, that had swept into the village on a northern wind across the Ochils on its way south. "Andreas, I think we are ready to go. Is there anything else you can think of before we mount up?"

Andreas looked over at his friend, and superior. "No Isaac, I feel good about my assignment. I think I drew the long straw in being able to continue here in Camelon. It is you and Bergamus who are having to start all over again."

"Good, good," said Isaac, and then paused a moment before looking right into the eyes of his young friend. "Andreas, it is pretty clear that you and Ninia are attracted to one another, even though you hardly know each other. You need to stay focused on your work, and try not to get too involved. While you were looking at her last night, her father was looking at you. Don't forget, Constantin is a tribal chief whose confidence in us is critical. I cannot imagine that he would countenance the possibility that his daughter might form a relationship with one of us." As always, Isaac was able to negotiate that fine line between friendship and authority.

"And one other thing, Andreas," said Isaac. "Whatever might or might not happen between myself and Coreen, is not even remotely like the situation that you have to deal with. Ninia is to all intents and purposes the King's daughter. Ninia is forbidden territory. That's the way it is, and there's nothing we can do about it."

Andreas could not hide his disappointment as he let the words sink in for a moment, then he gathered himself to respond, "I'll be careful Isaac, and you have my word that our mission comes first." He knew that Isaac was right, but there was a searing disappointment as he listened to his admonition, and some small part of him anchored on to the possibility that with the passage of time things might change in a way that would release him from this promise.

Isaac nodded, and looked over at Bergamus. "Anything I have missed?"

"No, I don't think so," said Bergamus with a smile. "Except the part where Ninia falls in love with me!"

Suddenly there was no more tension in the air, and the three friends hugged and shook hands. As if to bless their journey, the wind dropped and the rain chased itself away over the Slamannan Moors to the south of the village, and the trail to the west.

Andreas was alone again.

Chapter Seventeen
Cairnpapple

Although the sun rose later in the morning than Andreas was used to, and set earlier in the evening, he was becoming accustomed to the cycle of days and nights that framed the routine of his temporary existence in the heart of Caledonia. Now that he was on his own, he felt challenged by his responsibility to immerse himself in the culture of his host, and develop insights that would be of use to his Roman army, should they enter Caledonia to challenge the Caledonii tribe. Although his orders came from the army, it was Isaac who had earned his loyalty.

He no longer felt a conflict in his role here in the village, living and engaging with the local people, and yet here because of his assignment on behalf of a prospective invasion force. There had been enough conversations with Constantin by now to know that the confederation of tribes that were allied as a defensive force against a common tribal protagonist, if not enemy, seemed to be ambivalent about that invasion prospect. Traders from the south were remarkably consistent in their opinions. Along with their war machines, the Romans brought money and trade that lifted the local economies. Farm production increased. Sales increased. Labor needs meant jobs and well-earned coin that circulated among the local economy, and reduced the inefficiencies embedded in the barter system.

As he looked out his window, he could see movement in and around the houses, and hear the sounds of children already playing their games on the village green. His thoughts turned to Ninia, as he reminded himself before the start of another day to respect Isaac's caution, and of the need to keep propriety in their relationship. This was especially difficult now that Constantin had moved his family into their new home, and Ninia was always around the village, playing with the children, helping the women do the communal chores, and tending to the vegetable and flower gardens.

Just then, he spotted her walking slowly with an old lady bent over a walking stick, and holding on tightly as they made their way at a slow pace around the green. This was the first time that he had set eyes on Ninia's mother. She had succumbed in middle age to some kind of dementia that robbed her of her mental faculties, and she spent most of the time inside. Andreas quickly washed his face and hands, wiped them dry, and stepped out the door and into the surprisingly warm morning. The good weather must have brought them out.

He waved ahead to Ninia and tried to temper the happiness in his step, as he carefully approached them with a nervous smile. "Good morning, Ninia, how are you today?"

"Well, thank you, Andreas. This is my mother, Karla. Mum, this is Andreas, the visitor from the south."

She peered over at Andreas and fashioned a smile. "What visitor? I didn't know we had a visitor. He has nice blue eyes. Nice blue eyes, nice, blue eyes." Ninia looked almost apologetically at Andreas as she squeezed her mother's hand and began to lead her along the path. "It was nice to see you, Andreas, we'll be on our way. Take care."

Andreas watched them continue their walk, as a sudden wave of wind caught the material of their dresses, billowing them out for a brief moment, then it chased away as if searching for another quarry. Isaac was right. The wind in Caledonia was like nothing he had experienced before. The wind was a movement, with its own spirit.

Before he went inside, he looked around the village and waved to a couple of young lads acting up before a girl from one of the nearby houses. He had come to know many of the villagers by now, among the one hundred or so people who made up the population. He could tell that they all took pride in helping him learn to speak their language, and live in their ways. He was taller than all the men, and broad of shoulder rather than stout. and he was the subject of much conversation among the young women who lived there. They speculated about his relationship with Ninia, and wondered if he had a sweetheart in the country that he came from, or if he might favor one of them.

Entering the house, he went through to the bathroom, and looked out his copper razor to trim his beard. It was another constant reminder of his past, from his days as a young man in Patras. It was on his 16th birthday that his father had given it to him, and it had been passed down from his grandfather. If he let his beard grow it would become unmanageable and uncomfortable, and he preferred to have it follow the outline of his jaw.

He suddenly had the inclination to sit down for a while, and think about what Bergamus had said about the lay of the land between east and west of central Caledonia. There really was a central valley that separated the north and the south of the country, and that had huge implications for how an invasion force might think about deploying their forces against an enemy to the north, or even defending their territory to the south, should that be the state of play between the antagonists.

As he pondered the implications of this insight, it became clear that the ability to defend the south required either a significant commitment of troops, enough to be spread across about fifty miles or so of territory, or enough of a defensive barrier that it could be defended by a lesser commitment of soldiers, relying on the accommodating topography to make the difference. He thought back to his service in the Armenian campaign, and how the Romans were always looking for ways to let the natural lie of the land provide the advantage, rather than throwing vital human resources in the line of fire. There was an idea germinating here, but all he could sense was the essence of the idea. He would need to mull this over for a while, and see what develops.

Returning to the kitchen, he packed a bag with enough to get him through the day. Bread, cheese, berries, some salted meat pieces, and an empty cup that he would fill with water from a stream. Unlike the interior of the Peloponnese, in this country, cold clear drinking water was easily found. It was almost sweet, and tasted rich in minerals. Lastly, he spent a few minutes sharpening his knife with a piece of whetstone, rubbing firmly along the bottom of the blade, up the curve, and then to the point. He suddenly remembered one of the men in his unit in Caesarea, who used to say, "what's the point of sharpening the knife, if you don't sharpen the point?" and he had to smile at the thought.

Carrying his supplies in a satchel, he walked across the green and over to the communal paddock and stables, and waved to his friend Brude, who was on duty this week. "How are you, Brude? Is there a horse available today?"

Brude pointed to a brown filly that stood munching some hay in the corner of the barn. "She is good to go, Andreas, as long as it is not overnight. She is ready to breed and we might want to try her out tomorrow when the stable-master visits."

"That's fine. It's just a day trip. I thought I would have a look at Cairnpapple Hill. Can you give me directions?"

Both men chatted easily for a few minutes, and Andreas felt confident enough with the lay of the land to take on this day trip on his own. The village of Camelon lay around a hillside, part of a ridge that ran in an east-west direction, and faced the Ochil Hills that lay to the north, across the Carse, and the River Bodotria. Brude helped him saddle up, and he headed up to the ridge line and joined the trail toward the east.

It was mild and breezy, and he did not feel the need to hurry. With nine miles or so until the junction, and then about three more miles south from there, he could trot at a pace that would give him time to stop, should something catch his eye. He had only been in the saddle a few minutes, when he spotted the first landmark that Brude had alerted him to. The trail veered to the left around a stone-built ruin that lay in an exposed position on top of the ridge. He ambled over and tethered the filly, all the while murmuring softly to keep her calm.

It was hard to tell the original shape of the building. It appeared to be like Constantin's Broch, but the walls had caved in on themselves. He had never seen stones composed quite like that before. They were a typically gray color, but were speckled all over, and it was almost a dark green color that highlighted the stone base. Brude had volunteered that it was probably a holy place of the Druids so long ago, that no-one was alive who would know. It was certainly a commanding position, looking straight over to the Ochil Hills in the far distance, although the ridge line fell away gradually so that it probably did not lend itself to a military purpose.

Andreas mounted up, and picked up the pace. The filly seemed happy to be at exercise, and Andreas was enjoying the journey. There was enough change in the contour and the vegetation to make it interesting, so that sometimes the trail would disappear into a forest of oak and conifers, each fighting for their share of ground space that would determine their access to light. Then the forest would give way to fields, and Andreas realized that the ridge-line was no longer evident, as it was now over to the north.

Along the way he met the occasional traveler, usually on horseback, or riding a horse-drawn cart, and he exchanged greetings and waves of the hand with children traveling in the wagons. There were some red-headed and freckle-faced boys and girls of all ages, but the majority tended to have brown or sandy hair, and fair complexions. They stared at him as he passed by, knowing that he was different.

Eventually, he saw the shimmering blue signature of a loch, in the distance, and a settlement of houses on the rising ground to the south. This would be the village of Linlithgow, and the junction with the trail.

As soon as he made the right turn, he was on an uphill track, and the filly snorted and blew as they made their way against the slope. The land was definitely rising to the south, and he noticed an intermediate hill off to the right, forming a perfect triangle against the sky, that Brude had told him about. Then he crossed a bridge over a river running down to the north, making its way noisily toward the Bodotria. In a few minutes the filly was tested against a steep hill on the trail, which crested along the base of another hill, and continued toward the south. This was the bottom of Cairnpapple Hill, and Brude had advised him to lead the filly up the path rather than tether her at the gate. Andreas led her through, closed the gate carefully, then stepped out along the path.

The distance to the top was only a few hundred feet, and as Andreas got closer, he could see signs of human activity, but no-one around. The indistinct shapes on the hill-top proved to be huge stone markers, or grave-stones, and clearly there for some purpose. Although of irregular form, they were spaced around the crown of the hill at even intervals. Then, within the boundary there were some smaller stone obelisks, rudely shaped but clearly also in positions of purpose.

There was an opening into the crest of the hill, formed by foundation stones and lintels, and the summit was grassed over. A wooden hand-rail set into the dark opening led down into the hilltop that roofed the interior, and there was a solid door attached and swung over in the open position.

Before entering the area, Andreas left the filly un-tethered, but happily munching on the sweet grass in the field around the hilltop structure. As he approached the closest of the stone markers, he suddenly stopped, as he realized that perhaps there was a reason for the boundary. There surely had to be some religious purpose to the site, and perhaps he might not be authorized.

He had grown up in the Peloponnese, where every town had a temple of some description, and invariably with rules about how to worship, and who could worship. The Jewish Temple was even more structured, and in the Holiest of Holies on Temple Mount in Jerusalem, no ordinary man could enter, on penalty of death. And certainly, no woman.

He decided instead to walk around the exterior boundary, and as he progressed, he noticed that the slope leveled off to the south, and had a stone building on it, with smoke coming from a chimney. Staying on his circular route around the top, he had almost completed the circle when he remembered that on clear days, such as this, it should be possible to see the massive volcanic rock off to the east that marked the entrance to the Bodotria, and was their rendezvous point next Midsummer's Day. Constantin merely referred to it as the Bass. It was periodically visited by Votadini sailors as a source of eggs and meat when the fishing was poor, and when returning to port without a catch was an unacceptable option.

Looking due east with the sun overhead, he could see where the Bodotria widened out, and a round topped hill on the land that they had noticed on their journey in. He knew that the Bass was on that line and should be visible given the right conditions, but as clear as it was today, it was not enough to render a view. He also saw in much clearer definition, a combination of hilltops framing a ridge that ran across the intermediate horizon to the east, that would surely have strategic value to the Votadini, as it lay in the heart of their territory.

As Andreas walked over toward the filly, which had strayed toward a rock-strewn pit, he saw a man come out from the house, and heard the sound of his voice alerting someone inside. In a moment two other men came out, and waited. Andreas chose to stay put, nuzzling the filly and keeping the men in his vision. He could not help but notice the pit, which on closer inspection was full of dry soot and cinders, roughly in the shape of a square. And in the center, the burned remains of an old post jutted out from the ground.

Looking up, he saw the three men walking toward him, so he elected to wait and see what would transpire. He knew that the Druids lived by Cairnpapple, and that they were greatly feared by the common people. He couldn't help but feel for his short sword, to know that it was by his side, and ready to use if needed. He didn't quite know what to expect from these priests.

All three men wore a sleeved under-garment, covered by a black ankle-length cloak, that had a cape attached around the shoulders, and was tied at the waist by a rope. So different from the style of clothing worn by many of his own people in the Peloponnese.

The oldest priest had a round metal band with a curved cross-piece, that fitted on to the crown of his head, and kept it secure. Around the band of metal were sprigs of leaves. Andreas knew them to be of oak or mistletoe, from conversations back in the village.

Andreas addressed them as they approached. "Good day Sirs, my name is Andreas and I am pleased to make your acquaintance," spoken in perfectly worded language, but clearly indicating a foreign tongue.

Their leader replied, in an accent that reminded him of Bergamus. "My name is Gyrd, and this is Adrian and Diyar," as he nodded over to identify each of the men. "You must be one of the Romans that have been talked about around the villages recently."

Gyrd was of medium height, appeared to be bald, and his eyes were dark lines, as if he always had something to worry about. His narrow shoulders made him appear as if his head was too large for his body. By reputation he was absolute in his beliefs, and known as a fair but uncompromising priest.

Adrian was tall and thin, but much younger, and had a permanent scowl on his face. No one knew much about the life he led before his conversion to Druidism. That would always be his secret. As a young man he abused women, and could never hold a job down. He gave up on his family in the north, before they gave up on him, and went on the road, living from day to day, and profiting only at the expense of others. He lived on the edge for several years, but that all changed when he almost died from intoxication, and was saved by a Druid who managed to convince him to put away the alcohol and change his ways. He became an acolyte of the priest, and spent years learning the faith of Druidism from his mentor.

As a converted sinner he became a devout priest, and a zealot. He had been a misfit as a humble citizen. As a priest, he always looked for the worst in people. He was feared by the villagers that he ministered to, and they tended to look the other way when he was around, making jokes behind his back about his broken teeth and splayed feet.

The other priest, Diyar, was the youngest by looks, and his body language betrayed his constant deference to the other two priests. He had red hair that was cut to loosely circle his crown, and was awkward in his general appearance, with a slight lisp that made communication a challenge. Like the other two priests, he wore a full beard.

Andreas responded in a firm and positive tone. "Well, I am not Roman, but I do represent their Auxilliary, along with two of my fellow soldiers. I hope I am not trespassing. I just wanted to see the magnificent view from up here. I am a guest of Chief Constantin, and will be staying around here for a few months."

Gyrd looked at Andreas with a penetrating stare, and tried to inject a measure of civility into his voice. "Why don't you come over to our house, and we can have a seat outside and talk for a while. I would like to know more about where you are from, and what you can tell us to add to our limited knowledge of the Romans."

"Well thank you, I will," said Andreas.

The men turned around to walk back, and Andreas stepped over and secured his horse to the post, then followed them a few steps behind. There had been no warmth in his words, and Andreas resolved just to be polite. He walked behind them at their pace, and they soon reached the house. There was a wooden table in front of the house, with a bench on either side. Diyar went into the house and brought a tray with one cup, and one pitcher of water, then poured a measure into the cup, which he placed before Andreas.

As Andreas nodded his thanks and lifted the cup, Gyrd waited a moment, giving him time to drink. He leaned back in his chair and looked over at Andreas thoughtfully, then spoke in an even pitched voice. "I have always been surprised by the Romans in the way in which they worship their many gods, and from time to time change their allegiances to some other god. It is as if they have the world upside down, where the Romans behave like gods and the gods are subservient to their own adherents. How odd!"

Andreas had no trouble in seeing the point of view, but was puzzled and bemused by such a strange opening. He could respond by making light of it. He had even heard similar remarks in the marketplace in Patras, but he chose to answer seriously, and give the priest the benefit of the doubt. "There is a lot of confusion about the role of religion in the Roman hegemony, and it is probably because of the way in which Rome is governed, and in turn governs the provinces. The role of Emperor of such a powerful nation state, with no other like it, vests absolute power over much of the civilized world. There are few men who can deal with such an awesome responsibility. It has led to the obsolescence of humility, and the inevitability of hubris."

Andreas paused for a moment, saw no change in the severe expression of his inquisitor, and continued. "While the Emperor rules in Rome, control of the provinces requires delegated power that is greater than held in most independent nations. So, the Governors rule by example, and their word is God." Andreas stopped there, and took a breath.

The Druid focused his eyes on Andreas while he was speaking, and was both surprised and impressed. He had not expected that. Then he remembered that he was an Auxiliary soldier, which meant that he was not a Roman citizen.

"So, you are not a Roman. Your voice tells me you are not from Gaul. So where are you from?"

"There is a Roman province known as Achaia in the eastern waters of the Mediterranean Sea. That is where I was born, in Patras, and where I lived until I was conscripted into the Roman army."

"You seem to have a keen grasp of Roman statesmanship, for a common soldier." The priest sat forward and rested his arms on the table, looking over at Andreas as if to challenge his own words.

"Well, when you spend months marching with your fellow soldiers on military campaigns, it is a form of entertainment to argue and debate about the one thing that is a constant in your life. We see the best of Rome and the worst of it, in the men that serve their Emperor, and we all form opinions. There is almost no point in having an opinion unless it is shared. Don't you think?"

Gyrd knew fine that this young stranger had challenged him. "Perhaps what works for the man in a Roman tunic might not apply to the worker in these fields, who commits his life to the work of farming, and leaves the business of spirituality to those who are trained in the art of it." He looked directly at Andreas, then added, "Don't you think?"

The priest made no attempt to hide his contempt for Andreas. That was clear from his attitude and his words. As Andreas was about to stand up and leave, Gyrd leaned over and pressed his arm, as if to restrain him. "I have heard much about a people known as Jews, who are spread throughout Rome's eastern empire. What can you tell me about them?"

Andreas was taken aback for a moment, but then decided he had no good reason for declining to respond. "The Jews are a semitic tribe known as the Israelites, from a place called Judea at the far end of the Mediterranean Sea, whose history goes back over a thousand years. They believe in God. One God."

Andreas could not resist, and continued. "My father was Jewish, but by the time I was born he no longer followed that faith, as he had been converted to a new form of faith, as a follower of Jesus Christ of Nazareth, also in Judea."

His protagonist looked at him as if slightly puzzled by this information. "I understood the Jews to be believers in their single God. Who is this Jesus of Nazareth, and how could he possibly usurp a religion that has sustained itself for centuries?"

"Because he is the Son of God, of a virgin birth by a woman in Bethlehem. His coming was foretold in the scriptures of Judaism, and there were signs in the heavens that pointed to the place of his birth. Most of the Jews still proclaim the old faith, but for the past twenty years there has been a growing movement around the Jewish biblical lands, to convert to the new faith of Christianity. My father, Andrew, was a Disciple of Jesus Christ, and spent his life as a missionary spreading the Gospel of His words, and ministering to the poorest and weakest in society, as Jesus had commanded them to do." Andreas sat still for a moment to see the reaction from the three men, who were obviously learning about Christianity for the first time.

Suddenly the second priest spoke up, and could barely restrain the anger in his voice. "So, you arrive in our land with all this history and nonsense about a new religion, in the guise of a Roman soldier. Are you here to fight or to preach, that is what I want to know?"

Andreas paused for a moment, as Gyrd looked over at his novice with an admonishing shake of his head. He clearly wanted to control the dialogue, whereas Andreas was quite enjoying the give and take. "I am a soldier, but make no mistake about it, I believe in the divinity of Jesus Christ, that he is the son of God, and is part of a holy trinity of God, Jesus, and the Holy Spirit. I do not worship as I used to, now that I am a soldier, but I follow the tenets of the faith. I believe that makes me a better person. What is it about your faith, or your beliefs, that make you a better person, or perhaps that is not a requirement of Druidism?"

Andreas watched Gyrd contemplate, as he was clearly deciding whether or not to close the conversation. Had he done so at that point, Andreas would have had the last word. That would not be right.

"Your personal beliefs are only of academic interest to me. We are part of a movement that recognizes the spiritual aspects of life, and how these are embedded in everything that nature ordains. The people here could not exist without us. We are their spiritual conscience, their healers, the keepers of all knowledge that is unknowing to the rest of society. Without us there would be no laws, and no way for the people to be represented against kings. But above all, we understand the flow of life and death, and the constancy of the soul, that never dies."

Andreas could tell that Gyrd was now ready to keep on talking, and decided to try and bring the conversation to a close. He was hungry, and he wanted to think about what he had learned, and how it might relate to their mission. The Druids clearly had some kind of control over the people, and in their few months in Caledonia he had not really been aware that they were so omnipresent.

"Well, it seems to me that the Holy Spirit that is at the essence of Christianity is not so different from the soul that lies at the heart of your faith. I hope we can agree on that." With that, Andreas slipped along the bench and stood up, looked down at the three men, and said, "I thank you for your hospitality and your willingness to listen. I have not had much occasion lately to think and speak of matters of a higher order. Maybe we can talk again sometime."

Andreas held his hand out to Gyrd and they shook hands briefly, as Adrian turned away rudely. Diyar leaned over awkwardly to shake hands, and came closest of the three to showing any kind of congeniality in parting. With that, Andreas turned and walked back down the slope toward his horse, still grazing around the edges of the fire pit.

In a few minutes he was through the gate and back on the trail toward Linlithgow, only this time he turned to the right at the junction and headed over to the village. It was smaller than Camelon, but really pretty, with a row of established houses along the banks of the loch, and other houses sprinkled around the inevitable village green. He ambled over to a bench and some seats that were arranged in a communal area, and waved to a bunch of children playing on the green in the pleasant autumn weather.

He opened up his satchel and took out his lunch, which he spread out on the bench before him, then looked first for the cheese, to get that initial boost of energy. He noticed a nearby stream, what they called a burn, meandering down toward the loch, and went over to fill his cup, drinking a cupful there, and filling it again to take back to the bench. Then he walked the filly over to the burn for her turn to drink.

As he sat quietly enjoying the scene, and eating at random from the bread, cheese, and berries, he saw a young man heading over toward him, and as he got closer, he reached out his hand toward Andreas, who was quick to respond.

"This is a well-used stopping point for travelers heading east, are you bound for Traprain in Votadini country?"

"No, I'm heading back to Camelon, where I am staying as a guest of Chief Constantin. I am Andreas, good to meet you."

"I am Dylan, and live here with my young sister Senga. That's her over there. The one with the long red pigtails." Andreas looked over at the young girl, who looked to be barely a teenager, and waved his hand, prompting a fit of giggling from her group of friends.

Andreas pointed to the food to encourage Dylan to eat something, and he took a few of the berries and slipped them one by one into his mouth.

"I just came from Cairnpapple, and it was clear enough up there that I could see the far horizons in all directions. I could even see rain showers over the Ochils, and the view was incredible."

"Well, what they say around here is that if you can see the Ochil's then it's going to rain, and if you can't see them, it's already raining." Dylan laughed at his own joke, and Andreas had experienced enough of the local weather that he could easily see the irony.

Andreas continued. "I would have liked to have seen inside the cairn, but I wasn't sure that would have been allowed, and just then I met the three Druids who live nearby. Do you know them?"

Dylan hesitated before responding. "Not all of us know them personally, but they all know who we are. They are assigned to our villages, and they make it their business to know what is going on in the communities. Most of our people are afraid of them, but they have been part of our tribal rituals for generations, and they keep the sacred knowledge that governs our lives, and our destinies."

Andreas could sense that Dylan was being careful to be politically correct, and not overtly critical of them, but there was still an undertone of resistance that he obviously could not hide. "I sat down with them and talked for a while, and they seemed interested in what was going on in the Roman provinces. I don't think they took kindly to having a foreigner in their midst, and we didn't find much to agree on."

"It is hard to argue against them. The people live in fear of them, but fear life without them, and there is not much that goes on in the villages that they don't know about. We need them to tell us when to plant and when to reap, or how to get recourse if we are robbed, or how to cure a sick child." Dylan looked over toward his sister, and waved his hands to get her attention as he stood up from the chairs and offered his hand to Andreas. "Thanks for the snack, and the chance to talk to a stranger. I hope we meet again."

As Dylan turned away, Andreas picked up the remains of the food and, placing them on his hand, he offered it to the horse. After a final stop at the burn, so that the horse could drink, he mounted up and headed over toward the trail home. Home. It actually felt like home. He smiled to himself, as he held the reins lightly and let the animal carry him at its own pace toward Camelon.

It was an uneventful ride back to the village, and he got there before the clouds closed in and the rain pelted down. Returning the horse to Brude, he picked up his empty satchel and walked back to his home as he felt the spits of rain.

As he sat by the fire that night, he felt a bit leg weary after the several hours of riding, and took his time to savor the sweet tasting ale, that washed down a meal of boiled potatoes and chicken meat, prepared over the open fire. It occurred to him that he hadn't had fish for some time, and he made up his mind to spend the next few days fishing the river. He woke after a few hours, and leaning over, he broke up the cinders so that they would not spark in the night. In a few minutes he was fast asleep in bed, impervious to the rain that lashed against the roof in the early hours of the morning.

His plans for fishing were put on hold due to the continuing inclement weather, so the next two days were spent doing jobs around the house. There was always a need to shore up any points of penetration by the effects of the weather. Room by room, he took his patching materials and his trowel, filling in any gaps, and once filled, he then went round the entire walls applying a new coat of blue woad that had been thinned to a light blue color, that looked better on the inside walls. Taking advantage of gaps in the rain, he inspected the roof and made some repairs that might otherwise have resulted in some damage.

As he worked along, and especially when applying paint without having to concentrate too hard, he thought about the journey that he had taken to find his way here, and inevitably to the open question about the future. They were several months away from the rendezvous at the Bass, and at this point there were so many unknowns at play that it was easier to just focus on the present. But as he did so, there was really only one reality that concerned him, and that was his relationship with Ninia. And so, he ended up as he always did, telling himself that he would take each day as it comes. But still, he couldn't wait till tomorrow, and the chance of seeing her.

But when tomorrow came, he awoke to the noise of a knocking on the door, and the sound of Talorg's voice as he called out. "Hey Andreas, it's a fine day for fishing, and I thought that maybe you and me could take your wee boat out on the river and see if the trout are ready for a change of scenery."

Andreas was immediately enthused about the prospect, and welcomed Talorg in, while he sorted out his clothes and supplies for the trip. The small boat that they had brought from the ship was available to any of the local men, and Talorg had put the word around that he needed it today. Within the hour they were pushing off from the sandy beach and heading downstream, to the estuary at the Bodotria, but not before Andreas made a mental note to carry out some repairs and re-caulking to the hull, which would soon need some attention.

The small collapsible sail was enough to give them motion in the skirling winds, and they were able to tack around the estuary without going too far out into the main river, and set out their lines that were baited up to tempt the plentiful supply of fish.

By the time they pulled up on the sandy beach it was late afternoon, and the winds had gone. The clouds parted, and then dissolved into streams of white, and they too dissipated until there was nothing left but blue skies, and a bright and warming sun that had left it too late in the day to make an impression. And when the sun set, the clear dark skies remained and were suddenly host to a myriad of stars, so that folks who would normally be indoors, settling in for a night in front of the fire, were gathering outside, to indulge in conversations with neighbors, or just quietly enjoying the clear balmy autumn evening.

Chapter Eighteen
The Sign

As long as men have lived, they have looked to the heavens and wondered. The night skies told a tale that men shared with each other, coming to agree on the nature of the stars, the sun, the planets, the moon, and the Milky Way. And along with the constant and inevitable journeys of these heavenly bodies, men sometimes observed flashes of brilliant light in the night skies, and paused to marvel at these displays of awesome energy, that came and went in an inkling of time.

No-one then knew that they were the remains of huge pieces of rock and ice and minerals and metals that had met and clung to each other as they hurtled through the solar system, on a course that was choreographed at their place of birth. For those that were ultimately captured by the gravity of the Planet Earth, their birth of fire and light in the heavier atmosphere surrounding the planet became their very death, as they flamed across the endless sky, burning up into cosmic dust, to end as they began.

The streaking light appeared on the horizon then traversed across the sky, in a blaze of fiery red and gold, with a tail of sparkling emanations that trailed behind, then dissipated into nothing. It entered the sky from the north-east, and sped toward the south-east, before disappearing into the far horizon. The people on the ground, observing this unusual and terrifying spectacle, hurried indoors, caring not to talk to neighbors. They knew this was a signal, that would soon be given meaning.

The Druids on the hilltop of Cairnpapple had a bird's eye view. This was an event of significance that they would discuss into the early hours of the morning. All three priests were taught by different teachers, and they would need to reach a common position on what they had witnessed, and the response that would be appropriate.

At noon the next day, the three priests walked over to the cairn, and when Gyrd stepped down into the interior, his acolytes lifted the wooden door into the closed position. The candles were always lit, and had been replaced when Diyar prepared the vault earlier that morning. Gyrd knelt on the smooth dirt floor among the grave-stones, his head touching a worn stone marker in submission.

The two priests returned to the cairn at sunset and raised the opening, so that Gyrd could climb up the stairs and into the open. They followed him back to the house, and sat with him around the table. Diyar had an air of excitement around him. Adrian withdrew into himself, his dark eyes looking straight ahead but not seeing, as if in a trance.

Gyrd had washed his hands and face on entering the room, and he took his time drying them with a coarse towel. After throwing the towel on a nearby chair, he spoke decisively. "This message would have been observed in all of our villages, and while we sit here tonight the people are all wondering what it means. Our responsibility is to interpret the sign, and dictate the response. Here is what we need to do. Adrian, you will go to Linlithgow. Diyar, you will go to Torphichen. I will go to Camelon. We need to talk to the people about the events of that particular day in the villages. What was going on in their lives? Were there any deaths? Any births? Anything unusual about the livestock?

"Anything else of a salient nature in their lives, that could enable us to determine a course of action. At times like these, the people expect us to calm their fears and render a judgement. Diyar, go to the stables in Torphichen tonight, and bring the horses back with you. We will travel to our villages tomorrow, and be back here by noon on the day after. Have something to eat and drink now, and get some sleep."

As Gyrd rode to Camelon the following morning, he pictured his actions once he arrived at the village. He would pay his respects to Constantin, out of courtesy, then visit with one of the villagers, Galan, who was the best source of information on life in and around Camelon. He was appointed by the chief to record everything of significance that happened in the village, and report to the Druids if requested. Galan was an Elder of the tribe, who was trusted by the chief with this important role. While the normal occurrences of birth, life, and death were among the matters recorded by the Elder, and advised to the

Druids, he was also expected to know and to report on any other event of significance in the lives of their people. It was up to the priest to take note of the information, and intervene if necessary. Both Adrian and Diyar had their own sources in their villages.

When Gyrd arrived at Camelon, he first approached Constantin's house, and asked to see him. While he waited, he looked out over the village and saw people attending to their chores, washing clothes, carrying supplies of kindling and wood from the cart, nursing babies, and playing with their children on the green. He turned round as he heard Constantin come outside, and welcome him to the village. "I have been expecting you," said Constantin. "The people have been wondering about the flash in the evening sky, and I have tried to calm their nerves. They know that sometimes these signs can be a precursor to something good, or perhaps an omen of something bad."

"We shall see," said Gyrd. "I will talk with Galan, but in the meantime, I wanted to ask you about the Roman soldiers who are staying in the village. I met one of them the other day, a young man named Andreas, and we had an interesting conversation. I was under the impression that the Romans were merely in the area to trade with the tribes, but I heard no mention of trading in our conversation. This man, Andreas, has different interests than trading, and I would judge that they are more of politics than bushels of corn."

Constantin was surprised it had taken this long for the Druid to mention the visitors. "Well, it would hardly fit the reputation of Rome to send mere Auxiliary soldiers to negotiate with the tribes of Caledonia. They are merely here to get some understanding of our relationship with the Caledonii, who have been identified by the Brigantes as a potential threat. The Meatae and the other tribes have no dog in the fight, as it were, and we do not consider the Romans a threat. In fact, we know of the economic advantages that a Roman presence can have, and so our position now is one of guarded co-operation. The three men who are here will be visiting with all of the tribes in the alliance that is centered around the Meatae, and will do so with our support. I will let you know personally if there is any change in that position."

As Gyrd turned to leave and go about his business, pondering this unexpected information, Constantin was left shaking his head, reflecting his frequent impatience with the Druids. The relationship between the tribal chief and Druid was always tense. There were no rules of order, no treaties or binding agreements. Only a tradition going back generations.

The presence of a spiritual advisor was as much a requirement by the people as the chief, given the narrow boundaries of their daily lives, and their lack of control over their future. They could understand the notion that everyone has a soul, but could not endure the possibility that it might disappear on death. The promise of a return in a future life as the host of their soul was something they clung to as being fundamental to their existence. Without that promise, the hardships and consequences of life would be hard to bear. And that notion was propagated by the Druids at every opportunity.

While Gyrd was making his way through the village to see Galan, the other two priests were similarly engaged with their Elders in Linlithgow and Torphichen.

Diyar had the easier assignment, as Torphichen was the smallest of the villages, and was located just a mile or so from Cairnpapple. His Elder, Aod, was the oldest resident, and had often asked Constantin if he could be replaced. He was an articulate and highly respected Elder, and would likely keep his position till his death. He was also a good match for Diyar, who was hardly the most problematic of the three priests. Aod was always patient with him, and played the role of mentor.

It was not so simple in Linlithgow, where Adrian was meeting with Allyn. The priest was spotted as he picked his way on horseback down the trail toward the village. The children were all scared of him, and they quickly broke up their games and ran to the relative safety of their homes. Adrian could see this from a distance, and spat angrily as he prodded the horse into a quicker pace. He was anxious to talk to Allyn, and would no doubt have to pry information out of him, as usual.

Adrian took the seat that was offered by Allyn, in the yard of his small and impeccably kept house. He could hear Allyn's wife whistling to herself as she washed dishes, and created a symphony of household noises as she did her chores.

Allyn looked over at his interlocutor, and mentally prepared himself for an awkward conversation. He had nothing good to think or say about Adrian, but in the nature of things he had to keep his own counsel and do his best to assuage his guest. "So, Adrian, I imagine you are here to talk about the light in the sky. Our people are wondering what it was, and what it means. What can you tell us?"

Adrian was expressionless as he replied, trying to reduce the possible importance of the matter so that he could acquire the most information. It was not easy, as Allyn had a history of challenging the Druids, or pushing against them if there was a sensitive issue to be dealt with. Adrian had to be decisive. "Allyn, you saw what happened in the night sky. We know from our history and teachings that events like this have happened before, and will no doubt happen again. We must determine if the event was merely a show of energy from the heavens passing through our world by happenstance, or some other expression of matter that speaks to our people. Tell me all that was going on in and around the village in the past few days. Leave nothing out."

Allyn had an important role in the secular life of the village, and for the larger Meatae tribe in general. Linlithgow lay in a pleasant valley close to the extensive forests that clung to the hills and braes to the south, and provided the wood for the community that was so essential for building and repairing, as well as a constant supply of fuel for their fires, to augment the peat. Experience had shown that the forests had to be farmed, and if left to the people, the hills would be bare of trees in a generation.

Allyn knew where the new saplings were growing, and where over-production had stressed the land so that it had to be replanted and nurtured, with manure and water. He could look at a forest of trees, and tell which species should be culled to permit the better growth of the remaining trees, and if some trees showed signs of disease or stress, then how best to treat them. "Well Adrian, since we buried old Tam about two weeks ago, there has been no need for ceremonies of any kind around the green. We do have a pregnant lass, wee Nola, who is showing signs that she is close to her time, and the midwife is keeping a close eye on her. We did have a wee problem up by Turkey Hill two days ago. An old oak tree that was clinging to the cliff-side lost its roots in a gust of wind, and when it fell a dead branch snapped off and speared a wee calf that was away from its herd. That's about it."

Adrian was looking for any sign that Allyn was hiding something, but it did not appear so. Still, in a village of over one hundred people, something of significance must have occurred. His belief in his faith was absolute, and he did not doubt. Something must have happened either before the event or after the event, to complete the natural order of things.

"Allyn, it's only been three days since it happened. Are you sure there's nothing else?" Adrian mind was scrambling, trying to latch on to something that might trigger his memory. "What about livestock? You mentioned the calf that was struck. Was that all?"

"Well now," said Allyn, "there was a strange co-incidence over at the north fields. A cow and a horse both birthed new young on the same day."

Adrian shook his head impatiently, and sat still, waiting for more information.

"Let me see," said Allyn, "was that Monday when the children all ran away from the green? Yes, I think it was. Poor Senga, she was so embarrassed."

Adrian's eyes focused in on Allyn, willing him to continue. "There were about half a dozen youngsters, all around seven or eight years old, playing games together, and being watched over by Dylan's wee sister Senga, who must be about twelve years or so. Anyway, she suddenly fell to the ground, clutching her stomach, and then her dress began to show her woman's blood, apparently for the first time. The children thought she was dying, and they ran away, leaving her lying on the grass. Fortunately, it was just the first time that she had bled, and once Dylan picked her up and took her back home, she was fine."

Adrian was calm on the outside, but jubilant on the inside, as he listened to Allyn. This was it. It had to be. He suddenly realized that he should not show too much interest in the event. "So, Allyn, anything else, or is that all?"

"No, I think that's about all. If I think of anything else, I'll be sure to let you know."

Adrian couldn't wait to get saddled up, and back to Cairnpapple. The young lass only became a virgin by shedding blood, and did so as a prelude to the signal from the heavens. Surely that was it.

When he got back to the house, Diyar was there, and in all likelihood Gyrd would not be home till much later. When Diyar asked him about his visit, Adrian was visibly excited, but unwilling to talk about it. Diyar had nothing to report, and moved over to the kitchen area to organize dinner, while Adrian's mind was turning over, as he tried to put the events in context. Only then would it be possible to arrive at a response commensurate with the sign.

It was well after dark when Gyrd returned, and he would have been longer were it not for the full moon, shedding enough light to keep him glued to the trail. The only tricky part was the bridge over the Avon, when the moon was lost among the clouds, and he had to dismount and feel his way to the other side.

The next morning saw a change in the mild weather, suddenly turning colder, with winds battering the exposed summit of Cairnpapple, and sweeping down to the house of the priests on the nearby hill. After breakfast, when not much was said, in keeping with their usual start to the day, Gyrd built up the fire as Diyar cleaned up. Adrian paced around nervously, tidying up where possible, in a house that was spartan in appearance, and lacking any ornamentation other than sprigs of oak and mistletoe over doors and windows.

The white milky sheen of the berries on the mistletoe betrayed its recent cropping from the branches of its host tree. The berries of the mistletoe were a magic elixir used by the Druids to cure such disparate infirmities as infertility and poisoning. And sometimes as a paste applied to the vaginas of young women by their mother, as a prophylactic against penetration.

Finally, Gyrd moved over to the table, and as they sat down, he extended his hands so that the other two priests could join him in contemplation of the task ahead.

After a few moments, Gyrd reported on his visit with Galan, and was brief and to the point. "There was nothing that happened of any particular import. One birth at full term, and no birth defects, just a healthy baby. No deaths, and nothing out of the ordinary. Galan takes his responsibilities seriously, and I trust his word."

He looked over at Diyar, who nervously scratched at his beard before taking a deep breath to try and control his stutter, and then related his conversation with Aod. "There was nothing to report. The village was quiet, as the men were away on a hunting trip, and only the old men and the women and children were about. The men came back just as I was leaving, and they had brought down a huge boar, so they were in a mood to celebrate."

Gyrd was exasperated as he chastised Diyar for failing to recognize the importance of the kill. "You know that the boar is sacred to many of the Druidic sects. Having said that, I fail to see any particular connection between the hunt and the heavenly event. Killing a boar is not an unusual occurrence, and worthy only of a celebration by the people for the taste that they covet."

"Well Adrian, what have you to say?" He could tell that whatever Adrian had to say, his mind was already made up. He was not someone to hide his emotions.

Adrian stared straight ahead as he prepared to deliver his message, which he had been turning over in his mind ever since he became aware of it. "There is no doubt that an event in the village that day, just a few hours before the celestial fire, was directly connected to it. A young girl shed her woman's blood for the first time. At that moment she became a virgin." He paused after the word, letting it speak for itself.

"The fact that the flash came after is what makes it significant. There was a message contained in that fiery display, there always is. This is telling us that her virginity is special, and for her to continue in life as a young woman would require that virginity to be taken one day. She must give that virginity as a sacrifice now. That is surely what was intended. She must be brought to the pit and burned, in order to complete the natural order of things. Ashes to ashes, dust to dust."

While Gyrd stared at Adrian, processing what he had just heard, Diyar was fidgeting again, twisting the rope around his waist and looking down at the table, clearly uncomfortable about the immensity of what was being proposed. A burning at the pit was something not done lightly, unless it was a result of a heinous criminal act. This would be a sacrificial death, and of a young girl. Diyar could not cope with the possibility. Surely Gyrd would say no.

Gyrd stood up from the table, and looked down at Adrian. "There is precedent. A similar thing happened when I was an acolyte at our spiritual home in Anglesey. I was only a young boy, but I was chosen to be part of the ceremony. There had been a lot of controversy among the people because of the ruling, and even within the faith there were divisions. After a few days the priests came together, persuaded by the arguments of one of the most important of our leaders. The young girl was burned at the stake, and the next year the villages around all experienced record harvests, and bountiful yields from their crops."

Adrian could not believe it. Not only had Gyrd lined up in favor of his recommendation, he had substantiated the argument that he, Adrian, had propounded. He was almost giddy with excitement.

"This is not going to be an easy thing to do," said Gyrd, "so we must act carefully, and in concert with the civilian authority vested in Constantin. I will leave here this afternoon for Camelon. I plan to bring him with me to Linlithgow tomorrow, so you two should go there in the morning and wait for us. We will be there at mid-day. Do not do anything until I arrive with Constantin. Use the rest of today to prepare the pit, and replace the candles in the cairn. The virgin will stay there tomorrow night, and we will have the ceremony at noon the following day."

Diyar and Adrian went outside to prepare for the event. Diyar brought with him a supply of candles and headed over to the cairn, while Adrian fetched a spade and an axe from the outhouse and walked to the pit. He could visualize the scene, and wanted everything to be perfect.

By the time Gyrd set off on his journey to Camelon, the winds had dropped, but it was still chilly. He was well wrapped up, with a heavy blanket over his robe, and a pair of fur mittens to keep his hands warm, as he mounted his horse and nudged her forward. He had made this trip many times, and he always enjoyed the solitude of traveling alone, giving him the opportunity to reflect on his mission. A lot would depend on Constantin, and his reaction to the judgment.

It was almost dark as he approached the village of Camelon, and headed over to the annex by the stables to request a room for the night, and to see if Constantin was available. The young lad on duty had never spoken to a priest on his own before, and couldn't hide his trepidation. He mumbled something to the effect that there was a room always ready for a guest, and then ran away, presumably in the direction of Constantin's new house.

Gyrd walked the horse over to the paddock gate and tethered it, then removed his personal effects and walked over to the guest room, which he had used many times in the past. Just as he went back outside, the lad arrived with Constantin's daughter Ninia. "Welcome to Camelon, Gyrd. My father is waiting for you at our new home. Please follow me."

As they made their way over, Gyrd could not help but notice how much she had grown up in the last year or two. Daughters of chiefs were a prized commodity in the federation of tribes, and invariably required to wed the son of one of the other chiefs, cementing the alliance. As a priest, his innermost thoughts were his alone, and the only place where he could indulge, answering to no-one. He noted the fullness of her breasts, stretching the lace of her bodice as her shawl was parted by the wind, and contemplated what could never be. Just then Constantin stepped outside, and he was able to gather himself, before offering his hand and passing through the door, with just a lingering hint of conscience.

Their last meeting the day before had been perfunctory, and he sensed that Constantin wanted to make amends. He ate dinner with the family, including

Constantin's ailing wife, and suggested some herbal remedies for a leg strain due to a fall. There was no medical or spiritual prescription for dementia, other than keeping her comfortable, and stress free. Once the ladies had retired, they were able to talk freely.

It did not take Gyrd long to get to the point. "We were able to identify several events throughout the villages that had occurred around the time of the flash, but there was a singular event in Linlithgow that we believe to be directly linked."

When Constantin heard him tell the story of the young girl, Senga, he braced himself for the verdict. The spilling of a girl's first woman's blood had always been seen as having a spiritual meaning quite apart from the endowment of virginity.

But Gyrd was in no hurry to reach his conclusion. He felt the need to add context to a verdict that was not going to be easy for Constantin to deal with. "We have become accustomed to the endless and predictable cycle of the heavens, whose journeys through space and time mark every birth and every death. The seemingly random display of light, wrapped in a cloak of fiery red, is never random. Everything in the cosmos is ordained, and so we must search for meaning in all that we witness."

Gyrd's locked his fingers together as he paused, then continued. "This girl is now a woman, capable of giving birth, and for reasons that we will never know, the soul that enters a child of her mating must be denied. That is the meaning of the signal. And we have no option but to sacrifice her virginity and her life, by returning her soul to the fiery depths of hell."

Constantin knew that this was the likely outcome, and had braced himself for the possibility. Now it was official, and would be seen by the people as a seminal event. For those that were angered and troubled by the prospect of the sacrifice of a young girl, there were others who would not hesitate to laud it, as a necessary surrender of life that would bring favor to her people.

"She will be burned at the stake on the day after tomorrow, at noon. My priests are readying the pit at Cairnpapple. I will travel to Linlithgow tomorrow morning to take the girl into custody, and would prefer that you travel with me, to calm the people if needed. I believe she has an older brother, so we will need to act judiciously to avoid conflict."

Constantin stood up from his chair as he responded to Gyrd. "Are you absolutely sure that you must go through with this?" He stood looking at the hearth, seeing logs that were freshly cut just a few minutes ago covered in flames, and collapsing into the coals as the fire did its work. The picture in his mind was devastating.

"I have no doubts, Constantin. There is precedent, even in my own experience," and then he recounted the incident at Anglesey, and its aftermath. "I leave it to you to provide security in case there is resistance in Linlithgow. Let's leave tomorrow morning so that we get there before mid-day. My priests will meet us there, and will bring a horse to carry the girl to Cairnpapple."

Constantin stood by the door and watched Gyrd walk over toward the annex, then shook his head just as Ninia came into the room. As Constantin turned to her, she saw the look on his face, and stepped over to hug him. As they stood together, he told her what had happened, and the outcome. She closed her eyes and had begun to cry on his shoulder when he moved with a start, as he realized that he knew the little girl. "He said, she lives with her brother, and her name is Senga. That's the girl whose parents died in a house fire two years ago. Don't you remember?"

Ninia did remember. How could she not. The little girl with the red hair cut in pigtails, and her older brother, who was barely a man. She had attended their parent's funeral.

Father and daughter closed up the house and retired to their respective rooms, each of them heartbroken at the thought of what was to happen.

Next morning, Andreas was up early and busying around his home, contemplating the day ahead. He had no firm plans, and thought he might get a horse and go exploring to the south of the village. There was a place the villagers called the Blaeberry Mare, covered with bushes of different berries. As he stepped outside to check the weather, he saw Constantin and the Druid Gyrd on horseback, and heading toward the trail to the east. He wondered what that was all about.

He had just finished shaving when he saw Ninia coming toward his house, and stepped outside to greet her. As she got closer, he saw that she was clearly upset, and wondered what was wrong. She carried a white handkerchief which she used to dab her eyes, and as she looked up at Andreas, she tried hard to maintain control of her emotions.

"It's the Druids. They are requiring a sacrifice in response to the flash on Monday evening, and have chosen a young girl in Linlithgow, who had her first woman's blood just before the skies lit up. They are going to burn her at the stake tomorrow at Cairnpapple."

Andreas drew her into his arms without even thinking, and consoled her as she pressed her head against his chest and cried. Once her sobs were controlled, she looked up in his eyes and suddenly realized what she had done. Had anyone saw her?

He gently released her, and she wiped her eyes dry. "My father doesn't want me to go, and asked me to stay here and take care of mother, and be available should any of our own villagers need comfort or support. There are a lot of families with relatives and friends in the other villages. How can this be? Senga is such a beautiful and happy person. How can they do this?"

Andreas suddenly realized that it must be Dylan's sister. "Is it Senga, the girl with red pigtails? I met her and her brother in their village a few days ago, on my way back from Cairnpapple."

"Yes, that is Senga," said Ninia. "She can only be twelve years old!"

Andreas resolved at that point to travel to Linlithgow, to offer his support to Dylan in any way, and told Ninia so. She thanked him, and waved lightly as she turned away. He was so strong and comforting, and she was glad she had gone to see him.

Andreas packed his saddlebags with extra food, as he had no idea what might happen. He suddenly remembered about the oats that were boiling on the fire, and just managed to remove the pot before it boiled over. Adding some salt and milk, he ate his breakfast standing up, his mind going in many directions at the one time.

He got one of the horses from the annex and was soon on the familiar trail again. It was overcast but without rain, and he kept his rain-proofed cape wrapped with a piece of rope and slung over the bridle, ready for any inclement spell that might develop.

He was about a mile short of the village when he met Constantin, traveling alone on his return journey. They shook hands while still on horseback, and chatted for a few minutes about the situation in the village. The girl, Senga, had already been placed in the custody of the Druids, and was astride one of the horses on the way to Cairnpapple. She was old enough to understand what was to happen to her, but not to understand why. Dylan had to be restrained by several of the villagers, and finally he relented when Constantin went over to him and ordered him to let his sister go. There was no way to resist what had been decreed by the Druids.

As Andreas reached the village, the rain had started to pelt down, and he could see the people begin to return to their homes. They had gathered all day on the green, and watched as the Druids took Senga away. Dylan was still outside when Andreas got there, and they shook hands awkwardly in the manner of new friends, missing the familiarity. They both went inside and Dylan pointed to a chair by the fire, which had not yet been lit. Dylan used his fire lighting tools to ignite the moss and twigs, and then drew up another chair opposite Andreas.

As Dylan looked over at his new friend, he felt a sense of trust, even though they had only just met. As physically imposing as he was, the easy cadence of his voice and his light blue eyes softened his appearance. Dylan was no different than most people, who intuitively felt comfortable in his presence.

"Thanks for coming, Andreas. They've taken Senga to the cairn, and plan to burn her at the stake tomorrow. I just can't believe this is happening to my wee sister. She doesn't have a bad bone in her body, and yet they say they have to put her to death to restore the natural order of things. What does that mean? What nonsense is that?"

Andreas knew that these were not questions directed at him, but rather an outlet for his emotions. Still, Andreas felt the need to say something in response, and he naturally looked to his own faith to try and make sense of it.

"You know, Dylan, that I come from a land far away to the east, and am only here because I am a soldier of the Roman army. In some ways the dual authority of the tribal chiefs and the Druids over the lives of the people are similar to the situation in my country. The land I come from, the land of my father, has for centuries struggled with the conflict in their lives of being spiritually bound to a single, divine God, and yet forced to live in an environment of political and religious persecution by a foreign nation state.

"My mother was imprisoned, raped, and then hanged. My father was crucified, nailed upside down to a cross, after being whipped on every part of his body. The only thing that enables me to overcome the loss of the only people that I have ever loved, is that their deaths will not be in vain. The religion that they followed does not guarantee immunity from persecution. But it does give hope of an eternal life after death, in the presence of a divine God.

And that one day the persecutors will come to that same God, and beg forgiveness."

Dylan was hanging on to his every word, desperate for anything to latch on to, but his grief ruled out any rational thoughts, and as Andreas finished speaking, he managed to whisper, "I'm sorry!" as he put his elbows on the chair rail, and his head in his hands, face down. He was clearly emotionally beat.

Andreas watched him sit there for a while, as he poked at the fire and threw on some extra logs. Nothing he said could have made much of a difference to Dylan. He knew that his reference to his own faith, and the tribulations in his life, would only go so far in assuaging the incredible emotional pain and hurt that Dylan was dealing with. What would his father have said? He would have known what to say, and how to say it, in a way that would comfort the brother of a dying sister, or the mother of a dying son. A sense of inadequacy coursed through him, as he looked over at a broken man.

As Andreas willed himself to be strong for Dylan, he looked around the modest home and saw the evidence of the young girl who had lived here. Freshly laundered clothes in a pile on a cabinet. A broken piece of looking glass that was resting on a side table, along with a comb and a nest of ribbons. A box in the corner that had small shoes and sandals. And a neck garland of oak and mistletoe resting on a shelf.

Just then, Dylan looked up, wiped the tears from his eyes, and tried his best to manage a smile and an apology. Andreas was quick to respond. "Not to worry, Dylan, there's not much I can do to make you feel better, but I came prepared to stay overnight and be with you tomorrow. Would that be ok?"

That night Andreas stretched out on a cot in the corner of the main living area of the house. He and Dylan had shared a meal, and drank some ale, as they spent the evening before the fire. It was a restless night for both of them, but inevitably they made it through till the morning, and nature's clock in the form of a neighborhood cockerel put paid to any notion of sleeping past dawn.

Chapter Nineteen
Andreas

Looking out the door of Dylan's home, Andreas watched the villagers gather and talk together on the green, and then there was a general movement toward the trail to Cairnpapple. The throng of people left on foot, preferring to walk together rather than ride, as they sought comfort in their togetherness. This was something out of the ordinary from their routine and uneventful life in the village.

The loch was a placid mirror of dark blue, with a trail circling the loch-side that looped around a small harbor area. There were small row-boats and single sail boats that had been dragged up to the higher ground, and just a few in the water tied to a small dock. Looking past the loch, to the north, Andreas could see the ubiquitous Ochil Hills, protecting the land of the Veniconii. Today they were clearly visible in the morning sun, a collage of green and gray, as the drifting masses of cumulus clouds bounced along the hilltops.

After breakfast, they went outside and walked over to a common area, where the men of the village brought wood from the forests, and cut them up as a source of communal firewood. Following Dylan's lead, Andreas took an axe from a shed, and they both spent a while chopping wood, passing the time. Dylan had suggested that they wait till mid-morning, and then take their horses on the trail. He did not want to get there too early. "They will keep Senga in the cairn till the last minute," said Dylan. "That is what normally happens when there is a burning. The prisoner has to spend the last night alone, supposedly to commune with the spirits of the dead."

Dylan was like an automaton, as he lifted each log, placed it on the stump, then swung the axe into the heart of the wood. Picked up and stacked the two pieces, then moved the blade up and down to release it. Eventually he tired, and they both sat for a while, each to his own thoughts, until it was time to leave. In a few minutes they were on the trail, and to Andreas's surprise, it wasn't busy.

"The folks from the villages around Camelon, to the west of here, will take a different trail, by going south to another bridge over the Avon, and then turn east along the ridge line for a straight run into Torphichen, and then Cairnpapple. It's easy to get lost going that way, so that's probably why you were advised to travel via Linlithgow."

They arrived at the familiar gate, which was the formal entrance to the hillside and the cairn on top, and at Dylan's bidding, tied their horses in a copse of trees about fifty paces short of the gate. Before they began the short walk, Dylan put his hand on his friend's arm and stopped him. His voice was trembling as he lowered his voice.

"Andreas, I need to tell you this now so that you can take precautions. I am going to try and rescue Senga when the Druid brings her out of the cairn. The crowd will be massed on the other side of the hill, toward the pit, and no-one is allowed inside the perimeter of standing stones. I cannot allow my sister to be put to death like that. I just can't. Once you get up there just move away, and you will not have to be involved. This is not your fight."

Andreas didn't hesitate a moment before responding. "I am with you Dylan. Let me help. I'll seize the Druid and tie his hands so that he can't move, while you take Senga back to the horses. I'll catch up with you both before Linlithgow, and then you can move on from there."

Dylan was elated. He turned, took a length of rope from his saddle, and passed it to Andreas. "Please don't kill him, Andreas. It would be the death of you."

Andreas nodded, and he followed Dylan slowly up the rise toward the cairn. As Dylan had said, there was no one within the perimeter of standing stones, and most of the people were on the other side of the hill. It was now just a few minutes short of mid-day, and Dylan had timed their walk to get there before the Druid came out of the cairn. That would be their opportunity.

They stalled in waiting by the stones for several minutes, just a few paces from the cairn. Suddenly the wooden hatch on the cairn opened with a bang. Then, Druid Adrian appeared with Senga in his arms at the top of the steps, struggling to carry the limp body of the little girl. He stumbled on the last step, and Senga came out of his arms and fell motionless to the ground. The stub of a candle projected from her mouth, seemingly stuck in her throat. It was obvious to her brother, and to Andreas. She was already dead, her face a ghostly white, and her beautiful features desecrated by the molten wax that spilled from her mouth.

Almost without thinking, both men ran the short distance toward Senga, as Adrian looked up in surprise. Before he could do anything about it, Dylan had lifted Senga into his arms, causing the candle to fall out, and he crushed her against his chest and kissed her head. As he turned to run back down with her body, Andreas grabbed Adrian with both hands, moved a foot behind his leg, and pushed him over to the ground. Leaning over, he punched him twice in the jaw, rendering him impotent, if not unconscious, then flipped him over and wrapped the rope around his wrists, quickly tying a knot.

This was second nature to a soldier of the Auxiliary, having done it countless times at the training camp in Caesarea. Then, taking the candle stub, he jammed it into Adrian's mouth, and turned away to sprint down the hill.

This turn of events had been witnessed by some of the crowd, who had been pushed further along the hillside by the throngs of people, and soon their cries signaled their confusion with the turn of events. They reached the perimeter and spread along the circle of standing stones, not daring to enter the holy space.

At the base of the cairn, Adrian regained consciousness, and managed to eject most of the candle from his mouth, spitting and sputtering as he almost choked in the process. He was furious, and to the crowd he appeared delirious, as he stumbled to his feet shouting all manner of curses and depredations. By the time Constantin and Gyrd had made their way through the crowd, he was able to tell them what had happened.

"She committed suicide by forcing a candle into her nose and throat during the night, and was dead when I opened the cairn. When I brought her out, I was attacked by her brother and the Roman, Andreas. They must have gone back through the gate and on to the trail north."

Constantin looked over at the crowd of people around the perimeter, and walked over to a grassy ledge that gave him a slight height advantage over the crowd. In a voice that was strained to reach as many as people, he told them what had happened. As the news worked its way among the throng, Constantin spoke directly at a group of people in front of him. "Spread the word, and tell everyone to head back home. There is nothing more to be done today. I will meet tomorrow with my Elders and determine what, if anything, needs to happen. Please, go on home."

Meanwhile, Andreas caught up with Dylan about half way toward Linlithgow. He was sitting on his saddle, motionless, cradling the body of his sister. As Andreas reached him, he leaned over to her pale forehead and made the sign of a cross, as he closed his eyes for a moment.

Then looking across at Dylan, whose eyes were still locked on the limp body, he reached over and touched his arm. "Dylan, what do you want to do? We need to move quickly."

"They will want her body back, so that they can fulfill their wishes and burn her. I can't allow that. I want her to be buried, as it should be, and it needs to be away from the village. Somewhere they won't find her. When we get to Linlithgow, let's take the trail to the west toward Camelon. That road will be deserted for at least a while. I'll bury her at the ruins on the hillside before Camelon. The Broch with the speckled stones. They will never expect that."

"Alright," said Andreas, "But you go on ahead, and I'll find you later. I'll stay here, just off the trail, for a while. Druid Adrian will be in pursuit as soon as he is freed, and I'll stop him in his tracks. Then I'll catch up with you on the trail, either before or after you have buried your sister."

As Adrian watched Dylan continue down the sloping trail, he whispered to himself. "God bless you, Senga."

Turning his horse, he galloped back up the trail to the crossing point of a gurgling, rock filled stream, as he knew that Adrian would have to slow down to get across. In less than a minute he had tied his horse off the trail. Removing his knife, he crouched behind a wall of Alder trees, whose lower branches were adorned in lichen, that gave him a line of sight up the hill but still kept him hidden from view.

After a few minutes he saw a man on horseback cresting a hillock, then hitting his horse's flank to pick up speed. There was no mistaking Adrian, his figure defined by his dark cape and a cowl covering his head. As he eased up before approaching the stream, he was a tormented figure on a black horse that snorted and squealed, not used to being ridden hard.

Andreas rushed out of his hiding place toward the horse and grabbed the reins, pulling the horse to a stop. As Adrian cursed him and tried to kick him away, Adrian grabbed his leg, and hauled him off the saddle on to the ground.

As the horse reared up and turned away, he brought his knees down on Adrian's chest, straddling him and immobilizing him completely.

As he brought his weight down on Adrian's chest, he put a choke hold on his neck with his left hand, and drew his knife with the other. Adrian was terrified, but was powerless to do anything about it. His eyes opened up in horror as Andreas brought up his right hand clutching his knife, then turned the razor-sharp point down and into Adrian's forehead. His screams of terror were muffled by the strong hand around his neck, as Andreas carefully cut into the skin and tissue, tracing the outline of a fish across the entire forehead. He could feel the straining movements of the body below, but he was too strong and too heavy to be denied by the thin and weak torso of the priest.

For a moment the profile of the fish was perfectly drawn by a line of red, and then, before the linear form disappeared in a pool of blood, Andreas made a cut slightly inset of the main cut, and followed the profile around the outline of the fish, ensuring a scar that would be taken to the grave.

As Andreas released his chokehold and rose up, Adrian screamed in fear and pain, expecting to be stabbed to death. Instead, Andreas pulled on the rope of Adrian's cassock, and when it released, he easily flipped him over, and tied his hands behind his back, only this time he kept enough free rope to then encircle his legs. Once he tied the knot, Adrian was virtually immobile.

Moving over to the stream, he made his way quickly along the bank to where the horse was at rest, drinking the cold, clear water, and brought it back to the prone body of his captive. Grabbing the front of the cassock he pulled Adrian up and push him over the saddle, so that he was balanced, and then wrapped the rest of the rope around the nozzle on the front of the saddle. Leading the horse back across the stream, he slapped the flanks and watched it head back up the trail. It was all over in about three minutes.

He caught up with Dylan just after the left turn at Linlithgow. The village in the distance behind them showed no sign of life. By now the clouds had reclaimed their more familiar territory over the carse-land of the Bodotria, easily visible from the trail along the coastal ridge, and they were met by disparate squalls of wind and rain as they closed in on the ruins. The place was deserted. The villagers from Camelon were hours away from their homes, still walking, but this time with the sloping braes to their advantage.

Dylan had obviously planned the burial on the journey, and was purposeful as they reached the site of the ruined Broch. He carefully swung down from the saddle, balancing the small form of his sister in his arms, and then, feet planted on the ground, he held her close to his chest, as his tears spilled over the face of his beloved Senga. He then placed her gently on the ground and pulled out his knife, looking around for the right spot, which he found at the base of the ruins close to the falling edge of the grassy slope.

Andreas followed his lead, and they used their knives to pry up some half-submerged stones, which they placed to the side, until they had an open area large enough to accommodate her body. Then, kneeling in the grass, they stabbed the ground and used their hands to pull out the damp sweet smelling earth, and in a few minutes, there was a hole long enough and deep enough to contain the lifeless form of the girl who four days ago had become a woman.

Dylan rose from his knees, and then lifted the still form into his arms. Kissing her face, and wet with tears, he turned to the saddle and pulled out a length of a heavy woven cloth that was always packed in case he needed it when away from their house. He let the cloth fall to the ground, then placed Senga on it, carefully wrapping it around her entire body.

With one tearful last look at her pale face that only emphasized her blazing red pigtails, he covered her head, and placed her in the earth. Andreas helped him shovel the earth back into the grave, which they tamped down with their hands and feet so that it was even with the surface. Then, following Dylan's lead, Andreas helped him place some of the stones almost randomly around and on top of the earth, leaving no indication that this was anything other than a ruin. Finally, they collected leaves and branches from the nearby bushes and hid any sign of the fresh dirt.

Before they left, Dylan asked Andreas if he would say a prayer to his God.

"I already have," answered Andreas. "The soul of an innocent passes to heaven, and heaven is eternity. Her soul is at rest, forever."

Dylan looked to the grave, and turned away purposefully, as if a weight had been lifted from his shoulders. "Let's go to Camelon, and wait for Constantin to arrive. I have no idea what to expect, but there's no point in running away from it." The two friends, now bound by the tragedy of death, after a chance meeting of two strangers on a village green, mounted their horses and picked up the trail for the short ride into the village.

When they got there it looked deserted, but for the young lad in the stables, tending to the horses. A few of the old people had stayed behind in their homes, but even the children were at Cairnpapple. "No-one has returned yet. Miss Ninia is at her home, looking after her mother," he said to Andreas.

Andreas looked over at Dylan, and said, "I'll be gone for a few minutes," then made his way over to Constantin's house. It stood out among the others because of its size, and the brilliant blue paint that had been applied to the trimmed woodwork around the stone walls. It did not hurt that the garden in front of the house was a mass of diffused colors from the flowers that were hanging on to life before the season turned, and put them to rest.

On the front door was a horseshoe that Andreas had attached to it, resting against a square piece of blackened metal, and he used it for the first time, relieved that it worked properly. In a few moments he heard a muffled voice call from within the house, and then Ninia opened the door. She was stunning. Her blond hair cascaded across her shoulders, and her face was a perfect pallet of colors, made so by her blue eyes, the rich ruby of her lips, and the smooth unblemished cream of her complexion.

He didn't quite know if he should shake her hand, hug her, or just do nothing, but she made it easy for him by reaching for his hand and drawing him into the house. "Andreas, it's good to see you. Please come in."

He stepped inside to a room that was warm and comfortable, with a fire blazing in the hearth, and accented by a large matted floor rug. Odd pieces of furniture were placed around the interior, each of them functional, but also made by design. A large couch bordered one side of the fireplace, with scatter cushions to accent the dark brown polished wood frame. A pair of armchairs girded the other side of the fireplace. One corner of the room was a dining area, with a round table and four chairs. He had never seen a round table before, yet it looked perfectly in tune with the rest of the décor.

She released her hand so that she could she could walk over to the couch, then sat down, patting the cushion beside her for him to sit with her. "Andreas, it must have been awful at Cairnpapple. I can't imagine. That poor girl."

Andreas looked at her, and was momentarily distracted by her beauty. Then, he spoke softly and evenly, hiding his emotion, as he took her through the events of the day right up to his re-union with Dylan just outside Linlithgow. "All that you need to know is that Senga was buried by her brother, and it is better for all concerned that the site be kept secret. Dylan is here with me in Camelon, as he wants to explain himself to your father, and take responsibility for his actions."

They sat side by side, looking at the fire, and thinking their thoughts. "So," said Andreas, "I am waiting with Dylan to see your father. After all, I am involved. I just feel the need to tell him that I supported Dylan at Cairnpapple, and I hope that he will understand."

After a moment's hesitation, he stood up and warmed his hands before the fire, then reached out for her hand, pulling her to her feet. Then, as she stood expectantly before him, he put his arms around her and leaned down to kiss her. She melted into him, as she responded to his lips with hers, and felt her tongue tingle as it met his. It lasted a few moments but the intensity was undeniable. With one kiss everything unsaid was said.

And then she surprised him by pulling him back down so that he could kiss her again, with an urgency that was unmistakable. Then she broke away with a forced smile. "You must go, Andreas, you have work to do. Take care."

Andreas walked slowly back to the annex, and tried to stop thinking of her. It was not easy. She had clearly responded when he kissed her, but then she had clearly backed off, as if some kind of taboo had been broken. There was no mention of her feelings for him.

Just then he heard a voice call his name from the direction of the trail. It was Constantin, leading a group of other villagers on horseback, returning from Cairnpapple. He dismounted carefully, legs and back stiff from the long ride down and across the moors.

They shook hands, and Andreas spoke to him softly, before he could bring up the subject. "I brought Dylan with me. He wants to explain himself, and so do I." Constantin dropped the reins for one of his men to gather, and walked into the annex.

Half an hour later the three men were still seated at the table, at the point in the conversation when all the questions had been asked. Only one question remained unanswered. Where was Senga buried?

Constantin looked over at Dylan, and reached out his hand to clasp his. "Dylan, I know what you are concerned about. If Gyrd knew where Senga is buried, he might want to disinter her, so that they could at least put her body to the fire. Let me put your mind at rest. I don't need to know. If I don't know, then I can't tell, and he will have no leverage over me. Perhaps at some time, many years from now, you might want to tell me, and then I can go to her graveside and pay my respects. But that is for another time. For now, just keep it to yourself."

Their body language spoke volumes, as Constantin shook hands with each man, and then turned away for the short walk home. As he walked, it suddenly occurred to him that when he first saw Andreas he was walking across the green from the direction of his new house, more than likely having visited Ninia. He needed to talk to Ninia first, and then Andreas.

After a while Constantin returned to the annex, and found Andreas and Dylan seated by the fire. "Dylan, could you give me and Andreas a few minutes?"

Dylan stood up right away, and indicated for Constantin to take his seat. He left the room silently, and walked toward the stables, so that he could check on his horse. He had begun to think of his return to Linlithgow, and realized that he had a lot of things to take care of.

Constantin looked over at Andreas, as he began to speak softly and earnestly to the young man. "It has been obvious for some time that you have feelings for Ninia, but something significant has happened in the last few days, and I wanted to tell you in person."

Andreas was both surprised and concerned, but did not know what to think.

Constantin continued. "Ninia has reached eighteen years of age, and will soon be married to the son of the chief of the Votadinii people." He let his words sink in, as he looked into the eyes of the young man, clearly shaken by this news.

"There was a messenger from Traprain Law waiting for me at Linlithgow. He carried a letter from Chief Artair signifying his agreement to the marriage of his son with my daughter. This is a marriage that has long been in the making, Andreas, and will strengthen the bonds that already exist between the tribes. I am sorry, Andreas. There could never have been a future for you and Ninia."

Andreas was stunned, but did his best to take the news in stride, and not give way to an expression or sentiment of ill will. He looked over at Constantin, and although his words and his bearing expressed understanding, the sadness in his eyes betrayed the real extent of his feelings. "Thank you, Constantin, for telling me this news in person. I know enough of the tribal structure here in Caledonia to appreciate the significance of this announcement. I hope you will forgive me for seeming to be somewhat in awe of your daughter, and I suspect that could be said for many of the young men among the tribes. Please tell Ninia that I am happy for her, and wish her well."

Constantin made to rise from the chair, and Andreas quickly stepped over to offer him a hand up. "I'll tell Ninia that we spoke, Andreas, and pass along your good wishes."

Andreas walked with him to the door and they shook hands one more time, as Constantin turned toward his house at the other side of the green. Ninia would be waiting for him.

As Andreas lay alone in his bunk later that night, his mind kept taking him back to his brief meeting with Ninia. He could sense the passion in that first kiss between them, and that there was an underlying emotion on both sides that felt so complete and natural. But he had to admit to himself that the essence of their relationship now was much more a factor of that second embrace. He wanted to believe that her heart was with him, but even so, everything else was wrapped up in the exigencies of the tribal alliance. There was no future together.

It took a long time for Andreas to finally get to sleep, as he kept replaying the events of the past few hours in the hope of finding something he had missed, that would put their relationship in a place that had a future. Eventually he had to accept the fact that Isaac was right. Whatever the future held for him in Caledonia, it did not include Ninia.

His last thoughts were the product of his conditioning as a soldier of Rome, posted to a location at the extreme of the Empire, and bound by oath and loyalty to the mission.

The End

Printed in the USA
CPSIA information can be obtained
at www.ICGtesting.com
LVHW020616150124
768656LV00006BB/447